# Praise for *Tru*

"A compulsively readable debut." —*Kirkus Reviews*

"*Trust Me* pulses with intrigue, thrills and distinctive humor, all while remaining vividly rooted in the landscapes, cultures and complexities of the American Southwest. Santos' writing is as bright as the New Mexico sunshine." —Francisco Cantú, author of *The Line Becomes a River*

"Santos conjures a vibrant, vivid New Mexico full of menace, dark humor, false fronts, mutable histories, regrets, wild hopes, caches of gold just out of reach and characters who—to the reader's great benefit—just can't get out of their own damn way. A high-velocity, compulsively readable novel that crackles with energy, narrative drive and its author's unmistakable joy in storytelling. A hell of a debut." —Doug Dorst, *New York Times* bestselling author of *S.* and *Alive in Necropolis*

"A multi-tentacled, cinematic debut that will pull you into its winding labyrinth." —Fernando A. Flores, author of *Tears of the Trufflepig*

"White men scheming to build an airport on tribal land, Santa Fe's art scene, Apaches represented by an attorney, what's up with Geronimo's ghost and where precisely is he buried—Richard Santos' debut novel has the anarchic energy and slick characters you'd expect to find in a tale told by Elmore Leonard. *Trust Me* offers every reader a fun ride. My advice is: take it." —Tom Grimes, author of *Mentor, a Memoir*

"Best debut I've seen in about forever, best New Mexico novel I've read in a good while, far and away the best airport novel I've ever read, and not even close to the last Richard Santos I'll be reading." —Stephen Graham Jones, author of *Mongrels* and *The Only Good Indians*

"Richard Santos has written an extraordinary story with great craft and an exquisite use of language in this, his first book. It reads like a breath of fresh air after living in a stifling box of recycled themes and tired tropes, and will hopefully mark a shift for the future of American Latino literature." —Domingo Martinez, author of *The Boy Kings of Texas*, National Book Award Finalist

"With crisp, cinematic dialogue and insight into all that's duplicitous and corrupt (and juicy and thrilling), Santos kept me turning the pages late into the night."
—Dina Nayeri, author of
*The Ungrateful Refugee* and *Refuge*

"A story that sinks its teeth into a crooked land development deal in New Mexico with reverberations all the way to the seats of national power. This is great, tense writing."
—Michael Noll, author of *The Writer's Field Guide to the Craft of Fiction*

"*Trust Me* is a suspenseful and thoroughly enjoyable novel that explores the themes of betrayal, deceit, redemption and cultural collision in modern-day New Mexico. Santos draws on his own political background to create a web of manipulation and intrigue that ensnares his characters in a world in which trust itself becomes dangerously suspect. Even the New Mexico landscape, which Santos carefully paints, seems to hold its eerie and misleading secrets."
—Tim O'Brien, National Book Award-winning author of *Going After Cacciato* and *The Things They Carried*

"An earth-shattering meditation on new beginnings, happiness and the dark complications that sometimes arise. Richard Santos is a masterful storyteller. The small moments in his characters' lives matter just as much as the big ones; they contain entire worlds that tell us about the best parts of ourselves, the worst parts of ourselves."
—Daniel Peña, author of *Bang*

"A gripping novel with layers of political intrigue, class exploration, love, land and redemption. Santos' searing debut keeps the pages turning and the guesses coming."
—Lara Prescott, *New York Times* bestselling author of *The Secrets We Kept*

"*Trust Me* is a nimble blend of high-desert political thriller, noir and crime drama. The plot, folded tightly with twists and revelations, never veers far from its vivid and layered characters—reckless oil barons and unsavory political operatives, powerful single moms and redemption-seeking deadbeat dads, ambitious artists and weary veterans—characters who, in Santos' generous hands, glow with warmth and need and life, who risk everything they've got in end-of-the-line attempts to become who they believe themselves to be. An engrossing and insightful debut from a truly exciting talent."
—Joseph Scapellato, author of *The Made-Up Man* and *Big Lonesome*

# Trust Me

**Richard Z. Santos**

Arte Público Press
Houston, Texas

*Trust Me* is funded in part by a grant from the National Endowment for the Arts. We are grateful for their support.

*Recovering the past, creating the future*
Arte Público Press
University of Houston
4902 Gulf Fwy, Bldg 19, Rm 100
Houston, Texas 77204-2004
Cover design by Mora Des!gn

Names: Santos, Richard Z., author.
Title: Trust me / by Richard Z. Santos.
Description: Houston, Texas : Arte Público Press, [2019] | Summary: "Charles O'Connell is riding an epic losing streak. Having worked in politics since college, he is used to losing races, but he never imagined that his most recent candidate would end up in jail and that he would also need an attorney. His euphoria at not joining his boss in prison is short-lived-no one will hire him now, his credit cards are maxed out and his marriage is on the rocks. An unexpected offer to work in Santa Fe, New Mexico, doing public relations for a firm building the city's new airport feels like an opportunity to start fresh and make connections with powerful people out west. But when the construction crew unearths a skeleton, Charles' fresh start turns into another disaster. Soon, a group of Apache claims the site holds Geronimo's secret grave. Soon Charles realizes everyone has an agenda-and numerous dark secrets threaten to erupt. Gabriel Luna, one of the laborers present when the skeleton is unearthed, is willing to do just about anything to reconnect with his teenage son. Cody Branch, an ambitious, powerful millionaire, plans to leverage the deal to enrich himself. And there's his wife, Olivia Branch, who has a surprising connection to Charles' past and desperately needs his help. Surrounded by deception on all fronts, including his own lies to himself and his wife, Charles falls into a whirlwind of fraud, betrayal and double crosses. This riveting novel barrels through the New Mexican landscape in an exploration of innocence and guilt, power and wealth, and the search for love and happiness. RICHARD Z. SANTOS received an MFA from Texas State University. His fiction, essays and reviews have appeared in multiple publications, including The San Antonio Express-News, Kirkus Reviews, The Rumpus, The Morning News and The Texas Observer. Previously, he was a political campaign operative. A high-school English teacher in Austin, Texas, this is his first novel"—Provided by publisher.
Identifiers: LCCN 2019058191 (print) | LCCN 2019058192 (ebook) | ISBN 9781558859043 (trade paperback) | ISBN 9781518506253 (epub) | ISBN 9781518506260 (kindle edition) | ISBN 9781518506277 (adobe pdf)
Subjects: GSAFD: Suspense fiction.
Classification: LCC PS3619.A5985 T78 2019 (print) | LCC PS3619.A5985 (ebook) | DDC 813/.6—dc23
LC record available at https://lccn.loc.gov/2019058191
LC ebook record available at https://lccn.loc.gov/2019058192

♾ The paper used in this publication meets the requirements of the American National Standard for Information Sciences—Permanence of Paper for Printed Library Materials, ANSI Z39.48-1984.

19 20 21     5 4 3 2 1

# FRIDAY

# ONE

CHARLES O'CONNELL avoided his wife's hopeful, excited gaze. Addie walked towards him, a small drip coffee in her hand.

"That was quick," she said. "Is quick good?"

Charles swung his eyes towards her, then to the rental car. A year ago, they had been pricing new hybrids. Now, he was paying for a matchbox car by the hour and was embarrassed by the company's logos plastered on the windows.

His mother worked in the bank's original, red brick building. She'd claimed it instilled confidence if the bank president was in sight. Whether this confidence meant to be instilled in the costumers, the employees or maybe his mother herself, Charles never knew. Addie had taken a rare afternoon off, and they were going to celebrate his loan with a few drinks before he left Washington. After months of searching and a wallet full of maxed out credit cards, he had a job. All he needed was a little cash to keep him floating his first week in Santa Fe. Of course his mother would help him out. No question.

Addie slammed her door. "Tell me she did not turn you down."

He put the car in gear but left his foot on the brake. "She smiled while doing it. Took me awhile to figure out why. I'm asking for money. A chance to put my life back together, and she's beaming. Beaming, but not *really* looking at me."

"How much did you ask for?"

"I did exactly what we talked about. 'A small one,' I said. I never even gave a number. 'Until my first paycheck.' Nothing. Smiling . . . smiling the whole time, like we were on Oprah. But when I left, I saw her office blinds were open. All her little min-

2

ions saw her and her son grinning up a storm like a happy pair of . . . chipmunks."

Addie almost spit out her coffee. "Your mom is not a chipmunk."

"She's a vole. Are voles scary and judgmental?"

"Not like her."

Charles pulled into traffic. He wanted to keep the moment light, but they settled into silence as they crawled towards the beltway.

Charles was not mad at his mom for denying him. He was mad at himself for thinking his losing streak was coming to an end. He had worked in politics since college and lost plenty of races. Losing is fine. Political careers can handle a loss here and there. Even scandal is easy on the staffers. If your candidate gets caught hopping into bed with an intern, your career survives—unless you're the intern. But the Hunt campaign was the worst of all worlds. Charles' candidate was in jail. The Senate seat in Delaware went from an automatic win to a pick up for the other party. And Charles himself was forced to hire a lawyer because an ambitious US attorney was convinced the corruption ran up and down the chain of command. For a few days, Charles broke the cardinal rule of campaign staffers: he became the story. The euphoria of not following Hunt to prison was short-lived. All his old connections had dried up and blown away, and now even his mom thought he was a bad bet.

Charles picked up Addie's coffee and took a gulp. "What else is there to do?" she asked.

"I'll get paid two weeks after I start. I can make it two weeks on peanut butter."

"But where are you going to live?"

"They're giving me a place to crash. I think it's furnished. I can make it work."

Charles was not going to ask her for money. He never needed to because she always offered. Charles was living on a hundred dollars a week left on the kitchen counter every Monday morning—no note, no explanation, just five twenties and the unstated expectation that the cash would not be there long.

"Do you know anyone else out there?" she asked.

"My buddy Thompson. I think you met him at . . . a fundraiser or something. He doesn't even know I'm coming."

"Maybe you should ask him for a loan."

Charles merged onto the highway, feeling intimidated in the tiny car. The radio was still tuned to NPR but the volume was down to a murmur. "Ruined local man forced to beg his wife for money," he could almost hear.

"That'd be pretty awkward, don't you think? Haven't spoken to him in years."

"Then let's make sure this still makes sense."

"What do you mean?"

"The job in Santa Fe is a corporate gig. You'll be doing PR. There are corporate PR jobs in DC you never even considered."

"I'm working for a group building an airport. They ran into trouble on the construction site. They're not pharma or tobacco."

"That's not what I . . . " Addie massaged a spot in the middle of her forehead. "I don't know if this makes sense anymore."

"These people in Santa Fe reached out to me. You know how that feels? After Delaware, none of my friends talk to me. No one returns my emails. People pretend to get lost in their phones when they see me."

"I can't give you any more money. I won't. You've put me here. I have to say no."

"These people are funding a brand-new airport, they can connect me to people. I've never worked out west. That congressman out there, Solís, he's a star, and he's young. I can rebuild."

"That's what you keep saying, but . . . it's not going to be worth it."

"Well, it better be."

Addie's eyes scanned the road. Her breath began to catch as if the words were slicing her open as they came out.

"We've been through so much this year. Delaware, being so damn broke, and I don't think I can make it through you being gone for a year. It'll kill whatever I'm still clinging to."

Charles kept his eyes straight ahead. His face started to burn with shame and more than a little anger. "I have a plan," he said. "I have a chance. DC is dead for me."

"I'm in DC."

Charles looked at her. He put a hand on her leg, and her hand went back to her forehead.

They were quiet all the way home.

෫ළ ෫ළ ෫ළ

To Charles, the worst part of the scandal, something he would never tell Addie, was that his bold, consistent mantra—he was innocent, he reacted to the scandal like a sane, competent professional—was all a lie. Charles being right and the US attorney over reacting had developed into the twin pillars of his personality and self-worth over the past year. Now, those pillars were rotting from the inside.

They returned the car and walked to their Capitol Hill townhome. The neighborhood held an old confidence that Charles envied. He wanted to sling his arm around Addie's shoulders and smile with exaggerated cheer.

Addie wore sunglasses, but Charles saw her expression all too well. During the scandal, she had been his head cheerleader. Now, she was out of encouraging words.

"I saw my cousin in the bank," he said. "You never met him. He used to be a Wall Street guy. Now he's behind the counter. Can you believe that?"

"At least he has a job."

"I have a job."

Addie turned to him in front of the townhouse. "You have two weeks," she said. "In two weeks I'm flying out there, and we're deciding if this job is worth it."

He nodded.

"You're not going to say anything?"

"I agree. I agree. Two weeks. I'll know so much more in two weeks. I'll know if I have a way forward."

Addie hooked both hands around the back of her neck, her elbows pointing at Charles like stake posts.

She turned and walked up the steps to the front door. "Go for a walk," she said.

"A walk?"

"A walk."

She shut the door. Charles heard the deadbolt slide into place from the sidewalk.

Cigarette smoke hit his nose. Charles looked up and made eye contact with one of the junior staffers that were all shacked up two doors down. Not that he had ever hit anyone, or been hit himself, but Charles felt an urge to walk up to the kid and punch him right in his freshly straightened teeth. The smoker gave Charles a quick nod and went back inside.

Charles looked up and down the street, wondering how to kill twenty minutes.

# TWO

HELL OF A WEEK FOR GABRIEL LUNA. First, he was fired from a job he hated. Then, he discovered his mean bastard of a father gave him bone cancer.

Driving a dump truck on San Miguel Pueblo did not pay well, but it did pay. Gabe was helping to build Santa Fe's first major airport and, although the dust gave him headaches and he hated the hours and the heat, he occasionally felt something close to pride in the work. Then a bulldozer dug up a skeleton where there was not supposed to be a skeleton, and the whole site went to shit. A man with shiny shoes climbed onto the bed of a truck and, with shaking hands clasped in front of his mouth, sent everyone home. Gabe and the other laborers were given vague corporate assurances that the site would reopen after "a swift investigation into the origin of the artifacts." He wasn't holding his breath.

Holding his breath might be better than letting the bone cancer tunnel through his body. The same cancer had worn his father down to nothing but pain and sweat. Gabe would not go out that way.

The diagnosis came from Shaman Jeff, whom Gabe called *Jefe*. Wearing his customary blue Halliburton cap and smoking a cigarette, Jeff had said, "Yup, that's cancer . . . to the core. Can damn near see it dripping from your nose."

Gabe imagined his dying old man spitting bone cancer cells like pollen spores, special delivery, aimed right at the son who was never there. Granted, no actual doctor had diagnosed him. Jeff's diagnosis came after poking a few lymph nodes and lighting a can-

7

dle, but in fifteen years, he had never steered Gabe wrong. The cancer was chewing on Gabe's bones—that was for sure.

Now, a couple weeks after that one-two punch, Gabe pulled up in front of Jeff's trailer and killed his bike. Time for his second treatment.

Jeff came outside carrying a red backpack and a gallon of water. "Jefe," Gabe said, "you going to invite me in for a beer?"

"I don't let Mexicans drink before ceremonies. Causes trouble."

"Damn, do all you old Indians hate to share, or just you?"

Gabe put one arm around Jeff and slapped his back.

"Shit," Jeff said, "maybe if you people had left us something to share."

Jeff lived alone a few miles onto the Isleta Pueblo. For a fee, he dosed friends, and friends of friends, with Native-grade mushrooms. All a "patient" had to do was sign a paper converting to a Native religion and hand over two hundred bucks. Legal and above board. Gabe had been indulging in this mental enema at least twice a year for almost a decade. After the diagnosis, Jeff talked him up to the full deluxe model for two-fifty: drums, heat, smoke and a mushroom tea that tasted like rotten meat but sent Gabe to the moon and back.

Jeff claimed it purged toxins so the body could fight the cancer, but Gabe never believed in miracles. Still, a dying man needed to have some fun on his way out. He had taken two treatments in less than two weeks.

Jeff reached into his backpack and handed Gabe a gallon plastic bag packed tight with dried mushrooms. "You know who this is for."

Gabe laughed at the bag's heft.

"Where do you find this stuff?" he asked. "And what if I pounded all this, right now? Just shoved fistfuls down my throat?"

"I grow it in cow shit under the trailer," Jeff said. "And, if you ate that much, I'd have to shoot you before you pulled your own face off."

Gabe turned to hide the look on his face. Since the diagnosis, gut-shaking bouts of fear and paranoia would freeze him in place.

Jeff's treatments helped bring some calm back into his life, but nothing else made much of a difference.

He unzipped his saddlebag, took out a soft plastic lunchbox filled with the money and handed it to Jeff. Gabe never thought of himself as a drug dealer, no way. He was the middleman who introduced Jeff and his mushrooms to Frederick, a friend of Gabe's since high school who most definitely *was* a drug dealer.

"Our friend says the last batch was almost too strong," Gabe said. "Some of the customers complained. You believe that? Anyway, Frederick ended up charging more, so you got some extra in there."

Jeff took his money inside. He never talked details, never counted the cash in front of Gabe, never asked any questions. Gabe supposed the Indian was ashamed. Escorting friends through a religious experience was honorable, but blowing the minds of teenagers? Not worth a single word.

Gabe leaned against Jeff's truck, pulled a soft pack from his leather vest and slipped a cigarette behind his ear.

After Jeff had stowed the lunchbox inside, he came back, almost limping.

"We're breaking down like old horses," Gabe said. "We going to end up in the same rest home for broke Indians?"

Jeff pointed to his new truck. "Who's broke? And who's an Indian?"

"Hey, my great-grandma had a braid of black hair down to her ass and that pissed off face you always wear. Fifty bucks says I've got more Native blood than you. Call me Tonto."

"That's about as far as this will go."

Gabe stepped up into the cab, feeling a twinge in his bad ankle. He had always felt kinship with the Natives. New Mexico was bursting with light-skinned Latinos holding their pointy noses in the air like a bunch of matadors munching on olives and calling themselves "Spanish." Nope, not Gabe. His skin was brown as the Rio Grande, and his brother Lou was even darker. There were Indians hiding in his family tree, Gabe felt them. Not that he could prove it or apply for benefits or anything—he had tried—but extended family was family nonetheless.

Jeff pulled the truck down the dirt road that led to the sweat lodge, Gabe took the leather bandana off his head and shook out the dust onto the floorboards. He ran his hands through his mustache, sending grit to the floor.

"What kind of focus you want?" Jeff asked.

"I don't know. I'll see what I see. Hey, that eagle from last time, you remember? Bring that guy back."

Gabe popped the cigarette into his mouth and dug for a lighter.

"That was a vulture, not an eagle, and I'm not in charge. Except in this truck. No smoking."

Gabe rolled his eyes but tucked the cigarette back behind his ear. "Damn things have been hurting my chest anyways. Feel like I'm back in middle school."

"You tell your boy yet?"

"Working on it. Our schedules haven't quite aligned."

Jeff snorted.

"Hey, the kid's sixteen. Kids are busy little bastards nowadays." Gabe looked out the window. "And his mom doesn't always want me to see him. Hey, tonight, can we be outside? I've been itching to get up in those hills."

Jeff looked over at him and raised his eyebrows.

Gabe sighed. "I'll tell him. I know, I have to tell him. It's not that easy."

Jeff's cell phone dinged, the sound digital and fragile in the truck. "I didn't think those worked out here," Gabe said.

"Dude, we don't live in the nineteenth century."

Jeff pulled his phone off his hip and glanced at the screen. The truck swayed back and forth across the divider line, but there was no other vehicle for miles.

"My phone never worked out at the construction site," Gabe said.

"Those bones really did a number on y'all, huh? I'm still going to bed happy, thinking about millionaires with their dicks in their hands."

"Hey, I needed that job. And my brother works for the head millionaire. You better hope they get building soon or there's going to be broke Lunas as far as you can see."

"Lou will just go back to the force if he needs to."

"Kicking and screaming."

"White men buying up Indian land to build an airport." Jeff sneered. "Karma's a bitch."

"Don't say it like it was my idea." Gabe sat forward. "Wait, you don't think that . . . I don't have this shit inside me because of that skeleton, do I?"

"An Indian curse? That's what you're blaming this on?"

"They dropped the dude's skull into the back of my truck. I saw the damn thing in my rearview mirror. That has got to be bad karma."

"You're not sick because of that skull. You're sick because you're blocked in here." Jeff thumped his chest.

"Oh, that's sweet. You should put that wisdom on a T-shirt."

Jeff shook his head. "I can sweat your ass down to a nub, but if you don't unlock whatever's going on inside you, then you may as well wander into the woods and curl up under a rock."

"Whoa, a little harsh, man."

"You, of all people, can take it."

Gabe wondered if that was a compliment. He hated it when Jeff got too mystical. After being stuck in Catholic school until he turned fifteen, and one-too-many religious-themed beatings courtesy of his pious father, Gabe had lost or abandoned most of his superstitions. The ceremony tonight would not heal him. All he wanted was to round off some of his edges and, maybe, buy himself a little more time.

Gabe reached into his shirt pocket and counted out the money. He was supposed to pay $250, but Gabe pocketed a twenty and slipped the rest into Jeff's ashtray. If he called him on the missing cash, Gabe would claim a frequent flier discount.

They rode in silence for a few miles, the land rolling under the wheels and the horizon so unchanging that Gabe felt they were spinning in place. The sweat lodge was a log cabin at the end of a dirt road. If Jeff's trailer felt like the middle of nowhere, then the

lodge might have been on another planet. The hills that became
the Manzano Mountains started behind the lodge, and the flat,
rocky plain in front of the shack eventually turned into the Chi-
huahua desert that stretched thousands of miles south. At times,
when Gabe was high on the mushroom tea, the lodge itself
seemed to bind the continent together, fusing desert and mountains with its own split logs and packed dirt floor. That was when
even in the darkness every step was illuminated, Jeff turned into a
shaman and Gabe became something better than the wreck he had
grown into.

Jeff started a fire under a hole in the cabin roof. Water boiled
in a pot and he muttered a Native language Gabe only heard during ceremonies. Nervous anticipation flashed through his blood.
He wanted the show but the formality made his squirm. Last time,
an eagle did fly into the lodge—no vulture, Gabe swore—and cir-
cled the room before landing in the corner, sitting on its tail feathers and crossing its leg like a human. "Someone who died, trying
to send a message," Jeff said. During another vision, years earlier,
the dirt floor transformed into a woven expanse of tiny, perfectly
formed interlocking people supporting Gabe, supporting everything. For the next week, Gabe kept his yard immaculate, did not
even throw a cigarette butt on the ground. Life was always a little
different afterwards. Gabe would call his brother, send Helen
some child support, be nicer to strangers, visit his father's grave.
But eventually, the lesson would leak out of him, the yard would
go wild and Gabe would sink a little deeper into his own life.

Jeff sprinkled powders into the water, then poured the tea into
a metal thermos. After Gabe sipped until it was empty, time turned
rubbery and difficult to track. Jeff beat a drum, but when Gabe
looked, it was gone. The smoke still pulsed with the beat. Then,
Gabe was outside with Jeff still drumming. Gabe walked into the
hills, knowing where to step, knowing which rocks were loose
enough to turn his ankle, stepping around cactus even when
clouds covered the moon. Then, a line of fire spread along the top
of the hill, thin as thread. The orange thread thickened and rolled
forward. Trees that were not there cracked and exploded from the
heat and the pressure. The fire line grew stronger, advancing as if

on wheels, smooth and unstoppable. The flames, tall, perfectly shaped into a point, stopped inches in front of his nose. Gabe skimmed the flat of his hand over the edge of the flames. Fire is natural, nothing to fear. Forests burn and grow stronger. Gabe might burn and come back stronger.

Jeff grabbed his wrist. "No further. Not yet," he said. "Your marrow is not your own, and you're not ready to go."

Gabe looked back at the wall of flame. The flames turned pain black. At the center of the flames, he saw his dying father. Lou was there. Lou was the good son at the end, tying his father's wrists to the bedrails against the animal delirium. No Gabe. Fire ants tunneled out of his father's body and formed a line marching straight towards Gabe.

"Pop," he sobbed, "I meant to visit. Couldn't you have found some other way to punish me?"

The flames vanished, leaving Gabe red-faced and cold in the middle of the desert. At some point, Jeff had stopped drumming.

"You've got to tell your son," Jeff said, then turned back to the cabin.

Gabe hesitated, looking back to where the flames had been, as if there could be a different answer. Then he turned and followed Jeff, stumbling on the gravel beneath his boots.

# MONDAY

# THREE

CHARLES FACED LONG DELAYS on each of his flights to Albuquerque. In DC, he passed the time in an airport bar, drinking sour martinis, trying not to think about his fight with Addie. In Houston, he slogged through memos covering the history of the airport and the skeleton the contractors had discovered after breaking ground. His last night in DC for weeks, months, and he and Addie had barely spoken. When he told her that Thompson would pay him a couple hundred for some consulting work—basically just a conversation over dinner—all she did was nod. He wanted Addie to tell him if he should stay and fix their marriage or stay and mercy-kill it.

His binder full of memos and background papers on the airport was too boring to distract him, but it was better than being left with his own thoughts. A county ballot initiative had set aside funds to buy the land. The tribe assured the developers and the county there were no artifacts or burial sites in the area, only boulders and dirt, so this was a very large fly in a very expensive bowl of soup.

As he boarded the final plane to Albuquerque, Charles lost track of which person was the liaison for which tribe and which agency governed what organization. Politics used to be his drug, but this gig was a corporate labyrinth.

Maybe Addie would start up an affair. Charles cracked a smile. That would be the best option. She would tearfully confess her love for a co-worker, maybe even the congressman she worked for, and Charles would walk away from the marriage a wounded victim. This was roughly the story with Olivia Reyes, his first wife.

After one more drink, Charles settled into boozy dreaming about the young, hotshot Hispanic politician he might meet out west. A charming man with a killer smile and no accent, someone Hispanic but not *too* Hispanic, with his sights on national office. Someone Charles could build.

cᴓ cᴓ cᴓ

By the time the plane approached Albuquerque, Charles' throat had dried out and his head was pounding. He was sweating stains through his newest, old shirt. He had expected dunes and tall, red rocks—a John Wayne movie. But all he saw out the window was low, ambling hills and brown, dusty terrain.

A dark part of him relished how low he had sunk.

Charles muttered, "Hi, I'm a political junkie, and I've hit rock bottom."

The Albuquerque airport was small and almost deserted this late. It appeared old and vaguely Spanish Colonial. The airport shops had names like "Trader's Outpost" and "Turquoise Depot." To him, the exposed ceiling beams and pink and blue trim running along the walls looked like something out of Epcot.

Charles spotted his driver right away. The man was a wide pitbull in a simple black suit. His hair was a fuzz too short to tell its color, and the sign with Charles' name on it looked small against his chest.

"That's me," Charles said. "O'Connell."

The driver titled his head an inch, his expression set in stone. "Mallon. I'm taking you to Santa Fe."

The driver walked out of the terminal and towards an idling black town car in front of the airport. A thick palm on his shoulder steered Charles into the backseat, and Mallon went back inside for the luggage. The car was luxurious and clean—not just clean but spotless in a way only the very rich can maintain. The organization funding the airport had agreed to drive him from Albuquerque to Santa Fe and put him up in a house for the job's duration. On previous gigs he would be lucky to get a ride from a teenager with a hatchback. Hey, what's the point of selling out, Charles thought, if it doesn't come with perks?

He cracked the window and watched for the driver's return, already forgetting his name. Airport security waved other cars through, not letting anyone else park in front of the terminal, but they never even glanced at the town car.

Mallon returned, carrying Charles' large, square suitcases under his arms, the garment bag, hooked to one of the suitcases, dragged on the ground.

"You could have rolled them," Charles said.

After Mallon settled behind the wheel, he turned his head, and his wide little eyes blinked.

"The suitcases have wheels," Charles offered again.

"Need anything else, sir?"

Charles shook his head, and the car pulled away.

At night, Albuquerque looked like any other city—highways and strip malls. It looked like Phoenix but with more potholes. At the edge of town, the highway went dark and traffic dripped to a trickle. To the left, Charles saw scattered lights. To his right, nothing but stunted, bristly trees among the dirt and rocks. He cupped his hands around his eyes and held his face to the glass. No moon. No houses, no small towns in the distance, no cars on country roads.

Nothing past the knotted three-foot tall imitations of trees on the shoulder. It was like riding in a saddlebag. Charles smiled. Twenty minutes in New Mexico and he was already thinking like a cowboy.

"Where are we?" he asked.

Mallon made no indication he had heard, so Charles asked again.

"Between Albuquerque and Santa Fe," he mumbled. "It'll take an hour."

"No, but, where are we? What's around us? There's nothing here."

"To the left is tribal land. To the right is a mountain."

Charles looked again. High above the car were a dozen evenly spaced, tiny red dots. He shifted, but the lights stayed in place. Radio or cell towers, he figured. The blackness took on a new shape, not empty desert, but a thousand feet of solid rock.

He tugged at his seatbelt. "I didn't think the drive would be so long."

Mallon pulled up his shoulders as if Charles were a mosquito, an annoyance. "If the drive were any shorter, Santa Fe wouldn't need its own airport."

Charles laughed. "Good point. You from New Mexico?"

"Ohio."

"Ohio. Ohio. The Buckeye State. I've spent more time in Columbus and Toledo than any sane man ever should."

Charles looked for a response, a smile, an acknowledgement of his existence.

"Sure is a nice state though," Charles said. "Good people in Ohio. Real good people."

"Look, save it for the press."

"I'm sorry?

"You're not trying to convince me of anything. Save the PR hand jobs for the reporters and the tribes." Mallon continued muttering under his breath.

"What was that?" Charles said.

"We've all got trouble we're trying to beat. We've all got jobs to do, and mine isn't spending two hours in an airport parking lot."

Charles rubbed his eyes. "Right. You're right. I should have emailed my new arrival time. Hey, spending extra time in Houston wasn't exactly paradise."

A small building with a tin roof and siding like Tupperware appeared to the right. The words "Indian Casino" blazed in purple neon. Farm trucks and beat-up cars dotted the parking lot. Just past the casino, three weathered Christmas wreaths hung on white wooden crosses along the shoulder.

A car with darkened headlights entered the highway and swung in front of them. Mallon slammed on the brakes and swerved. As they whipped around the car, Charles saw the driver's eyes narrowed to drunken slits

"Did we hit him?" Charles yelled.

He turned around and watched the drunk struggle to stay in a lane. He wanted to puke up all the vodka in his gut. "There that many drunks out here?"

"Drunks everywhere, aren't there?"

"Yeah, but . . . "

"Look, pal. You want me to say we've got a bunch of alkies?" Charles threw his hands into the air. "What is it with you?"

"I'm worried you're going to mess up like you did in Delaware."

Charles laughed. "Who even are you? No offense but you don't know shit."

"I know this state. I know these people. And I don't think you're up for this."

"Well, I know you're here to drive."

Mallon stared at him in the mirror until Charles had to blink and pull out his phone. Off to a great start as always. He wanted to call his wife, but it was so late in DC. She would have found a way to charm this guy.

After a few minutes, the driver tapped a finger against the glass, indicating an unremarkable patch of rock and darkness. "That's the airport construction site. Mr. Branch will want you out there soon."

Charles saw a gate and a few metallic glints but didn't know what he was looking at. "Who's Branch?" Charles asked. "I've only been in contact with Diana Salazar."

Mallon looked in the mirror. "Your house isn't ready, sir."

"Why's that?"

"I'm just a driver, remember? Mrs. Branch told me it wasn't ready, so I'm taking you somewhere else."

Charles tried to stay agreeable. "Okay, good enough, that's fine. Mind if I ask where I'm staying?"

"With Lou Luna, a state trooper. Works security for Mr. Branch, like me. Also a driver. He's expecting us."

Streetlights reappeared on the highway as they passed the Santa Fe County line. With valleys on both sides of the car, Charles began to get a sense of space. He had travelled the political circuit: urban Chicago, suburban Ohio, New England city-states. Electoral-sized bites and small, manageable groups of voters were easy to comprehend, but New Mexico's empty space—the sheer, insane distance between people and cities—threatened to melt his brain.

Before Mallon exited, the drunk zoomed past. His headlights were still off and he was driving fast, too fast, weaving his way north.

ഇ ഇ ഇ

They pulled off I-25 and followed a two-lane country road. Charles lost the lights of Santa Fe behind hills. They were moving away from the city. Rocks and dried-out mesquite trees crowded the road. Bluish lights in the distance marked houses trying to make a dent in the darkness. Mallon accelerated around curves. The land on the sides of the road rose and fell, exposing layers of stone. Small, tangled clumps of paddle cactus grew sideways out of the rock and reached for the car. Out here, Charles' phone had one flickering bar of service.

"Hey, what is this? I'll pay for a hotel."

"Lou's is better."

A single light appeared. A man in a glass booth wore a military uniform and cradled a machine gun. For a second, Charles thought they were crossing into Mexico. The soldier dropped the gun onto a desk, ran out and lifted a long, yellow metal arm with a sign that read: *Stop No Trespassing US Government.* The soldier saluted as the car drove through the gate.

Charles laughed. "Is this a joke?"

"This is a National Guard base." Mallon sounded a little too pleased.

Angular shapes that looked like giant bugs were set in the shadows off the road.

Helicopters. Charles' mind reeled.

"Why am I staying on a military base?"

"National Guard. This is where Lou lives."

"I'm here a few days?"

The road turned to gravel and they stopped in front of a double-wide trailer, the only building in sight. The car kicked up a cloud of white dust. A yellow bulb cast a weak glow onto three handmade wooden steps leading to the trailer's door.

"You're kidding," Charles said.

Mallon got out, loping to the trailer in hunched, angry strides, and slammed his fist against the plastic front door. Charles stayed close to the car. The driveway held a small, dirt-covered Toyota and a black town car identical to Mallon's. There was no sound other than Mallon's pounding. There was no wind, and the air smelled cold and empty. The dim glow of Lou's trailer only brought out the blackness, the way cigarette smoke brings out light.

"Goddammit, Lou." Mallon pounded the trailer.

When Lou opened the door, Mallon pulled him close and whispered. Lou was big, strong, but Mallon towered over him.

He came back for Charles' bags and carried them into the trailer.

Lou stayed in the doorway, looking at Charles with sympathy. "Come in," he said. "You got a bedroom."

The floor near the front door felt thin, as if it might give way if he jumped. Charles could see the entire trailer with a turn of his head. A green suede couch and a massive TV dominated the center. To the left was a small dining area, a kitchen and a closed door. Charles thought about how funny this would all be later. Another story of the road and its indignities. His politico friends would laugh and share their own horror stories. His mother would cringe. It would be hilarious. At some point.

Lou walked down a short hall to the right. "This is you," he said.

Charles followed, surprised that trailers even had hallways. Lou dropped the suitcases on a full-sized bed. A small nightstand and lamp filled most of the remaining space. The room was cold and felt unused.

Lou put his hands on his hips. "It's clean."

Charles smiled. "It's fine. Thank you. But . . . the people I'd been speaking with didn't say anything about staying out here."

Lou walked back down the hall. "Yeah? Who you talking to?"

Charles followed. "Diana Salazar and Jordan Reilly. I'm working on the airport. Is that what you do?"

Mallon was standing in the far corner, talking into his phone. Lou went to the fridge and pulled out a couple of beers. Charles could not remember the last time he had been so excited for beer so cheap.

Lou pointed his beer can to the closed door on the other side of the kitchen. "Jordan's here." He lowered his voice. "Guess we should be quiet."

"Oh." Charles nodded. "Right, right."

Mallon put his phone away. "My ride will be here soon. I'll wait right here if you don't mind."

"Wherever," Lou said. "Want a beer? A chair?"

Mallon shook his head.

Charles dropped onto the couch. The walls were covered with photos of Lou and a woman skiing, hiking, swimming. The woman's skin was white, papery, and she had red hair.

"Is this Jordan?"

"Sure is," Lou said. "She loves to do that kind of thing. You know, outdoorsy things?"

"I always mean to do stuff like that," Charles said. "But I don't."

"We can show you where to go. My brother lives south of town . . . he really knows the mountains. I'll connect you two."

Charles smiled and nodded. His eyes kept slipping to Mallon near the front door. He noticed Lou do the same. They sipped their beer.

"So," Charles said, "you don't work for Salazar, then? Or do you?"

Mallon made a noise from his throat. "Told you he'd say something stupid."

Charles froze with his beer halfway towards his mouth. Lou raised his eyebrows and scratched the side of his neck. He made quick eye contact with Charles and nodded.

"I'm a State Trooper, but I've been assigned to Mr. Branch. Mallon here also used to be a trooper but came on full time a few years ago."

Charles sipped his beer and realized no one knew where he was—not even him.

"So, I'm the new guy," Charles said. "And kind of an idiot, evidently. Help me out. What can you give me? At this point, I'll take anything."

Lou laughed. "It's confusing. Okay, I'm one of Mr. Cody Branch's security guys. Mallon runs the operation. Big compound, cars, a plane. Sounds impressive, but really I drive Branch around, make him snacks, carry his Louis Vuitton bags. Hell, a few weeks ago he made me turn on his shower for him."

"Lou, that's enough."

Charles tried not to look at Mallon, but he was standing so still, no fidgeting with a cell phone or shifting back and forth, pure statuary. Charles pulled his eyes away and saw an older, framed photo on the wood paneling. It showed a pair of teenage boys in jean shorts and T-shirts with the sleeves cut off. The thinner one looked like Lou. He held a small rifle on his hip, and both boys glared into the camera. They looked so country, so wild.

Charles wondered if Lou and Mallon were like these kids, acting tough. Or should he really be scared?

"So, Branch is helping fund the airport?"

"Wow, you really don't know," Lou said. "Yeah, he funded the campaign for the bonds, your job, Salazar's job. He'll fund construction and he's funding the sun coming up tomorrow."

Headlights beamed through the frosted plastic window set in the door.

"And that's another one of his cars right now."

Mallon opened the door and signaled to the driver. Before leaving, he tossed Charles a set of keys.

"The town car's yours while you're here. Keep it clean. Mr. Branch hates it when his cars get dirty. *I* hate it when Mr. Branch's cars get dirty. GPS knows the way to the office. Be there by 9:00 PM."

As Mallon turned, Charles yelled, "AM. You meant AM, you said PM."

Mallon paused on the front step, nearly filling the entire doorway. Lou stood up and put his hand on the doorknob. Charles felt the beer gurgle in his stomach.

"See you in the morning," Lou said to Mallon's back. "I got this."

Mallon walked towards the waiting car without turning around.

Lou shut the door. "Watch the smart-ass comments." He leaned back against the door and sipped his beer.

"Are you scared of that guy?" Charles asked.

Lou looked down into his can for a moment, chewing on something. Then he locked the door and walked through the kitchen into his bedroom.

Charles sat alone on the couch and finished his beer. When he turned out the light in his bedroom, the silence was so absolute that he stayed up for twenty more minutes, looking for a white noise app on his phone. He fell asleep before deciding on one.

# WEDNESDAY

# FOUR

OLIVIA BRANCH HATED ESPAÑOLA. She grew up there but left as soon as possible, and her skin crawled each time she returned. The town still had two distinctions, other than being very easy to leave: the lowrider car was supposedly invented in Española, and it often led the nation in drug overdoses per capita.

The town also had a little house that had been empty for months. Back when Cody was building his empire a few houses at a time, he had snapped up pockets of real estate across northern New Mexico. Some were on the market now, but many were still empty and waiting for renovation. Olivia was back in town to walk Andrea and her two kids into one of those empty houses. Being married to a rich man did not make Olivia rich, but it did give her access to the properties that her husband owned. This was the third house Olivia had snuck Andrea's family into.

"It's not as glamorous as the house in the mountains," Olivia said.

Andrea shook her head. "Oh please, I spent the whole time scared the kids were going to break a window. This is better."

"No, it's really not, but it's yours as long as you want it."

The kids touched the sides of the TV, opened cabinets and rummaged through closets, but they did it quietly, with the subdued energy of kids who'd been evicted three or four times in their lives.

Andrea and Olivia grew up together and started calling each other "sister" when they were ten. Going on twenty-five years, they were just as close, despite their not sharing a drop of blood between them. With a mom only remembered as a car pulling away and a dad who spent his life drinking and wondering what the hell had happened to him, Olivia had to find family where she could. Yet no amount of bond, familial or otherwise, would diminish her husband's wrath if he found out what she was doing.

"I've said 'thank you' so many times it doesn't mean anything anymore."

"No, no, no," Olivia said, "I can't do much but I can do this."

Andrea's hair was still growing back but had been stuck in a stubborn phase for a couple months. The treatments were over, for now, but the bills never stopped coming. She ran her fingers through the few inches of growth, curly and soft as a baby's.

"I've got to get these kids back in school."

"I'm sure the lessons you've been doing with them have helped." Andrea shook her head. "My mom was the teacher, not me."

Olivia had gone shopping the day before, so the kitchen was already stocked. She helped Andrea unload their few boxes.

Andrea seemed so tired, but this time Olivia knew it was the moving, the uncertainty, and not the cancer.

"This is temporary," Olivia said.

"You don't need to remind me."

"No, I mean it. This is going to be the last house. I'm really close, really close to finding a way out."

"Don't stay with him for us, girl. Walk away when you need to. We'll be fine. Wait too long, you won't get what you want."

"We're all going to get what we need."

One of the little girls, Ellie, only five years old, ran by and Olivia scooped her up.

"All of us," Olivia said and tickled the girl.

Ellie squealed with delight and more than a touch of fear.

"Be careful," Andrea said. "She's not used to that."

Olivia swung the child down as if she were dropping her.

"Oh no," Olivia said and then smiled as she held fast. "Oh no, oh no," again and again.

∽ ∽ ∽

On her way home, Olivia stopped at a gas station with a view of sloping, bare valleys. When she slammed her door, a sound came from the engine block. A clunking piece of metal had fallen from somewhere under the hood and landed with a crunch on the concrete.

She reached under the car and grabbed a black box, not much bigger than a book of matches. The metal was still warm. Wires snaked out of the top, there was a red LED, and a little switch. She flipped the switch but the LED stayed dark.

Olivia opened the hood. When she was a kid, back before everything was sealed inside little computers, she had worked on cars with her uncle, but this engine looked impenetrable, like it could navigate the ocean floor. She poked around the edges of the engine block, but the designers had hidden everything away, compartmentalizing and layering the parts. The engine was aesthetically pleasing, clean and one hundred percent useless to her.

A man in a work cover-all came out of the gas station. Olivia felt his condescension before he said a word.

"Everything all right there, ma'am?"

She didn't look up from the engine. "Everything is just dandy."

"You out of gas?"

Olivia glanced up. "Out of gas?"

"It happens. Some ladies find themselves pushing that tank a little too far."

"And I'm sure you come to their rescue."

"You'd be surprised."

Olivia turned and locked eyes with the man long enough for him to fake a cough and turn away. He pulled out a flashlight.

"So, can I do something?"

She held out the black box. "This fell out. Maybe an airbag sensor? I'm just wondering where it goes."

"Must be a government vehicle, huh?"

Olivia looked back up at the man.

"What with the little tracking device," he said. "GPS."

Olivia gripped the black box and forced a smile. "Could you help me reconnect this?"

∽ ∽ ∽

Back in Santa Fe, Olivia drove in circles around the Plaza for the better part of an hour. She hoped Cody's men would spend hours trying to make sense of that route. Maybe the stop in Española would blend in with the other miles on her car that day.

How did the tracking work? Did Cody get a printout of her route every day? Mallon would be the one watching her. He always watched her. She pictured him lurking like a smog cloud in the compound's guard room—a *casita* with cold Saltillo tiles, two rooms, a kitchen and a bathroom. Perfect for an old mother-in-law, a sullen teenager or her husband's increasingly militarized security apparatus. Cody had made millions in the past ten years, but he seemed to enjoy life less and less. Since the airport project started last year, his sullenness had sunk into anger and seclusion.

Maybe he knew she was on the way out. Olivia had to be careful. A divorce would be easy, but she would have to fight and claw for any kind of settlement.

Cody and Olivia lived next to the governor's mansion in a sprawling home in the mountains north of downtown. The house and grounds pooled like a rockslide on a slight clearing and extended up the hill. Parts of the house were higher than others, small flights of stairs leading between rooms and up to a roof deck designed to ensure a better view than the governor's.

She refused to acknowledge the slight nods from the security guards. Stay mad or you'll fold, she told herself. She was going to demand answers, the truth, even an apology.

Mallon was upstairs, sitting in a chair next to the roof deck. He was always nearby. God forbid Cody's pet strayed far from his side. Olivia kept her eyes straight ahead, trying not to let her hair stand on end. Mallon looked at his watch and made a mark in his little black notebook.

Cody was at the edge of the deck in a chaise lounge. The sagging slope of his shoulders and the folds in the back of his sunburned neck made her sad. She had married a bull, but he was aging into a cow.

"We have to talk," she said.

The wind was so strong she thought it might have taken her words away.

Cody's hands were folded across his gut—yet another development that was rapidly growing.

"Shoot." He sounded half-drunk already.

Olivia chewed on her words. If she yelled, he would just storm off. If she went soft, he would soothe her but wouldn't do anything.

Neither looked at the other. The city was close enough to see cars on the streets, but from this distance they took on the quiet air of insects skittering across a floor.

She thought about putting her hand on Cody's neck, coaxing him back from the edge. "Sometimes I think you don't even like this house," she said.

He slopped half a bottle of wine into a beer mug. "It's the most beautiful place in the world. Beats the view back in Hobbs, that's for sure."

"You always say that."

"It's always true."

"Hobbs was only eight years ago."

"No, no, no. Those lean days were lifetimes ago." He took a deep gulp of wine. "I'm thinking I should get the kids to drive us up to Taos this weekend, get out of the city."

"Don't call them 'kids.' They're grown men who carry guns. They work for a living."

"I pay them. I'll call them what I want."

A few years ago, he would have meant that to be funny.

"I want to talk about my car," Olivia said.

"What about it?" He held up a hand. "Oh, that friend of yours made it into town the other day. Charlie? Charles? The dweeb from DC."

Olivia took a breath and thanked God that Cody was looking at the woods and not her. He knew she had been married before, but not to Charles.

"Not a friend," she said. "Just someone I remembered from way back. It's good you're taking a chance on him."

Cody laughed. "His old boss is in prison. Maybe your boy was dirty, too, but he kept out of the clink. I like that. Nerves."

Cody pressed the palms of his hands into his forehead and took a deep breath. "We've got to start building again."

The motion was honest and terrified. Olivia was mad about the GPS but this timing was all wrong. She had lied about her connection to Charles, and her husband had been too busy to dig up the truth. She needed to leave, and Charles would help her.

Cody's cell rang. It was his private phone, the one only a handful of people were allowed to call. The noise seemed to surprise him. Olivia took a step back as he dug in his pocket.

He jammed the phone hard against his ear. "What?"

Olivia stepped towards the house. Cody hung up the phone, took a slug of his wine and then coughed. The coughing turned into laughing—a deep, maniacal laugh. He had never sounded like that before. Olivia slipped into the house as Mallon walked onto the deck, braced for bad news. Even inside the house, she still heard Cody cackling like it was the end of the world.

ఆ ఆ ఆ

The men had all stormed out of the compound like a herd of elephants. It all happened too fast for Olivia to ask any questions. She caught scattered mentions of the construction site, the skeleton. Then they were gone and everything went quiet.

Olivia was never home alone. Someone always lurked in the shadows. Now she crept from room to room, making sure they had all left. Her laugh echoed off the windows. This felt like a game of hide-and-seek. She heard a ticking clock and a bird outside. Horror-movie quiet. Olivia went into her studio and turned on some music. She also switched on a TV for good measure and cranked both volumes. She ran into the master bedroom and jumped on the bed. She bounced a few times and then dropped onto her back with a whoosh that pulled the air from her lungs. The memory foam hurt when she landed.

Olivia pulled the duvet over her head. The weighty softness was almost too heavy, smothering. If she left, Cody would hold on to every stitch. She threw off the duvet. Bartending at night and painting during the day had worked before. Selling a painting here and there would give her some extra cash. She could do all that again. It would work if she wanted it to.

Olivia rolled off the bed, went back into the studio and turned off the noise. All her freedom and energy drained and she started pacing and fidgeting. Cody and his goons were still there. Signs of their presence—coffee cups, spare car keys, a smell of hair gel and gun oil—could never be cleaned away.

Her eyes flicked towards one of the security cameras as she went into her room. Cody claimed that camera was angled more towards the hallway than her bedroom, but she'd never believed him. For months, Olivia's world had steadily narrowed. The kitchen and dining room were gone. She moved out of the master bedroom step by step. First, she only dressed in the spare room, then read there before bed, then slept alone one night a week, then two, then four, now seven.

She caught her own reflection on a window. Andrea's mother had been Olivia's art teacher. She had a favorite piece of advice: *Move with intent, move with intent.* Olivia pulled out her dresser drawer and set it aside. Weeks earlier, she had bought a burner phone and taped it to the inside of the dresser. Olivia had a plan. All she needed was knowledge, sensitive knowledge that her rich and soon-to-be ex-husband would pay her to hold onto. A parting gift of a few million dollars seemed reasonable. That would be enough for her to leave town, set up somewhere new—Aspen, Austin, Olympia—paint, start a gallery, donate to schools. More importantly, it would pay for Andrea's treatment and give her kids a shot at a life outside Española. Olivia's stomach churned. She hated leaving them in that city.

The burner phone held only a few numbers: Andrea, an uncle who lived near Los Alamos and Janice Chávez, Cody's first wife.

"Hey," Janice said. "It's been a few days."

"I didn't want to call unless I had something to say."

"You all right?"

"Bored." Olivia lay down on the floor and put her feet up on the bed. "I am always bored."

"Don't be one of those rich ladies complaining about being rich. Boredom means you're not spending your money right."

"Like you?" Olivia asked.

"Excuse me, I do not complain. I enjoy every dime of Cody's money."

"I'm sure you do."

Cody divorced Janice right after making his first few millions. He was not a reflective man and he never dwelled in the past, but the importance of pre-nuptial agreements was one lesson Cody Branch definitely learned.

"Look, something's going on," Olivia said. "I don't know what, but he stormed off. I think all the drones went to the construction site."

"Oh? All of them?" Janice bubbled with excitement. "Could be all sorts of drama. No word on what?"

"Something big. He didn't even seem mad, more . . . surprised."

"That's even worse. I'll ask around."

"I'm getting nervous. He's going to figure me out."

"You're more on the inside than I am," Janice said. "Poke around. Find something."

"Hey, you're not the one tracked and filmed every second."

"There's got to be a room somewhere they forgot to secure. If you're finally alone, rattle some drawers."

"I'll talk to you soon."

Olivia always felt like a child when Janice scolded her. No one else knew what being married to Cody Branch was like, but Janice always found a way to make Olivia feel foolish. Janice banked information like a currency, so far she had lent Olivia plenty, but Charles was Olivia's big secret.

Bringing him to Santa Fe had started as a crazy notion, but Cody had been desperate and seemed to like how crooked Charles had become. Before she knew it, Charles was heading to town and Olivia was supposed to make sure one of the rental houses was cleaned out and ready for him. It had taken days to scrub away all traces of Andrea and the kids. Charles could sleep there tonight, and so could Olivia.

But first, she would visit the one room where all the cameras pointed outward.

Since he built it five years ago, the guard shack had never been empty. There was always at least one guy watching the monitors. Computer stations filled most of the space, as if her husband's men had emails to send and reports to read. She rattled the door of the gun rack in the corner. Locked.

The computers were all password protected. She tried a few phrases—Cody's birthday, "password," obvious stuff—but nothing worked. A bank of TVs along the wall showed the grounds, the hallways, the roof deck. She found the monitor that showed the entrance to her bedroom and shut it off. There were also a few screens that showed the offices near the Capitol and the construction site.

Olivia sat down to watch the show but could not tell what was happening. Media vans dotted the construction site, and the office was buzzing. She was at the center of her husband's world, yet she was totally blind.

She scanned the monitors for Charles. He was out there somewhere, and she would keep watching until he showed up.

# FIVE

GABE STOOD IN HIS LIVING ROOM with one hand against the wall,
testing his bad ankle. Since Jefe had told him about the cancer,
weak points had emerged in Gabe's body. He pictured a little man
swimming through his blood, sawing on support wires. That
morning, when Gabe got out of bed, the pain in his ankle had
knocked him back onto the mattress. By now it was a dull ache.

Gabe dropped onto his couch, reached into a gallon-sized
plastic bag full of marijuana and started rolling a joint. It took him
a few seconds longer than normal. No, no that's not a skill I can
lose, he thought. Gabe lit up, puffed a few times and exhaled as he
rolled onto his side.

His father used to treat the leather twice a year with mineral
oil, but Gabe let the couch fade and crack, like so many other neg-
lected things around the house. His father was an ugly man who
had built a beautiful home. Inheriting the property fifteen years
ago had been a surprise to Gabe. He never knew why it went to
him and not Lou. Helen was pregnant when they moved in, and
they imitated a happy couple for a few years.

Gabe looked out the sliding glass door. The house sat at the
back of a triangular plot. The front door opened to half an acre of
scrub, an old barn, remnants of dead gardens and assorted non-
sense his dad had tossed out.

New housing developments penned Gabe in to the rear. He
lived in the country, but the yuppies next door lived in the suburbs. They must hate Gabe, and he hated them right back. They
would drive him out one day, he knew that.

He released a cloud of smoke. That was tomorrow's problem. Today, Gabe needed to drive into Albuquerque to pick up his money before everything shut down. Gabe was owed his disability check and also a final payout from the construction company. Helen had been riding his ass about child support, and Gabe needed to pay up if he wanted to see Micah the next week. Spring Break was coming up and maybe the kid would want to give the bike another chance, or ride horses up to Bosque Peak. Something, anything. It was time.

Gabe pushed himself up, found some paper in a kitchen drawer and made a list. *Things to do with Micah: 1. Ride Horses. 2. Ride the bike up the mountain. 3. Things that kids like.*

He balled up the paper and tossed it in the trash can.

Gabe heard steps in the grass, muffled but heavy, right outside the back door. He tried to breathe through his paranoia. Dog, it must be a dog, he told himself. Or nothing at all.

A man, fat and tall, appeared, banged on the doorframe and yelled, "*Órale*, it's the police, we're here to fuck your shit up!"

Gabe coughed out the breath he'd been holding. Fucking Rey. The lawyer with a degree from Georgetown was standing in the dirt, dressed like a Hell's Angel and giggling. Rey's mustache was long with waxed tips, which shook even more than his belly when he laughed.

"One day, *güey*, I'm going to shoot your ass," Gabe shouted from the kitchen.

"Nah, you couldn't even hit a target big as me."

Gabe unlocked the back door and sat down. "I'm going to electrify my windows," he said. "Keep psychos like you from screwing around."

Rey filled the room with his presence. At six-foot-four and well past two-hundred-and-fifty pounds, Rey was always the biggest and loudest guy around.

"Like the time you were going to put land mines out front?" Rey asked. "That's still a good idea."

"Until you blow off a meter reader's foot."

"It would have been fireworks. Just enough to, you know, make people leave me alone. You know those yuppies next door are walking their dogs in my field? They ripped a hole in the fence. Should have you sue them."

"At least they're fertilizing the land, right? Whoa." Rey whistled and pointed at the fat bags of weed on Gabe's coffee table. "What the hell is all that?"

"Get me an orange soda and I'll share this joint with you."

Rey stomped into the kitchen and came back with a Fanta and a beer. "Now, what's up?" Rey picked up one of the gallon bags and hefted its weight. "This isn't real, right? These are movie props."

Rey's presence made Gabe feel less like an old man burning up the day alone. This was now a social engagement.

"Frederick gave it to me."

They had all gone to high school together thirty years ago, and even as kids no one ever called Frederick Freddie or Fred—there was always something formal about him, even when he was slinging dime bags to farm hands. Only one kid broke the rule. Junior year, new guy from the city called him Fred the Head. No one knew what it meant, not even that dumb kid, but Frederick made sure that was the last time anyone called him anything but his full, God-given name. Rey gripped the bag like it was welded to his hands. "He just up and gave you a pound?"

"Two pounds."

"Like a going-out-of-business sale, or what?"

Gabe handed Rey the joint. "Don't even say that. No, I earned this. Jefe out at Isleta grows . . . "

"No, no, I don't want to know what you two are up to." Rey took a drag and set the bag down like it was made of glass. "But, Scarface, don't leave this out on your coffee table. You got to hide the illegal shit. The cops bust in, make it at least a little tough for them to nail your ass. You got like three or four ratty sheds out there. Put it in a paint can."

Gabe groaned. "I'm not going to keep my weed in a shed. It'll look pretty weird for me to walk out to a shed three times a day. Besides, coyotes or something will get to it. I don't need stoned coyotes trying to eat my ass."

Rey looked at Gabe for a second and then burst out laughing, causing Gabe to do the same.

"Oh, dude," Rey said, "I know someone looking for a bed frame. Willing to pay. You still got that big one upstairs?"

"No, that thing's been gone for a couple weeks. I got five hundred for that. Rosie told me to take a photo and helped me put it on Craigslist. Some white couple drove down from Santa Fe."

Rey whistled. "Five hundred."

"Handcrafted, man. Only the best."

"I mean, at this rate you'll be sitting on milk crates in a few months, but whatever."

"You sound like my ex. I wasn't using the old man's furniture anyways."

"You find a job yet?" The joint looked small smashed between Rey's fingers. He inhaled a third of it in one drag.

"Nah, they'll start building again soon."

Rey shook his head. "I don't know. White developers plus Native land and bones . . . I'd look for a new gig, man. Did they really dump the skull in your truck?"

"No bullshit. I saw it. Fucking skull."

Gabe dropped his mouth open and rolled his eyes back into his head. His skull impression had scored Gabe a few rounds of beers over the past couple of weeks.

"Did y'all stop digging, or were the bosses pushing you to keep going? Who were the foremen out there, by the way?"

Gabe reached for the roach, what Rey had left of it, at least. "You sound like Courtroom Rey."

Rey let out a burst of laughter. "All right, look, don't tell anyone, but I got this case."

"Cool."

"No, you don't get it." Rey leaned towards Gabe. "I got *this* case. Real money. I'm telling you to find a new job. My clients are riding this all the way. Did you get severance pay or anything?"

"The tribe's going to move the bones, and we'll go back to work. I didn't get a severance because I haven't been severed. It's . . . paused."

"They should have given you something."

"I've got to go grab my last check in a minute. And my disability."

"You're still getting disability for that busted ankle?" Rey laughed. "I never should have helped you with that."

"I'm going to cash those checks until I die or the government runs out of money."

"When they ran you off the site, how'd they do it?"

Gabe smoked what he could from the roach, then popped it into his mouth. He swallowed, feeling pleasant heat in his chest.

"I'm not testifying, I'm not . . . whatever you're trying to do."

"This is important, man. These land developers don't care about the tribes or the workers. You don't owe them. *They* owe *you*."

Gabe shook his head. "You know I'm not into that stuff."

"You don't even know what's going on out there."

Rey took a swig from his beer. He had been talking revolution since high school, even carried a gun in his car and a knife in his boot. Gabe never bought it, even when he was a kid. There were not going to be any revolutions in New Mexico anytime soon.

"I need work," Gabe said. "I got to see Micah soon. Everyone needs this airport money. Your San Miguel clients need it most of all."

"I didn't say my clients were San Miguel. I'm heading to the construction site. Want a lift?" Rey stood up.

Gabe shook his head, and stretched out, resting his head back on the armrest. If he left for Albuquerque by two, he should have plenty of time.

"You don't get it," Rey said. "Trust me, my clients are very serious people, and this airport is not happening."

Gabe cracked one eye open. "No one cares about an old Indian skeleton. Don't fuck up my job with your asinine schemes."

Rey laughed. "*Asinine?* Where'd that shit come from?"

"Fuck you, man. I didn't go to law school but I know things."

"Don't get mad, Gabriel. Just joking around."

Gabe closed his eyes again. Pop used big words like that. Gabe must have inherited more than death from the old man.

"Fine." Rey guzzled his beer. "Thanks for the fortifications. Let's get a drink soon."

Gabe nodded without opening his eyes. A few minutes later, he heard Rey's truck start up. He must have left it at the end of Gabe's dirt road. Gabe hoped he stepped in dog shit. It never occurred to him to tell Rey about the cancer. How do you start telling people? Cancer. The whole idea of cancer was . . . asinine.

⁣ᴂ ᴂ ᴂ

The phone was ringing. Gabe looked around. How long had it been ringing? He rolled off the couch and found the phone under a pizza box in front of the television.

Helen.

Any other day he would let his ex-wife's call go to voicemail. Gabe took a breath, remembering that wall of black fire he'd seen in the sweat lodge.

"Hey," he said.

"Hi. Hello, sorry. I wasn't expecting you to answer."

"It's a phone. That's what you do."

"No, that's what *other* people do."

Gabe lay back on the floor and sighed.

"Are you at work today?" she asked.

"Not today," he said. "Day off."

"Good," Helen said. "Two things. First, can you pick up Micah from school today? He's staying late for a club meeting. He'll be ready at 4:30. It's fine if you don't want to. You weren't my first choice."

It was already two. Gabe would have trouble getting both checks and making it to Micah's school on time.

"Fine, yeah, no problem," he said.

"Really?"

"Of course. Damn, I haven't seen him for, what, a month?"

"Two. And bring that old truck. I don't want him on the Harley."

"Can he stay with me this weekend?"

"I mean it about the bike," she said. "And why does he have to stay up there? There's more to do in the city."

"Not the same. I want him up here. He should remember what his grandfather made."

"And what you've trashed by now."

"No, no, they're paying me pretty good on the building site, and I hired some *mojao* to scrub the house out. Looks real good."

Gabe sat up, pushed himself to his feet and grabbed a handful of beer cans. He tossed them in the trash.

She sighed loud enough to fuzz his phone's speaker. "Look, he's going to ask for your help. Some money. His friends are going camping at the end of the school year. Maybe if you come through, then he can go up next week during Spring Break."

"How much money?"

"He needs boots, outdoors stuff, the whole deal. I told him he could go if you paid for the gear."

Gabe knew Helen. This was her way of keeping Micah home and setting Gabe up for failure. She would be furious if he somehow came through with the cash.

"How much does he need?"

"Well, there's also a fee to get onto the campground and gas money."

"Numbers."

"Six hundred."

"Six? He wants a gold-lined sleeping bag, I bet. Lou and I used to sleep on old horse blankets."

"I knew it," she said. "Never mind, I told Micah you couldn't."

"Hang on, I've got it. I'm picking up two paychecks today. Two."

Helen went quiet again, searching for another excuse to say no. Gabe had heard them all: "Your house is dirty," "You're too far away," "He hates the country." They all meant, "Please, God, don't make my son start liking his father. Don't turn my son *into* his father."

She used to love Gabe's craziness. When Helen graduated from high school and met Gabe with his bike and his country attitude, she threw herself into his life head-first. Of course, she assumed marriage and kids would mellow him. Fun, crazy Gabe turned into just crazy Gabe after he hit thirty.

"It's been months," Gabe said.

"Months since you paid child support."

"He's sixteen."

"That makes him free?"

"No, that's not . . . " Gabe took a breath. "Okay, I'll give you the cash today. Six hundred."

"You owe us thousands."

"I'll give you a grand. One thousand dollars, today. That's all my construction money plus most of my disability."

It felt like a cattle auction. Before hanging up, they settled on a thousand today and a thousand next week when Gabe came to pick him up. Unless Micah said no, in which case Gabe would be out two grand and one son.

Micah would want to see him. He had to. If the kid was getting into camping and hiking, then no one could teach him better than Gabe. There were dozens of old trails up in the mountains that no one used anymore. Gabe knew them all.

He grabbed his keys and tested his ankle again. All good. It was 2:30. That meant two hours to get his construction money, cash his disability check and pick up Micah.

Paying Helen a grand today was easy but, with construction stalled the next thousand would be tricky. A handful of odd jobs might get him two or three hundred. Rey might float him a tiny bit. Gabe ticked through some options and did his best to not think about Frederick, Jefe out in the desert and the bag of weed that he was now squeezing so tight the seal at the top had opened.

It was a gift from Frederick for bringing Jefe's mushrooms onboard. Selling the weed would raise quick cash, but it would also quickly get his arms broken. If Gabe became Frederick's competitor, then the bone cancer would have to get in line.

Gabe shook the thoughts away.

Outside, the sun clung to his skin, hot and sticky. Despite Helen's request, the bike was the only option. The old truck, a boxy, steel beast that would have run forever if Gabe had done even a little bit of maintenance, was under a stack of tarps and busted tools on the other side of the barn—the engine locked. His small-frame Harley Davidson Sportster SuperLow was the nicest thing he had ever purchased, but now it was limping along like him.

Gabe looked up his long, dirt driveway, closing one eye and then the other. By the time he hit city traffic, he should be sharp again, sober.

"This will work," Gabe said.

He backed out of the barn. The sun warmed his skin. He kicked over the engine, lifted his bandana up over his mouth, and drove down the driveway. His spine buzzed and he felt alive with possibilities. Gabe wasn't dead yet.

# SIX

---

AFTER TWO DAYS IN THE OFFICE, Charles wanted to sneak out and get a job selling turquoise to tourists in the plaza. Or he could spin a roulette wheel on a reservation. Anything could be better than this.

From the start, he knew this gig would lack the high-wire energy of a campaign. Even his title reeked of corporate drudgery: Public Relations Supervisor. Diana Salazar, his boss, made it clear that his job was to write press releases about how much the developers respected native traditions. If he were lucky, Charles would run a meeting where the biggest challenge was kissing all asses equally.

The office made him look more important than he felt. Headquarters occupied a mirrored, two-story building adjacent to the state capitol, The Roundhouse. With the flick of a switch, the glass doors of the conference room became frosted for privacy. Even the cubicles occupied by sharply dressed young people in the center bullpen were made from thick oak. Charles himself had a commanding view of the mountains, which he had spent far too much time admiring.

Jordan knocked on his doorframe. "You busy? Can we go over the press release?"

Her office was ten feet away, yet she held her phone in one hand as if the president of the United States might give her a ring.

"Sure, but I'm leaving for lunch in a sec." Charles motioned to the chair in front of his desk. "My buddy runs Thompson Financial Services. Heard of it?"

"Heard of it, I think," Jordan said.

He had been sleeping in Lou's extra bedroom for two nights, and Jordan had fallen into the habit of coming over late at night and leaving at dawn. She seemed determined to avoid seeing Charles in the trailer at all costs.

"First, I have a question," Charles said. She raised her eyebrows.

He pointed over her shoulder. "Who are all those people buzzing around in the bullpen? They're dressed so nicely."

"Most work for Mr. Branch's other businesses. I don't pay any attention to them."

"They distract the hell out of me. They're like fish in an aquarium. Well-dressed, lawyerly fish."

Jordan formed an obligatory smile. "The dispute over the skeleton is coming to an end. I think the press release should make that more clear."

"How much more clear can I be?" Charles asked. "The first sentence is: 'Archaeologists have not found additional remains or artifacts at the construction site for Santa Fe County's future international airport.' The end. Some poor bastard got his ankle stuck in a rock a thousand years ago. Crisis over. Can I take credit?"

"Well, we've still got to be careful," she said. "Let's make it clear that the relationship between the developers and the Pueblo is solid. Strong. I have a few suggestions."

Charles knew the "let me tweak this" game. Hell, he might have invented that game. The kid had the self-consciously furrowed brows of someone dying to be a bitter old-timer.

"How many campaigns have you worked on?" Charles asked. "Political ones, not stuff like this or, you know, student government."

"Three. You wrote 'ancient burial ground.'"

He shrugged.

"That's too, I don't know, too Indiana Jones." She picked up a pencil from his desk. "I'm changing this to 'burial sites.' It's more neutral. Don't make these people exotic."

He stood up and grabbed his jacket from behind his chair. "Don't lecture me about being sensitive. I choose my words carefully."

"Diana wants us to be even more careful than usual. What if the whole airport goes down the drain?"

"An archeological survey cleared these parcels, and the tribe is saying we can restart once they relocate the bones. The drains shall remain free of airports. I'm heading to lunch," he said. "I can walk to the plaza, right?"

"How long will you be gone?"

"Not long enough for anything to happen."

ᴄᴤᴑ ᴄᴤᴑ ᴄᴤᴑ

Outside, Charles told himself to stop needling Jordan so much. Young people with limitless energy made the world go around. He knew he was probably jealous. Jordan still had a whole life to ruin.

Headquarters was on the edge of downtown and the historic plaza. Most of the adobe buildings had twentieth-century small-town facades, but the area dated back to the 1500s. The Spanish Governor's Mansion, an ancient, empty brick structure that was now a museum, didn't look too different from any other window-less administrative building. Charles imagined bearded, frustrated Spaniards in full armor wrestling with jammed copiers.

Wandering tourists looked lost in their pink gift shop sweat-shirts. Addie might have called the city quaint. The clock had started ticking on her impending visit. Less than two weeks.

He was meeting Thompson in a restaurant called Zuni. The plan was for Charles to be labeled a freelance advisor—somehow this would help Thompson write off some income. An hour catching up with an old friend and telling him about the most boring job in the world was worth a couple hundred dollars. Hopefully Thompson would buy lunch.

From the outside, Charles could tell the restaurant was nicer than he had assumed. A small army manned the valet, and every-one stepping out of the cars looked crisp and cool. Charles started to feel sweaty and overheated.

Despite the southwestern flair—paintings of Indian braves slumped in defeat, curved oval fireplaces in the corners and blankets nailed to the walls—the restaurant was familiar. Dim, wood-paneled restaurants where the powerful, or those who aspire to power, gather to revel in comfort and scotch were all pretty much the same, and he loved every single one of them.

Thompson had a goblet of white wine and squinted down at his phone through thin reading glasses. Charles was struck by his friend's age. The angle of Thompson's head caused his chin to bulge into a shiver-inducing pouch. Charles stroked his own neck, afraid of what he would find.

"Oh, you're so important," Charles said. "Can't put down your phone to say hello to a stranger."

"Don't ever think you'll escape idiots when you escape politics," Thompson replied without looking up. "They cling to all surfaces like oysters."

"You mean like barnacles."

Thompson pointed at his phone. "I mean like Republicans on financial advisors."

Charles leaned in for an awkward handshake and a crouching pat on the back.

Thompson left politics five years earlier. For a time, Charles dismissed his old friend as greedy, even traitorous. Another man cashing in his ideals for a few private-sector bucks.

"I can't believe you're out here." He slid the drink menu to Charles. "The land of retirees and breakfast burritos."

Charles hesitated over the drinks. The waitress appeared at his shoulder with water and flatware. A glass of red wine on a slow day was acceptable.

"It doesn't feel real," Charles said. "I've never had a gig out here: The Wild West. I did a House race in northern California, but that's not quite the same thing."

Thompson grinned. "It is not."

They had met when Charles was still in college. That race was his first campaign and Thompson's second. Over the years, they had worked together a couple more times, and always tipped each other off to good jobs. One time, late at night in a campaign office in Iowa, they locked arms and made drunken promises to keep fighting until they elected a good man president. They lost that race, and neither one mentioned the sloppy moment again.

The wine arrived. Charles ordered a dish that involved chicken and cheese.

"You got married out here, right?" Charles asked.

"Indeed. You were invited."

"I think I was in Delaware fighting for my life."

"No, it was before your misadventure in Delaware, but you sent some nice shot glasses. You're still married?"

Charles nodded. "Of course. Going great."

"Whatever you say." Thompson raised his hands as if to make peace. "So what's your gig out here? Congressman Solís?"

"No, not Solís, although maybe afterwards if all this goes well. . . . I'm working on the airport. PR stuff."

Thompson raised his eyebrows. "Oh, you didn't tell me that. I thought you were doing campaign work. Why would you be working for the airport no one wants?"

"Why don't people want it?"

"Because we don't need it," Thompson bellowed. "Northern New Mexico is growing, I guess, but it's not growing that fast. Nothing in this state has ever grown fast. You should have tried for . . . something else."

Thompson tapped his fingers on the base of his wine glass and avoided Charles' eyes.

"I took the best offer," Charles said. "Hell, I took the only offer."

Thompson looked around and smiled. "Yeah, yeah, you'll be fine. You know the game."

"Were you expecting me to tell you about Solís?" Charles was worried. "Is this airport info not something you need?"

Thompson shook his head. "Oh, no, no. In fact, the airport's all my clients can talk about. Half of them love it because they see an opportunity. The other half hate it because they see an opportunity that will make our little jewel of the mountains even more crowded."

Over the years, Thompson had developed a habit of punching certain words with exaggerated emphasis. It was almost hypnotic. Maybe the old sell-out was making too much money and had taken on the persona of all those rich donors that cling to politics like, well, barnacles. A second wine glass appeared next to Charles.

"Well, everyone's going to have to get over it. The skeleton is being moved. Both sides are ready to restart."

"Are they?"

"Sure are." Charles nodded. "Okay, tell me the truth. Do you miss the game?"

Thompson opened his eyes wide and threw his head back in mock, silent laughter. "Miss it? I do not miss it and I do not come close to politics. I'm in witness protection. If these people knew how much experience I had, they'd draft me onto every finance committee and every PAC for every asshole between here and Portland. I'm helping people make money and pulling in a good amount myself."

"Sounds nice."

"You have no idea. I vote, I recycle my wine bottles, I go to bed before midnight and I cut a check once a year to assuage my guilt. That's it." Thompson lowered his voice and leaned in close. "Besides, word to the wise, the game out here is a little too unsanitary for me. I feel much cleaner in finance, if you can imagine."

Charles sipped his wine. Thompson's point hit a little too close to home.

"Dirty politics?"

Thompson bobbed his head like he was trying to make up his mind. "*Dirty*? Not really, not like back east. Most of our politicians aren't powerful enough to be dirty. The people with money, on the other hand, they could be cleaner."

Charles looked around the restaurant. There was a hum of power and wealth in the air, but Thompson's words were hard to believe.

"Is there enough money out here for it to be dirty? What's out here? Gift shop moguls?"

Thompson looked surprised. "Oil. Gaming. Federal contracts. That enough for you? Plus, a desert big enough for plenty of bodies."

The food arrived, and Thompson cut off his words. Both plates struggled to contain a wash of color and soft textures.

Everything was covered in a green sauce flecked with black pepper, and Charles had no idea where the rice and beans began and where the chicken ended. Thompson ordered gin martinis for both of them.

"A guy named Cody Branch is calling the shots," Charles said, "Haven't met him but he's got all the gold, from what I hear."

"Yeah, and he's tough. Came from nothing to richer-than-God in about ten years. He made a boatload on fracking, then he made another boatload selling fracking clean-up supplies to the EPA and the state." Thompson took a bite of his food and kept talking. "If someone builds an outhouse north of White Sands, Branch makes a dollar."

Charles put his fork down. "Look, man, I'll be straight with you. I'm broke. The cash you gave me saved my neck, but can I make some real money out here?"

Thompson took Charles' honesty with ease. "Cody Branch has made a lot of people rich, but never out of kindness. If he wants you in the real money, he'll have an angle. He invests a dollar expecting five back. Tell me more."

Charles wondered how much of a return Thompson was expecting out of him.

"We're in a crowded office, nice place, real nice, next to the Capitol. But the only people working on the airport are me, a young research assistant and a woman named Diana Salazar. Supposedly I'm the PR manager, but Salazar's in charge of it all. She cuts through the bullshit."

"Damn right, she does." Thompson finished his wine. "I didn't know about her involvement. Should have guessed, though."

"Why is that?"

"Branch and his friends, which includes the governor and a senator or two, and a few people who are actually important, go to Salazar when they want something done right."

"Am I working for *crooks?* I can't work for more crooks."

"I would not say 'crooks.' Others might, but I would not." Thompson laughed. "The silver-haired lady in question was chief of staff in DC for Senator Baca. Managed his campaigns out here, managed the gubernatorial race a few years ago. Kingmaker

Salazar. Old school. And she's been skating a hair in front of investigations and allegations for years. Nothing crazy. It's never anything crazy, right? You know that. Favors for donors, state contracts to supporters, maybe a few salaries that get paid out of multiple campaign accounts over multiple years. Most of it probably isn't even illegal."

"You had me thinking I could make some money out here. Now I'm worried my boss will go to prison. Again."

"Hey, I'm probably exaggerating. This isn't *The Godfather*. You're working for people who push the rules. What else is new?"

"I suppose." The food felt heavy in his stomach, and Charles began to hate the lingering taste of spice and heat.

"Although, a few of Branch and Salazar's previous employees have found themselves in trouble."

"Prison trouble? Or resign-in-wealthy-disgrace trouble?"

"Usually the second, but not always." Thompson lowered his voice and Charles leaned forward. "Their two most recent big projects were a mall and a new racetrack. At a certain point Branch's company forms a new organization to finish the project. Totally separate on paper. The money is still going to Branch, but the connections are more obscure. New Mexico takes corporate privacy very serious."

"They form a shell corporation?"

Thompson rolled his eyes. "Nobody calls it that, but kind of. So, when things go wrong, and in those two examples things went wrong, the newer, smaller organization goes down and the head of that organization falls on his gold-plated sword. Branch and Salazar live to fight another day."

"But the Feds would notice that. Someone would notice that pattern."

"They come in, sniff around, can't quite put anything together. Federal law enforcement works on immigration and drugs out here. Short attention spans for millionaires in the mountains. The little guy gets a fine and probation, then moves to Montana and dissolves the corporation. Branch buys another neighborhood."

Charles put his fork down "What the hell? Why can't I just get a straight job?"

Thompson laughed. A waiter cleared their plates, giving Charles a minute to unclench his jaw. He took a sip of his martini. It burned his mouth.

"Maybe tread lightly," Thompson said. "Has it occurred to you that your new employer knew about your troubles and maybe thought, 'Now there's the kind of gentlemen not above telling a teeny, tiny fib or two?'"

"No, that had not occurred to me."

Thompson smiled. "You'll be fine, but keep me updated. I know the angles."

"And your clients pay for only the best angles."

The bill arrived. Thompson dropped a card onto the table and slid over a plain envelope full of twenties. Charles' consulting fee looked dirty but felt so wonderful. As they walked towards the door, Thompson clapped Charles on the back. The gesture felt both familiar and condescending.

"Living in the mountains has made you melodramatic," Charles said. "I'm here to do a job. Although, you make it seem like I'm involved with people that could make my future much more . . . remunerative."

"That you are," Thompson said. "Myself included."

They stepped outside into bright daylight. The comradely grin on Thompson's face was drenched in sunshine. "And, speaking of money, would you happen to know if Branch's airport contract has any limitations on gaming?"

"Gaming?"

"Gambling. People have noticed the airport is located on a Native American pueblo. Might some enterprising folk build a lovely, upscale casino resort nearby? Maybe, even, on the top floor of the new terminal?"

Charles laughed. "Why would I know that? I don't know about gaming. Besides, even if I did know, wouldn't this be entering into that 'insider information' area? That *federal prison* area?"

"Is it? Oh, that's such a vague area." Thompson thrust his hands into his pockets. "I have a lot of clients, wealthy clients. And they are convinced that a cute boutique hotel and a cute casino and golf course, right next to this cute little airport, might start exercising credit cards. Everyone wants an invitation to that party. If someone had that information, or any relevant information about the project, then that person might be hired on as a consultant. A freelancer, if that person would prefer. Cash, if that person is worried about taxes or debt collectors."

For the first time, Charles smelled the trees, the thin mountain air.

"You said you felt more sanitary working in finance. I'm not sure you should feel that way."

Thompson smiled.

Charles was getting sick of his friend's smiles.

"You stopped being sanitary well before Delaware, my friend, and what do you have to show for it? Stay in touch."

ぐ◎ ぐ◎ ぐ◎

Strolling back to the office, passing so many happy tourists, Charles breathed deep through his nose to dispel the booze.

For years, he ate rubber chicken dinners and cold pizza, slept on lumpy hotel beds and drank too much with kids like Jordan. Money flowed through politics like blood. Every palm was greased, but never his.

There would be nothing to it, nothing at all. Glance at some paperwork. Call up an old friend. Maybe get onboard with Branch as well. Two streams of income, two sources of stability, two guarantees for the future.

What time was it? He turned his phone on. Four missed calls, two voicemails and three text messages—all from Salazar or Jordan: *There's a problem. Get back here. Where the hell are you?*

Getting rich, he thought. Finally.

# SEVEN

GABE LIVED HALFWAY between Albuquerque and Santa Fe. On a good day, before the construction started, he could zip downtown in under thirty minutes. Once it was complete, the airport could push the trip to an hour. His small town had become the suburbs, but Albuquerque was getting farther away. That new geographic math confused the hell out of him.

Traffic slowed as he approached the construction site. A line of news vans was pulling into the gravel lot. Everything had been shut down for weeks, but now the site hummed.

Gabe cut in front of the vans and gave his name to a man in a hard-hat. The way this new guy scanned his clipboard made Gabe nervous. Being hunted for in official-looking papers made him nervous. After too long, the guy grunted, then tapped his pen against the page.

"Eh, there you are." He sounded disappointed, like Gabe's money was coming out of his own paycheck. "Go to the trailer where you clock in. Bobby's got your check."

"What's going on?" Gabe asked. "We starting back up?"

The guy pulled open the gate for Gabe to wheel his bike through, then shut it fast, as if the hordes were clamoring to get in.

"Nah," he said. "It's about the bones. I don't know. Was quiet until today."

The site looked different. Slick cars dotted the parking area and news vans were raising satellite dishes. Suited men moved in clumps, like gangs sizing each other up. Maybe Rey was up to something after all. Inside the fence, Gabe started his bike and rode to the foreman's trailer. Reporters interviewed a group of older Native Americans, and a handful of nervous-looking men in suits stood to the side. Gabe climbed the steps to the trailer, his bad ankle flaring.

Bobby, the assistant foreman, was peering through the blinds. He snapped back when Gabe opened the door.

"Gabey, Gabe, Gabe, you never learned to knock?"

"Don't mess with me, Bobby. I'm just here for my money."

Bobby huffed and grabbed a stack of white envelopes off the desk. He pressed his meaty thumb against his tongue and flipped through the checks.

"You going to lick them all or just mine?"

"You're not here." Bobby dropped the stack and went back to the window.

"No, don't mess with me, you remember I get cash."

"Oh, right, then you're in the other stack."

Gabe picked up the stack of envelopes meant for the guys without socials and people who had negotiated being paid off the books. He flipped through six or seven envelopes before realizing there was enough cash right here to make his problems go away. Quick scenarios flipped through his head. Grab the cash while Bobby had his back turned. Everyone would know he took the money but maybe Gabe didn't care. Hit the road with ten grand and a bushel of marijuana. Start a new life with a new name and die somewhere in Utah. Alone.

Gabe dropped the envelopes back on Bobby's desk. Feeling that money leave his hands almost hurt.

"Dude, you look like you're peeping into the girl's locker room," Gabe said.

"Something's happening out there, Gaber, and damn if I like it. What I like is getting paid for sitting on my ass."

"Don't call me that," Gabe said. "So we starting back up?"

Bobby slid open the window and leaned out on the sill. "They stopped telling me shit yesterday."

Bobby shut the window. "Can't hear a damn thing, anyways. You haven't picked up anything, huh? You always hear something."

"I've been hearing my couch break under my ass."

"You know, most guys who come in here aren't this happy. They get all squinty and sweaty when they see the checks. I'm tired of hearing about sick kids and empty gas tanks."

"Guess you have one of those fat, trustworthy faces," Gabe said. "Today is your lucky day. No sob stories from me. Hey, maybe that makes me the lucky one?"

Bobby shook his head and picked up a clipboard. "Yeah, Gabe, that's you. The lucky one. Let me know if you hear anything."

Back outside, the reporters were talking to the guy who had been driving the bulldozer that scooped up the rocks and bones. He swept his hands through the air and pulled broad faces like he was recreating what happened. Gabe sat on his bike, watching the scene. They found the skeleton weeks ago. Who the hell cared what some bulldozer saw?

Yet another news van pulled in. Gabe revved his engine once, twice. At the noise, the bulldozer operator looked up, recognized Gabe and pointed in his direction. The cameras and reporters swung around as if on a pulley and started advancing towards the trailer. His first instinct was to bolt, get out of there before they spotted him. Gabe straddled his bike. The reporters stepped through the dirt and rocks on their tiptoes. The women wobbled on their high heels, and the men looked like they thought the ground would give way.

Bobby opened the trailer door, smoothing his shirt over his belly and touching the sides of his hair. The crowd swarmed in a semi-circle around Gabe and his bike.

A small woman with eyes more white than blue thrust her mic forward. "Sir, Mr. Lula, how do you feel about this latest development?"

"Luna," Gabe said, "I'm Luna."

The reporters seemed taken aback.

"But this latest development?"

Gabe assumed she was talking about the airport.

"It is what it is, not that I like what it is." He tried to spot someone laughing, someone who would admit this was a prank.

"Not much you can do about it, though. Change, you know? It is what it is."

"What are your thoughts on Geronimo?" another person asked.

Gabe grinned. "Haven't jumped out of a plane in a while, so I don't know that I have lots of them."

A few people chuckled. Gabe started to relax. "I'll be on the news, I guess?"

"After what you saw, yes sir."

"You mean out with Jefe on the rez?"

Gabe wanted to kick himself. It was the first thing that popped into his head. The reporters made eye contact with each other, with the cameramen, no one quite understanding.

Another reporter held his mic forward. "Sir, a group of Apaches is now claiming that Geronimo's skull was dumped into your truck. Geronimo. How does that feel?"

Red lights glared from each camera.

"Right, this shit ain't funny no more. Rey set you up on this?"

No one moved. Gabe was still straddling his bike, hunched forward over his handlebars. He felt pinned to the ground, stakes driven through his boots. "Sir?" a voice asked. "Don't you have something to say?"

A life of accusations came back to him. *Can't you explain yourself? Don't you have a reason for the things you do? Say something.* Gabe started his bike. The gaggle took a quick step back.

"I didn't do shit," Gabe shouted. "I don't know shit. And I didn't do shit." He peeled out, kicking dust up around the cameras, and sped off the construction site.

ᥰᥰ ᥰᥰ ᥰᥰ

After hitting traffic and a line of broken-down people picking up disability checks, Gabe was an hour and a half late to Micah's school. The check-cashing places were all closed, so all he could give Helen was the cash from the construction site.

Micah was slouched on a concrete bench near the main building. His hair was cut into a style almost devoid of style—short on the sides, a little long on top, combed to the left. Gabe had never seen the kid in T-shirts or ripped jeans. He looked like a stockbroker stuck in high school.

"Mikey, what's happening, man?"

Micah caved in like a crushed beer can when he saw the bike. He stayed seated for a beat and looked around to make sure his friends weren't watching, or maybe not watching.

He pulled out an earbud. "You're late."

"This is when your mom told me to be here. She said you had a thing after school."

"I thought you were bringing the truck," Micah said. He hooked his thumbs on the straps of his backpack and rocked his head to the side. "I don't even fit on the bike anymore."

"Nah, hop on, there's plenty of room."

Micah worried the earbuds like an old woman with a rosary. By the time Gabe was sixteen, his personality was set. That kid who skipped school after lunch never went away.

Maybe Micah would be the same. Scared of the world at sixteen and scared of the world at sixty. "What about my helmet?"

Gabe looked back at the bike. The helmet was behind the blue recliner in the living room, where he had bowled it after the previous failed attempt to get Micah on the bike. That was a year ago, and he had hoped the kid would at least have grown curious about the Harley.

"I thought we could get you a new one," Gabe said. "One that fits better."

Micah arched an eyebrow, wanting, for a brief moment, to believe his father. He pulled out his phone. "Whatever. It's fine. Mom'll be off work in thirty minutes, anyway."

"No, no, it'll be cool. We'll go slow, take surface roads, no highway. Slow."

"Mom said you were supposed to have cash."

Gabe straightened. "She's not supposed to talk to you about that stuff."

"She said you'd help with the camping trip."

"Here." Gabe unzipped a side pocket in his leather riding vest and pulled out the envelope. "I got paid. I'm giving the cash to your mother today."

Micah nodded and looked at the ground. Gabe knew they had crossed some sort of boundary there. His son talking about money, about his father's deficiencies. It stung.

A man emerged from the school and made his way towards Gabe and Micah. He wore a striped white shirt tucked into slacks. He approached them at a casual angle, as if to look less threatening. Ray used to describe that move as "White Man on Patrol."

Gabe jammed the money back into his vest. "Everything fine here, son?" the man asked.

"Son?" Gabe interrupted. "My son, not yours. Unless his mother has something to tell me."

"It's okay, Mr. González. This is my dad."

González looked at Gabe and tried to keep his face neutral. Since growing his hair long and letting his mustache go wild, Gabe had seen that look ripple over countless faces. Some people, the best people, never blinked twice, but everyone else shook their head and tried to wish him away.

"Nice to meet you, sir." González smiled.

Gabe nodded and kept staring at González but didn't say anything. His presence made Gabe realize how different he and his son looked. They had the same sharp nose, and everyone said they had the same eyes, but Micah was light-skinned and his hair was dark blonde. The kid looked white, like his mother.

González grew very interested in his keys and drifted away. "Can you believe that guy?" Gabe asked.

"He's fine." Micah shook his head. "Not a lot of motorcycle parents here."

"You mean not a lot of *badass* parents here."

Micah smiled and let out a quick dismissive laugh through his nose. Gabe felt the impact in his gut.

"You know, if a girl sees you getting on this thing, she'll want to . . . she'll be impressed."

Micah's body posture thawed. "What makes you think I don't impress them already?"

"Get on the bike, smartass."

Micah sat on the bike and leaned back, away from Gabe, but when they pulled out of the driveway, he hunched forward and hooked his fingers through Gabe's belt loops.

Gabe focused on the road, keeping his distance from cars, stopping at yellow lights, not pushing the speed. Micah had been on the bike a handful of times. To Gabe it felt like they were sharing a secret language better than any words. Not that Micah acknowledged feeling any connection.

They stopped at a red light behind a white pick-up truck.

"Hey, your mom said you'd come up to the house this weekend," Gabe shouted over his shoulder. "That'd be good, don't you think?"

"This weekend?"

"Yeah, we'll hit the mountains. I mean, I heard you're getting into camping."

"Why does it have to be this weekend?"

Gabe took his left hand off the handlebar and turned around. "You haven't been around a lot and we should talk."

Micah leaned back and looked at the sky. "Mom said you'd be pretty weirded out by all this. About the camp and the church."

"Wait, you're going to a *church* camp?"

Micah nodded, then opened his eyes wide and pointed forward. "Whoa, whoa, Dad . . . "

Gabe snapped around and saw the truck's reverse lights. For an instant, he thought the bike was sliding forward. He gripped the brakes hard and grabbed the handlebars, but the truck kept backing up like a dumb slow animal. Gabe shouted but he didn't have time to wheel back, so he grabbed Micah by the collar and pushed him clear of the bike. At the same time, Gabe swung himself off and tried to lay the bike down without getting caught underneath. Cars around him honked and he jumped back.

A man in a starched white shirt came out of the truck cab and put his hands over his face. "Oh, buddy," the man said. "What happened here?"

"Fuck yourself, what happened here? I've got a kid with me and you start back . . . back . . . "

Gabe lost the words. His legs wobbled. Where were the words? His hands should have been around this man's throat. The sun beat down, but Gabe went cold. This is it, he thought. The first time the body truly betrayed him.

The driver waved his hands. The world came back to Gabe in a loud whoosh, and he heard a voice yelling at him. It was Micah, slumped against the curb.

He looked red-faced and younger than his years. "Dad, what did you do? You threw me to the ground to save your piece of shit bike?"

"No, no, I was helping. I was saving you."

"I can take care of myself."

"Look, buddy," the other driver said. "Maybe we should call the cops or something, but I didn't see you there. You must have come up fast on my tail."

Gabe pointed at the man. "You could have killed us."

"I don't think we need that sort of talk."

Micah stood up and brushed his clothes off. "I should have waited for Mom." His voice shook. "This is just so, so you."

The white truck pulled away and Gabe had to keep himself from hopping on the bike and chasing the man down. Traffic backed up behind them, and more cars were honking. Micah pulled out his phone and called his mother. By the time Gabe righted the bike and wheeled it onto the sidewalk, Micah was at a bus stop down the street, waiting for his mom to save him.

Thirty minutes later, Helen pulled into a parking lot beside the bus stop. Gabe's heart had stopped pounding, but Micah would not get back on the bike. They both sat in silence, feeling the heat radiate from the street. Micah kept his head down and avoided looking into passing cars. He swatted away all of Gabe's attempts at explanation. Micah stood when he saw his mom.

"No, no way," Helen said. "Where's his helmet?"

"We're okay," Gabe said. "Some idiot . . . "

"A helmet is basic . . . basic sense."

"We got in a wreck," Micah said. His voice shook.

Gabe saw the teenager trying to hide the little kid.

"Not a wreck. This truck was in front of us . . . "

Helen, still gripping her keys, pressed both hands against the sides of her head and looked down at the ground, breathing hard. Micah climbed into Helen's backseat. A wasted day. Who knew how many Gabe had left, yet this one had rotted away.

"He doesn't like the bike. Never has. Even you must have seen that by now."

"I didn't cash my check," Gabe said. "I didn't have time, but I have money. The construction crew paid me out."

Helen raised an eyebrow. "You lost your job?"

He shook his head. "No, it's temporary. Everyone's out of work, and that gives me time to come pick him up next week."

"You don't have a job. You got in a wreck. What makes you think you're seeing him next week or any week?"

"I'm sick," Gabe said. "I think it's serious. I need to see him."

Helen's mouth dropped open and her eyes went wide. "You're fucking sick, all right," she said. "You've never had a fever in your life. Don't pull some 'I'm scared of turning fifty' shit with me."

"Let him decide about this weekend," Gabe said. "Maybe he still wants to. I'll melt this bike down if he wants me to."

Surprise flashed over Helen's face before she locked back into her anger and got into her car.

Gabe leaned into the back window and shouted to Micah, "Dude, watch the news tonight, they interviewed me about the airport. I didn't even get to tell you about the skeleton."

Micah's eyes swung his way, then back out the window. Gabe saw strains of himself in that angry look.

Gabe turned to Helen. "I've got cash from the construction job. It's not a grand but it's close. I need to cash the other check . . . all the places were closed."

"Money isn't enough," Helen whispered. "You can't buy your way into being good for him."

"You said you wanted money. That was the deal you made."

"Deal? You only respond when I hound you. If I hadn't said go pick him up, be a father, you wouldn't have gone. I have to scare you, or you don't come through."

Helen shut her eyes. Gabe noticed the cracked, plastic steering wheel and the layer of dirt on her car. He reached for his vest pocket, but the zipper was undone. He reached into the other pocket. He patted his jeans and jammed his hands into his hip pockets.

Helen raised an eyebrow.

"During the accident," Gabe said, "my vest was unzipped." Helen started the car and faced forward, ready to leave Gabe in the dust.

"Both envelopes were here. Right here," Gabe said. "They were in my pocket and . . . "

Helen cut him off. "You're not even listening."

Gabe looked at Micah, who had his earbuds in and was retreating into his music, or was pretending to.

"I can do it. I can get the money. A thousand dollars." Gabe smiled. "It's me, you know I can do it. I can always do it when it matters."

"Guess what, Gabriel? I don't care anymore."

# EIGHT

CHARLES WAS HEADING BACK to the office with his head spinning. The meeting with the Apaches at the construction site had been brief—not much more than a handshake—but he had taken their numbers, and they knew his name. Good enough for now. Before hopping in the car, he had sent Addie a quick text: *Things are changing out here and it's good. Tell you more soon.* She had been calling and texting him excited questions ever since.

Charles cracked his window and let the air wash over him. Geronimo? He knew the name but only had a vague sense of the history. None of that mattered to him right now. When Salazar filled him in after lunch, Charles laughed and called it a hoax. He still assumed that was true, but he knew the truth would not matter. A good story buzzed, and this felt like a huge one.

He was so distracted that he missed the exit for the plaza and his office and spent twenty minutes doubling back. Since Delaware, Charles had been telling himself his career was not over, but this was the first real evidence of his survival.

 conabor conabor conabor

Finally, pulling up to the office building, Charles hopped out of the sedan. The sun was setting and the office was almost completely empty. Branch's cubicle fish must have been sent home. Jordan sat at her desk, and they eyed each other without a word. She had been visibly upset when Salazar sent him and not her to deal with the Apaches.

Indistinct voices came from Salazar's office. A man's deep rumble, followed by silence, then the man's loud voice again. The voices became clear as Charles went up to her door.

"We don't have a report yet," Salazar said. "Once we hear from the Apache . . . "

"I don't want a report. I want them to run them off. I am not letting anyone else in on this deal."

The man had a faint Texas twang Charles had not yet heard in New Mexico. Then the door snapped open and a man filled the doorway. He wore a chambray shirt tucked into jeans and a bolo tie that made his head look rotund, like a twist tie on a round loaf of bread.

"Boy, if I'd wanted coffee, I'd have pulled it out of your ass myself."

Salazar came from behind her desk and waved Charles forward. "This is Cody Branch, our fearless leader and the man spearheading the airport development. Cody, this is our man Charles. Hell of a first week for him."

Branch twisted the lower half of his face into a rictus resembling a grin. He wrapped both paws around Charles' and pulled him into a moist, meaty handshake. Branch was wide in all directions, a charging rhinoceros.

"Diana here's been sucking your dick for the past twenty minutes. She thinks you'll be able to get these Apaches out of our hair before sunset."

"Cody," Salazar warned, "Charles isn't quite used to your sense of humor yet."

Branch kept a hold on Charles, who felt he would be absorbed into the larger man's body if he didn't stand his ground.

"Listen, Frank, you came highly recommended. Highly. You're here to put out the fires, and these redskins are dancing with a leaky can of gasoline."

Charles' head spun. Did he call him Frank? There were two ways to deal with egos like this: set them back on their heels, or cower and hope they grew tired of smacking you around.

"Hell, I'm trying," Charles said. "Everything's happened so fast, but their story won't hold up. That's obvious."

"Good news," Salazar said.

Branch released his grip, stepped back into Salazar's office and settled onto the couch, looking every bit the emperor on expensive leather.

Charles cleared his throat. "I think you called me Frank. Name's Charles, but that's okay."

"If these Apaches aren't serious then what the hell do they want?"

Branch and Salazar looked to Charles as if he had all the answers.

"I didn't have a lot of time with them today. Laying the ground work, introductions and so on."

Branch's jaw was set and his eyebrows lowered. "Ground work? Frankie, this stoppage has, to date, cost me about twenty million dollars. No time for ground work."

"Well, San Miguel are okay with us starting back up, but the Apaches are a new wrinkle."

Branch looked at Salazar and cocked a thumb towards Charles. "Does your boy always do that? Tell you the obvious? Report on the wetness of water?"

Charles ran a hand through his hair. He thought he had done a good job on the site. He could not let Branch mess with him.

"It's a stunt," Salazar said. "They're raising awareness on Native issues, or they'll ask for federal recognition. They cannot really think that Geronimo was buried in the mountains outside of Albuquerque."

Branch sneered at Charles. "But how much to make them go away? Did you, or did you not, get a dollar amount?"

Charles felt the room slide under his feet. Maybe he should have stayed in Bethesda, at his mother's bank, asking customers if they wanted their money deposited into checking or savings.

"It wasn't the right time . . . "

"Sí or no?" Branch said in loud, mangled Spanish.

"No. But I met them, I met their lawyer, a big caveman kind of guy. They're coming in tomorrow or the next day. I tried to pin them down on a time but they blew me off."

"Of course," Branch said. "They're stringing this out. Make us sweat. I'm telling you, Diana, they're going to want money, they're going to want all the god-blessed money in all the god-fucked world."

"What about the reporters?" Salazar asked. "You told the press we were working with the tribes? You assured everyone we were in control?"

Charles felt his phone vibrate in his pocket. It was probably Addie.

"I did. I did all of that. They filmed the Apaches, then they interviewed a few construction guys who . . . "

"You're allergic to simple answers," Branch said. "Am I going to see your smiling mug on the news tonight?"

"They didn't seem interested in filming me."

"You weren't asking them to the prom, son. Diana, this guy doesn't have the nerves for this."

Salazar sat back, looking like she agreed.

"Wait," Charles said. "Wait one goddamned second. The press wasn't out there to talk to me or anyone connected to the airport . . . not even you. You could be building a hospital for paralyzed vets and not a reporter in the world would care. Don't you get it? This Geronimo story is going to be national, international, in an hour. It was a circus. But I got their lawyer's name and I set up a meeting, that's pretty damn good. And my name is not Frank."

Charles exhaled through his nose twice in a row. The sound loud and almost obscene in the small room.

Branch laughed from deep in his chest, and Salazar cracked a small grin. Charles pulled his mouth back into a quick smile.

"Well, Diana, your boy here can get it up when he needs to, huh?" Branch turned to Charles. "I've sunk vast wealth into this project and I need to know, right now, this second, if you have the guts to get us back on track."

"I do."

Branch held up a palm. "Wait. Not so fast. There are forces at play here that will swallow you if you let them."

"Cody," Salazar interrupted. "Let's keep some perspective. Charles doesn't need to . . . "

"The only perspective I need is my cost turning into a profit, and don't act like you're any different, Diana."

Charles hooked one hand around the back of his neck. "This doesn't sound like an airport anymore."

"Oh Frankie, you do stumble into the truth sometimes, don't you?"

Salazar leaned forward. "Cody, there's no . . . "

"We're not building an airport," Branch said. "We're building a casino."

Salazar stood up, walked behind Charles and closed her office door. "We didn't need to go there yet, and you know it. Charles, sit down before you fall down."

Charles blinked a few times and tried to clear his head. "A land development bond was posted by the county." He grabbed a chair and pulled it towards Branch. "Santa Fe voted for an *airport*. San Miguel agreed to an *airport*."

Branch waved his hands in front of him. "We're going to build an airport, too. But it'll be smaller than originally planned, and at the same time we'll be pouring some extra asphalt, that's all."

Charles rubbed his forehead. He had sat in on this meeting before. A boss had told him too much before, and it had cost him everything.

"You lied to the voters."

"No, no we did not," Salazar said.

"No way," Branch said. "Most of the casino will be built with private funds."

Charles groaned. "After the county has paid to run utilities out to the middle of nowhere, expanded the highway and has done everything that will make the casino possible."

Branch swung off the couch and was by Charles' side in an instant. He crouched down, looked Charles in the eye and put a hand on his shoulder.

"Son, I am going to make an unholy amount of money, and there will be plenty to go around for those who *believe* in this project. You can see why I'm anxious to get building again."

"We were going to tell you," Salazar said. "Bring you fully onboard, months from now, after you'd established yourself." She looked at Branch. "Seems we've sped up the schedule."

Branch fiercely held Charles' gaze, but betrayed no anger. Charles could not look away.

"Let's work on one of those simple answers," Branch said. "Do you believe in this project?"

Charles felt himself nodding before he realized it was happening.

"I do."

"Are you willing to invest yourself? Truly commit your time?"

"I am."

Branch smiled and cuffed a hand on the back of Charles' neck. The contact felt strong, reassuring. In Delaware, Hunt was sitting in prison because of a single meeting. Other men with Charles' same experiences had parlayed their careers into high-dollar consultant work and think-tank salaries. For years, Charles' prize kept slipping through his greased-up fingers, but now he had it. No, Cody Branch had it, but Charles was going to claim his fair share.

# NINE

GABE STAYED ON THAT STREET corner for an hour; turning his pockets inside out, convinced that if he looked in his vest pocket, or in his shirt pocket, or his hip pocket, again and again, then the money would reveal itself.

The accident had barely touched them. Micah scraped his elbow, Gabe maybe strained his calf a little, but that was nothing. The old man would have told him to forget it, say one prayer, give God his bit and move on. But Gabe could not shake the fear that had a grip on his stomach and he had stopped talking to God years ago.

Back home, the fear blossomed into panic. He roamed from empty room to empty room. He imagined every scenario: the wheels crushing Micah. His head banging hard against the curb after Gabe pushed him off. Or the truck reversing, pinning them on top of each other. That was the worst one: Gabe knowing he was crushing his son, while the muffler burned his face and he twitched his arms under the truck.

After a few beers, the terror receded, but the day's real conclusion became unavoidable: he was screwed. It would take weeks to get a replacement disability check, and no way would the construction company pay him twice. Any philosophical or religious debate about why they had survived, or where the money had vanished to, or even the disease nibbling at his bones, was burned away and replaced by the very real, very solid figure of one thousand dollars. Helen needed money, and Gabe needed to see his son.

Around midnight, after hours of pacing and smoking and running his fingers through his beard, Gabe headed to The Pig. Either he would see some friends who could help him out, or he would get drunk enough to stop worrying. Both sounded great.

The Pig was a double-wide trailer out on Jarales Road, where the town thinned out and gave way to ranches. Angie, the owner, had knocked down the interior walls and built brick columns to hold up the roof. Faint outlines of wall joints were still visible on the plastic floor. There used to be plenty of bars around town where Gabe felt comfortable. They were places with simple rules: don't touch the waitress, don't hit anyone, don't piss in the parking lot. But half the old places were shut down now, and Albuquerque yuppies had taken over all the downtown spots and turned them into cocktail "lounges." The Pig and Lucero's place near the highway were all that was left. Everywhere else had a valet or was an Applebee's.

This late, The Pig was quiet and dappled with the colored light of neon beer signs. Most of the floor lamps were off. A boom box behind the bar played Angie's favorite whispering, female radio DJ, spinning love and break-up songs. Guys Gabe knew from high school drank Bud Light in the corner, as usual. At the bar, Angie poured wine for Rose. Sitting with the guys would have pulled him into chatter about the old days—all they ever talked about. Rose was more fun. She was consistent. She may not have been in The Pig every night, but Gabe saw her every time he was there. They had dated in high school, even went to the prom together. They never stopped flirting, but nothing had happened between them in decades.

Rose flashed Gabe a quick, distracted smile. Angie handed him a beer before turning back to Rose. "Girl, come on, this isn't so complicated. Your son is your son and should do what you say. Simple."

"I know," Rose whined. "But, what, I'm supposed to say yes to him joining the Army in six months, but he can't stay out past midnight this weekend?"

Angie shook her head and leaned back against the wall. She turned to Gabe. "Did your mom flip out when you signed up?"

Gabe looked over to Rose, who blinked away. His mom had vanished years before Gabe enlisted.

"Oh, I'm sorry." Angie put her hand on her forehead. "I forgot. I just forgot."

"No sweat." Gabe turned to Rose. "And don't let your boy join the damn Army. God knows why I did. He wants some *pendejo* to yell at him, tell him to come cut my grass."

Rose screwed her face up. "He'd go AWOL right now if he thought he'd end up like you. Bum at work, bum at home."

Gabe bristled. "Hey, I'm a good dad."

Angie laughed, "That so, Private Luna?"

"I saw Micah today. He's into camping, and he always wants to ride. Can't keep him off my damn bike."

"*Mentiroso*, you told me he hated that thing."

"Nah, when he was a kid. He's stronger now. Older. We're going to ride to California, and I wasn't a damn private . . . not for long."

Gabe smoothed his mustache. The Micah stories felt good in his mouth. They even felt like they could be true. One day, Micah would wake up and want to hop on the bike. It could happen. Angie handed Gabe another beer.

Rose raised her wine glass in a mock toast. "Well then, you're Father of the Year, Admiral. My boy hates school. Fine, the high school's crap. It's the same rundown buildings and the same mean teachers we had, but he's pretty good at math. Not great, but pretty good. So, he says, 'Ma, the Army can teach me math better than any college, and I'll get paid.'"

"The Army doesn't have admirals."

She rolled her eyes and turned back to Angie. "So I ask him: 'You think you'll get paid more if some fucking psycho blows your head off? You think the Army ain't sick of paying off the families of dead Mexicans?' He shuffles his feet and mumbles, like always, right? Kid thinks he's bulletproof."

"My Army was boring," Gabe said. "I was lucky. Slipped in and out between the wars like a snake."

"I've heard you tell people you were in Desert Storm," Rose said.

Gabe shook his head. Had he spun a whole tale about fighting in the desert?

"Take your son to see Mrs. Baca," Angie said.

"Baca who?" Gabe asked.

Angie and Rose looked at him like he had pulled out his dick.

"What do you do all day in that big house?" Angie walked away to tend to the other customers.

"The local kid," Rose said. "He died, you know, somewhere over there. It's been on the news." She sipped her wine. "So, Lieutenant, Mr. Best Parent in the Universe, do I tell him no or do I let them ship my baby to the desert?"

Gabe finished his beer. "We got deserts here."

"The wars in our deserts are over."

Gabe shrugged. "Hell, I don't know, Rose. Wars can't last forever."

They dropped the subject and drank side by side. Gabe wanted to come straight out and ask. Being honest with Rose had worked in the past. If he got a few hundred from her, a few hundred from some other friends, then Gabe might be on his way. But now he couldn't do it, not after bullshitting her about how great everything was with Micah. Angie brought drinks, then more drinks. Gabe told dirty jokes that made Rose laugh and made Angie shake her head. The knot of anxiety in his chest slowly loosened.

An hour later, Rey showed up dressed in full motorcycle leathers: chaps, a long-sleeve leather jacket, even a leather bandana around his big head.

"Now that was a goddamned day to remember." Rey's voice was loud enough for half the bar to glance up. "Did you see those guys shaking in their loafers?"

"Rey, it's late, don't get all worked up." Angie handed him a beer.

"Hon, we brought down an airport today. Who should we go after tomorrow?"

"Hey, *carnal*," Gabe said, "can we talk?"

"I saw you out on the site." Rey settled onto his stool, his bulk threatening to splinter the wood. "These Apaches are no joke, huh? You were on the news for a second, did you see it?"

Gabe nodded towards the corner. "Real fast."

Rey sighed. All his leather creaked when he stood back up. If Rey wanted to be an activist, then here was one dude in particular he could help. They went to a white plastic folding table in the far corner under a Smokey the Bear sign on the wall.

"You know it was Latinos who found that cub in the forest, right?" Rey said. "And they didn't name him no Smokey. They named him *Humo*. But, no, we can't have *Humo el Oso* telling white people what to do, so they changed his name."

"I lost my money," Gabe said. "Lost it. Didn't spend a dime, not a dime."

Rey put his hand on his chest. "You mean, you don't want to hear about my crusade for justice and the rights of indigenous people? I am shocked."

"Micah and I were in an accident."

"Look, get your story straight. Pick one: you were in an accident or you lost the money."

"I got to see my kid. Give me a job for a couple weeks."

"You a lawyer now? Congrats. I'll put your name on the door." Rey pointed a finger at Gabe's chest. "If it's so serious, then sell your house."

Gabe wanted to slap Rey's hand away. "That's my everything, man. And it'll take too long, I don't have time."

"The bike, then. You could sell that tonight, in an hour, if you wanted to."

"Be serious, how would I get around?"

"Do you want help or not?" Rey laughed. "Christ, you know what to do. You've got pounds of weed sitting on your coffee table, man. Serious stuff. It makes what the rest of us smoke seem like *piñón*. Sell that, and you've got your money."

"Of course, but," Gabe looked around and lowered his voice. "I can't sell Fredrick's weed out from under him. You want to get me killed? Hire me, I can help."

"I'll let you know if my clients need anyone to smoke them out. Until then, you're fucked. You have one thing, and one thing only, that you can sell very quickly for a lot of money. Hell, even *I'd* buy some from you. What else you going to do?"

Rey's solution made Gabe too damn nervous. There was the law. Not the actual law, not Officer Smith with a nightclub, but the law of being friends with a drug dealer. Don't cut into his territory, not even for a nickel.

"I've got to go," Rey said. "I'm still working, if you can believe it. I thought stopping in here would be relaxing. Those Apaches are running me ragged, but man we can use this to recruit more Chicanos to the cause."

Gabe finished his beer. "A bunch of whiny wetbacks and Indians ain't a cause."

Anger crossed Rey's face, but then he smiled. "Oh, Gabe, I'm trying to make this world better, even for *pendejos* like you."

Gabe stayed by himself in the corner, finishing his beer and signaling for another. Angie turned off the open sign but wouldn't kick anyone out. She wouldn't even lock the door. She would keep serving as long as people were there. He rubbed the bridge of his nose.

Rose drank by herself at the corner of the bar. Gabe steadied himself and made his way to her side.

He folded his arms on the bar. "You know, I'm not going to be around forever."

Rose kept playing a game on her phone, lining up jewels into a pattern.

"Oh please, you'll be drunk and dancing at all our funerals. You're one of those guys. Unstoppable."

"No, no, no it's about time to stop," Gabe said. "All of it. Smokes, drinks, everything. That's what my old man did. Said that he used to drink too much, after the war, but then one day he stopped. No more beer, no more cigarettes. Fortitude. That was the word he used. Said all it took was some fortitude. Not that it mattered when the cancer came along. So why should *I* quit, right? I'm getting another beer, want one?"

"I can't get past this level." Rose made a face at her game. "Gabe, you're not making much sense. I don't think either of us needs another drink."

"For. Ti. Tude. Damn old man was full of words like that. Pronounced them slow and perfect, like casting a spell." Gabe laughed and lifted his empty bottle in the air. "Cast a spell he did. Thanks, Dad."

"Did you really see your son today?"

Angie was ignoring him, so he put his bottle back down. "I did. I did. Damn near killed him. I don't know the boy, but, you know what's worse than that? He thinks he knows me."

"Spend more time with him."

"I'm trying."

Gabe's voice was louder than he'd meant. Rose flinched and looked up.

"I'm trying to see him this weekend." He scratched the side of his face. "It's important."

"Good, just don't take him to a stock show or out on the Harley. That's not him, that's you."

Gabe snapped at her. "You don't know shit about us."

She blinked a few times. "What's that?"

"I'm trying to carve something with my own hands. You people are drowning me."

Rose slid off her stool, unsteady. "You know what, Gabe? This is why your son hates you. Good luck fucking up his life, too. You're bound to do it one day."

She flipped him off and went outside.

Angie came over. "Hey, you yell at her or anyone else like that again, Gabe, and I'll kick you out for good. ¿Entiendes?"

"Ange, you know, if I die, I'll leave you some cash. You know that, right?"

She turned to wash glasses in the sink behind the bar.

"I was thinking I should work here," Gabe continued. "With you. I could clean up and do whatever you need."

Angie shook her head. "No, no, no. You're fun, Gabe. Most of the time. But I'm not giving you access to alcohol or cash."

"Damn, that's harsh."

"You think you're the first drunk to try to charm a job out of me? If I say, you're hired, then you ask for an advance on your first paycheck. Right? A small one?"

"When I'm gone, y'all are going to feel damn shamed of your-selves."

"Take a deep breath."

"Just trying to help you out."

She pointed to the empty bottles. "You do plenty."

Gabe turned and rested his elbows on the bar. The place was emptying. A group of men in the corner played drunken dominoes, and two of the tables held solitary drinkers peering around at everyone else. One of the men looked ancient, skin stretched apart by time and sun. The other solo drinker was younger than Gabe, with a field worker's crisped brown skin. Gabe told himself he was different from these guys, alone and drinking away their lives.

Right then, two white boys, college kids or maybe high school seniors, very young, came into the trailer. They tried to keep a straight face. Gabe knew what they were doing. Going on a safari, slumming it, seeing how the Mexicans did things. This was how the bleaching started. First, it was a couple white boys thinking they were conquistadors. Then, they would tell their friends about funny old drunks and a place that never closes. Gabe would have to find another bar. Everyone in The Pig felt their presence. The closed-circuit had been disrupted. Gabe realized what separated him from his friends and the other drunks at The Pig. He was willing to act.

The kids sat down at a table. Their eyes were stoned slits and they could barely contain their high, condescending smiles. Gabe enjoyed watching them tense as he grabbed a chair.

"¿Burqueños?" he asked. The kids nodded obliquely.

"From Albuquerque?" he repeated.

"Yeah, yeah," said the boy wearing a yellow knit cap.

Gabe pointed over his shoulder. "You order at the bar."

The boy in the red hoodie stood up. "I'll go."

Then the other kid stood up. "I'll go with you."

"There's only two types of beer here," Gabe said. "Need to vote on it? Hold hands?"

The hoodie sat back down. Ah, Gabe knew this was the tough one.

"Yeah, go get me whatever, man. I don't care."

"You two been in here before?" Gabe asked.

The kid tried to fake being relaxed. "First time. Heard it was a cool place. Name's Tyler. People call me Smokey."

"No, they don't. No one calls you Smokey. Don't even try that shit here."

Knit Cap came back to the table but remained standing. "We got to go, dude. She carded me."

"What?" Tyler-Smokey asked. "What'd you say to her?"

"I asked for a beer, and she carded me."

Gabe looked over his shoulder. Angie was glaring at him, her hands on her hips. "Yeah," Gabe said. "Time for us all to go."

The stoners tried to hold it together, but Gabe could smell their nervous sweat. He followed them out of the bar. Rose was smoking outside, and Gabe tried to lead the kids away from her.

"Shitty place, anyway," Knit Cap said.

"What kind of weed are y'all smoking?" Gabe whispered.

The kids looked at each other, scared.

"We're just chilling," Tyler said.

"Yeah, sure, chilling. But you can't be smoking nothing too strong, or you wouldn't need beer."

"What you know about that smoke, Cowboy?"

"Man, let's go," said Knit Cap.

"I got weed that'll put you on your ass," Gabe said.

"How much?"

"Two hundred an ounce. No, I'm serious. This is all you need. Here." Gabe gave the kid a joint out of his vest. "Come back here tomorrow at two PM for more. One thing . . . " Gabe pointed at the bar. "After you buy from me, you don't come back here."

"We wouldn't drink in there if that bitch paid us."

"Tomorrow afternoon."

Tyler nodded. The kids got into their car and drove away. Gabe closed his eyes and took a deep breath through his nose.

The early spring nights were still cool. A breeze from the north carried thin mountain air down into the valley. The wind smelled like a mix of sweet *manzanilla* and cloves mixed with the dirt coming off the soybean and wheat fields. Southern breezes held the desert in them and almost no scent at all, but the mountain breezes filled Gabe with the even certainty that this was his spot. Then he swayed on his feet and needed to open his eyes before he fell over.

When he turned around, Rose was smoking a cigarette and watching him. "Were those kids friends of yours?" she asked.

Gabe shook his head. "Giving them directions back to the highway. They were lost."

She nodded. "Yeah, they looked it."

He strolled to his bike, making sure she could see how the chrome gleamed. In the sunlight, you could see scratched paint, cracking handlebars and balding tires, but in the moonlight Gabe imagined the Harley looked coiled, powerful. Sometimes, women he met drinking wanted to have sex on the bike, which Gabe avoided because it required a combination of balance, arm strength and a lack of concern for the side-stand. He'd only successfully managed it twice, but those experiments had convinced Gabe that running his fingers lightly over the seat was enough to pull most women towards him.

Rose snorted, dropped her cigarette and went back inside.

⋘ ⋘ ⋘

Gabe knew it was late, but there was no light on the eastern horizon, so that was a good sign. On the ride home, he noticed the Baca kid's name everywhere. Gas stations, car windows, even fast-food restaurant signs that usually said "$1 Cheeseburger" now said, "Thank you, Eliseo Baca."

Gabe sneered. Thank you for being shot, really nice of you to go get killed. No signs had sported the old man's name when he came back from the Pacific. No one thanked Gabe when he came back, either. No matter the only blood Gabe saw was when one of the kids in Basic broke his own arm on purpose. Poor bastard had grown stronger without realizing. When that scared kid brought his forearm down on his footlocker, one of the bones popped right through the skin, making a slicing *thwick*, like a piece of paper torn in half. At least, that was the story Gabe told everyone.

Sludgy tension crept into Gabe's mind. He could see the truck's reverse lights from the accident with Micah. He was convinced those white kids were the sons of cops. Or they might blab. Blabbing would be worse because blabbing would get back to Frederick. Gabe had crossed a line with those kids.

Walking back into his house used to make Gabe feel better, but tonight it felt empty and cold. Most of the lights were blazing because Gabe hated coming home to the dark.

There was crystal in his freezer. He had only smoked it once before with some chick he had met at Lucero's. It was fun. Like swimming. Like almost drowning. He kept the shards wrapped in foil in the freezer, the same way the old man did with batteries and medicine. He sprinkled the plasticky slivers over a few grains of weed in his pipe and set it ablaze. A burnt smell filled the air and his lungs.

At first, it felt good. Gabe sat on the couch and closed his eyes. The room spun to the left, then paused and came back to the right—smooth, like a swaying boat. It reminded Gabe of the ship he had been on in the Marines. Wait, no, Gabe shook his head. He was Army. His dad was the Marine, six feet of pure Mexican Marineness.

Gabe scratched the side of his face—it didn't hurt then but he would notice welts in the morning. It must have been the accident that brought up all those memories. Most World War II veterans came home and never spoke about the war, but Gabe's father never shut up. Riding horses through the mountains, he would tell Gabe and Lou, "those Jap planes dived so close I could see the pilot's teeth filed to points." Bedtime stories for the boys were about his ship sinking and him treading water for twelve hours. "Warm water, comfortable," he said. "Fucking paradise water full of blood and sharks."

Gabe's dad wore a life jacket, so he lived. Most of the other men panicked and jumped in without one. The old man said he felt a shark's nose press into his back, but he stayed still, so the shark moved on to some poor bastard who was all flailing limbs and pissed pants.

"How'd you know it was a shark?" Gabe once asked.

"Well, it wasn't a fucking mermaid."

That was his father's wisdom. You have to jump? Jump with a life jacket. If a shark touches you, pretend nothing's happening. It drove the old man crazy, of course, floating with nothing but southern constellations above and the blood and twitching remnants of his friends below.

A siren went off. Gabe opened his eyes. A fire alarm, maybe a tornado. Each fiber of the carpet swayed in the wind from the ceiling fan.

Gabe sat up and his head cleared long enough for him to feel sick. The meth was too old, spiked, poisoned. He needed to catch his breath. He needed help, but he was all alone. He dug through beer cans looking for cigarettes, but all he found were piles and piles of beer cans, enough to build a stinking mansion.

Once, when he was a kid, Gabe came to his father and told him he had heard something outside the window. His father said, "Maybe it's the devil. Now, go back to bed." The siren boomed again, loud enough to shake his skull. It was the police arresting him for the disability scam. No, the man in the white truck came back to finish Gabe off. Geronimo wanted his skull back. Or Frederick. Those kids told Frederick.

Maybe it's the devil. He should go to bed. The siren wailed, and Gabe's arm hairs stood on end. Guns, he had guns in his bedroom. Gabe took the stairs faster than he had in years. He heard his name. A woman's voice held out the syllables, stretching the vowels to insanity. *Gaaaaaaaaaaaaaaabeeeee*. He locked the bedroom door. Guns in the closet. Lots of them. Hunting rifles, a couple handguns for protection and one big monster assault rifle. Now he heard footsteps on the stairs. Slow, thumping steps. A shotgun in his hands, but he forgot how to check if it was loaded. He looked down the barrel. The pounding moved to the bedroom door. The frame shook and cracked. He locked himself in the bathroom, crawled into the bathtub and cradled the shotgun. He heard wet steps outside, the swish of a current, and the demented wailing didn't stop.

"I told you the sharks would get you one day, Gabe."

Gabe cocked the gun, pressed back into the wall, trying to disappear, his feet slipping on the wet ceramic tub, and he pointed the barrel at the door.

"I'm going to do it," Gabe shouted. "I'm finally going to do it!"

The top half of the bathroom door evaporated into a cloud of dust. In the silence after the gunshot, the siren's wail eased into the ringing of a cell phone. It was ringing in his own pocket.

Rose.

Gabe held the phone in one hand, the shotgun in the other, crouching in the bathtub. He dropped the phone. The world finally went quiet. Dark mold was growing in the space between the tiles, and grey hairs clogged the drain like daisies in concrete. Someone had called him; someone was checking on him. And Gabe was alone, cradling a loaded shotgun. But that was okay. Being alone was okay. It all made more sense that way.

# THURSDAY

# TEN

CHARLES WAS HUNGOVER, and the road to his new house snaked up the side of a mountain, so his first act in the house might be puking in the toilet. If he could wait that long. Salazar had given him the house keys last night in the office, but he had crashed at Lou's.

When he went back to the trailer to grab his suitcases, Lou was drinking beer and watching TV. Charles sat down to have a quick one. Then one turned to two, turned to three, turned to Lou and Charles bonding over how much Diana Salazar scared them. The beer was thin and yellow, and the cop show they watched was boring. Perfect. All of Charles' DC friends, those who still spoke to him, only talked about politics. He needed a dumb night with a crate of piss beer.

Charles' stomach churned as he remembered Lou and Jordan were coming over for dinner on Saturday night. Full of drunken good cheer, the invitation had seemed like a good idea. Now, he was unshowered and almost late for work.

This road was torture. He was up the side of a mountain just outside of downtown. Juniper and mesquite trees hung low over the street and buckled the asphalt. The houses themselves were set behind adobe courtyards, and Charles had no way to tell if this neighborhood was run down and abandoned or ancient and luxurious.

When his phone rang, he knew it was Addie without even looking at the screen. Charles answered, put the phone on speaker and placed it on the console next to him.

"Hey," he said. "I'm driving. What's up?"

"Calling to see how it went yesterday," Addie said. "You got so excited, then I never heard anything."

"You haven't seen the headlines? Things are blowing up."

"Yeah? I didn't notice anything, but I'm glad something's up. You were worried the gig was all over."

"Definitely not worried about that anymore."

Charles had a secret. He could tell her about the casino and Branch's plans for world domination and wealth. He should tell her. He knew there was no reason not to tell her, but he held back.

"I think this is going to work out for me," he said. "There's a ton going on. I don't even know where to start."

"I'm glad you're happy. You driving to work?"

"Dropping my stuff at the new house first."

"I got my tickets," she said. "I'll be there next Friday."

Her voice was neutral, waiting to respond to Charles' emotion. His silence lasted maybe half a second, but that was long enough.

"Yeah, yeah that's good." He said it loud, as if he could make up for his hesitation. "Things'll be less crazy by then. I can show you around."

"Yeah, okay. Great, I guess."

Despite her frustration, she was still too generous. Charles knew Addie would work for their relationship, keep sacrificing past all reason. Cold threads of guilt wrapped around his bones.

"I really," Charles paused, "I know this is hard, but this job will be worth it. There are real opportunities here."

As he drove up the mountain, the houses became more spaced out and the land between them more wild and dense with trees and brush. He found the correct street and pulled into a short, gravel cul-de-sac on which there were only two houses.

"There's another thing," Addie said. "It's not good."

Low walls jutted out of the narrow, adobe house, like two arms reaching forward in protection. A thick wooden door looked like it opened onto a courtyard. The initial impression it gave was of cloistered luxury. A monastery in Beverly Hills. Charles hopped out of the car and almost left the phone behind.

"Babe, I've never seen a house like this. It's out of a magazine."

"Can't wait to see it, but I have to tell you about your friend Jim Hawley."

The courtyard door had been repurposed from an old church. Through a cross-hatched grill, he could see a spread of cacti and coarse desert grass. In the courtyard, the air smelled dark and fertile with overgrown plant life.

The front door was frosted, corrugated glass. Inside, the thick plaster walls were smooth as icing. The ceiling was lined with walnut-brown *vigas* and the floor was slate, cool to the touch. Charles wanted to caress the smooth surfaces and take it all in.

"I'm listening, I swear," he said. "But this place is unreal."

"Jim was arrested in Syria," said Addie.

Charles noticed a pair of high heel shoes by the front door. "Hello?" Addie asked.

"I'm here, but what do you mean? Like, *Syria* Syria?"

The shoes were out of place, left behind, but they also looked at home, arranged as if the owner knew exactly where to put them.

"Some NGO work," Addie said. "I'm not sure. Democracy-building stuff, but the Syrians came in, busted it up, accused everyone of spying."

Charles looked down the hall towards the bedrooms. The house was empty. It had to be.

"You don't seem concerned," she said.

"Well, Jim Hawley had a temper. Every campaign he punched a hole in the drywall. Every campaign. He did it to make a point, but it became a joke after the fourth or fifth time he did it. Probably decked a Syrian senator. Do they have senators?"

"Charlie, he's being accused of spying. Everyone else was released, but they're going to make an example of him. State has threatened to pull the ambassador."

One of the bedroom doors was cracked open a bit, and Charles pushed it open all the way. He felt the ground cut out from under his feet. He knew he was standing, knew he was awake, alive, but this had to be a mistake or a dream.

Only a dream, a bad dream, would explain why he was looking at his ex-wife.

Olivia pulled the blankets up around her neck. He had awakened her, and she was blinking at him like she was the one seeing a ghost. A bottle of champagne and two glasses, one empty, sat on the nightstand.

Olivia smiled. "Well, you're a little late, dear."

Charles heard Addie's voice from far away. At some point, he had lowered the phone to his side. He brought the phone back up to his ear. "Sorry, sorry, you cut out on the last part."

"This all just happened," she said. "But I figured you'd want to know. I thought he was your friend."

Charles and Olivia had not seen each other for more than ten years. He took a tiny step towards the bed, feeling like a lion tamer whose act had started to go sideways. They had met in Chicago when they were both in their twenties. He was working a campaign and she bartended at the bar near the office. She hated politics, and he was kind of a stiff. For a few months, it was perfect. Then, it stopped being perfect. She cheated. He cheated shortly afterward. They split, and he almost never thought of her.

Finally, he managed a few words to Addie. "Hawley was a jerk. I wouldn't worry about it. He was probably drunk and rubbed someone the wrong way. He'll sleep it off."

Olivia laughed, sat up and smoothed her hair back. She was wearing a black nightgown. "Is that your wife?" she stage-whispered.

Charles covered the phone. "Look, I'm really losing you up here. Can I call you later?"

Addie sighed. "You seem annoyed that I took the time to tell you."

"No, no, no. I'm just running late and need time to process this."

Olivia reached for the champagne and poured herself a splash. She offered the bottle to Charles, who smiled and shook his head.

"Call me later?" Addie asked. "I want to hear things."

"Definitely. For sure."

Charles hung up feeling guilty.

"Welcome home, husband."

He looked down at his phone. "I just got bad news about a friend. A guy I worked with a while back. But I can't even think about it." He looked around the bedroom, wondering who else would pop out. "What's happening right now?"

"I'm in bed. You're standing over there. We're in a million-dollar house on a mountain."

"I knew you'd say something clever like that. How are *you* here?"

"I'm from here. What are *you* doing here?"

"This isn't a coincidence."

"Can't get anything past you." She rolled her eyes. "I knew you were staying here and I wanted to see you. Then I fell asleep. You're the one who walked into my bedroom."

He shook his head. "No, no this house belongs to my, to, to . . ."

Charles turned around and walked into the living room. He sat down on one of the couches. His best hope, really his only chance at this point, was if she never walked out of that bedroom. If no one was there. If she was a ghost or, if he was lucky, a tumor chewing through his brain.

Then, he heard her bare feet coming down the stone hallway.

Olivia had thrown on a pair of jeans and a white button-up shirt. It was so much preppier than anything Olivia wore back in Chicago. Now that she was out of bed, Charles got a good look at her. She used to have more of an edge. He could see traces of it in her walk. Ten years had turned her into a woman with money.

"Oh, I thought you'd be a little happy to see me. A smidge?"

"I've been working with these people for almost a week, interviewing for two weeks before that. Your name did not come up."

"You're mad. I get it. You're mad because we're both losers." She made an L out of her thumb and forefinger and placed it on her forehead. "Remember when people did this?"

"I'm not a loser."

She laughed and shook her head.

"That laugh," he said. "That little snort you do. It used to sound nice. Do you work for Branch and Salazar? Those are the only people in the state who know me, and don't give me a sarcastic answer."

"Don't we all work for him?" She rolled her eyes. "Fine, sorry I didn't tell you, I'm married to your boss."

"Cody Branch is not my boss."

"Oh, Charlie, you've been out here long enough to know better than that."

He curled up on the couch. The room was on its side and felt quiet and cool. The leather couch smelled like money, and the entire house hummed as if vast machines toiled in the basement. This whole job, airport or casino or whatever, really had been too good to be true. Of course, the signs had been there. Thompson's skepticism. Addie wondering how they got his name in the first place. He had shrugged it all off.

"This is stalking," he said. "Manipulation. You got me this job but didn't tell me."

She laughed. "Stalking? I mentioned your name to Cody. That's all. You got yourself hired."

Charles thought of his mother. This was the kind of stunt she used to pull all the time.

When she donated stacks of cash to party committees or to PACs in states where Charles had taken jobs, she referred to it as "voting with her pocketbook." Soon, bald men wearing gold rings were gripping his shoulder and introducing him as Lena O'Connell's son.

"You can't do stuff like this," he said. "You're not allowed to sneak into my life."

"I'm from here," she laughed.

"You could have sent one email. 'Hey, heard of a gig. Interested?' But I didn't even get to decide if I wanted to owe you a favor."

Olivia sat on the couch's arm, but he stayed curled up on his side.

"Look, all I did was give my husband a name. That's the truth." She came closer.

Charles looked at his watch. "I've got to go to work."

"Were you always this whiny? Diana won't be mad if you tell her we were together."

"I am not doing that."

"You really don't have a sense of humor anymore. Did you ever? I can't remember."

Charles pushed himself up and looked at her. "Why would you marry that guy? Don't say money."

She stood up and put on her sunglasses. "Not only a loser but a judgmental loser." She walked to the door. "If I said he used to be different, would you believe me?"

"No. No, not really."

She slipped on her shoes. "Look," she said, "you could use a friend out here, and I'm a little short on allies myself. I have a show, an art show, at a gallery tonight. It's my first solo. You can come. I left a postcard on the counter."

"Does he know about our past?"

Olivia snorted and opened the door. "Would he hire you if he did?"

She grinned, and Charles could almost see a wink behind her sunglasses. Even the smooth way she locked the door behind her dripped with nauseating confidence. Charles pressed his face back down on the couch, the cool leather calmed his stomach. When he wondered if Mr. or Mrs. Branch picked out the color, he went to the bathroom and finally lost all the beer he had drank with Lou.

# ELEVEN

JUST BEFORE SUNRISE, with the dregs of the meth still burning out of his system, Gabe felt an insane desire, almost a biological need, to clean. This had happened before. The meth come down zeroed out his focus and pushed him into the minutiae of cleaning. If he was scrubbing green and black mold from sinks and bathtubs, he could ignore his blood falling from boil to simmer, and his jaw would slowly unclench. He took what remained of the bathroom door off its hinges and dragged it to the curb. In the kitchen, he scraped and put away dishes that had been accumulating for ages. He dug out the vacuum cleaner and sucked up so much ash and dust from the carpets that their color turned from grey to sand. Each obliterated stain and tossed-out beer can brought him one step closer to Micah.

Long after the sun came up, Gabe climbed back into the bathtub for sleep. The smell of bleach clung to his skin like plastic film, but the porcelain was clean and cool. He slept hard and still. His back curved to fit the shape of the tub.

In the afternoon, climbing out with a tortured groan, Gabe felt sick. The state of the house should have cheered him up, but the hangover had seeped into his bones, and his head felt gummy. It was a hangover with moral dimensions and no dignity, as if his kidneys and liver were so clogged with toxins that his soul had shriveled.

He looked around the house. Nothing was different, not really. The rot and dirt had been papered over with a thin layer of respectability and disinfectant.

Gabe winced when he saw the coffee pot. He had filled the machine with water and ground coffee the night before. A note was taped to the pot: *Just press start.* Some kind of gift from his high self to his hungover self. Then he saw the next note, this one stuck to a mug: *To Do Today: Sell Kids to Drugs, 2 PM.* He supposed it was funny.

That kid called himself something idiotic. Sketchy? Smokey? Tangling with teenage potheads. Gabe shook his head. "No, thank you."

There were other ways to raise cash. He imagined Frederick sitting in his lair, peering into a crystal ball and smiling at Gabe's wise decision.

He took his coffee upstairs and felt shards of pain in his knees, as if the drug had left flecks of rust in his joints. Fragments of memories came back to him. He'd spent time in Micah's old room. He pushed open the door. The room had been empty, but Gabe must have dragged in the air mattress and a few things Micah had left behind: a box of toys, a clown lamp, a milk crate. The toys were scattered. Posters of long-retired wrestlers, growling and pointing at Gabe, hung on the walls. He had also thrown an old poker table under the windowsill and put some pencils and construction paper on the padded, beige top. It looked like a crime scene or a bad movie set. Micah would hate it. Gabe hated it.

His chest tightened like a serpent had wrapped around him. He needed to sit, but his legs barely fit under the poker table. This side of the house looked out on his overgrown half-acre field. The barn out there was half-caved in, and flaking red paint would occasionally catch the wind and blow like red snow into his neighbor's yard.

He used to have a couple of horses in that barn—helpful for odd jobs working cattle, taking tourists up the mountains or meandering through the woods. He had sold both horses and got a good deal on a power-washing rig. The plan was to build a life blasting dirt out of the world's cracks, but he sold the power washer last year.

He took a pencil from the coffee can and tapped it on the table.

A few notes to Micah, Gabe decided. Simple explanations to help clear the air. He rubbed the light blue construction paper between his thumbs and forefingers. It felt child-like, more suited to games than a meaningful confession.

*Son, I'm not sure my own father ever loved me. The old man was damn near a mute and I can't say we ever had more than a handful of honest to god conversations. I always wanted to be better than that to you.*

Gabe read it two, three times. Whiny. He crossed it out.

*In my life I've tried to do what I thought was right but there's no denying I made bad choices. Done things, seen things, lived lives other people couldn't imagine.*

Gabe balled up the paper. That was turning into bullshit—tall-tales and half-truths. Gabe tried again. Again. Each time he approached some honest appraisal of his life, some true feelings, the writing veered into boasting about bull riding or the Army. Balls of colored paper piled up around his ankles.

He needed some help. Gabe found his phone under some blankets in the closet. Lou was the articulate brother, and he was bound to have something to say.

"Hey, man," Gabe said. "Glad I caught you, what you doing?"

"I don't like the sound of that," Lou replied. "What do you need?"

"Everyone's messing with me lately. Maybe I'm just calling to call."

"Sure, yeah." Lou cleared his throat. "Calling to call. What are you up to? Let me guess, chillin'?"

"No, no, no, Micah's coming down this weekend, and I'm getting the place ready for him. You should see it. Place'll knock your socks off."

When the will was read, no one expected the house, their father's only object of pride, to go to Gabe. Lou was the one who stayed there, cared for their dying father, maintained the house and held the whole world together. But Lou was never mad. Getting out of that house gave Lou his life back.

"I've wanted to go into town," Lou said, "take Micah to lunch, but it's hard to find the time."

"Then you should come here this weekend," Gabe said. "Come down, join us. The kid's getting into camping. Going into the mountains. Must run in the blood, I guess, right?"

"I don't know. Things have been tough at work." Lou paused. "What was it you needed?"

There was never a big showdown with his brother. No conscious decision to stop seeing each other, at least not on Gabe's part. One day, he looked over and his brother was gone, like a boulder broken in two by dripping water.

"How would you describe Pop?" Gabe asked. "Like if someone asked for the truth, how he really was."

"Sounds like you've got another project going on. Remember when you were going to trace our family back to the conquistadors?"

"I'm serious. I want to talk to Micah about the family."

"Look at you." Lou whistled. "Getting all thoughtful down in that big house by yourself." Gabe wanted to throw his phone across the room.

"Nevermind, I'll figure it out."

"Oh, *pobre* Gabriel," Lou said. "Pop's gone. He was complicated. That's the word I'd use. Then I'd change the subject. He dicked around, so Mom split to God-knows-where. Hell, he probably beat her ass like he did us."

"He only hit us when we deserved it."

"Yeah, keep telling yourself that, brother." Lou took a loud, deep breath, as if he could exhale the conversation. Sure enough, he was onto another topic. "Hey, I know a guy, he works with my girl, and he wants to go into the mountains. I told him you'd show him around."

"He'll pay?"

"Yeah, charge him. He'll talk your fucking head off."

"Come down, we'll hit an old trail or something."

"I wish I could but I've been working like a dad, so when I have a day off, I take a day off."

"Like a dad?"

"You fucker, I meant to say 'dog.' Now you got Pop on *my* brain. I'm not writing my life story. I don't need those memories."

"What about Mom?" Gabe asked.

"You trying to ruin my whole day?"

"Hang on, I've been wondering about her. About him too, both of them."

Lou went quiet for a few seconds. "You still there?" Gabe asked.

"It's too late for these questions, man," Lou said. "Right after she ducked out, I tried to tell myself stories about where she went, and you, not Pop, *you* beat the shit out of me for it."

"Nah," Gabe said. "That's not . . . no."

"I said she was in Hollywood, or singing in Vegas, and you knocked out two of my baby teeth."

Now it was Gabe's turn to be silent. "I don't remember that," he admitted. "Hey, I didn't mean for you to deal with Pop all by yourself."

The words came out in a rush, and Gabe wondered who they were supposed to make feel better.

"That's it," Lou said. "Goodbye, I'm done. I'll text you the guy's number. Call him if you want. Or don't, that's fine too."

Lou hung up.

Gabe felt a pain in his gut, not in his stomach, but straight through his guts. Gabe always thought that when the time came, and he knew it would come eventually, turning everything around would be a breeze. Making amends, reaching out, asking for forgiveness, rebuilding his life, all of it: snap. Done. But now it was getting late, and he needed to get to The Pig.

# TWELVE

EMBARRASSMENT CLUNG TO OLIVIA LIKE TAR. Driving out to Española, she imagined Andrea howling with laughter at the thought of Olivia popping champagne and posing on the bed, only to fall asleep when he never showed up.

Olivia let out a small, sad laugh. She wanted to upend Charles, but he had practically tumbled down the mountain and onto the highway.

Leaving Santa Fe and heading into the mountains relieved a tension Olivia had been trying to ignore. She had spent years wanting to be a city girl, but those valleys outside of town had a power over her.

She pictured Taos. That's where the four of them—Olivia, Andrea and the girls—would likely end up. Olivia had her eye on a house in the mountains a short drive from town. A few years down the line, maybe she would have a gallery with her name on it, and the only time she would think about Cody Branch would be when she saw his name on a new development. Or maybe when he was finally handcuffed and marched away.

Olivia looked to the right of the highway as a passing cloud sent a shadow racing over the valley. Her stomach filled with nerves and she drove fast. If Mallon had noticed the disabled tracker, he was keeping it quiet. She knew that would not last long. She turned on a podcast, something juicy that followed a series of murders in a Texas bordertown. She wasn't listening, but the words filled the air and made her less scared.

The house looked empty and dark. The blinds were drawn, and from the sidewalk there was no way to tell a family lived there. No toys in the yard, no blaring TV you could hear from the street, even Andrea's car was parked four houses down.

They had gone through this before. Andrea would settle in and then get paranoid. She would decide they were about to be kicked out by Branch's men, or that the debt collectors would find her, so they would hunker down and wait for the end.

Andrea answered the door, already raising her hand to Olivia's objections.

"I know, I know," Andrea said, "you hate it when it looks like we're hiding."

Olivia put her keys and phone on a table near the front door. "A hermit with kids draws attention. This is your house, go meet your neighbors, send the kids outside to play, open the windows."

Andrea shook her head. "But this isn't our house." She pulled her sweater tighter around her shoulders and pointed towards a back room. "Let's keep it down, they're sleeping, or at least they're talking very quietly."

Olivia picked her keys up. "I brought some food."

Andrea followed her outside. Olivia resisted the urge to compliment her on the steadiness of her gait. The last time she had, Andrea almost hit her with her cane and said, "It shouldn't be impressive to walk without falling over."

Olivia grabbed three of the grocery bags. She saw Andrea try to do the same but then grab a pack of paper towels instead.

"You have to stop buying us so much stuff," she said. "I'm not *totally* broke. I still have money from Mom, and we've moved so many times, I'm not even getting hospital bills anymore."

"I know, I know," Olivia said. "But I have an 'Entertainment Budget,' and there's no reason not to use it."

When Olivia put the groceries away, she saw most of the previous food she'd brought last time was still untouched. Andrea said, "The kids are on a grilled cheese and cereal kick this week, and I don't have an appetite for much."

"That's fine, just let me know. I'll get the best grilled cheese fixings I can find. Let's get some thousand-dollar cheese. If they sell that anywhere, it's in Santa Fe."

Andrea laughed and sat down. She would never actually give Olivia a grocery list. She needed what Olivia was offering, but she was too proud to place orders. Olivia grabbed vegetables out of the fridge and started assembling a salad.

"I hope that's for you," Andrea said. "I just ate."

"Nice try. What'd you eat? A handful of jelly beans?"

"I like jelly beans, and every tray of hospital food comes with a soggy iceberg salad. For real, the tomatoes are white and the croutons can crack a tooth. Kind of put me off salads for a while."

Olivia tossed the spinach with cherry tomatoes, cucumber slices, feta cheese and olive oil. She put the bowl in front of Andrea. "You'll suffer through this one. Now, where are your keys?"

"I don't want to park in the driveway. What if a realtor drives by and they know this place should be empty?"

"There's no realtor," Olivia said. "This is your house."

Andrea picked up the fork. "But you know it's not."

Olivia sighed. "I've got a show tonight. I can send a car out here. You can . . . "

Andrea took a bite of salad and shook her head. "Uh-uh. Nope. I'm not going to go to some Canyon Road gallery. Cody will be there, and I'd end up breaking a wine bottle over his head."

"Go for it. You might win an award."

Andrea pointed with her fork towards the front door. "So, listen to me, I've got some cousins in town willing to get us out of here. They'll put me and the girls up for . . . "

Olivia shook her head. "No, no, no. We're not staying in this town. Give me a couple weeks. I'm so so close. I'm right there. There's a guy helping me, and we're going to figure out how to get what we need."

"The girls need stability, and you're taking too many risks for us."

"No such thing."

"You got a week tops, girl. You've been great to us, but after a week we're figuring something else out. This isn't good for any of us."

Olivia nodded and smiled because if she stopped smiling, she would burst into tears.

# THIRTEEN

CHARLES PROPPED THE POSTCARD up against his computer monitor. *Fields of Play: New Oils by Olivia Reyes Branch.* She had painted back in Chicago, but it had seemed to be more of a hobby. He wondered if Branch owned the gallery. Charles knew there was no way he could go tonight.

Yet, every time Charles tried to focus on his emails or news coverage of yesterday's press conference, the postcard distracted him. She had been waiting for him. In his bed. Charles stood and shook his hands, as if he could fling her off his skin. Of course she would reenter his life with a splash. That manic energy floored him when they had first met, until it started to drain him.

According to the legal documents, Charles' marriage to Olivia fell apart because she had an affair. He appreciated that juicy detail because it was humiliating enough to wring sympathy from family and friends. Her infidelity kept anyone from asking if he, too, had cheated.

At the time, he had been grateful to escape. They met while Charles was on a campaign. Usually, campaign tunnel vision reduced the universe to what was a foot in front of your face. Anything beyond your duty to your candidate—family, friends, life—blinked out of existence. But Olivia burned brighter than his campaign. As the candidate drank more and the poll numbers slipped and slipped, Olivia became a sign of other things Charles could have in his life. They were married after Election Day—a loss, of course.

One month into the marriage, Charles knew the whole thing was a mistake. He saw the same look on *her* face, as if there were a vague, rotting scent in the air. After the flush of hurried love had subsided, Olivia grew bored and Charles realized the momentum that had swept her up in their relationship would reverse and carry her away. He landed another campaign in Chicago, so he could be close, but she was always asleep when he came home and gone when he awoke. Then, she stopped being home at all.

Divorced at twenty-two. Someone once told him that being divorced when he was barely of drinking age made him seem mysterious and world-weary. They had immediately lost touch with each other, and Charles could not even imagine what terrible chain of events led her to Cody Branch. He looked back at the postcard. Maybe he should ask.

Charles snapped his head up when Salazar stepped into his office.

"I woke up this morning hoping it had all been a bad dream," she said. She stood inside the doorway with her fingertips clasped at her stomach. "Bones of an old warrior dug up and causing trouble? My kids used to watch 'Scooby-Doo.' I swear I've seen this one."

Salazar walked around Charles' desk and admired the view out the window. It was a deliberate pose. She looked more comfortable in his office than he did.

"Press coverage has been light," she said. "The local papers and channels are all over it, of course. Decent impact in Arizona and Oklahoma. Only capsule stories, so far, in *The Times* and *Post*. I'm surprised there's not more nationally, but that's good for us. It means no one believes them. Online activists are a bigger threat. We're not the bad guys yet. Let's keep it that way."

"This is complicated," Charles said. "I love it. It's exciting. But it is complicated."

"Look, last night Cody told you more than he needed to. I'm not happy, but it happened. Stay focused. Today is only about the Apaches."

"I get it. I'm focused." He wanted to defend himself, talk about all the secrets he could have told over the years, but he held back.

Salazar faced the windows again, as if she were lecturing the mountains. "You also signed an NDA. We'll enforce it if we need to."

Charles put his notepad on top of Olivia's postcard.

"I've been researching all morning," he said. "There's no historical connection between Geronimo and the San Miguel tribe," Charles said. "Or even between Geronimo and New Mexico, really."

"Of course," she said. "Jordan's been finding the same. She knows how to get on Wikipedia too."

Salazar turned and leaned her back against the window. Charles spun his chair completely around. Somehow, he had become a visitor in his own office.

"Their claims don't make sense," she said. "The official Apache nation has no idea who these guys are, but Jordan thinks maybe they're not lying. Maybe someone convinced them that Geronimo's their uncle and they should reclaim their birthright. This sort of thing has happened before."

"Is that any better? If they were lying, they could be tripped up. But if they're committed to something that's not true, they're fanatics."

Salazar gave him a slight nod of approval, and Charles felt like he had won a medal.

"You and Jordan need to stop whatever bickering is happening. Work together. You get paid too much to silo yourself."

"Hey, I'm trying. I even invited her and Lou over to dinner."

"Oh, I just hate to miss that."

"Until the Apaches show us proof, can't we go ahead and start building again? At a different part of the site, away from the grave. We have San Miguel's permission."

"It's not a grave. It's a body in the wrong place." Salazar shook her head. "Restarting right away is what Cody wants, but we can wait a little longer. We need to hear the Apaches out. If we go around them, they'll sue us to hell and back. Sometimes these groups only want someone to listen."

It could be weeks until construction restarted. He considered asking Thompson out to lunch again. He might not tell his old friend about the casino, not yet, but a few crumbs could help everyone.

"Can I ask about Branch?"

Salazar's face drew still. She looked too steady, too ready to lie. He knew he needed to focus on what was in front of him, but his thoughts kept running to Olivia. How she had married the type of man she used to rail against: mean, loud, blind to others. It had been bothering Charles all morning. He took Salazar's silence for a go ahead.

"Last night he seemed to take it all so personally," Charles said. "And he's put so much into this operation. The house is phenomenal. The cars. The offices. But even if the *other* project falls apart, he'll be okay. Getting a cut of the airport parking alone could double his wealth, right?"

He hoped Salazar would spill more about the casino, but she stayed quiet.

"Why does he care so much?" he asked.

This time her silence was more weighted, less contemplative than before. Charles had always wanted to master the knowing pause, but he could never hold back. He always kept trying to weave words into a solution.

"Do you care about money?" Salazar asked.

Charles shrugged. "Who doesn't?"

"Him. Not at all. If he cared, he'd be too timid to make any. Thirty years ago, a twenty-something kid borrows money from his first wife and buys a patch of dirt south of Albuquerque. Just a little square that wasn't part of the Isleta reservation and that no one else even noticed. Terrible location. No utilities. An accident on the map. He didn't have any plans for that land. It was worthless, but it was his. Then, he bought another patch and sold cars. An actual used car salesman, but that didn't matter because now he owned even more land."

"Doesn't sound like the man I met last night."

She agreed. "About ten years ago, that strange ugly dusty patch of ground starts pumping out millions. It's all his."

She spoke as if the power of the words could transport them back to the primordial ooze that Branch had emerged from, coated in dollar signs and luxury.

"The next year, one of his other patches struck oil. Then he bought another patch and did it again. And again, the year after that. The rest of us are venal and ambitious. Cody Branch doesn't have to lie to himself about what he wants."

"Now, he wants an airport and . . . "

Salazar broke eye contact and started towards the door. "The Apaches' lawyer found my cell phone number," she said. "They'll be here tomorrow morning. I'll run the meeting. Jordan will provide historical perspective, but it's up to you to get them to spit out the number. Cody's going to write a check. We need to know how big. Then, Geronimo can hitchhike back to Oklahoma."

Salazar walked out of the room. Charles still struggled with all the moving pieces. There was power here. Wealth without any of the baggage of east coast money. No ancient alliances or unions or half-remembered favors waiting to be cashed in. Thompson said it was dirty and then bragged about his comfort. Maybe this was Charles' kind of dirty.

He tossed the notepad aside and picked up Olivia's postcard. Tonight, Mrs. Branch would be able to answer some questions.

# FOURTEEN

THE PARKING LOT WAS EMPTY, and Angie never showed up before six pm, but Gabe was still paranoid. He brought two ounces for the kid. Not enough to decimate his own stash, but enough to earn him a good chunk of Helen's money. He put the baggie into his vest pocket and had double-checked the zipper at every light.

Gabe felt damp. He was still sweating out the meth. He wondered if he smelled like disinfectant and plastic drugs.

Heat shimmers danced in the soybean fields across from The Pig. The bar itself looked rundown, even abandoned in the daylight. He resolved to buy back that sandblaster. It was hard work, and the sand cut up the inside of his nose and mouth, but cleaning driveways had to be better than waiting out in the open for some dumb kid.

Gabe looked up and down Route 116. This was too obvious. There was nothing else out here. A truck went by, taking some guys out to a field. They all turned their heads to look at him, and one guy waved.

When the kid's red Camry appeared in the distance, Gabe tracked it with his eyes, worried it was someone else, worried it was the kid. The car pulled up next to Gabe's bike. Music, really only bass, boomed from the car. The kid left the engine on and the music running when he opened the door. This gangster looked like a baby in the daylight. Gabe hated him. He hated the acne clustered on his chin. He hated the tight hemp necklace and he really hated that knit cap.

The kid flicked his chin up in the air. "'Sup?"

"Four hundred!" Gabe shouted over the music. "Two ounces."

The kid pushed out his lips and shook his head. "Nah, I think three-fifty."

"Four. You tried it. Let's get this done."

"You in such a hurry, Pops, then we can do it for three-fifty."

Gabe pictured the kid using this story like a cudgel against his friends. *Fuck you, guys, I'm the one with the balls to go deal with the old Mexican.*

"You trying to negotiate?" Gabe shouted.

"I think you need to sell this shit, and I don't think you're a real dealer."

"This isn't a flea market, kid."

The kid shrugged and turned around. "Fuck yourself, then. Our stuff wasn't that good. I'm not trying to stress right now. You're old, and you're weird."

The kid stepped towards his car and opened the door. The music boomed louder.

"You came all the way down here," Gabe shouted.

Gabe stepped to the kid, hating his arrogance, hating his beat-up car pumping out that brain-rattling music.

"Three-fifty, fine, but I'm pinching a bud off."

"Nah, I can get smoke in town from people who know what they're doing. I don't trust you."

Before the kid could duck inside, Gabe grabbed his arm. "Hang on a second."

The kid flinched, one foot still on the ground and the other in his car. "Dude, get off me!"

"Let's talk about . . . "

"Get off me!"

He shoved Gabe in the chest, rocking him back and sending a twinge of pain through his ankle.

Gabe reached forward and grabbed the kid by his throat. He squeezed just enough to silence him. The kid's eyes went wide and almost bulged in time with the music. The hemp necklace felt rough against Gabe's palm. The kid shook his head very slightly and brought a hand up to Gabe's wrist, softly, not clawing or pushing. The wrist hung on Gabe's arm, barely skirting the skin, like a bird on a wire.

Gabe let go. His chest ached like *he* had been the one holding his breath.

The kid screamed. Not a word or a cry for help, but the high-pitched scream of a child stung by a wasp on the playground. A sound to make any decent person look up.

"Okay, okay," Gabe said. "Okay. It's okay."

The kid screamed again and fell in the dirt, hitting the back of his head on the open door.

He sat on the ground, rubbing his head and sniffling. He reached into the pocket of his hoodie and handed over a wallet and phone. Gabe opened the red plastic wallet, took out four hundred and tossed the bag of weed into the car. The kid scrambled into the driver's seat and slammed the door before Gabe could hand back the wallet and phone. Gravel and dirt kicked up into Gabe's face as the kid peeled out of the parking lot.

Everything went quiet. In seconds, the Camry disappeared around a curve in the road.

Gabe had the cash. He also had the kid's cheap wallet and cell phone. When he tried to light a cigarette, the tip kept bouncing out of the flame.

That happened. It happened, and now it was over. Gabe could shrug it off. The kid would get high later and tell his friends a story, maybe impress a girl. Everyone got what they wanted.

The cigarette was gone, so Gabe sat down in front of The Pig and smoked another. Then, he saw a car on the horizon coming his way. His hands were still shaking and he was a little dizzy, but Gabe flexed and relaxed his fingers until he caught his breath. He tossed the kid's phone and wallet into one of his saddlebags. When he glanced at his own phone, there was a text from Rose: *Hey youre kinda famous right now. Online and stuff.*

He stashed his phone, double-checked all his zippers and looked over his shoulder. It was okay. "No one saw," Gabe muttered to himself. "I'll make it. No one saw."

# FIFTEEN

INSTEAD OF PREPPING for the meeting with the Apaches, Charles spent the afternoon googling Olivia and practicing his disinterested look. It seemed Branch had not yet been deserving of splashy coverage when they got married. Since then, she appeared in the background of countless photos: groundbreaking ceremonies, events where Branch handed over large checks to children's hospitals and so on. It was not enough to answer any of Charles' questions. Back at the house for a shower, Charles almost expected her to be waiting again. His eyes jumped, looking for her shoes by the door. Nothing. That's a good thing, he reminded himself.

The show was on Canyon Road, which was lined with art galleries and souvenir shops inside pink adobe buildings. Paintings of sunsets framed in thick, blocky wood frames stood in windows, and *ristras* of dried red chili hung from each doorway. It was impossible to tell which buildings were old and which had been sanded down to provide an authentic feel. Waiters buzzed around the party with glasses of champagne. Charles knew no one and felt self-conscious in his plain black suit. Most of the crowd was older and had the shiny skin and relaxed designer clothing of early-retirees. White men with long hair and blue jeans, but also Rolexes and hand-made shoes, stood next to women, most of them younger by quite a few years, wearing simple dresses with so much turquoise jewelry that Charles was impressed they could walk in a straight line. Actually, Charles noticed quite a few people were already having trouble walking straight. Did the wealthy of Santa Fe always dress like old hippies, or was this the art gallery uniform?

He wandered away from the crowd and picked up a flyer.

*Olivia Reyes Branch is a New Mexico native who studied art in Chicago, Paris and Los Angeles. The artist describes her work as 'ultra-realism' because it uses the fantastic to portray the truth about humanity's daily existence.*

After grabbing another glass of champagne, Charles turned to a painting: a bright acrylic rendering of a decrepit house with a torn screen door and a wooden porch with holes in the planks. In the front yard, a family of skeletons was throwing a party. One skeleton grilled bones, a skeleton kid in blue shorts and a red T-shirt jumped rope, while a skeleton girl in a frosting-pink dress swung a broom handle at a piñata hanging from a tree made of beer bottles. The skulls wore expressions that ranged from joyous to terrified.

The room filled and the crowd started to relax. Sometime after his second glass of champagne, a man started talking to him about which restaurants to avoid. It seemed like he listed every restaurant in the city. Another person listed the hotels in Taos with the worst views. The glad-handing, the mood that accompanies important people mingling but not dwelling on important matters, not yet, felt familiar to him.

An older woman with curly red hair and tight, high-waisted blue jeans approached him. The man Charles had been speaking to quietly slipped away. The woman's hair was above shoulder-length but pulled back in a short riot of a ponytail.

"Fresh victim?" She pointed at Charles and arched an eyebrow.

His champagne stopped halfway to his mouth. "Excuse me?"

"I'm afraid the same people always come to these things, and I've never seen you before."

"Guess I stick out," he said.

"Sure do." She smiled. "Name's Janice Chávez."

"Charles O'Connell."

He shook her hand. She was one of the few women not wearing thick bracelets or a turquoise watch. No jewelry at all, Charles noticed.

The woman's smile was probably twenty years older than his, but her jeans hugged her body, and she seemed to be coiled, full of energy. Her lack of interest in the crowd was compelling.

"How are you finding our fair mountain city?"

He let out a quick, involuntary laugh. "Takes some getting used to. Haven't really seen much of it, to be honest. Mostly working."

"On what? Something classified by the government?"

"Yes, I'm building a UFO death ray." Charles smiled at his joke. "No, it's the airport."

Janice sipped her champagne. "Well, don't worry. Your secret's safe with me. These people might cast you out if they discovered your shameful occupation."

"I hadn't quite realized until the other day there was any real opposition."

She gestured around the room with her glass. "People are always scared of 'the new.'"

"I'm working with Cody Branch," he said after a moment. "And Diana Salazar. You familiar with them?"

"As much as anyone can be. Those two keep close counsel." Janice smiled and looked toward the paintings. "Have you seen the art?"

"I have. It's nice."

"I hate it. The woman's not as talented as we've all been led to believe. Alas, if you're wealthy enough, you can inflict your hobbies on poor innocents like us."

Charles noticed people doing their best to look at the two of them without actually looking at the two of them.

"I'm afraid we all have to pay fealty to the oh-so-talented Mrs. Branch," Janice said. "It's expected. The governor's likely to slither in any moment now."

Charles tried to sound neutral. "You seem to have strong feelings about Mr. and Mrs. Branch."

Janice exchanged their glasses for fresh ones. Her mood became as bubbly as the champagne. "Enough of that, we must talk about your job. I'm sure it's the most fascinating thing."

Her excitement flattered him. "No, no, no. Not until yesterday."

"Is it really him? Geronimo's vengeance all these years later? Quite poetic, don't you think?"

"We don't think it's him. We're taking the Apache claims seriously, of course, but, you know, what are the odds that it's actually

Geronimo? Is *Mr.* Branch definitely going to be here? I thought he might be too busy."

Charles looked around the room, distracted by the thought of Branch and Mallon stalking in behind him.

Janice laughed. "Oh, he doesn't let her go out alone. But if they believe it's Geronimo, and if the press want to believe it's Geronimo, then it *is*, right?"

"Funny, I said the same thing today, and Diana agreed." Charles smiled, but Janice twisted her mouth.

"So, what do you do?" Charles asked. "Other than look at art you don't like?"

"I spend most of my time trying to gouge my ex-husband for more money. It's both my vocation and avocation."

They laughed. He started to realize why people seemed to avoid this woman. She clearly did not give a fuck, and it was amazing. He pictured her drowning in champagne with pool boys and cowboys half her age. Tonight, she would buy a painting she hated, just because she could. Maybe she would burn it and put out the fire with a bottle of wine.

"You must allow me to buy you dinner soon," she said. "I'll tell you all the juicy bits that Diana keeps close to her wizened breast, and you can tell me about your work."

"I'm not sure my job is a good trade for 'juicy bits.'"

"Oh, working with the people you're working with? You're bound to be next year's absolutely juiciest bit. Who owns that land, right now?"

The question came fast as a needle, but Charles kept smiling. "Well . . . the tribe, San Miguel, sold it to the county. So, it's county land, mostly."

"But the county handed it over to an airport authority, correct? To run the actual operations."

Charles thought of the suited cubicle dwellers. "Right," he said. "Yeah, it's pretty technical stuff. Janice, I'm sorry I don't know that I should be . . . "

"Jan. It must be Jan."

Her smile started to look as if it had been crafted in a desert workshop. He should stop drinking champagne. Charles found it difficult to explain himself in New Mexico. It was as if the air rendered normal words obscure.

"And now the Apaches," she said with an air of finality.

Jan's eyes caught on something over Charles' shoulder, and her energy drained away. Diana Salazar had walked in. Brief, unpleasant surprise flashed on her face when she saw Charles and Jan—only to be quickly folded and put away.

"Well, Charles," Salazar said. "You know how to make the social rounds, I see. Hi, Janice."

"Hello, Diana. Don't worry. I'm keeping my hands to myself."

"Jan was going to tell me about the paintings," Charles said.

"Another time, perhaps. I'll leave you two to discuss your work. I will take that dinner date soon, dear."

Jan tilted her head gently and made her way deeper into the gallery, now looking much older and more unsteady on her feet.

"You meet the most interesting people, don't you?" Salazar asked.

"When will Mrs. Branch arrive?"

"Which one?" Salazar flicked her eyes at Janice's back. "You were just speaking with the first."

Charles almost spilled his champagne. "Jan? Janice? At Olivia's show?"

"Janice goes to everything." Salazar's voice had a touch of disgust. "Small town, lots of people do, but she comes to stuff like this to get under Cody's skin. It works. She's about the only one that can do it. Not even the current Mrs. Branch has that effect on him. You speak with her long?" Salazar did not look at him when she asked.

"No, not really. She asked about the airport, but I didn't say anything. She said her name was Chávez."

"She took back her family name after taking Cody's first million or so."

The questions, the smiles, what had Janice wanted from him?

"With that red hair she doesn't look like a Chávez," Charles said.

Salazar nodded very gently and took a deep breath through her nose. It was her talking-to-a-child face. "Yes, well there are all sorts of stories out here, aren't there?"

Charles grabbed another glass of champagne off a passing tray.

# SIXTEEN

OLIVIA AND CODY sat in the back of the town car. She looked into a small mirror, too nervous to even see herself, but needing to keep her hands busy. Cody wanted to wait until the right moment. He would stare at the doors, clock the people going into the gallery, then, when *he* was ready, they would make their entrance. Olivia waited.

Finally, he grunted and reached for the door. She stepped out of the car, holding the loose fabric of her dress in one hand. She would not let Cody ruin tonight.

Some of these paintings had traveled to Chicago and back with her. Others started as sketches she had first drawn in high school. Her first show by herself would also be her last as Olivia Branch. The paintings were good. Most of them. She knew maybe three or four would have been left out of a show at an impartial gallery, but she had earned this. Selling a few canvasses tonight would be enough to get another show on her own.

Cody muscled through the gallery door ahead of her.

"Okay, okay folks. Make way, the *artiste* is here."

A circle formed in the middle of the gallery. Cody lifted Olivia's hand and walked her into the center.

For a second, and only a second, she felt like it was her show. Like these people were here to see her and her work. Then, Cody slithered his arm around her waist and pulled her against him with a comic *oomph*. She crawled inside herself and set up a fence thin enough that no one could see.

"Can she throw that paint around or can't she? I can't understand a damn thing about them," Branch yelled. "But people like what she does, so I tell her to keep pumping them out."

She looked down at her shoes. From that angle, only the tips were visible under the long, black dress. Most of her paintings were black, and she wanted to look like she could glide right into the canvas.

The crowd laughed, looking so pleased under the soft lights. She knew her photo op smile looked convincing because she had years of practice. Olivia took a step forward, and Cody's arm caught for a second on her waist.

"Thank you so much for your support," she said.

The crowd went silent, maybe surprised the wife could speak.

"I've been working on these paintings for a long time. They're about me. They're about New Mexico. And that means they're also about each of you. I want to thank Morningrise Gallery for helping me select the right canvasses and for giving me this chance. Thank you for being here."

The crowd clapped. Olivia smiled. Most of them were strangers but that was fine. They were here and they would look at her work, and her work would curl up somewhere inside them, and that was the point.

Cody disappeared into the crowd. Olivia saw Jan leaning against a table in the corner, a little drunk, and not even trying to hide her disgust. She saw Charles towards the back, looking like he'd seen his crush holding someone else's hand. She avoided eye contact with both of them.

Olivia had resolved not to let herself get stuck in conversations that were actually meant for Cody. A lobbyist wanting to talk about reforming commercial zoning laws, she thanked him and walked away. An accountant talking about the services he could offer, she thanked him and walked away. A reporter wanting an update on the airport, she thanked him and walked away. Each dodged conversation made her feel better than the last.

Only a handful of people seemed to really engage with the paintings. Olivia basked in their time together, luxuriating in conversations about brush strokes and her inspirations. She gave these people everything. Whenever Mallon came over and delivered a message from her husband—almost always a call to join in a conversation that could make him money—she dismissed him in favor of a curator, an art collector and even a few lost tourists excited to be speaking with a real, live Santa Fe artist.

In Española, Olivia was always the girl who could draw better than everyone else. Her dad worked two jobs, three if you counted drinking, so Olivia had time to herself. She filled sketchbooks, designed the yearbook cover, the homecoming banners, dance posters, all the little graphics that gave her school an identity. Back then, she had no idea nights like this were even possible. She thought artists drew cartoons for the newspaper and, if they were lucky, designed fast food cups. Andrea's mom showed her this world existed and spent years convincing Olivia she could make it. She looked around the gallery. This is what making it looked like, she supposed.

෨ ෨ ෨

Olivia checked in with the gallery owner. They had sold three paintings. Not a huge splash, but three was her goal.

Charles was still in the corner. She took pity on him.

His eyes went too wide, his smile too big as she approached. Olivia paused, tilted her head a fraction of an inch, just enough to send a warning. Charles wiped his mouth. For this to work, to even come close to working, they needed to be strangers.

She touched her glass to his. "There's so much champagne in this city, I love it."

Charles glanced around the room. "So am I living in your guest house? Your party cottage?"

She laughed, a loud social laugh.

"*He* writes me a check, a big one, and I get to play house. Most get rented out to tourists, but you're stuck in that one. Sometimes, I have a little party before they go on the market. Kind of thrilling to think about families from California moving into a house that a few days earlier was filled with my drunken, debaucherous friends."

"Well, there's no family there now, just me."

"Just you?" She smiled. "And your wife."

Charles folded one hand over the other, hiding his ring. His eyes darted around the room, and Olivia knew he was scanning for Cody or Diana. He was still a flirt who enjoyed playing the game more than the victory.

"I don't know how to do this. Everyone's watching you," he said.

Olivia made eye contact with a different gallery owner over Charles' shoulder, gave a big-toothed smile and twinkled her fingers at him.

Charles marveled. "You used to hate crowds like this. Now, you're really good at them. That wave. That was meant for someone you have no intention of actually speaking with."

"It was the person who Cody pressured into showing some of my paintings a few years ago. He hated them, and he was right, most of them were crap."

"Your husband's quite the patron."

"Watch your tone," Olivia warned. "We can talk about everything my husband is and isn't, but not here."

Olivia noticed Jan push away from her table in the corner and make a straight line their way. Time to cut Charles loose.

"I see my husband speaking with the governor of San Miguel Pueblo. I imagine I should put in a good word. I do hope you're enjoying the property."

Charles nodded. "It's lovely. You'll have to tell me more about some of the architecture, the design details."

"Yes, maybe soon. I do have a key."

As Olivia turned away, Jan, stinking of the liquor she had been slipping into her champagne glass, brushed her arm. Was it a warning? Or a signal that she had her back? Maybe both.

Olivia avoided Charles the rest of the night. They had connected. He was interested. God help her, she wanted to see him again too.

# SEVENTEEN

AFTER LEAVING THE PIG, Gabe went home and stashed the money in a bowl in a kitchen cabinet. It was not much money. But it was a start.

He tried calling some friends, but no one answered. He left voicemails asking for work, but after three calls, he got embarrassed and wished he could go back and delete the messages. As the day wore on, Gabe paced around the house and only felt calm when he sat at the card table in Micah's room.

He tried to squeeze out another sentence in his letter to Micah. There were too many unanswered questions. Did Dad find peace at the end? Where was his mother?

Gabe shook his head. He needed to get out of the house.

He remembered Rose's text message. The thought of calling her back made him nervous. A tight, fluttering drum beat behind his breastbone, which he could not blame on the cancer.

Gabe spent ten minutes standing next to his bike, smoking cigarettes and looking at her orange living room curtains. It was dusk before he got up the nerve to knock.

Johnny answered the door. Rose's kid had bulked up and was taller than Gabe but with a thin joke of a mustache.

"Mom, your stalker finally knocked," Johnny announced over his shoulder.

He returned to a recliner and un-muted the TV, leaving Gabe in the doorway. Rose came out of the kitchen, drying her hands on a towel.

"We heard your bike, you know. I thought you'd leave after a few minutes but Johnny said you'd knock. Now I owe him five bucks. Thanks a lot, Gabe."

She waved him in. On the TV, someone in a white lab coat was pointing lasers at a skeleton.

"Wait, should I go to my room?" Johnny asked without taking his eyes off the TV. "I can, you know, if y'all are going to be gross."

Rose threw the dishtowel at his chest. "Such a smartass. What do you think, Gabe? Should he go? Are we gross?"

Gabe tugged at his jacket. "No, no, I'm just swinging by."

Her house was small and overflowing with furniture and lamps. He loved it. Religious paintings covered one wall: an angel tilling a field for a praying farmer, Guadalupe appearing to men on horseback in the mountains, adobe churches that radiated light into the desert. On another wall, there were photos, mostly of Rose and Johnny with the kid's father popping up here and there, looking more strung-out in every picture.

They sat on a couch angled away from the TV. Gabe's back was to the screen but he could see the light flicker over Rose's face. His whole life, Gabe had always thought he was comfortable any-where, with anyone, but now he was fidgeting. Johnny sat in his recliner, looking like a dad ready to strike if Gabe tried anything.

"So, how's your week been?" he asked.

"Fine," she said. "We went out to dinner tonight. That was nice."

"That's good, real good."

Johnny muted the commercials, sinking the room into silence. When Gabe exhaled through his nose he thought it sounded like a tornado. He made eye contact with Johnny, but both turned away.

Rose smiled and rubbed her hands together as if they were aching. She kept running her thumbs over her fingertips, nails painted bright red.

"Want something to drink? Think I've got some beer."

Gabe nodded and followed her through an archway into the kitchen.

He whispered, "Hey, Rosie, you know there's no way I would have acted that way last night if my head was right. I've been trying to do something for my kid, and it's running me raw."

"You were dark, mean."

"Today's different. I'm starting to see how I actually want everything to be. I got some news that changed how I..."

"Oh my god!" Rose screamed. "Johnny, the *news*. Show Gabe the news video. I can't believe we forgot."

She rushed out of the kitchen and play-slapped her son on the shoulder. "Show him already."

Johnny rustled in his pocket for his phone, the action reminding Gabe of the teenager with the knit cap digging for his wallet.

"It's like you're two different people," Rose said. "That's why I forgot. Like, the one on the news was someone else, and you're just you."

"Man, I figured you'd already talked about that," Johnny said. "It's some funny shit."

Rose pushed a finger into the side of Johnny's head. "Funny stuff. I said 'stuff.'"

Rose smiled at Gabe. "Have people been giving you a hard time about this?" He shook his head, not knowing what she meant.

Rose laughed and bounced up and down like a kid. "Why didn't you say you were on the news? Someone could have pulled it up at Angie's."

"I just forgot. I've had a lot going on."

"Did you find it?" she asked. Johnny nodded.

"Okay, well, you know the interview they ran last night and this morning?"

Gabe smiled at Rose's happiness. "No," he said with a laugh. "There were reporters at the site, but I didn't know what was happening."

"Okay, well come look at this. I went and bought the paper today because it was so weird."

She turned to a side table near the door and pulled a newspaper out from under her purse.

*Geronimo's Bones Found in Secret New Mexico Grave?*

There were pictures of the pit where the bones were found and of serious men standing in a line on the construction site.

"I was there when they found the bones."

"Yeah, I know, everyone knows. They mention you in the paper. They say you guys dug up Geronimo. On the news, they said the Apaches want the whole land. That it's theirs."

He scanned the article.

"Am I in trouble?" he asked. "Are these guys going to come to me to pay for this?"

Rose shook her head and kept smiling. "No, no, no. That's someone else's problem. Johnny, explain how this video thing works."

He turned towards Gabe and Rose and sighed like he was explaining water to a fish.

"Here, look, I found a video that combines all three. I don't even know when someone had time to do this. The remix has only been up for a few hours."

Gabe started to sweat. People had been talking about him, looking at him.

"Wait," Rose said. "Let me get us our beer."

"Mom, can I have a sip of yours?" Johnny yelled.

"A sip!" Rose said from the kitchen. "You hear that, Gabe? Boy thinks he's slick and pretends he just wants a sip."

She walked back in with two beers and handed one to Gabe.

"Go get your own," she said to Johnny. "I'm not serving you beer until you get a job."

Johnny scrambled out of the recliner and into the kitchen.

"Only one," Rose said after him. "You sure move fast when you want something."

Gabe pictured Johnny and Micah watching TV, slapping each other on the arms at the funny parts. Did Micah drink beer yet? That was a thing a father should know. Johnny would be the older friend that intimidated Micah. The kind that handed him a beer, then laughed when the kid hated the taste.

"Okay." Johnny sat back down. "So the news only showed like two seconds of your interview. Then, late last night, the station posted the entire interview to YouTube. The extended cut or something, you know?"

Gabe did not know.

"And . . . " Johnny smiled and cleared his throat. "It's pretty funny, you just seem real freaked. And that shit took off. People all over started watching it and commenting. Like from around the world. Everywhere. Then, someone, you know, remixed it. You. Remixed you."

"Show him," Rose said. "Poor guy looks like a ghost." She put her hand on Gabe's arm.

"Right." Johnny handed Rose his phone. "Just hit play. But don't read any messages I get."

Johnny turned back to the TV, and Rose pulled Gabe into the corner. She touched the screen and the video started.

It was him. At the construction site, hunched over his bike, but he was boxed in by the logo for the station and his name. Along the top of the screen were the words: "Geronimo's Secret?" The first clip lasted just a second. He looked scared and all he said was "Luna. I'm Luna." Then it cut to other interviews and a reporter explaining the story.

There was another second of black, then it was the full recording.

No wonder the news only showed him saying his name. Nothing else made any sense. He made a joke about shouting Geronimo when you jump out of a plane. Then he mentioned being high on the reservation with Jefe. Then, after a mention of Geronimo, Gabe curses and peels out. For a second, the camera pans to catch him speeding away like a criminal. It was less an interview and more a crazy man rambling and answering questions no one had asked. Gabe worried Micah had seen this.

Rose looked concerned, like the surprise party had given the birthday boy a heart attack. "Okay, so that was bad, but trust me, this next part's good."

It was the same shot of Gabe hunched over his bike but with music, a deep, simple bass line, something electronic that Gabe hated. Boom, boom, boom, boom. He thought of the kid at The Pig. "Luna," he said in the video, then the video started over, and he said it again. "Luna. Luna. Luna. Luna," each time with the beat till it formed some demented dance song.

Then another noise joined the beat, a cymbal crashing, and the words changed again. "Luna. I'm Luna." Boom crash. Boom crash. "Luna. I'm Luna." Over and over.

Then the song got more frenetic, more beats were layered over it and some effect was placed on Gabe's voice, making it high and rhythmic, like he was singing. "It is what it is." Then, "Luna. I'm Luna." Boom crash. Boom crash. "It is what it is. Luna. I'm Luna." Then a stutter came into his voice, and the music sounded like it was being played backwards. "Not much you can do. Not much you can do. Not much you can do." Boom crash. "Luna. I'm Luna."

Rose was giggling, high-pitched and squealing. "Gabe, go with it. This is so funny."

"Not much you can do." Then the music fell away and it was just Gabe's voice echoing impossibly, like he was falling. "Haven't jumped out of a plane. Jumped out of a plane. Jumped out of a plane." Pause. "In a while."

Then everything crashed together and the song exploded faster. "This shit ain't funny no more. This shit ain't funny no more." Over and over. Then all his words were strung together, all out of order.

He glanced over at Johnny, who was doing a little dance in his recliner.

The words came faster, and higher, and faster, and higher. Then it all dropped away, leaving only Gabe's voice with a rhythmic, echo effect: "I didn't know shit." Each vowel was stretched out for an impossibly long time, his voice a squeaking whine. "Knoooooow shiiiit. I didn't doooo shiiiiiit." Then everything went quiet. The video went normal, and Gabe said, "Change, you know? It is what it is."

Then it cut to a shot of him riding away.

Gabe dropped into a brown, thin wooden chair near the front door. Gabe had only felt vertigo once. It was sixth, maybe seventh grade, and his father had taken Gabe out of school to go for a hike that day but left Lou behind. That felt so special. They hiked a familiar trail. Near the peak, there was a rise that looked out

across the valley below—not a steep drop but you could see forever. Gabe had seen it countless times, but this time he swung his
head and lost his stomach. He felt like the valley was folding up
to crush them. When he dropped to his knees, his father looked
worried for a split second before shaking his head and turning
away.

Gabe blinked a few times before realizing his eyes were open.
Rose was kneeling in front of him.

"Damn, I'm sorry, Gabriel. I didn't think it was a big deal."

He liked the way she said his full name, full of rising Spanish
vowels.

"Not your fault." Gabe ran his hands over his face and opened
his eyes wide. "Things have been confusing lately. I should . . . I
should head home."

"You won't make it five feet on your bike." Rose pulled him up
by the hands. "Sit with us."

Gabe sat at the far end of the couch and Rose took up a spot
closer to Johnny. "I thought you'd get a kick out of being famous,"
she said.

Johnny held up both his hands like he had a major announce-
ment. "Bet you five bucks someone's already selling shirts that say
'This shit ain't funny no more.'"

He laughed, and Rose went to swat at him. "Bet you five bucks
you're not going out this weekend if you keep that up."

The kid smiled and sipped his beer. "Just messing with y'all."

Gabe appreciated the way the kid backed down. Johnny had
to know he could storm out whenever he wanted, drink whatever
he wanted and talk however he wanted. Another show started on
the TV, and Gabe heard sitcom music and saw a family standing in
a kitchen. Rose's eyes flicked towards the screen. She watched a
few seconds with a half-smile on her face and laughed.

"Stupid," Johnny said with a laugh.

Gabe came here to apologize, to tell Rose he had been thinking about her. Had he said it? Rose poked Johnny and pointed at
one of the characters. "That was your *tía* growing up."

Johnny shook his head and snorted. Gabe turned to face the
TV, sliding closer to Rose. He had never seen the show, but it was

easy to pick up the story: small family crisis, meaningful conversation, one character who's always a clown. In the end, all their
problems were solved.

Afterwards, Johnny slinked into his room, calling goodnight
before he shut the door and turned on his music. Gabe pictured
himself doing the same thing in high school.

"Well, should we . . . " Gabe looked at Johnny's door. "Should
we watch more TV?"

Rose shook her head. "No, no more TV. I'm off all week. I
don't have to be up early tomorrow."

꿍 꿍 꿍

On the ride to his house, Rose folded her arms across Gabe's
stomach. She was relaxed where Micah had been tense. Some of
the gas stations mourning Eliseo Baca had replaced their memori-
als with cigarette and beer prices.

When Gabe tried to see the house through Rose's eyes, he
thought it still looked nice, even with the overgrown yard and
peeling shingles. But the contrast with the empty, smoke-stained
interior was harsh, and Gabe felt bad about Rose's clear disap-
pointment.

She strolled into the living room and examined the last few
pieces of furniture. He threw a shirt over the bags of pot and carried the bundle into the laundry room.

"I remember your dad building this house," she said. "I'd
drive by and watch the frame go up. Seemed to take forever."

"He moved slow."

"Deliberate, he moved real deliberate."

They stood next to the couch, as if waiting for some force to
push them down.

"He died here," Gabe blurted out. "In the old dining room
through the kitchen. Empty now."

Rosemarie raised her eyebrows.

He laughed out loud and said, "Oh sorry, I don't know why I
said that."

They both laughed and Gabe felt a bit better.

Rose sat down on the couch. "Yikes, I just realized your house smells like my son's room. You smell like a teenage boy, you know that? Cigarettes, beer, man-stink all let loose."

"We can get some fans going, open a window." Gabe opened the back door.

"No wonder your son likes it here so much."

Gabe sat down next to her and felt like they were back in high school. Was he supposed to put his hand on her knee?

"He really does. He's a guy, so he doesn't care about the furniture. Gives him room to breathe, run around."

Rose smiled. "I don't know why you're still talking about your son that way. This house is all you. It's too you for anyone else to like it here."

"Hey, it was my father's house."

"Ages ago, on a whole other planet."

The two of them sat back, their shoulders touching and heads resting on the couch. Gabe thought about the pages he had written for Micah. Maybe Rose would like to see them.

"Okay, maybe it's been a while since Helen let him come up."

"I knew you weren't going to rodeos or whatever."

"No, no we did that." Gabe laughed. "Once. The kid hates animals. Bitched the whole time and listened to his headphones."

"That's their specialty."

"Is the thing online actually funny? I sound so . . . confused and old. Sick."

She tried to hold back her smile. "Yeah, it is. It's really, really funny. You seem so freaked out. I mean, you're not that way normally, so that's why I think it's funny. Mr. Cool got all weirded out by some cameras. It's pretty cute."

"Can't believe people are watching it, watching me."

"You love it when people watch you. You're that guy with the stories."

"Half of them aren't even true," Gabe admitted. "I've never said that before."

"You think it's a shock?" Rose sat up straight and looked at Gabe. "Angie warned me, said you'd ask for money, that you asked her."

"No, no. I asked her for a *job*."

"Why do you care about being a father all of a sudden? You're Gabe, lazy and alone. Always have been."

"People change." He stopped and tried to shake that anger out of his voice. "Things can happen to make people change."

"I don't know. People can change for a minute, then they go right back."

Rose's eyes sunk into Gabe's blank walls. She got lost in whatever she was thinking about: her son, or her ex, or something a million miles away in the desert. Gabe put his hand on her arm, around her bicep and tugged her back to where they were. She smiled and laid back so her head was resting on the arm of the couch. Gabe pressed his mouth against hers. He pushed his weight down on top of her. She grunted and wrapped her legs around him. Her hands tangled in his hair, then ran over his shoulders and down his back. Gabe's mustache left red patches on her neck. She smelled of smoke mixed with perfume and a layer of powder or soap underneath. It was so strong, so female. She brought her hands under him and unbuttoned her blouse. Gabe leaned back to take off his leather vest and T-shirt as Rose unhooked her bra. The smell of their bodies met in the room, filling the air with something new. He looked at the stretch marks along her round stomach. Her torso was paler than her face. Her breasts pressed flat against her body, and a thin trail of black hairs, a dozen or so, sat like fallen eyelashes in a line snaking down from her belly button. His own beach ball stomach was covered in patches of kinky hair that had started to grey. Thick moles dotted his skin. The muscles in his arms were beginning to unravel, and his chest had gone flabby and loose. He remembered their young bodies and could feel where the skin had loosened and the muscles softened; it felt like she was more his that way. Gabe pulled her hips down so that she was flat on the couch. He pressed their soft stomachs together. Her eyes were shut tight, so tight the sides of her face spider-webbed, like she was trying to shut out the world and focus the universe's energy on the course of Gabe's mouth.

# EIGHTEEN

CHARLES LOOKED AROUND THE HOUSE, her house, and felt like the skeleton girl from her painting was swinging that broom into his guts. The year since the Hunt campaign had been an exercise in finding new, more humiliating lows. His ex-wife acting as secret benefactor was a level of pity and sadness new even to him.

Addie had been so full of concern for Hawley that morning. That girl swung the broom handle even harder. He dropped onto the couch and pulled up Addie's number on his cell. It was nearly midnight back in Washington. She was home, brushing her teeth or sitting quietly in front of the TV with her hair pulled back. Or maybe, like him, she was looking around a house that could never really be home.

Charles turned on the TV and put his phone away. He hoped Addie was out having fun and flirting with men nicer than her husband. He flicked through the channels and found what appeared to be a softcore porn channel.

"Whoa," Charles said to himself. "Old-school."

The flick had only the thinnest thread of plot involving spaceships and female aliens with large breasts. The military kidnapped the aliens, but the aliens seemed to enjoy it. The sex looked wrong, staged, the bodies not at viable angles. It all seemed uncomfortable for everyone. He muted the sound and kept watching.

Before letting herself in, Olivia tapped her fingernails on the glass door. The quick, familiar rhythm sent a shiver through his bones.

She wore the same black, floor-length dress she had at the gallery. The fabric clung to her hips and flared near her feet. Her single exposed shoulder danced with the medley of freckles that Charles remembered so well.

She tossed her handbag on the shelf near the front door. "I had to escape," she said. "The newspaper editor thinks he's Truman Capote, and everyone is laughing at each other's jokes."

"Does your husband know where you are?"

Olivia's eyes went to the TV and she fell apart in giggles. "Lonely?"

He scrambled for the remote and turned off the muted porn. "No, it was . . . I was flipping channels."

"Whatever gets you through the night."

He could feel every inch of space, every molecule of air between them. Her presence and those damn freckles on her shoulder infuriated him. She walked into the kitchen and grabbed a wine glass.

"What do you think of the tile in here? Took me forever to find enough for the whole house."

"I don't think anything about it."

"Okay, okay," she said out of the corner of her mouth. "Tough crowd."

She strolled into the living room and pointed to a painting next to the windows. She studied the canvas and then looked over her shoulder, raising her eyebrows at Charles. The painting showed the sun setting behind a mountain range. The rocks and trees in the foreground, from a certain angle, looked like a skull.

"It's a beautiful sunset," Charles said.

"It's a sunrise."

"Are you ready to tell me what's going on here?"

"It's the sunrise. Happens pretty much every day."

"No, you need to . . . "

Olivia rolled her eyes. "I already said sorry. I already said I should have told you I had a line on a job." She filled her wine glass. "You're welcome for the fully stocked bar, by the way. Or, at least, it *was* fully stocked."

Her brown eyes focused, became devious, when she smiled. She walked into the living room, sat down, slipped off her shoes and leaned back into the corner of the couch. She pulled her legs up against her chest and tucked her dress between her knees, the fabric drew impossibly tight. He moved to the far side of the couch.

"You don't seem to find this very funny," she said.

"Ask me to come up with a list of people I'd find in my bed in Santa Fe, you'd be towards the bottom."

"Well, that's because we know so many people. We're old now."

"We're not old. I'm not old."

"Nearly forty is old. It's not as old as we'll get. But it's older than we were."

Charles made his way to the kitchen and the bottle of wine. "You're really from here?"

"Española, just up the road."

"I didn't remember that."

Olivia nodded her head like it was the answer she expected. She smiled and rested her head on the back of the couch, staring at the ceiling.

"Were we really dumb enough to marry strangers?"

"In the courthouse. My mom was mad at me until we divorced."

"It was good for a few months."

He leaned against the kitchen island. He wanted to move back to the sofa, but he held off.

"You were impressive," he said. "I'd been surrounded by politicos for years, and you were amazing."

Olivia closed her eyes and looked for a second like she could sleep. "We didn't actually like each other. I was crazy. You were . . . boring. It's what we needed. Now, I'm here. Painting. Playing house."

"Must be a happy marriage," he said.

She opened her eyes. "I knew you'd dig at me for marrying Cody before you actually asked why I married him. I knew, *I knew,* I knew that's how you'd do it."

Olivia rested her glass on her stomach. The wine threatened to spill over the side with each breath. She ran her fingernails along the rim.

"I know how this looks," she said. "He's almost twenty years older. He's rich. I'm wearing a fucking ball gown."

"Back in Chicago, you made me promise not to drag you to fundraisers because you couldn't stand the exact same people who were in the gallery tonight. Different accents, different names, but they are the same people."

"I get it, Charles, Charlie, Chuckster." She drew out each of the syllables in the nicknames. He had always hated the way she called him that and he hated it even more now.

Olivia set the glass on the coffee table, sloshing wine out of the side. "We're exactly the same. Neither of us really knows how we got here or how to get out." She leaned forward, closer. "These people have everything you've ever wanted. You're up against the heart of it and you can't even see it. But you are an outsider and you're going to have to take what you want."

Charles felt much drunker all at once, like his brain was bringing back all the wine, all the champagne and booze he had drunk since he had landed here. He tried to ground himself, to think about Addie, but what came instead was Jim Hawley in Syria and the sound of boots marching down a cinder block hallway.

"These people like me," he said. "I can help them, and they'll help me."

"There's money out here, but you're going to have to carve out your own space. Learn what's important. Find the secrets they're keeping from you. That's what you cash in."

Charles thought of the casino and Branch's grip on his shoulder. "Oh, they're telling me plenty."

Olivia groaned. "After everything you still think you're the lucky one. Cody's not dumb and he's not generous."

Olivia stood up and grabbed her handbag. She had walked in, kicked over all the furniture, left her fingerprints and her breath all over everything, and now she was going to leave. As she slipped into her heels, Charles walked up behind her and put his hands on her hips.

She flinched and then leaned her head back against his shoulder. "I have got to go home," she said.

Charles felt dizzy with the scent of her hair, the crinkle of the fabric under his hands. He moved his mouth towards her neck. Olivia pushed back, and Charles tried to hold on tighter, but then she was walking away, towards the door.

"I have your number," she said over her shoulder. "I'll be in touch."

And then she was out the front door and gone. Charles ran his hands over his face and then locked his fingers behind his head. He grabbed her glass of wine and poured what was left of it into his. Roaming the house, nosing in the cabinets and drinking another bottle of wine did nothing to calm him down, but he did it until he passed out.

# NINETEEN

MALLON STOOD ON THE COMPOUND'S roof deck and poured out a Ball jar full of Cody Branch's piss. Tonight would be rough. Branch was drinking himself into insanity. Mallon could smell the craziness in the air, like something was on fire high in the atmosphere. He looked over the city. The lights seemed ready to rise off the ground and enter orbit. It would be a good start, he thought. No one would complain if the whole city blew away in the wind.

"Come on, girl," Branch hollered. "Don't sip it. Just bring it back now."

Mallon looked down at the trees below the house, wondering if the grass had died. Six months ago, Branch asked for his usual bottle of brandy plus a large jar. Over the past couple months, he must have dumped ten gallons of piss over the side.

Mallon figured Branch would pass out within the hour. He placed the jar to Branch's right, then re-filled the jar to his left with brandy. At some point, Mallon was sure the drunk would get confused and drink out of the wrong one. He took a seat in a chair behind Branch.

"You're like a goddamned hound dog sometimes, you know that? Setting there watching the trees. What is there to see?"

Mallon never responded because there was nothing to say. Once, he had responded to a lieutenant in Anbar Province, then spent the afternoon sweeping the highway ahead of the lieutenant's Humvee by himself. For hours, Mallon was out in the open, poking dead dogs and piles of trash, trying to spot the wires before they tripped. It was a job they used to pay the locals twenty bucks to do, and half the time there was no one left to pay out.

Mallon swore he lost ten pounds of sweat on that walk. He looked so hard his eyes dried out and blinking hurt. He could see the individual fleas, desperate for one more pulse of life, bouncing off the muzzles of dead dogs. He could see his legs getting blown off or fire chewing up his face. He could see a crying ten-year-old who had been tracking Mallon for months, slipping in and out of the shadows, desperate to pay Mallon back for a destroyed house and a fried family.

Later, when he was in his bunk and his throat had cracked and his legs kept beating time on their own, he heard that stretch of highway had been cleared a few hours earlier. Mallon never found out if the lieutenant had known that, but the lesson stuck.

"These past days were like something from the Book of Fucking Revelations." Branch coughed from deep in his chest and spat on the ground next to him.

Mallon folded his hands in his lap and leaned his head back to scan the sky for satellites.

Branch picked up a thread of conversation from an hour earlier. "Then he said, he 'didn't think so.' You believe we hired someone like that? The world is an imperiled place. *Imperiled.* Yes. Yes, sir."

Branch had always been tough, but the past six months were different. His anxieties were edging up day by day, and Mallon had trouble keeping perspective. Branch's anger was seeping into his own pores, changing him. He had wanted to hurt that little guy from DC. He saw him tonight at the gallery and he *still* wanted to hurt him. It would have been so easy. All because of a wasted night at the airport and because Branch's paranoia had infected him.

Unless Mallon was right to be suspicious. He had no idea anymore.

"Not that you care. You get paid, that's all you want, that's all everyone wants." Branch's voice had taken on a swollen quality. "But, I'm serious. . . . When did you last speak? Was I there?"

"I speak when you ask me to."

Branch's laugh started in his throat, then moved up to his nose and into a cough. "That's good. That's a trained response. 'I speak when you ask me to.' Well, now I'm asking you to speak. Speak to me about my wife."

Mallon had spotted a second satellite when he brought his head back down. "She's been following her usual patterns. Visiting those friends of hers off Cerrillos Road. The shops. The drives west of town have continued, but they seem aimless."

"Seem?"

Mallon was concerned about the stop in Española, but he decided not to say anything.

Once did not make a pattern, and only deviations from patterns were worth reporting.

"You not going to answer my question?" Branch turned around in his chair. Something he almost never did.

"I trust her," Mallon said.

"You do?"

"I do."

"Well, she had something on her mind tonight, that's for sure." Branch laughed and poured himself more brandy. "But it was her night, so I'm probably just being an asshole. I should go wish her goodnight."

Branch looked out on the city and then slumped his shoulders. Mallon could see the darkness creep up on him. It looked painful.

Mallon thought of his own home, which he had not seen for days. The cot in the guardroom was closer, easier. He pulled out his notebook and made a note of the time and the number of brandies Branch consumed. He flipped through the previous pages. It all looked in order. No, yesterday they went to the campaign office at 6:30, not 7. Mallon made the edit and slipped the notebook back into his pocket.

Branch picked up another thread of his anger. "They are determined to make us bleed. All of them. Every single one. The Apaches are the latest and the messiest. But they're all circling vultures who don't even know what they're circling, but they know they want it." Branch raised one finger in the air. "That's our secret weapon, yes? Knowledge is money and strength."

Branch set his empty glass down and tipped it over.

"I trust Diana," Branch said. "I trust . . . you, God help me. I trust my dick when it works, and . . . that'll have to be good enough."

Branch stood up. He put his hands on his hips while his balance evened out. Mallon stood ready with a bracing hand.

"We need to be ready. There's going to be too much attention on us now that these Apaches are causing trouble. Look at their lawyer. Where does he go? Who are his other clients? Does he have secrets? Of course he has secrets. What are they? If he's rotten, find out how. If he's picking up girls on Central, I need to know what hair color he likes. You. Not one of the kids. You take the lead on this."

"Sir, we're already stretched very thin, and I worry . . . "

"Hire more people."

"Yes, sir."

Branch looked back at Mallon. "Do you think my wife will be in our bed tonight? Or will she be in that guest bedroom again?"

Mallon stayed silent.

Branch stumbled ahead of Mallon, who stayed a step behind him, hands out, just in case.

# FRIDAY

# TWENTY

ROSE LEFT BEFORE the sun came up. She laughed at Gabe's air mattress and said she would rather nap on the couch for a few hours. The leather still smelled like her sweat. Gabe drifted in and out of a light doze. After a couple hours, guilt pulled him up. He would rather wallow around in his memories than work on earning Micah's money.

When Gabe stood up, the pain in his ankle blasted everything away. He dropped back on the couch. The ankle—a horse had stepped on it years earlier—hurt most mornings and before it snowed, but not like this. Now, it felt bruised deep inside.

The night with Rose had been surprising. He forgot about cancer and his disinterested son. But now the sun was up and he was sweating. He was so far from having enough money.

Gabe fiddled with his class ring. Do something. That was the lesson he learned at The Pig. He pushed himself back to his feet. This time, his ankle held up. He grabbed his keys.

Gabe parked in front of the pawnshop. Andrés would give him a good deal. They had gone to school together, closed down countless bars countless times, and that better be worth something. Before walking into the store, Gabe heard a muffled, electric ding come from his saddlebags. Smokey's phone.

He ignored it. No reason to look at that phone unless he was going to throw the damn thing away. Or sell it. Gabe unsnapped the bag. He would sell it to Andrés. But the phone was scratched and worn; even Gabe could tell it was ancient, some hand-me-down from an older brother. There were a dozen missed calls: Mom Cell, Home, Karlee, Hunter. Kid names that made Gabe sick.

There were three texts from someone named Wilson. The latest one caught Gabe's eye: *You get the shit? Can your cowboy hook me up too?*

*Cowboy?* Gabe was okay with that.

No, Gabe stopped himself from replying. He threw the phone back in the bag.

In the shop, the first thing Gabe saw was a mountain of high school rings in a plastic tub.

He smiled at Andrés, who started shaking his head before Gabe had the ring off his finger.

"Okay, Luna, listen up. Some of you dudes chose cheap-ass bands with cheap-ass stones. That's a fact. Maybe your parents were cheap, maybe you were cheap. I don't know, I don't care."

"Uh-uh, nope, not this one," Gabe said. "No, sir. This is the real deal right here, brother."

Gabe had saved for his ring. He and Lou worked themselves to nubs bailing hay for the nearby ranches. It was hateful work. The backaches started early and lasted for days. The bailing wire dug into his palms, even through the leather gloves, leaving deep, red grooves in the skin.

Andrés pulled out a little tray with some tools and a few bottles of liquid. He held the ring against the light.

"Andrés, you're full of shit, man. This isn't an antique show. That's gold—with an emerald. I saved up."

He grunted. "Can I test the band?"

Gabe shrugged. Andrés dropped some liquid on the ring and then rubbed it against a stone bolted into the counter. His eyebrows went up.

"Okay, you got real gold here, 10k it looks like."

"Hell, yeah. I told you that shit was real."

Adrenalin beat through Gabe. If he could get four or five hundred for this ring, then he'd be set. "Thirty years old, that's nearly an antique right there."

"Hang on, Luna, slow down. If the stone's legit, I can give you even more, but I need your permission to test it."

"Sure, whatever, let's do it."

Andrés pulled out a pair of heavy-looking tweezers from his tray, grabbed the sides of the ring and squeezed out the stone. It slipped out easily, leaving a neutered space in the band.

"Whoa." Gabe reached for the ring.

"You said I could test it, *cabrón*."

"I didn't say you could fuck it up."

"*Cálmate*, it's not fucked up. I can get it back in there when I'm through." Andrés raised his eyebrows. "Probably."

Andrés held the stone up to the light and rubbed it between his fingers. Gabe cleaned that ring every month with a cloth and some jewelry polish he had slipped from Helen's boxes before she moved out. Now it looked tiny, cheap, and there was something obscene about the way Andrés was handling the jewel.

"Okay, like I thought. This ain't emerald. It's hardened glass."

"Bullshit."

Andrés didn't move or say anything.

"No, uh-uh," Gabe said, "I filled out the order form myself. I remember. Emerald. Gold band."

"Maybe 'emerald-style.' Those catalogs confuse you on purpose."

"I worked my ass off. That's a goddamned emerald."

Andrés exhaled. His patience had run out. Gabe was no longer a friend, just another asshole trying to scrape together some cash.

"I've got emeralds here. I can show you the difference."

He offered the eye-piece and the stone.

Gabe waved him off. "What does this mean?"

"It means you can pawn this and I'll give you fifteen dollars. Or you can sell it to me and I'll give you seventy-five."

"Andrés, you're . . . I remember the order form. I remember watching my dad fill everything out. I gave him the cash."

"Just because he ripped you off doesn't mean you can rip me off." Andrés stepped back, done humoring Gabe. "Those are the numbers. You know I get two of these a week? Some older and nicer than this. Most people walk out with shit."

"Seventy-five?"

"That's too much." Andrés pointed to the tub of class rings, all tinged mossy green. "Those fuckers didn't even have precious metal. Take them with you. Wear one of those instead. Wear ten. I give them out on Halloween."

"Why do you want to buy it then? Must have someone who'll take it."

"Don't be fucking stupid, Luna. I'm going to melt this down out back. It'll be earrings in LA in a month."

Gabe pinched the bridge of his nose and rubbed his thumb and finger into the corners of his eyes. It was not enough. Not for that ring. The stone and the setting lay on Andrés' counter, broken apart.

Gabe looked at the bin of other class rings. Would he even be around to help Micah pick out his own?

He pointed at the bin. "You got one in there from my year?"

In the parking lot, Gabe pulled out the kid's phone. He texted Wilson back—fast, before he stopped himself: *Dude hooked me up. He'll meet you in front of The Pig tomorrow at noon. 400 for 2 ounces. Worth it.*

It felt like someone else typed the message. Helen needed a grand. If he sold some weed to this other kid, he would be closing in on eight hundred. Gabe looked around the parking lot, worried someone had seen him. But what would they have even seen?

# TWENTY-ONE

STEPPING INTO HIS CAR, Charles knew it was all over for him. He looked in the rearview mirror and saw the mountains behind the house. Her mountains. Her house. Charles sighed. Her husband's rearview mirror.

He gritted his teeth. Olivia had been close enough for him to smell, to almost taste. The whole encounter felt gauzy, dreamlike, and he kept seeing the way her body had moved under that dress.

Addie would find out if anything happened. Mr. Branch and Salazar would find out, and his future would consist of a used Corolla and a pity job at his mom's bank. Charles pulled into the office parking lot. Olivia had been so close.

Today was the meeting with the Apaches. He tried to box Olivia up and put out the sparks she had fired up in his chest. This meeting could fully ground Charles in Branch's organization. Salazar had given Charles clear orders: listen, acknowledge any concerns, get a dollar amount. Mr. Branch invited him to the party, and last night Mrs. Branch confirmed it could make his future. He bounced into the office with an energy that even Jordan would admire.

Charles spent the morning with Jordan and Salazar. They rehearsed talking points and rejoinders, polished the historical details, anticipated the amount of money Branch would have to spend. It felt like a war council, and Charles buzzed. Jordan panicked when the Apaches showed up half an hour early. The cubicle dwellers sprang into action, offering water and chairs.

It was the same five men from the building site. Four Apaches and their lawyer, who wore a white suit that made him look like a thick, decorative candle. His face was hidden by a wild beard. Everyone else wore the same clothes they'd worn the previous day: two were in suits, two were in flannel, long-sleeve shirts buttoned to the collar. Had they coordinated looking professional and down-home at the same time? It would photograph well.

Hawley came to mind. Every negative press hit, every hitch in a candidate's step and gaffe out of their mouth became an occasion to yell, threaten and spit.

Charles had never mastered that blistering art of political motivation through anger. Hawley would have charged into this meeting laughing at the Apache's claims to ownership. He would have stayed standing, and the meeting would have lasted ten minutes. Hawley would have won.

Charles sat down at the middle of the table, the man in the white suit directly across from him. Jordan sat at Charles' side, but Salazar took a seat towards the end of the table, the kind of spot reserved for a note taker or an assistant.

The lawyer opened a briefcase and pulled out five copies of a thick, bound document.

He looked at Salazar and Jordan, but focused on Charles. "My name is Rey Baca. I've been brought on by the San Miguel Apaches to make sure their interests are looked after in this case."

"Well, I have a question already," Salazar said.

The lawyer lowered his eyebrows and craned his neck over to look at her.

"I'm familiar with all the pueblos and tribes in the state," she continued. "I've visited every single one, multiple times and have represented several of them in legal matters. I must admit, and this is quite embarrassing, I have never heard of the 'San Miguel Apaches.'"

Just as Rey opened his mouth, Salazar continued. "I'm sorry to interrupt but this is a related question. Do the San Miguel, a tribe we've been working with and that has no historical connection or shared customs with the Apache Nation, realize you even exist?"

Rey cracked a polite smile, then turned back to Charles. "The San Miguel Pueblo has received a copy of these documents, and we're meeting with them tomorrow."

"So, the answer is no. No one has heard of you, or your tribe, until . . . yesterday?"

Charles' control of the meeting had slid towards Salazar before he said a word.

"Ma'am, I am not a member of the tribe," Rey said. "I've been brought on to make sure their interests are looked after."

"Maybe, let's start at the beginning," Charles said. "You're a *new* tribe?"

It immediately felt like the wrong question. The men on the other side of the table shifted uneasily, and Jordan shot him a glance.

Rey opened the bound document to the first page. "They are an ancient people. It's all explained in our brief. When the United States government, in violation of dozens of treaties with First Nations people, relocated Apaches, and others, to Oklahoma, Arizona and so on, there were dozens of small tribes and sub-tribes erased from history through assimilation and extermination. It is our contention that these men here, and nearly one hundred other descendants throughout Oklahoma, Arizona, Texas and New Mexico, are entitled to official tribal recognition by the United States government. It is also their contention, based on a vast oral tradition and a series of letters written during and after the forced relocation, that their ancestral homeland is on what has erroneously been labeled San Miguel land."

"You're asking for *all* of San Miguel's land?" Jordan asked.

"No, ma'am." Rey pulled out a surveyor's map. "This marks out the land that the San Miguel Apaches are entitled to."

"And I'm sure it happens to include highway access and the airport site." Salazar dropped her pencil on the table.

"There are nine recognized Apache tribes in the United States," Jordan said. "Two of them already have land in New Mexico. How could they *all* have forgotten the San Miguel Apaches?"

Charles spoke up. "Gentlemen, I also think we've lost sight of the issue that first brought you to our attention and to the attention of the media."

One of the younger men wearing a flannel shirt spoke up. "We are entitled to that land. Many of the men who joined Geronimo's fight were San Miguel Apaches. They left their home and were murdered by the US Army."

"Excuse me, once again," Salazar said. "I'm trying to follow along. Correct me, if you will. The claim is that you *deserve* the land. Is there a legal aspect to your argument or is this about giving you something because you asked nicely?"

Rey shifted in his chair so he could face Salazar. The big man looked contorted and uncomfortable. The focus of the room shifted away from Charles and Rey towards her in the corner. It was a brilliant move and it seemed so obvious now.

She continued before anyone could respond. "We can come back to that question, I suppose."

"There are complicated tribal feuds and land disputes that go back thousands of years. It is our contention that the San Miguel Apaches were driven from their land first by local tribes, and then the US Army finished the job. Now, they are back."

"When did the local tribes drive the San Miguel Apaches from their land?" Jordan asked.

"The first expulsion occurred in the late 1700s, and the final removal was completed in the late 1800s."

There was silence around the table. Charles had trouble following all the details, but it was clear the men in suits next to Rey looked nervous, like something was slipping through their fingers.

"So . . . " Charles said. "If this started happening two hundred years ago, how do these men know they're related to what you claim is a lost tribe?"

"That's exactly what I was wondering," Salazar said.

"They've gone through the painstaking effort of re-creating tribal genealogy. Each of the people listed in this suit is related to a group of Apaches who were living on your construction site before the first expulsion. Construction on this airport must stop immediately because it was not San Miguel's land to sell. It has never been San Miguel land. It is Apache land. Once the property rights have been reestablished and the government has redistributed the land to the San Miguel Apaches, these men here today, then we can discuss whether or not we are willing to do business with your group."

"We've cleared that land and prepped it for development," Salazar said.

"The county already bought the land and handed it over to us," Charles added. "Is there a settlement that can be reached? Maybe a certain outlay of funds to an organization that represents . . . "

"We're not after a payoff," Rey said. "The county bought that land from someone not authorized to sell it. We plan on taking ownership. How San Miguel reimburses your investors is up to their tribal council."

"You do know they've paved roads, built health clinics and new schools with that money," Jordan said. "Half of it has been spent."

"The transfer of money between your organization and the San Miguel Pueblo is not our concern. You can try to get your money back, I suppose. But if I sell you the deed to Manhattan, the Mayor of New York won't give you his sympathies."

"You're taking away San Miguel's future," Jordan said.

Charles jumped in again. "A settlement offer could be arranged."

"Your organization did not do the proper research," Rey said. "We did not expect your organization to hand over the land. So, in an hour, we are filing this suit with the Bureau of Indian Affairs, the US Attorney General's Office and the proper local authorities."

Rey zipped his bag shut, but Salazar stood up a fraction of a second faster. It looked comic, this scramble to be the first to adjourn the meeting, but Charles knew it was important.

"We still haven't discussed the issue of Geronimo," Charles said again.

"I have a feeling Geronimo is resting peacefully in Oklahoma," Salazar said. "Isn't that right?"

"Geronimo was a prisoner of war buried in alien territory. Our documentation on Geronimo's request to be buried in his homeland has been released to the press," Rey said. "I'm sure if you open any news site you'll be able to read all about it."

"Of course," Salazar smiled and shook each man's hand like the meeting had gone according to plan.

The three Apache men trailed behind Rey. Salazar walked them to the front door, while Charles and Jordan remained in the conference room.

"And you thought we were about to lose our jobs," Jordan said.

Charles looked at his notebook. All he had written was, "a billion in investments." He had been sliding around like a kid on ice skates. These guys never raised their voices or broke a sweat. The meeting lasted less than ten minutes, but they'd blown up everyone's plans and had started a forest fire with Cody Branch's money. It was hard not to be impressed.

Salazar came back into the conference room. Charles could feel her suppressed anger.

"They're aggressive," she said. "Next meeting, we need to start with a number so big it'll shake their conviction. If we get two or three of those guys willing to take a couple million, then the rest will crumble."

"Where's that going to come from?" Charles asked. "Surely Branch won't pay it all himself."

"There are investors devoted to clearing this up. The money will be there."

"San Miguel will be ruined," Jordan said. "No one will work with them while this is happening. All those improvements, the school, everything will stop until this is settled."

Salazar spoke over her concerns. "If these guys are serious about this lawsuit, about petitioning the government, it'll take years. We just dealt with a tribe down south, seventeen members, who spent a decade trying to convince the US government they were real. And that was down south, away from the press, away from our delightfully liberal Santa Fe."

"Away from the ghost of Geronimo," Charles said. "That's not his body, is it?"

"I don't think it matters," Salazar said. "It's a great hook, but the press hasn't bit. If that changes, then this made-up tribe just became the most famous Natives in the country. We have to settle with them before the press decides to take this seriously."

The three sat in silence for a few moments. Charles decided to take a swing.

"Why do we have to work with San Miguel?"

Jordan didn't even look up from her notes. "A little thing called 'contracts,'" she said. "We gave them money. We gave them a cut of future airport profit."

Salazar put a hand along her hairline and looked down at her phone.

Charles knew he could keep pushing this, or he could be timid, fold, let someone else take the lead.

"But, let's say we *agree* with the Apaches," he said. "If we discover that it actually is their land, not San Miguel's, then can't we get the contracts nullified? We give the Apaches San Miguel's original share of future profit, maybe a few more points to sweeten it all, and move on with this tribe and not the original one. What's the difference?"

Jordan spoke up. "The difference is that San Miguel will sue us, San Miguel will be ruined and we'd have broken our word."

"San Miguel gets to keep the money they were already given. They lose *future* profits, that's all." Charles looked to Salazar, but she kept her head down.

"It'll be expensive," Charles continued. "And we'll have to make sure we can work with the Apaches, but this could go away. San Miguel will sue, but they'll take a settlement because they won't have a choice. And they'll be next to a major airport. That'll save their economy, right? And our long-term plans can still work."

Salazar speared Charles with her eyes. Then she stood up, smoothed her dress and pushed her chair back under the table. Jordan looked like she knew something had been left unsaid.

"I need to talk to Cody," she said. "You two keep digging into what you can find about these Apaches. Jordan, look at the legal details of our agreement with San Miguel. There may be a clause that can get us out of this. Charles, we need press releases . . . you know the drill: peace, harmony, love, respect. We're throwing around a lot of big plans like this is our money. Let's be careful about that. This isn't east coast politics."

Salazar left the room, leaving Charles alone with Jordan.

"We can't abandon San Miguel," she said. "Have you been out there? Seen the pueblo? They need this."

"Everyone needs something. I'm focusing on helping our organization."

Jordan shook her head and gathered her material. Her top layer of idealism was still thick and healthy. She thought there was a way for everyone to be happy in the end. Charles pitied her for that.

# TWENTY-TWO

MALLON LIVED IN A DUPLEX half the size of Cody Branch's roof deck. The place was simple, sparse and perfect for him. Still, he had been gone for days. When the job got busy, it was easier to crash on a guardhouse bunk. The hard canvas cot felt better on his back, and Mallon knew the importance of demonstrating his dedication and respect to the newer guys. Branch kept hiring more security—more than he needed. Most of them were sitting around, eyeing Mrs. Branch on the security monitors or strolling around the property like they were being paid to count mosquitoes.

The duplex was on Santa Fe's south side. The drive from Branch's compound took him from wealth, around the plaza, through the middle-class neighborhoods of coffee shops and yoga studios, and then into the Mexican neighborhoods of car repair joints and burrito places. These were his neighbors, but he never talked to anyone other than Claudia.

She lived in the other half of the duplex. Her old Ford was in the carport and her kitchen light was on. The first thing he did, before even turning on the light, was unlock the back door. She would hear him through the walls and slide in. That was how they first met. A year ago, she opened her back door, stepped over the two-foot high bush that separated their halves of the yard and walked right in. She asked why she could never hear his TV or any music through the thin walls, almost complaining about the quiet. After that, she came over once a week, and then several times a week, and now she visited pretty much every night he was in.

The living room smelled musty, so he cracked a window. He switched on all the lights, and when he turned on the swamp cooler, he could smell the moist air flood his home. Mallon had never bothered to replace the old machine with an AC.

Mallon lined up his shoes near the front door and hung his keys on a plain hook he had twisted into the wall. He walked around the house, making sure everything was as he left it. Even coming home had its own dedicated routine. After looking in on every room, even the empty spare bedroom, he dumped his clothes into the washing machine. The routine and the cleanliness soothed him. Clutter, loose ends, made him jumpy.

As he was loading the dryer, Claudia crept in the back door and dropped onto the couch. He heard her, of course, even though she made almost no noise. Claudia moved with the kind of practiced quiet he assumed she had needed to learn the hard way. She was holding a six-pack of tall beers and wore a long-sleeve T-shirt underneath a pair of overalls. She cracked a can and rested her sneakers on the arm of the couch.

"You look like an Amish kid," Mallon said.

Claudia took a sip and shook her head. "You have no idea what the Amish look like. Do they even wear denim?"

"Aren't you hot?"

"You keep this place cold. And, one day you'll get a job where you're wearing a g-string the whole time, and then I'll make fun of you for wearing a lot of clothes off-duty."

He started the dryer and sat in the chair he bought only after realizing that she tended to take up the whole couch.

"Here's where I ask about your day," Claudia said. "And here's where you tell me it was fine but don't really say much of anything at all. Ready? How was your day?"

"It was fine."

He smiled and she played like she was going to kick him. "You are such a jerk." She held out a beer to him, but Mallon shook his head, as she knew he would. "It's been longer than usual," she said. "Three days, easy."

Mallon nodded. "Work has been . . . demanding."

"I love our conversations because they make me feel so damn psychic. I can see it all." She balanced the beer against her side and held her fingertips against her temple. "I can see your words before they emerge."

"Have you fed the cat?"

Claudia dropped her hands. The beer can almost tipped over, but she caught it and held it on her stomach. "Damn, I thought you were going to ask about the shooting down the street."

"Shooting?"

"Down the street," she repeated. "Man got drunk. Man climbed a tree in his own backyard. Neighbor thought it was some kind of home invasion from the air." She made a cartoon gunshot noise. "Man fell from tree."

"That's funny," Mallon said with a straight face.

She laughed. "Yeah, I guess it is. Could have been me. I've climbed a tree before. Weird, if you think about it."

It had taken Mallon a year to stop being puzzled when Claudia was sarcastic. He trusted that she would help him find his way through her words.

"I heard some music I liked." Mallon said it fast, then pulled back, embarrassed. "But, I guess I don't know the name. It was a woman. Modern, I think, but a little jazzy and . . . dark? Is that . . . is that anything?"

Claudia smiled but didn't laugh at him. "That sounds nice. You'll have to find out who it was. I can download the tracks for you. You can finally use that thing." She waved her beer at the ancient boom box in the corner.

It had been a gift from the guys when he quit the Highway Patrol. They had lifted it from the evidence room. She was making a joke. He recognized it and smiled.

"Tell me another story about your boss," Claudia whispered. "I should have never told you any of that."

"Oh, but you did, and now they're my favorite thing of anything ever. Tell me one secret. Or, at least tell me about a time he got drunk and fell down."

Mallon kept secrets better than anyone he knew. But not from her.

"He thinks his wife is cheating on him."

"Ohhhhh. Tough one. Is she?"

Mallon folded his hands over his stomach. The movement reminded him of Mr. Branch, and he rearranged his hands. "I don't know. I hope not. She sleeps in the guest bedroom and is always driving around during the day."

"You going to follow her? No, hire me. I'll follow her. That sounds fun."

"You would not be good at that."

"What?" Claudia pretended to be shocked. "I am sneaky."

"You are. But you'd also want to get coffee and chat with her."

Claudia laughed. "Maybe that's what you should do."

"Mrs. Branch does not want to talk to me."

"I think you have a crush on her. Steal her away from him. Wow, I bet she'd snag a lot of money in a divorce."

Mallon felt embarrassed by Claudia's mention of Olivia. He stood up, grabbed a paper towel from the kitchen and wrapped it around Claudia's beer.

"I don't want to talk about her. And he's more scared of strangers swooping in and taking it all than he's scared of losing her."

"If he lost everything, it'd be terrible for you."

"And a lot of other people."

"Yeah, but I don't know 'other people.' Who is going to listen to my stories about creepy customers if you have to leave for some new job."

"I'll be here."

Claudia looked down at her beer and flicked the tab with her thumb. "You're barely here now."

Mallon swallowed. He had no idea what to do with his guilt. What he had with Claudia wasn't exactly a relationship but it was the closest thing he had to it, so he held his feeling in his chest and let it burn.

"He pisses in jars," Mallon said. "My boss."

Claudia's eyes went wide and her eyebrows shot up. "What the fuck?" Mallon knew that was too much to share, but at least she smiled.

"When he's drunk, he doesn't want to get up anymore, so I bring him an empty jar."

Her mouth dropped open.

"I don't even know that I can laugh as hard as I need to right now," she said. "That story has gone the full spectrum, over the bar on the swing-set, through laugher up to some type of higher level." She scrunched her eyes up and started to snicker. "That's the grossest, I—I can't."

He smiled. Three days was too long.

"One day, I'll be rich enough to piss in jars," she said.

Claudia finished her second beer and placed it on the carpet next to the sweating cans. No one else in the world could get away with that in his home.

She yawned. "I'm sleepy."

"I could sleep."

"You could, but you don't ever seem to."

"I get enough."

Claudia stood up and unbuckled her overalls. She left a trail of clothing that led through the house and into Mallon's bed. He gathered her clothes, folded them on the couch, then went room to room and shut off the lights. He found a clean undershirt and boxers and changed in the bathroom.

She always curled into a tight comma facing the wall. Then, when he got into bed, she rolled over and flopped a leg and an arm onto him. She smelled like lotion and a long bath, and her body was impossibly warm. Once or twice a month, they had sex. It was brief, even mechanical, yet necessary. Mallon had never been good at understanding his own feelings, much less those of other people. But he knew he and Claudia needed each other. She rested her head on his chest, and he placed his hand on the iguana tattoo that crawled up her side.

"Slightly fewer assholes at work, lately," she said in a sleepy voice. "Although this one guy showed up. I was giving him a dance. Normal, nothing special. But he, I don't know . . . They all try to touch me, that's the point. What I mean is, when they go too far, they all go too far in the same way."

Mallon felt himself go red with heat. He opened his eyes. "You got a name?"

"No, no," Claudia said, more awake now. "It's fine. The last time you defended my honor, I almost lost my job."

"You said that guy had been . . . "

"He was a jerk, but I'm sure that he, and his new set of dentures, are now treating women with much respect." Claudia settled back in under his arm. "No, this other guy. He wasn't rough. The opposite. He touched the side of my neck, very soft. Ran his fingertips up the back of my calf real slow. So, I turned around, because it didn't feel right, and then he skimmed his fingertips along my shoulder blades. Soft, gentle. He's been back twice, but I keep my distance. Hungry. He was so emotionally hungry."

Mallon tried, he tried so hard, not to let his voice give away his anger. "Let me know. A license plate. A name. Anything."

Claudia pressed her palm against Mallon's chest as if she could calm the storm. Soon, she was sleeping, and he held her tight, remembering why he worked so hard to preserve an ounce of order in the world.

# SATURDAY

# TWENTY-THREE

GABE HAD AN HOUR TO KILL before meeting the teenager. He was in a bad mood and could picture this Wilson kid showing up, calling him "Cowboy," and generally being a pain in the ass. This time, he would keep his temper. There was a goal, and Gabe needed to stay on track. Fortitude.

At the desk in Micah's room, Gabe tried to explain himself.

*I know it's wrong but it's what I got left. Get yourself to the spot where you don't have to pick and gripe and you won't have to do what you know is wrong. My whole life, I've been getting under people's skin. But that's not what gets things done. Don't be a prick. Or be a prick that takes on the bigger issue. That's what's good about Rey. That fat bastard busted his ass in law school so he could make people listen to him. I never saw the big picture, son. My father had a life jacket. That's why he made it out of WWII alive. But he never should have been on that boat to begin with. He should have been the guy back in the office—sending people to death. I don't know how to get there but I know you can. Maybe you're already on your way and you don't even need me or these pages. Maybe that's where my mother went. She found something bigger than my old man and two bratty boys. Hell, I guess that's why your mother left.*

Gabe stopped writing. Some of his problems he still had to avoid. He knew exactly when to stand up and walk away.

He called Helen.

She answered, which filled Gabe with absurd happiness. It meant he still had a chance.

"Hey," he said, "so can I see him next week?"

"Why are you doing this?"

"I want to spend a couple days with him. It's important."

"You're making me say no. You put him on the bike. You got in a wreck. You don't have a job."

"I have some money. Nearly the whole thousand. It's all for him."

"Did construction start again?" Helen sounded like she was only going through the motions of giving Gabe a chance.

"No, not yet, but soon."

"Having a job is not an unreasonable expectation. It's in the custody agreement, and you should be thanking me for not reporting that accident."

"It wasn't my fault, and it was the scariest damn thing ever."

Helen was quiet for a second. "Yeah, I know. He explained it to me a little more. I told him you were trying to help him. Don't know if he bought it." She dropped her voice. "He's still young. He got freaked out."

"When I pick him up, I'll borrow Rey's truck. No bike."

"Call me when construction starts again." She hung up.

Gabe almost threw his phone across the room. He rubbed both hands over his face. He had no idea when the site would reopen. Rey was doing his damnedest to keep it shut forever.

It was time to go meet this kid. A shiver of fear went through his guts. What if he got busted? Frederick had been Gabe's only concern, but if he got busted selling a couple ounces to a teenager, the courts would keep Micah away forever.

Gabe grabbed his keys and left before he changed his mind. Forever was not going to be for very long. It was only an ounce. Frederick would not find out. The cops would not find out. He looked over his shoulder at each light, and he drove up and down in front of The Pig four times before pulling into the dirt lot.

A few minutes later, Wilson's car pulled in. It was a silver VW with a decal of a baseball bat and his name on the back wind-shield. The kid poked at his phone for a few seconds after killing the engine. He never looked up at Gabe.

Something felt wrong. Cops would be laughing about this bust for years. "We got the guy by texting with him on a stolen phone." One count of assaulting a minor, two for dealing, one for possessing stolen goods, *and* then they'd find out about the disability scam.

Gabe walked back to his bike. But either his bike or his hand was shaking because he could not get the key into the ignition. He used both hands to guide the key into the slot.

Wilson got out of the car and jogged towards Gabe. "Dude, dude, dude, what's up? No, I'm here."

Wilson was barely five feet tall and maybe 110 pounds. His face was blistered with pink, nickel-sized bumps. The kid's chest was probably concave under his T-shirt.

"How the fuck old are you?"

Wilson looked down. "Old enough to have cash."

Gabe ran his hand over his face and stepped off his bike. "Let's get this over with."

"Awesome. Really, really awesome." Wilson pulled out his phone. "I need to take a pic with you. It'll be fast."

Before Gabe could step back, Wilson put his arm around his shoulder and held his phone out in front of them. For a second, Gabe saw himself on the phone screen, mouth slightly open, looking haggard and tired while Wilson smiled and held up a thumb.

"You're like a legend or something, you know? This is kind of a big deal." Wilson took a step back but didn't put the phone away. "I'm going to take a video so you got to do the thing you do."

The kid lifted the phone and held it out towards Gabe.

"Umm . . . do something." Wilson smiled. "Say 'this shit ain't funny no more.' That's your thing, right?"

"What the fuck is your problem, kid?"

"That's it, that's it! This is crazy."

He moved the phone closer, and Gabe pushed it out of his face. Wilson squealed, almost jumping up and down with excitement. He looked like a kid meeting Mickey Mouse.

"Smokey said you might do that! He said you tried to wrestle with him. He's telling everyone. Dude, tell the truth, do you like to wrestle teenage boys?"

Wilson pushed the phone back into Gabe's face then turned it off. He was feeling calmer, now that the camera was off.

"That was perfect. Wow, that was like exactly what I wanted to happen. Smokey said you'd get all mad and say weird shit like in that clip. This is awesome, the dudes are going to flip!"

Gabe felt sick. They were talking about him. High school kids in Albuquerque were watching his video, talking about his weed, building him into an urban legend. Gabe was some type of game or a test of strength and nerve. Who can meet up with the crazy Mexican from the internet? The next kid would bring along his girlfriend, and the kid after that would take a swing at him, just to say he was the one that knocked the cowboy into the dirt.

Gabe took a few steps back. "Two hundred an ounce, just like your friend."

"Fine, fine, I can totally do that." Wilson pulled out his wallet and started counting out the cash. The kid frowned and gave a long, theatrical grunt. "Ah, I got three eighty. I stopped and got some food after I hit the ATM. That's cool though, right, for two ounces? What's twenty bucks? I'll be back in a few weeks. You're too badass for me not to come back."

Gabe just wanted the kid to shut up and leave. That was worth the missing twenty. He held out his hand. Wilson slapped the cash into his palm.

"Get out of here. Don't try to come back here." Gabe reached into his vest and pulled out two baggies. "I'm not selling anymore. Tell your friends, tell whoever, I'm done."

The kid bobbed his head up and down, trying to look casual. "Man, I hope not, you're hilarious, and your shit is for real."

Twice was two times too many. Gabe headed to his bike. These kids were idiots and they were going to get him arrested or worse. Wilson had gone quiet, and when Gabe looked over his shoulder, he saw the kid had his phone back out, and was filming him. Gabe told himself not to peel out, not to flip the kid off and not to buzz by him so close the kid would fall back into the dirt. Of course, he did all three.

# TWENTY-FOUR

CHARLES WANTED TO STASH all the empty wine bottles before Lou and Jordan came over. There was no recycling bin, so he lined them up along a side wall in the courtyard.

Inviting them over had been a mistake. There had been no sign of Olivia since the night of the art opening, but what if there was a stray earring or a few long black hairs? Some tell-tale sign that Jordan would recognize? The nightmare scenarios were endless.

Lou and Jordan arrived right on time, which meant they could leave just as fast.

"Come in," Charles said. "I'm getting the food started. There's wine."

Jordan's eyes flicked around the house, seeming to catalog the furnishings and the décor.

Lou whistled. "Damn, boy. This is crazy."

Charles laughed. "I know. It's too much. Nearly all the floors are either heated or cooled, whichever you want. Even the toilet seat has a little heater."

Lou snorted, but Jordan's smile looked like something that had escaped from one of Olivia's paintings. As Charles showed Lou the speakers hidden in the walls and ceiling, Jordan went to the sliding glass door that looked down on the city. Olivia should ask *her* about the tile, Charles thought.

Everyone settled around the kitchen island. Charles leaned onto the marble countertop while Jordan and Lou sat on high bar stools. Lou took Charles up on a beer, but Jordan declined a glass of wine.

"Hey," he said, "we've got to get through this somehow, right?"

Acknowledging the tension caused Lou and Jordan to freeze up and then smile. "Yeah," Jordan said. "Sorry, I'm fine. This is just quite a house."

Charles insisted on serving her a glass of wine.

"It's not normally like this. On the road, I've shared sofa beds, slept on recliners in screened-in patios, all sorts of terrible places. So, I'm enjoying this spot as long as I've got it."

Everyone went quiet. The ticking of the oven timer seemed very loud.

"So, Charles," Lou said, "is it always 'Charles?' Not 'Charlie' or something?"

"I had an ex that called me Chuckster when she was mad at me."

"Right. Well, Lou isn't even my actual name. It's Guadalupe. Very Hispanic, you know, so 'Lou' is easier."

Jordan finally sipped her wine. "This is good. Thank you."

Charles nodded and looked at the oven timer, again. The three of them kept glancing at each other, and Lou and Charles were drinking a little too fast.

"So, do you like all this traveling?" Lou asked. "Going on campaigns and stuff?"

"It doesn't feel like 'traveling.' Not really, not in a tourist way. It's hard to see much more than office buildings." Charles smiled. "But I do like the road. Higher stakes, more alive than staying in one place. You know this, Lou. Desk job versus beat, right?"

"Being law enforcement is not the same as campaign work," Jordan said.

"Okay," Charles conceded. "Of course not, but campaign life is more fun than normal life."

"I don't know," Lou said. "I had my fun on the beat and now I like scrubbing Mr. Branch's balls. The work is less bloody and the pay is better."

The kitchen started to smell like food. Another drink. Dinner. One more drink. Then, he could show them the door. Charles finished his wine and topped off Jordan's without asking. Lou helped himself to another beer.

"And you?" Charles asked Jordan. "You going to hit the road? Get out of New Mexico and work some real campaigns?"

"I've done *real* campaigns. Maybe I'll work a presidential in a couple years. Diana can help me with that."

"How many times have you worked with her?"

"Several. She ran Governor Baca's campaigns, you know? I did research. Then she advised Congressman Solís on his races, so I went over there. That's where we got close. I also spent a month with her at the Roundhouse, but government work isn't for me."

"Exactly," Charles said. "Campaigns are more alive. You get what I'm saying?"

"I guess." Jordan smiled. "I don't know how she did it. Between running that campaign and being the governor's chief of staff? Just one of those jobs would wreck me."

Charles crossed his arms and leaned back against the counter. "Wait. She didn't do both jobs at the same time, right? You can't work an election and a government gig."

"There was a strict firewall in terms of resources. Different offices, cell phones. And she excused herself from a few of the hot-button legislative issues. I checked the rules myself. It was fine."

"I keep telling her to go to law school," Lou said. "Spends half her time digging through papers and archives already."

"No wonder Salazar keeps you around." Charles raised his glass to Jordan and laughed. "Hate to think what you found out about me."

"Oh, researching you was easy."

Lou raised his eyebrows, and Charles turned a little too fast to the oven. He opened the door and poked at the food with a wooden spoon.

"I was wondering about one thing," Jordan said. "Mayor Hunt had no real opposition in the senate race, so why would he do something so stupid? He didn't need that union's support to win. The corruption was pointless."

"I don't think he was corrupt."

"He went to prison."

"Wait, wait, wait," Lou interrupted. "Start over. One of you give me the story. Was it a hooker? Dick pics?"

"I wish," Charles said. "You can come back from that. No, Hunt had been mayor of Dover for ages, centuries. Everyone came to him for decisions up and down the line. Senator wants to push a wind farm, talk to Hunt. Alderman wants to redevelop a stretch of urban blight, talk to Hunt. He was King of Delaware because Dover is where all the money and the people who matter are. Finally, a senator retires and everyone knows Hunt is next in line if he wants the seat. Well, he wants it. Money pours in. Corporations, interest groups, they're all setting up PACs, 501c3s, c4s, the whole bit. One time, the owner of a furniture shop showed up with a trailer full of oak desks and bookshelves for the campaign office. Just wanted to give it to us. I had to go out there and say no. That hurt."

Lou jumped in. "You always bet a sure thing."

"Exactly. When you know with absolute certainty that a candidate will be a United States senator, you don't want to be the guy who gave him ten thousand dollars. You want to be the guy who gave him fifty thousand."

"Then he went too far," Jordan said.

"I'm getting there. About six months before Election Day, the sanitation workers' union came to him. There'd been an out-of-state company applying for permits to pick up garbage in Dover using private trucks and non-union workers. So, the union wanted Hunt to do something about it. They said they'd endorse, spend a boatload of cash and deliver the votes of every garbage worker in the state. In Delaware, this is huge."

"He got caught," Lou said.

Charles cocked his head to the side and raised his hands. "Well, the permits were denied and the non-union company got sent back to Kentucky, or to the mob, who knows? Then news of the meeting comes out. The opponent, some nobody with zero experience, jumped on it. We didn't respond fast enough, or in the right way, so when the press started running the story, we were behind the eight ball."

"It was the response that did you in," Jordan said.

"I still think it was the right response. I said, in a very televised press conference, that it didn't matter, that it was simple government work, simple politics. And it was."

"You did something for the money."

"The press made you believe that narrative. See, that private company would have been denied these permits no matter what. The union would have endorsed us no matter what. But Hunt and the union guys huddled. *That* was wrong. They were stupid for shaking on something that should have been understood."

"Were you in that meeting?" Jordan asked.

"As a campaign staffer I wasn't allowed to attend government meetings. Firewall, like you said."

Jordan obviously knew Charles was lying. Of course, he had been in that meeting. He had been in the corner, on his phone, flirting with one of the communication interns and not paying attention. That was the worst part. He never even saw the moment his life went to hell.

"So why meet?" Lou asked. "Why shoot yourself?"

"Because they were crooks," Jordan said.

"Everyone's a hair away from corruption at all times. There's a way of doing politics, of governing—same thing—that happens everywhere. Everyone thinks their race, their candidate, their policy initiative is more important than anything else. You fall in love. How could you not? You spend seventy, eighty hours a week working with the same people for the same candidate, and you lose focus."

"Your perspective changes," Lou said.

Charles nodded. Lou seemed to understand better than Jordan.

"I couldn't imagine getting like that," Jordan said.

"Yeah? Like being chief of staff and running a political campaign at the same time? But that's okay because she had two cell phones."

The oven timer went off. Lou took a deep breath. Charles gave everyone more booze and pulled the food out. Enchiladas and mashed potatoes: a combination that seemed obviously wrong, now that it was all oozing towards each other on the middle of the plate.

Charles found a radio station that played a mix of country and horn-heavy Spanish songs. The music cleared the air a bit, but everyone ate in silence, until Lou took one for the team.

"So," he said between bites, "what do you think the Apaches really want?"

"Money," Charles said. "Like everyone, right?"

"You sound like Mr. Branch."

"Parts of their story might be true," Jordan said. "Tribes were erased from history."

"Even if their story is completely true, and even if Geronimo actually asked these guys to bury him on site, they'll still want money. They'll still want a casino off the highway."

"Baiting the press with the story about Geronimo was so smart," Jordan said.

"You've got to be careful. You're going to start admiring some less than savory behavior."

Jordan set her fork down next to her plate. "Look, I'm not some kid."

Lou placed his hand on her lower back.

"No," she said, shaking off his hand. "It's true. Being from DC doesn't make him smarter than everyone else. I know Mr. Branch is a greedy slime ball. And I know that Diana would kneecap any-one in her way, probably me included, but we don't need to cele-brate it and we can help San Miguel build some fucking schools."

Charles looked down at his plate. "And the mashed potatoes were cold."

Lou laughed and immediately raised a hand over his mouth, but it was too late.

Jordan looked at him and rolled her eyes. "They were really gross mashed potatoes."

Charles laughed. "I saw a friend the other day and didn't rec-ognize him. People change on the road and don't even realize it, so thank you for being honest. My marriage is falling apart and my career is probably over, and that's why I'm going to open another bottle of wine."

"Now that's a toast," Lou said.

Jordan finally relaxed. Charles was glad Jordan had called him out. It was probably long overdue.

Then, someone knocked on the front door. Two long knocks and two short ones, which somehow sounded very intimate. Charles' guts turned to lead.

"Maybe it's for me," Lou joked. "Probably Mallon coming to drag my ass somewhere."

Charles walked to the door, then turned around and yelled back to Jordan and Lou, "It's probably a mistake. I hardly know anyone out here."

He waited another second with his hand on the doorknob, willing her not to be there.

But, there she was. Olivia Branch held a bottle of wine and cracked a smile that snapped into something formal and inquisitive, but not fast enough.

Charles told himself he would make this work. He could spin anything.

"Come in, come in. Glad you got my invite. Sorry your husband couldn't make it."

"Yes. Yes, of course," Olivia said. "We really wanted to check in, make sure you were finding everything satisfactory."

Lou's head was down, as if he was the one who should be embarrassed, and Jordan's mouth was gaping. Olivia walked into the kitchen with Charles a step behind.

"Sorry I'm late," Olivia smiled.

Her presence altered everything in the room; the colors intensified, the temperature rose, the weight of the air increased, and if Charles had been offered a cyanide pill just then, he might have taken it.

"Everyone knows each other?" Charles asked.

"Sorry you missed dinner," Jordan said. "It was very good. But we're about to head out. We . . . we . . . "

"I've got an early day," Lou said.

Jordan kept staring, but Lou just looked at the ground. As they walked out of the house, Jordan nodded at Charles while Lou shook his hand and smirked.

After shutting the door, Charles kept his hand on the knob and rested his forehead against the cold glass panel. Maybe if he were quiet enough, he would wake up on Capitol Hill with a wife and a ghost of a career. Then he heard Olivia pouring what sounded like a big glass of wine.

"Well," she said, "think they bought it?"

He turned around and leaned against the door. "This isn't funny."

"No, I suppose not." She sat down where Jordan had been and pushed the plate away. "What is this stuff?"

"You saw their cars out there."

"It's a cul-de-sac; they didn't park in front of the house. How was I supposed to know you'd make friends?" Olivia leaned her forearms on the island, she already seemed tired of the crisis. "Lou won't say anything. It's their job to keep secrets."

"Jordan wants my job."

"Fine, fine, this is a disaster." Olivia jumped up to sit on the marble countertop of the island and let her legs dangle. "You may need to kill her."

Charles positioned himself out of arm's reach. "Jordan will say something to Salazar. Lou spends a lot of time with Mallon."

"He spends enough time with Mallon to not want to have to deal with it." Olivia's smile reached out and pulled him closer. "And what can you do about it now?"

Charles' phone vibrated on the kitchen counter. He knew it was Addie. Olivia glanced towards the phone.

"You can get it," she said. "You probably should."

"No, I should not. She's going to be here next week."

"Good, show her the sights. Wait, was I supposed to get jealous? You're not leaving her. Or if you are, you're not doing it for me."

"You're leaving your husband."

"I'm not starting a trend. I'm leaving because there're things I need to do and I'm sick of his paranoia."

"Why is it so bad? Is he . . . dangerous?"

Olivia smiled. "You're oh so concerned. No, he's not dangerous. Not yet. He was great when I met him. You don't believe that, but it's true. Exciting, full of life. Having all his dreams come true seems to have broken something in him."

Charles turned his back to her and kept his hands busy with dishes and forks. "I could use this job to make some money, maybe get a new gig related to the airport. My friend Thompson indicated I could do pretty well. Maybe I stay."

"No."

Charles turned around. "No? You bring me out here, then you tell me to go home?"

"Look, I'm glad you're in Santa Fe. We can both benefit from you working for my husband, but pocket what you can and go back to your wife. Maybe do some things for me along the way."

"No one in Washington wants me."

Olivia jumped down from the island and slipped back into her shoes. "I bet your wife does. I shouldn't have come back over here again."

"Wait, wait, wait!"

Charles put out his hands to stop her, but she slapped them away.

"Do not do that."

He took a step back. "I'm saying I may be here longer than I initially thought, that's all. Your husband is doing some big things that could result in some real money, and I cannot afford to walk away. I'm not saying we're going to get remarried."

"Remarried? Are you crazy?"

Olivia grabbed her wine glass and walked into the living room. Charles wanted to trail after her like a puppy but restrained himself.

"You're too excited," she said. "There's something else going on. Neither of you could possibly care this much about an airport."

Charles met her eyes, then turned around and grabbed some more plates.

Her eyebrows went up and her voice rose with excitement. "Wait, wait . . . you found something. Look at you, little researcher. What'd you learn?"

Charles held his breath for a second, excited to share his secret, wanting her to be impressed, like it was the diamond ring he never bought her back in Chicago. "He's going to build most of the airport, then help fund a casino he'll run with San Miguel. Or the Apaches or whichever tribe shows up next."

Olivia's surprise looked genuine.

"Now that's devious," she said. "He's using the state and county money to get a head start on the project."

"People will fly in, gamble, fly out. Maybe never even leave that stretch of highway."

"The only way for a non-Native person to get some gaming money is to pay for something else. Do you have proof? A document or anything?"

Charles shook his head. "He told me, but I doubt there's anything in writing. He and Salazar are way too clever for that."

"There's got to be something."

The greedy look in her eyes made Charles nervous. "Olivia, if you want to leave him, then leave him. Find a lawyer. Hell, I met one the other day. Your husband hates him."

"You know he won't let me leave with a dime unless I have something that makes him nervous."

Charles put a hand over his mouth. "You got me this job so I could help you blackmail your husband."

"No, do not say that. I'm looking for a way out, and you can help me. There's nothing wrong with leaving on my own terms."

"You mean with money."

Charles put a hand on his forehead, then slid it to the side of his face. He wanted to slap some sanity back into himself.

She walked up behind him and whispered. "I will leave with dignity, with a life. I can use his cash for something good."

"You want it all." It came out more bitter than he had intended. "You want the money and the freedom. Branch's money conveniently without being attached to Branch."

She stepped closer. "I'm not being unreasonable. People are depending on me." She put her hands on his waist. "And you need to protect yourself."

Charles stepped away from her. He dumped plates into the sink, liking the clattering noise and hoping something would break.

"I'm fine," he said. "I'm on the inside. I can sell you out to your husband and he'll give me a raise."

"He will have Mallon skin you alive, and you know it. You're not out here because of your resume. If their casino falls apart my husband is not going to end up like Mayor Hunt. Diana Salazar will hold a press conference and say, 'We should have known better. We trusted this man. He fooled us like he fooled everyone in Delaware.'" Olivia caught her breath. She glowed with fury. "You can leave tonight, or you can stay and help both of us, but you need protection just as much as I do."

Charles wanted to argue. He wanted to say she was paranoid, that he deserved this job and he deserved Branch's trust. But then she was in front of him and he could smell her skin and his hands were on her hips and her mouth was coming closer to his.

# TWENTY-FIVE

CLAUDIA SLIPPED into Mallon's house sometime after four AM. It was later than usual, but not the latest it had ever been.

She crawled over his chest and curled up against him.

"Stop pretending," she whispered. "I know you're awake."

"You put your knee into my stomach."

"Are you tired?" She propped herself up on her elbows. "Because I'm not. Do you have the laptop? Let's see what we can see."

"What did you take? Why do you have so much energy?"

"I'm fine, don't worry. You know . . . it was one of those nights. Show me the cameras."

A few weeks ago, Mallon showed her the compound's video feeds. His laptop gave him access to everything: the cameras, the GPS, the dash cams, all of it.

He slipped out of bed and grabbed his computer bag. They spent forty-five minutes ticking around the compound. They saw raccoons, night birds, the trees swayed in the breeze and everything was cast in an eerie green glow. Something about the color mesmerized Claudia. She said it was soothing. Mallon knew it was inappropriate, but he enjoyed patrolling the perimeter and making sure all was well.

"I should set some of these up here, out back. Keep an eye on things."

"Nah, it's better to look at places that are far away. Too close would be too weird."

"Well, look at this. It's new." He opened the control panel for the vehicles and turned on the dash cam in his own car. Claudia sat up.

"See, this is weird." She put her finger over the bedroom window. "There we are."

"There we are," he repeated.

"All these rich people are going to get you in trouble one day. You could join the local police, you know. It'd be boring, I guess, but you wouldn't have to do all this."

"Being a trooper was nothing but handing out band-aids. Get one drunk off the road? He's out there the next night. If not him, then someone else."

"You must have done some good." She sounded like she was telling it to herself.

"A few drug busts. Some people who deserved to have their skulls knocked around. That's it."

"What? No evil mastermind with a dungeon full of innocent beauties?"

"That's not funny."

Mallon switched the camera view. Now, they were looking out of a dash cam at the compound. They could see the nose of another car parked directly in front of it.

"I pulled over a cargo van one night. No reason. I didn't like the look of it . . . that was the reason. Blacked out windows, dirty tires. Just as well I didn't find anything because it wasn't a legit stop. Driver was a little guy, ratty mustache, kind of looks like this loser we just hired."

Claudia pulled her knees against her chest. "What was in the van?"

"There were little rings embedded in the ceiling and walls, but that was it. Nothing else. Not a pebble. Not a speck of dirt, and that was the problem."

"*Your* place doesn't have a speck of dirt!"

"That was different. Guy got squirmy and started to sweat once I pulled him over. I drag him to the station, talking big about forensics and fluorescein. But no one had that kind of tech in the mountains. No one wanted to do anything, and the desk sergeant knew it wasn't a good stop. So this guy gets released. But I can't stop talking about him. I wanted surveillance, I wanted to go out to his house. I wanted us to do something. Two weeks later, I'm farmed out to the governor's security. That's how I met Branch and started working for him."

"Because of the little guy?"

"I think so."

"He was probably the son of a big shot. Or some witness protection guy stashed out in the woods."

Mallon shook his head. "No, I pushed too hard and people got sick of me talking about it, so they shipped me out. But, that van, something wasn't right."

"I bet he's still out there."

Mallon shook his head.

"How do you know? Creepy guys come into the club all the time. I see guys who . . . "

"No. I ran the plate, and the address came back as a little trailer outside Cerrillos, up in the mountains. Single wide, a few sheds out back, a dog tied to a post, neighbors were miles away."

The story was gathering its own momentum and was pulling out of his control. This man who was once tied up in a neat bow in the back of Mallon's mind, out of sight. Now, here he was again.

"You went out there?"

"I needed to. There was something. I *still* think there was something." Mallon ticked through the dash cams without looking at any of them. "Guy pissed his pants when he saw me. Tried to hide behind his recliner."

"So would I."

"No you wouldn't, you're innocent."

Claudia lay back down. "Sure."

"I couldn't find anything. Not a single earring or a fingernail. Not even any dust on picture frames. I still go through the trailer in my head, imagining this or that hiding place. I can see it all, the whole trailer, but there's nothing. Nothing out in the sheds, or under the trailer or in his old barn, so I must have missed it."

"Or not. Maybe he was just a weirdo who got the piss scared out of him. You're lucky he didn't sue."

Mallon's eyes refocused on the screen. Something was wrong. "He couldn't do that."

"Why not?"

He pulled up the cameras again. Something was out of place, but what? He looked at the GPS map. All the cars were accounted for. Mr. Branch, Mrs. Branch, the SUV, the van, were all at the compound. Then, he went through the dash cams again. One of the cars at the compound had a good view of the house and the driveway. The GPS map showed four vehicles parked outside of the residence. But Mallon was looking through one car's camera, and he only saw two other vehicles.

Mrs. Branch's car was missing, but her car's tracker said she was at home.

He turned on her dash camera. It was a black screen. He restarted the system. Nothing. He tried to pan and focus the camera. Nothing, as if she had put something over the camera lens. Finally, he remote-started her car and was able to activate the back-up camera. She was not at the compound. The camera showed a view of a house and some dense trees. It looked like it could have been one of those neighborhoods just outside of downtown.

When Mallon sat up, Claudia's hand slipped off his arm, but he barely noticed. He remembered the little guy in that trailer and his chance to do something good. He had promised himself not to make that mistake again.

He had never trusted this prick from DC, and now he knew why.

She was parked at his house.

# SUNDAY

# TWENTY-SIX

Olivia ignored the sadness pulling at her skin. She kept her eyes shut and felt Charles' body behind her. Their arms and legs were tangled and knotted without them actually holding each other. She knew they were holding everything they had lost in the past ten years.

Olivia tried to relax but it was no use. She could not stand the thought of opening her eyes and seeing her ex-husband, older and sadder and in over his head.

A phone started to ring. Charles pulled back, as if his wife had kicked down the door. Olivia rolled onto her back and looked out the bedroom's plate glass window. It took up nearly the whole wall and showed the view up the mountain: nothing but dense trees. Andrea told her they had seen deer outside the windows. She and the kids had piled onto the bed and watched the animals peck through the blankets of pine needles. Andrea was never happy here. No matter how many times Olivia pointed out the heated floors or the recessed speakers, or any of the pathetic little flourishes Olivia loved.

Charles moved back towards her, trying to put his arms around her waist, but Olivia slipped out of bed and grabbed a thick cotton robe out of the closet.

Charles attempted a sexy voice. "Well, that was amazing. Was I always that good?"

Olivia smiled. "You're awful. Some things never change."

Charles rolled his eyes. "Please. I'm faking it all. Every day I'm not working at my mother's bank is a day above ground."

"Hey, a job's a job." Olivia sat down in a leather armchair near the window.

"Oh, you're one to talk about jobs," Charles said. "What was the last one you had?"

She pulled the robe around her. "I work hard. I'm not bartending or anything, but I work hard."

"You look comfortable in that robe. Almost like you picked it out."

"What's the point of decorating a sex den if you can't have the things you like?"

Charles smiled, and his face went soft. "Come back over here."

"Stop it. You're trying too hard. We're almost forty. Let's not pretend to be something we're not."

He rocked his head back as if she had slapped him. "Wow, you're not as good at pillow talk as you used to be."

"You don't actually like me. You know that, right?"

"I liked you more about five minutes ago. We had a good time. A great time."

"You're trying to fall for me again. Don't. Let's have fun, let's help each other out and let's not go crazy."

Charles hopped out of bed and fished around for some clothes. "Too late."

He found a shirt but nothing else. "I'm not a fool. Our lives are terrible, and it was nice to forget all that for a night. I get it. But something that won't suck is the bottle of champagne I'm about to get out of your kitchen."

"You look ridiculous in just a T-shirt," Olivia hollered after him.

She pulled her hair back and looped it into a loose knot. Olivia had planned on sleeping with him from the start. It would pull him closer and carve out a blind spot for her to slip into. Charles was a romantic. He always pictured himself the star of a great narrative: scrappy underdog, crusader for justice, victim of circumstance and conspiracy, the great lover. He came back into the bedroom with a bottle of champagne and two glasses.

Charles climbed back in bed. "Neither of us should be here. How do we keep your husband from finding out?"

"That's up to me. Don't worry about that. You just be normal."

"Things haven't been normal for me since I got here. I can't tell if I'm positioning myself for a million-dollar raise or ten years in prison."

Olivia climbed back into bed, but turned her back to him and burrowed into his chest.

"I should have guessed casino," she said. "He's been obsessed with them for years."

"Well, he is *also* building the airport. The poker room might be bigger than the runway, but he'll build what he promised."

"I need your help. We have to talk about this."

"Is it too early in the morning for champagne?" Charles sat up and poured another glass.

"I'm not asking too much of you. Stay in New Mexico, if you want. Try to get rich, but get me something too."

"Are we really that scared of being poor?" he asked.

"I can remember being poor," she said. "I'm not going back there. And I have other obligations, other people to help."

"Is this when you tell me I have a lost child I never knew about?"

Olivia laughed and smacked the back of his head. "No, trust me, that's not it. I'm helping people. I'm going to buy a house for me and someone who's going through cancer. She's depending on me. I'm not going to only invest in bonbons and champagne."

"Who is this family?"

Olivia sat up. "It's my sister, diagnosed with lung cancer six months ago. She's got two kids, seven and eight years old. I've given them as much as I can, but it's not enough. I don't want to talk about them."

"Branch won't help?"

"He doesn't give money to charity unless the press is there. That's an actual quote. I've been looking for a way out ever since."

"That's when I fell into your lap."

"Oh, get over yourself." She got up and threw the robe on the bed. "You've got an opportunity out here, but it's not the one you think. My husband will burn you. Get off the bed."

Charles did not move, so she started tugging the sheets and pillows out from under him.

He stood up and grinned, convinced this was transitioning into some new game.

"You've spent your life not thinking about anything or anyone else," she said. "Now's the time to change that."

Olivia grabbed her purse and pulled out running clothes and a large black trash bag. She changed and then stuffed her dress from last night, the sheets, pillowcases, robe and her wine glass into the bag. "What are you doing?" Charles asked.

"Leaving," she said, as she hooked her purse over one shoulder and flung the trash bag over the other.

"Are you coming back? And why are you taking the sheets?"

Olivia moved towards the bedroom door but stopped. She came back to Charles and kissed him hard. "I want to come back. Make it worthwhile."

She walked out of the house and threw the bag of evidence into her back seat. She would find a dumpster on the way home.

# TWENTY-SEVEN

GABE WAS GOING to tell Rose the truth. He stood outside her front door with a bag of breakfast burritos and coffee. He had yet to decide if he would tell her before they ate or after. Wait, he thought and stopped himself from knocking, is having cancer the kind of thing you tell someone over breakfast?

Then Rose opened the door and waved him in. "Hey," she said. "Good timing. I think I found the site we should use."

She turned back towards the living room. A computer sat on an old hutch in the corner. Gabe set the food and coffee next to the screen and dragged a chair over from the dining room. She had called him the night before, convinced there was a way for him to make some cash from this airport video.

Narrow, red reading glasses hung from a loop around her neck. She squinted at the screen. Gabe tried putting them on her, but she made a *pffft* sound and waved his hands away.

"Such a weirdo sometimes, Gabe." She put on the glasses herself. "So, this site will give you 50% of the sale price of each mug or T-shirt and 75% of smaller stuff, like key chains and buttons. It's the best deal I've been able to find."

Gabe leaned forward as if being closer would help him understand better. "I don't really do this web stuff. They're going to sell what I make?"

"Not quite. I start an account. Then we upload a design, probably just a phrase from the video, because I don't know how to draw or anything. Then, people buy it."

"Why?"

Rose looked at the screen, then back at Gabe. "What do you mean 'why'? Because people buy dumb shit," Rose said. "That one video I showed you has half a million views, and there are other versions. If a hundred of those people buy a mug that says 'This shit ain't funny no more,' then you get some serious cash."

"No way!"

Rose nodded and started unwrapping her burrito. Gabe could smell the eggs and potatoes, but it made him nauseous. He couldn't even remember his last full meal.

"Aren't they making fun of me?"

Rose bobbed her head. "Well . . . let's say they're having fun with you. And don't read every comment below the video. Some of those people are crazy and racist, but . . . "

"Racist?"

Rose smiled at him like he was a dog doing something cute. She cupped his face with both hands, a maternal gesture that Gabe would have swatted away from anyone else. "What matters is that people are watching this and you should be able to get something from it. So, what do you want the T-shirt to say?"

He decided to trust her.

"How about, 'This shit ain't funny no more'?"

"Let's do two. We don't want kids getting busted at school if they wear your shirt. How about 'Not much you can do'?"

Gabe shrugged and reached for a burrito. "Whatever you think."

Rose straightened her glasses. "This will work."

"Don't get ripped off," Gabe said between bites. "Everyone online is trying to rip you off. I know that much."

Rose nodded as she squinted at the screen. She was already designing a T-shirt and matching coffee mug. "Send the first one to Micah. I'll write down the address."

"You know, I think we might be the ones doing the ripping off," Rose said. "If you make a single dollar off this, it'll be the easiest dollar you ever made."

"I doubt that."

Rose rolled her eyes. "My sister pays her rent from old cowboy stuff she finds in barns. It's our turn."

"*Our* turn? You think I'm giving you a cut, huh?"

"Damn right, you're giving me a cut," Rose said. "I'm breaking a sweat here. You'll pay me, somehow."

A steady stream of bass from the back of the house was the only sign of Johnny's existence. Gabe put the burrito down. He reached for the coffee but pulled back because his hand was shaking. This was the moment. Gabe tried to bite it back but then it was out, lying between them like a dead dog.

"I'm sick," he said. "Bad."

Rose kept clicking on the screen. She turned to Gabe. "You have to put in your address."

Gabe gave her a blank stare. She pointed at the screen and back to him. He started to peck out his address on her keyboard. Rose put her palm on his forehead, and Gabe wanted to melt down until he was so small she could cradle him in her palm.

"You feel fine. Trying to get the afternoon off?"

Gabe sat back, and Rose's face tightened as she really looked at him.

"My old man. It's him. Bone cancer tore him up. Fast. It was bad. Not that I was there at the end, which is the problem. Lou . . . " Gabe placed his fingertips on his chest as if he could pull the words out through his skin. "When I was with Jefe I saw something, and he told me it's because I'm sick."

Rose hooked her hand around the back of his neck. "Take a deep breath. Don't worry about your father or anything right now."

"That's why I'm doing all this." Gabe pointed at the computer, accidentally knocking her hand away. "Micah needs money to go on this trip, and I need to come clean to him. It's cancer."

Gabe stopped breathing. His breath tried to crawl out of his chest but got stuck behind his breastbone. Rose looked worried. She looked scared. Why did he do this to her? To him? Why start spending time with her as he was about to waste away?

Better not to have told anyone. Gabe got to his feet.

Rose reached up and hit him, more of a push than a strike, but it knocked Gabe back a foot.

"Why now?" she asked. "You cannot be playing these games anymore. You cannot be lying, to *me*, right now."

"Rose, I'm not lying."

"Of course, you're lying. Did you go to a doctor? Did you get blood tests and x-rays?"

"My buddy Jefe . . . "

"That guy is a conman and a drug dealer." She stood up and grabbed a slip of paper off a shelf near the front door. "You think you needed to lie to get me to help you? You think I didn't want to take you and Micah out to dinner this weekend? I was going to help you without you trying to trick me into feeling something."

She pressed the paper into his hand. It was a check for four hundred dollars.

"Let's skip it," she said. "Let's skip to the end, where I say I thought you had changed and that you were about to let yourself be happy. You're a grown man, you're an old man."

Rose shook her head. She leaned towards the computer and started closing windows.

"It's not a story."

Rose walked to the door and opened it. She stood with one hand on the doorknob, ready to slam it shut after him.

# MONDAY

# TWENTY-EIGHT

CHARLES GOT TO WORK EARLY. If Jordan was going to march over to Salazar with gossip about Olivia, then she would walk past his smiling mug. He had spent the morning practicing his denials, looking for ways to spin this back onto Jordan.

And then, nothing. Salazar slipped straight into her office. Jordan said "Good morning" and handed over a white card with "Thank You" embossed in silver letters. Both she and Lou signed the card, but it was otherwise blank.

The quiet was worse than a fight.

Even the cubicles seemed subdued. Charles poured a cup of coffee and walked into the bullpen. There was a heaviness in the air. People typed away, phones quietly trilled, yet something was different.

Then, Charles noticed two or three empty cubicles that had been occupied on Friday. There wasn't even a phone in some of those stations.

Salazar left her office. Charles sipped his coffee because his mouth had gone dry. She pointed over his shoulder. "Let's go into your office."

He turned and followed, bracing for the worst.

"The San Miguel Tribal Council is meeting today," she said. "We're going down there to address the council, keep everyone on board. A few members are getting worked up."

Charles took a seat in front of his desk. "We've got to smooth some ruffled feathers." She arched an eyebrow.

"No, I didn't mean feathers like that . . . like Native. . . . I meant the saying, you know?"

186

Salazar nodded and handed over a document. "Our statement. I'll read it, but you'll be there to help clarify and answer questions."

He scanned it and said, "This sounds good. I've wanted to get more involved. I feel like I'm part of this, like I can help."

"Most of San Miguel's anxiety stems from two possible outcomes. One, we're going to abandon the project and demand our money back. Or, we're going to turn everything over to the Apaches—the idea *you* floated the other day." She tapped the document in his hand. "There may be some concession offered to the Apaches, but we need to assure San Miguel we're still with them."

"How many people on the council are aware of the larger gaming plan."

"That's not something we're talking about today. Not in this public forum. In fact, you will never bring it up again. Cody made you feel special when he told you, but you better be focused on what's in front of you."

Charles nodded. Every part of him wanted to clarify what he meant, to talk his way into Salazar trusting him, but he knew it would be better if he held his tongue.

She continued, "We include our standard 'respect all tribal lands and privileges' line in the statement. They know that's a nod towards gaming."

Salazar looked at her watch and then over her shoulder. Mallon walked into the building.

"You think you can handle this?" she asked.

"Of course."

"Good. Me too. In fact, I think you can handle this on your own. Mallon will drive you. I've got to reach out to the Apaches' lawyer."

"Wait, I've never been to this council meeting."

"You'll be fine. It's a meeting. They're all the same. Stick to what's on the sheet, read it, memorize it, speak it. Answer questions with generalities and references back to the statement. You're going to be late if you don't get moving."

Mallon stood in the doorway. Charles grabbed his blazer and the talking points, but it felt like someone else was controlling his feet.

ৎᔢ ৎᔢ ৎᔢ

In the car, Charles tried to study the statement, but Mallon was too intimidating. The man even breathed angrily. He kept looking over at Charles, almost daring him to say something. His knuckles were white around the wheel and he was passing cars going ninety. For ten, then fifteen minutes, neither of them spoke.

Charles broke the silence. "What is wrong? Why do you keep staring at me like that?"

"I'm wondering how a rat like you could . . . "

Charles' phone rang. He had not been this happy to get a call from Addie in months.

"Hey," Charles said. "I'm heading down to the reservation. How are you?"

"Fine, but I have news about Jim Hawley. This hasn't hit the papers, but a friend in State called me. He . . . oh, baby, he's dead."

"What do you mean?"

"They don't know what happened for sure. But his body is being delivered to the embassy now. Everyone's expecting the Syrians to claim suicide, but the ambassador's not going to let this go. It all just happened in the past few days."

Charles turned away from Mallon and towards the window. The hills looked less like mountains and more like a loose pile of rocks.

"Maybe it's a ruse," he said. "You know, the CIA or something."

"No, honey, it's not. He . . . "

Addie's voice glitched then phased out. Charles looked at his phone.

"Through here you won't get a signal," Mallon said. "In about ten minutes, maybe."

Charles looked out at the miles of scrub. He exhaled loud, as if he could blow away the entire desert.

"That was bad news," Charles said. "A friend was killed in Syria."

Mallon shot him a quick look. "Military?"

"No, teaching political parties how to organize."

"So he was CIA."

"What? No, no, lots of political people take jobs overseas. We know how to talk to voters, and lots of countries don't."

Mallon furrowed his brow. He looked like someone told him that animals sometimes speak English behind people's backs.

"Like Doctors without Borders, but for political hacks," Mallon said.

"Is that a joke?"

"I don't know," Mallon said. "Maybe."

Charles burst out a guffaw and then held it back. "Yeah, I suppose it's like Hacks without Borders."

Mallon seemed to release some of his anger, but he kept moving his mouth as if literally chewing his words before spitting them out.

"You actually help others, or are you just American tourists partying?"

"I haven't done it," Charles said. "I'd like to. Hell, if my wife leaves me, why not? This guy, Jim Hawley, he was a prick with a temper, but even the worst of us still want to help people. Or, we started that way, at least."

"Then what turns you into assholes?"

"What turns some cops bad?" Charles quipped.

Mallon's eyes cast sparks of rage at Chris, who quickly looked away.

"I know it's not the same," Charles said. "I've already been warned against making that comparison."

Charles watched the land go by, noticing how the clouds on the horizon seemed to hover inches above the peaks of the distant mountains, as if they wanted to come so close, but were afraid to actually touch.

"It's the ego," Charles said. "The candidates and the electeds and the donors are all rich assholes, and that rubs off on you. Everyone wants to climb higher, closer to the center of power, but everyone loses eventually, and that also messes with you. Even when you win, you're out of a job the day after the election."

"But you keep working. You keep doing what you do."

"And then you end up taking a job in Damascus because you're looking for that next jolt, an injection of energy."

"I knew you guys in the Army and on the force. Itching for a battle."

"You're not?"

"I've been through battles." Mallon pointed his finger at the road in front of him. "If your friend had walked out of that prison, he'd be done with all of you. He'd be carving out his place."

Charles laughed, bitter and ironic. "That's what I'm doing out here, I guess. After my battle."

"That was not a battle you went through. A real battle changes you. You disappear. Can't get that back, not ever, not all the way."

Charles looked straight ahead, watching the highway curve around hills. "I think I liked you better when you were just scary."

"We're almost to San Miguel," Mallon said. "I'm giving you a chance that you don't deserve. Stop what you're doing. You know what I mean. You need to either focus on this job, or you need to go back home."

Charles' mouth went dry. Mallon knew about Olivia. Somehow, he knew.

Addie called him back. Only two bars of service. He ignored the call; he would only lose the connection again.

# TWENTY-NINE

OLIVIA PARKED HER SUV behind the Spanish Governor's Mansion and walked through the plaza. Men with leaf blowers were making a lot of noise but not moving too many leaves. She looked over her shoulder at the people on the sidewalk. She resisted the urge to duck her head or hide under a shawl. It was time to tell Janice about Charles.

For months now, Olivia continued to be surprised by how well Janice still knew Cody. That woman felt him in her bones, and it was useful. She was bound to have some ideas about what Charles could do. In truth, Olivia would never say she trusted Janice, but she trusted her anger. Her rage for Cody was pure, rational and unadulterated.

Still, meeting was risky because it would look so strange to anyone who knew them. Why would the two Mrs. Branches be grabbing a cappuccino together? They chose a coffee shop in a converted house near the commuter rail station. The porch creaked and the wall near the front door showed an Aztec mural of a warrior in front of a blocky, tiered pyramid. The Aztec's skin was unpainted adobe. He was holding a knife and wore a flowing headdress of white feathers.

The coffee shop was so dark, it tended to scare away any stray tourists. Olivia loved it. Coffee beans were roasting in the basement, giving the shop a faint smell of burnt popcorn. Olivia ordered a black coffee. Janice sat at an untreated picnic table in a side room. The old, grey walls were covered with photos of Pancho Villa, Emiliano Zapata and scowling men wearing bands of bullets.

Olivia sat down, always unsure how to greet the woman help-ing her leave her husband. They were much closer than a hug and a peck on the cheek.

"Did I tell you about the tracker I found in the car?" Olivia asked.

Janice nodded. "Not surprising. Unfortunate, but not surpris-ing. He's tearing his hair out. These Apaches are not taking a quick payout and I've heard San Miguel is terrified they'll lose every-thing."

"They should be. He'll go with whichever tribe makes it the easiest for him to cash in. Everything's moving so fast."

Janice tilted her head. "You know something."

Olivia sipped her coffee. "I have a friend. An old friend."

"Oh, I see. A very good friend, I'm sure."

"Not as good as he thinks he is." Olivia smiled.

Janice's eyes glimmered. "It must be that new fellow from back east, right? Dark hair, kind of looks scared all the time."

"Accurate description."

"And this friend knows something?"

"Wait, first, I need you to do something," Olivia said.

Janice picked up a spoon and idly stirred her coffee. She would not say yes or no without first hearing the request. Maybe Cody had learned more from her than he liked to let on.

"I need you to pay a lawyer a retainer, on my behalf. Give him my name, tell him it's a divorce, secure him however you need. I can't pay for that now, but you can."

"That should be easy enough."

"I also think you know more about Cody's finances then you've let on. Send me the banks, the account numbers, anything you have."

"Dear, you must already have that information."

"He divorced you as the money was coming in. You've seen accounts I haven't."

"And you're going to rob the bank?"

"I'm looking for transactions, embarrassing information. Don't say the word you're thinking of."

Janice smiled. "The B-word? Of course not."

Olivia looked around the coffee shop, worried someone had slipped in behind her. "I don't like what I'm turning into," she said. "But I am going to live my life after Cody Branch."

"That's what I said." Janice sighed, and her mouth pouted into an expression equally maternal and condescending. "You think I'm such a bitch for still being so hung up on him."

"No, I get it. He sticks to you. And I can still see him, the man I fell for, underneath all these layers of fat and ego."

"Isn't that the worst part? Knowing how good it could be."

Olivia saw Janice's anger differently now. She was not only furious about being left behind, she was also mad at Cody for having changed. Maybe helping Olivia leave—finally, a loss for the great man—would bring some of the old Cody back.

"I don't think he has any of the same accounts," Janice said. "His bankers would have set him up with a whole new portfolio, but I do recall the man loved his safe."

"Yeah, it's in the bedroom. Not very big."

"Do you know the combination?" Janice asked.

Olivia rolled her eyes.

"Dumb question," Janice continued. "Try . . . well . . . try *my* birthday."

"*Your* birthday? For the combination?"

"That opened it years ago, and Cody is, at times, both sentimental and lazy."

Olivia nodded. She took a sip of coffee and looked around again. "It's not just an airport. The plan is to help fund a casino, and Cody will use the different leases and airport commissions and tribal groups to mask his ownership. He's going to make millions."

Janice sat back and smoothed her hair. "Of course. What else could it have been? We're idiots for not seeing that earlier. Oh, your friend must be a really good friend."

"Cody told him personally. I'm not sure why. He either trusts him a lot or he's looking for someone to blame now, when construction has barely begun, which is earlier than usual. Charles is a good guy, and I'm hoping he'll get out of this fine, but he's desperate for recognition."

"What if he doesn't get recognition? What if nothing goes like he planned?"

"He's already hit rock bottom."

Janice put her hand on Olivia's arm. "Be careful. Be *careful.* Watch out for your friend."

Olivia pulled her hand away. "Stop. Cody's not dangerous, not like that."

"But the money is, dear."

Olivia didn't like the look in Janice's eyes—too concerned, too sympathetic. Guilty. Olivia pushed back from the table. "Should I not have told you?"

Janice looked down into her coffee and then raised her head, with a new smile like a pane of glass over a painting. "We should have never started telling each other anything, I'm afraid."

"Did you do something you shouldn't have? What did you do?"

Janice opened her mouth but closed it again. Olivia stood up and backed away, unable to turn her back on Janice and her glassy smile.

# THIRTY

CHARLES HAD NEVER BEEN on a reservation before. They passed a faded sign, hand-painted on a sheet of plywood: *Now Entering San Miguel Pueblo. No pictures allowed. This is a closed Pueblo and a sacred space. If you do not have official business here or have not been invited personally,* please *turn around. Open feast day is September 29.*

"You been out here before?" Charles asked. He and Mallon had not spoken since his veiled threat.

"For Mr. Branch," Mallon said. "June 25th. Last year. We needed to persuade some tribal elders that the airport wouldn't impede their way of life."

"Did it work?"

"We're here, aren't we?"

Charles could see a line of trailers up on a ridge. Some trailers had carports and attached patios, while others sat alone in the middle of the grass, as if dropped from above. They passed houses with cars under wooden carports and sheet metal ringing small yards. Wire penned in a few goats and chickens, and wood was stacked alongside blackened adobe ovens.

"What's the difference between a pueblo and a reservation?"

"None of these people were relocated. This is their ancestral land, but with a . . . perimeter around it."

They approached the edge of town, where the roads were freshly paved. Gravel cul-de-sacs holding five or six homes branched off the main road like seed pods. There were no sidewalks anywhere in town, and electrical wires sagged off their poles. Charles expected poverty, but he was surprised by the economic range the houses displayed: two-story jobs with brick facades and pillars, squat adobes with crude additions, patched-up trailers with sagging roofs. For every three farm trucks with rusted side panels and plastic sheeting where the windows should be, there was a new SUV.

"Look, why haven't they tried to build a casino or anything sooner."

"Bigger tribes lobby to limit new gaming licenses."

"Can't the tribes all work together?"

Mallon smiled. It looked strange, like his lips were accidentally glued to his back teeth. "Working together is almost as bad as working with us."

The tribal headquarters was in a white adobe building shaped like a southwest church, complete with curving walls, a bell tower and wide doors. The doors were propped open, letting in a stream of people. This was supposed to have been a small meeting, but Charles saw families, kids, elders, even teenagers shuffling in, as if they were going to see a new movie. He folded the statement, shifted it from his jacket pocket to his shirt pocket and then back again.

The room was lined with tribal flags and framed photos of smiling men in suits. Most of the seats were taken, and there was a microphone set up in the aisle. The tribal council was already seated on the stage, and there was an empty chair next to a man with a nameplate that read "Governor."

Mallon disappeared to the back, underneath a large aerial photo of the pueblo. Charles looked around, waiting for someone to save him. The governor got to his feet and waved him forward. Charles thought he might have been at Olivia's show a few nights ago. Charles went to the side of the stage.

The governor bent over and introduced himself, "Oscar Luján." He shook Charles' hand. "Is Diana outside?"

"No, she couldn't make it."

"We had this scheduled." Luján stood up and looked over Charles' shoulder as if he might be mistaken.

"I'm here."

Luján looked down at Charles. "Who the fuck are you?"

"Charles O'Connell. I'm with the airport. Salazar and Branch," he managed to spit out.

Luján put his hands on his hips, causing his suit jacket to stretch over his belly. "I guess you'll have to do. Come on."

Charles took the seat next to the governor and nodded at the other men on stage. They gave him curt, political smiles, the kind you get when someone has to hide the look they think you deserve.

Luján tapped the microphone, silencing the crowd. "Thank you everyone for coming on short notice. As tribal governor, I'm going to go ahead and call this meeting to order. This is a special session, so we're going to forgo some of the formalities. We're here to discuss potential changes to our agreement with Branch Development, the Santa Fe Regional Airport Commission and other related entities."

Charles saw a stenographer in the front row. There was also a man holding a video camera in the aisle. Charles wanted to wipe away his sweat, but he knew that would call attention to his nerves.

"We're joined today by. . . . " Luján grimaced at Charles.

"Charles O'Connell. Director of Public Outreach and Communications for the Santa Fe . . . " His mind went blank again. "I work for Mr. Branch."

Luján looked at the crowd. "Let's welcome our guest."

To call the applause that followed a "smattering" would be an exaggeration.

"I have a statement to share before taking questions." Charles smoothed the piece of paper in front of him and then held it in both hands. It seemed so insignificant now.

"The Santa Fe Regional Airport Commission and Branch Development have enjoyed a long, mutually beneficial relationship."

A snorting laugh came from the crowd.

"Recent developments have slowed our progress, but now that the San Miguel Tribal Council, supported by historical evidence, have approved our plans resuming construction, we hope to make up lost time and open the airport on schedule. In regards to the claims of the so-called San Miguel Apache . . . "

A few hisses came from the front row.

"We're not prepared to comment on their veracity or historical accuracy. We have an agreement with the San Miguel Pueblo that we plan to honor, as we're sure the tribal council will honor its agreement with us. We commit to respecting all tribal rights and privileges. If, pending future discoveries, the claims of the San Miguel Apache prove to have merit, then we'll discuss a concession to their rights. Until then, we hope to resume construction later this week."

Charles looked up, wondering if the room had always been this silent. He could see Mallon's dark shape in the back corner, like a water stain on the wall. Luján's thick face was pinched into a network of caves and bulging flesh.

Then, Charles looked back at the words he had just read. "A concession to their rights will be discussed." That was not what Salazar briefed him on. This statement opened the door to cutting in the Apaches in on the deal. Charles saw the stenographer tap out the last words of his statement.

A man sitting next to Luján finally spoke, "Can you say that last part again?" Charles looked at his nameplate: Otero, Lt. Governor.

"What I think it meant," Charles said, "was that we're excited to start building again and to open this airport so that the San Miguel Pueblo can benefit."

"Sure, sure," Otero said. "But you also said concessions might be given to the Apache fraudsters. How is that possible? And are we going to be the ones paying them?"

Charles was sitting there, in an uncomfortable folding chair in New Mexico, but he was also standing behind a lectern in Dover. The press could have been sated with a stern denial and the election would have been close, but they would have won. Then Charles would not be in New Mexico at all, he'd be in DC, chief of staff to a US senator. But he hadn't given that strong denial, he hadn't handled the moment properly. He had dug into his own ego and told the press that nothing was wrong and that everyone should go back to work. This time he would be firm.

"The Apache claims have zero reliability. None. However, it's possible, unlikely but possible, that they have a small, valid claim.

It's also possible we'll all be hit by a meteor before I'm done with this sentence." Charles paused. "So far neither of those things are true."

This provoked an actual laugh from the crowd. Sure, it was more of an acknowledgement of humor than a laugh, but it meant there was light ahead.

"We want this Apache claim to be laughed out of the state," Otero said. "We want our rights to be ironclad, but you're leaving wiggle room."

"Hang on," Charles said, "I don't control the Apaches. Who could? We want them run out just as bad as you. Lieutenant Governor Otero called them 'fraudsters,' and he's probably right. But they're a fact of life now, like a flooding river or . . . "

Otero cut him off. "You don't need to make nature-based metaphors for our sake."

Charles went red. His whole career had been one step forward and then two feet in his mouth. "What I mean is that we are all dedicated to working together. There are outside groups trying to slow us down—that's a fact—but together we can get through this. Together."

"Together seems to be the keyword there," Luján said. "Let's have five minutes of questions from the audience."

A woman with round glasses and curly gray hair came up to the microphone.

"My name is Christine Morales and I run the Women's Economic Initiative Program here in San Miguel."

Charles knew he was in trouble when she stopped addressing him and turned her attention to the audience.

"Look, we don't have to listen to them," she said. "Maybe this is a sign that we should stop. Wash our hands and move on."

"Ma'am, you can't just move on." Charles looked to the tribal council for help. "We have an agreement and construction is well underway."

Luján leaned forward. "Mrs. Morales is concerned that the airport won't actually provide jobs for the people of our tribe."

"We tried to put it into the agreements," Morales said. "But the council didn't want to push too hard. Can you promise this project will actually benefit our most vulnerable citizens?"

The crowd nodded in agreement. Charles began to realize why Salazar had sent him. The tribe had been toyed with and lied to for hundreds of years. He thought of Branch, waiting in the wings to sweep up all the profits. They had no idea. Charles took a sip of the lukewarm water in front of him. He knew it made him look guilty. That was okay. He was.

"This project will bring many jobs to the region. I'm sure the tribe will be well represented and adequately compensated."

"Let's build a casino," a man in the crowd shouted.

"No more outbursts," Luján said. "Our time for questions is almost up and if the council has nothing more to add, I propose that we . . . "

"No, no, one more thing," Morales said, walking towards the stage. "Sir, you don't get it, and that's okay, why would you? We have never viewed this land as something to dig up and pave over for money. Approving the sale was difficult. Painful. It's painful to watch the trucks drive on and off the grounds. Painful to hear the digging all over town, to taste the dust in the air."

"Christine, this is not the place," Luján said. "Lt. Governor Otero and I will be meeting with Mr. Branch ourselves in the coming days. We'll tell him our concerns."

"I don't know if you will, Sonny. We can't trust this. I've spent my life trying to bring jobs out here, and I'm worried this isn't the answer."

She turned to Charles, who started folding up the statement and tried melting into his chair. "They won't even look us in the eye."

"I'm adjourning this meeting," Luján said. "Thank you for attending. Thank you, Mr. O'Connell."

The crowd made its way out the front door. Everyone who had been seated around Charles walked away without even a backwards glance. Charles wanted to check in with the governor, ask how he had done, but Luján shook his hand and turned away before releasing his grip. By the time Charles slipped out the side door, the meeting room was empty.

Mallon was waiting inside the town car.

"That could have been worse," Charles said.

Mallon put the car in drive, and Charles noticed the phone pressed to his ear and the sour expression clinging to Mallon's face.

"Sir, this is a sudden change. Are you quite sure . . . "

Mallon went quiet. Charles imagined Branch at the other end of the line, howling in anger. They turned right out of the tribal headquarters, opposite from the way they had entered. Charles' eyes flicked towards the speedometer.

"I understand," Mallon said. "Will you need me to help with this delivery?"

Mallon stayed on the line, quiet, for a few more seconds before lowering the phone.

Charles got the sense that Branch had hung up on him.

"What's going on?" Charles smiled. "Last time I got a call like that, they'd found Geronimo at the airport."

Mallon hunched forward and kept his eyes straight ahead. They were speeding down a two-lane highway Charles did not recognize. It led them to the interstate in less than five minutes.

# THIRTY-ONE

AFTER LEAVING ROSE'S, Gabe sped home. He ran a light downtown and cut off half a dozen cars on the ride. At the house, he tried to roll a joint, but his hands were shaking and the weed kept slipping out the other end. He balled up the paper and threw it on the floor.

He wanted to punch holes in the walls, kick the doors off his dad's perfect hinges, but the doors were too thick and wrecking the house would only be one more thing he would fail at.

Gabe sat at the table in Micah's room. The papers on the desk looked childish and embarrassing. He flicked through them, knots growing in his stomach with each ridiculous page. There was nothing here. No wisdom, no story, nothing for Micah. At best, Gabe had four or five pages of stories that might make the kid crack a grin, call his dad a nut and then forget about him after he died.

Gabe wrecked the table. He tore some of the papers, smashed others into the carpet, broke half the pencils and left the room a mess. It felt good. Giving up felt good. He told himself Rose was a distraction and the papers were unnecessary. All he needed was some more cash.

He went back downstairs. He had some weed to sell.

eᴽᴼ eᴽᴼ eᴽᴼ

One of Gabe's great pleasures was the fact that Rey—fancy, college-educated, super lawyer Rey—lived in a house smaller than Gabe's.

"How can you even stand it here?" Gabe always asked the same question. "Damn wetbacks and homeless dudes would turn their noses up at this."

Rey held his stomach and pretended to laugh. "Funny, oh you're so, so funny."

As usual, Rey was working from his living room. He had an office on the main square, but spent most of his time in his recliner at home; books, laptops, and stacks of papers spread out on couches, chairs and the floor the way beer cans were sprawled throughout Gabe's rooms. Rey wore a blue, thick cotton bathrobe and was watching *telenovelas* while working. He dropped back into the recliner without clearing a spot anywhere for Gabe.

"Why do you watch these shows, man?" Gabe asked. "They're so damn cheesy."

"The women, mostly. And they keep me connected to my culture."

Gold-embossed law books lined one wall of the living room. Gabe pulled one off the shelf, releasing a small cloud of dust he felt in his nose.

"Culture, my ass. You're the least Mexican 'Baca' I know."

"Not the point, *cabrón*." He pointed at the TV. "I'm part of the larger Mexican . . . Nevermind. What do you need?"

"When am I getting my job back?" Gabe flipped through the thin, Bible-like pages of the law book. "Helen won't let Micah come down until she knows I'm getting a paycheck."

Rey pushed his weight back into the recliner. His bathrobe opened and fell loose around his gut. "I don't know, man. This thing is complicated, and there have been some new developments."

"This shit is witchcraft," Gabe said and put the book back on the shelf. He locked his hands behind his head. "Look, I'll be straight with you, man. I need some cash. Micah wants to go on a trip, Helen needs some money, I've got to buy the kid all this fancy camping gear."

"I told you, I can't."

"You lost me my old job. Give me a new one. I can go out to the site, report what I see there. I can go up to Santa Fe and, I don't know, ask questions."

"Sam Spade, huh?"

"Okay." Gabe pulled on his beard, the hair felt thin and rough. "Fine, buy some weed."

Rey snorted. "I've got some."

"Buy some more. You'll be helping me out."

"Hang on." Rey leaned over and dug under a coffee table next to his chair. His robe opened and revealed his underwear's white elastic. He pulled out a white cardboard box with a handle.

"See this? Milk chocolate, with peanuts. Five boxes of them around here somewhere. Five! All terrible! They taste like burnt cardboard, but my secretary's kid is on the dance team. Have to help the holy dance team. And this." He leaned back over and pulled a thick book from under a stack of magazines. "A coupon book. Dry cleaners and pizza and shit like that. They expire in a month, and I don't think I've used one of them, but my sister's kid is in the choir. Hell, thanks to some gimpy kid who knocked on my door, I've got a freezer full of the blandest green *chile* ever grown. Said he needed to go see a doctor in Pittsburgh. That stuff tastes like it was grown in Pittsburgh."

He tossed the coupon book at Gabe's chest, causing his robe to open more. "Spare me the lecture," Gabe said. "And the fucking show. Cover yourself."

Rey looked down at the opening in his robe but didn't close it. "Shit, you should be paying me for this view."

That open robe began to feel like a challenge, like someone poking Gabe in the chest, daring him to throw a punch.

"I am not asking for a handout."

"Frederick is going to find out," Rey said. "And he's not going to like it. No, let me rephrase: I'm sure Fredrick already knows."

"I'm being smart about this. I'm not slinging dime bags on the corner."

"We've both heard the stories, man. About him tying people to trees in the mountains. Drives them an hour into the Sandia, gags them, and leaves them there. That takes days and days."

Gabe shook his head. "I'm not his competition. I don't have a choice. You encouraged me to sell it in the first place."

"Not to *me*." Rey shook his head and pulled his robe closed. "I'm not going to buy any weed from you. I never buy weed from anyone. But I am going to leave some money on this table, and you might accidentally drop something next to it."

"Two ounces of something."

Rey lifted a single finger, then grabbed his wallet and counted out a stack of twenties. "You going to roll a joint before you leave?"

"Don't think I have a choice."

Rey dropped the cash on the table. "You're going to flash this to the wrong person. You're going to sell to the wrong person. When he stops being your friend, he's going to be a mean bastard, and Jefe's mushrooms aren't strong enough to protect you."

"How do you know about that?"

"That's my point. It's a small town."

Gabe sat down on the carpet in front of the coffee table. He kept his head down, working the rolling papers.

"When am I going back to work? These Apaches are full of shit, right?"

Rey rubbed his hand over his face. Gabe hadn't noticed until then how tired he looked.

"You know, man, they probably are full of shit. But, I don't know, they may be onto something."

Gabe looked up and lit the joint. "Geronimo is not buried outside of Albuquerque."

"Okay, so maybe the Geronimo stuff isn't ironclad. But these guys might have a claim on this land. There were so many different tribes. They deserve their history. You're playing a role in this. Might need you to testify about them dumping the bones in your truck."

"I'm not testifying for nothing, and you know it."

"People aren't paying attention to this now."

Gabe finished the joint and grabbed a newspaper off the coffee table. The headline was about delays on highway construction in downtown Albuquerque.

Rey sighed, "Media engagement is not what we hoped."

Gabe handed over the joint. Rey took a deep hit and went quiet. He looked over Gabe's head at the smoke, and the room seemed much heavier.

"I'm going to be straight, here," Rey said. "I might be out of my depth, man."

"Your ass is so big I didn't think that was possible."

Rey kept a straight face and Gabe was unsure how to handle his seriousness.

"You'll figure it out," Gabe said. "Hell, you have to. If you don't know what you're doing, then there's really no hope for my dying ass."

"When they came to me, the Apaches, they said they wanted their land but they'd take a settlement. Two million, maybe even one-five."

"Two million. You get a cut of that too, right?"

"That's not the point," Rey snapped.

Smoking had not done either of them any good. Rey had gone serious, and Gabe just felt numb. He took another drag.

"Okay, question for you." Rey seemed to perk up. "So, I bought this weed, two hundred bucks, to make you stop whining, right? To make you leave me alone. What would your reaction have been if I offered you five grand for one ounce?"

"Five? I'd have snatched your money before you realized you were an idiot."

"No, no, no, wrong move." Rey shook his head. "Wrong move. Offering you five grand means I *really* want you to stop whining. If I'm five-grand desperate for you to go away, then I'd maybe cough up seven, or ten."

"Hey, I'll take ten grand. No, we'll strike a deal, just one grand for me to leave you alone. Forever."

Rey sat up and leaned close to Gabe. "This morning, I got a call from the woman running the whole show. Serious, serious woman. She offered ten million dollars."

Gabe's mouth went dry. The fact that these sums existed in the world and that they could be conjured, offered, denied at a whim, confused him.

"Yeah," Rey said. "My reaction too."

"Take it. Take it. Call them now and take it."

"The Apaches are deciding on that. If they take it, you're going back to work very, very soon. But here's the thing you don't get. We never asked for anything. Never even put out any feelers about taking one or two million. Then, out of nowhere, ten? I got a call from the woman helping the Apaches. And she says to wait. Wait, because maybe they'll pay twenty."

Rey looked around the room, as if expecting someone else to be there, taking notes in the corner, listening.

"Take the money," Gabe said. "These guys aren't in the habit of handing over millions to Indians. I'm desperate for cash, but waiting for twenty feels like a dangerous mistake."

Rey looked at Gabe with a heavy worry. They were both getting so old. Gabe pushed himself up to his feet with a groan. He grabbed the cash from the table. Far from ten million, but it would do.

"This money will help."

"I'm a real lifesaver."

Gabe walked all the way to the front door before stopping. He knew Rey was back there, waiting for Gabe to leave.

"Don't ask me to buy any more," Rey hollered.

Gabe leaned his head against Rey's front door. "No, no, it's . . . could you help me find someone?"

"I'm not digging up customers for you."

Gabe took a breath and let it out through his mouth. "I meant my mom."

Rey did not respond. Gabe pictured him pooled in his armchair, laughing at Gabe's family. He opened the door, ready to slam it shut after him.

"Yeah," Rey shouted, "I'll try."

Gabe felt like throwing up. He wanted to tell Rey to forget about it, find another way to waste his time. Before taking a step outside, Gabe shouted.

"Hey, did you see the video? I'm famous online, like YouTube and stuff. There's a video of me singing, talking, like a million people have seen it."

Rey snorted. "Shit like that is why people never believe a damn thing you say."

Walking back to his bike, Gabe felt his legs go watery. Before graduating high school, he had looked in the phone book for a Celsa Luna. There was one in Albuquerque and another in Pecos. He sent graduation announcements to both. No one showed, and that was the last time he had tried to find her.

Gabe rested one fist on the seat of his bike. He needed to focus on Micah. He needed to sell a lot more weed.

# THIRTY-TWO

MALLON DUMPED O'CONNELL at the office and sped back to the compound. On the phone, Mr. Branch had sounded the alarm. "Pack your bags. We've decided it's time to move on," Branch said.

Who was 'we'?

Years of sitting in the corners of every meeting, hearing every phone call and delivering every message, either with a fist or an envelope, and he had never heard Branch talk about giving up. Someone had his ear, and Mallon doubted it was Mrs. Branch.

He pulled into the compound and jogged into the guardhouse before going up to Branch's office. No way would he walk in there without at least a little extra knowledge. Mallon hunched over a monitor and switched through the camera feeds. Mrs. Branch's bedroom door was open. He looked for any signs of movement. Through the doorway all he could see was the edge of a dresser. If she was packing, she was doing it quietly. The monitors at the office showed Salazar addressing the suited masses all gathered together in the center of the cubicles. They were being fired. O'Connell leaned in the doorway of his office, hand over his mouth, looking as confused as Mallon felt. The GPS trackers showed each car in Branch's fleet, except for O'Connell's, making their way back to the compound. The empire was being rolled up, and Mallon had no idea why.

He left the guardhouse and went into the main house. Branch would know Mallon had not gone straight to see him, and he would have a few things to say about that. In truth, Branch's abuse never bothered Mallon. He had made it through Basic Training, dealt with snipers and IEDs. He had faced down meth heads with cleavers. One millionaire's bile was easy.

The door to the office was open. It was never open. He pushed. Branch was in a recliner that he had pushed to nearly horizontal.

"Finally," Branch said. "I need your help finding this game. It's called 'Magic Run' or 'Run Magic,' I don't know. I thought I found it, but this screen is so small."

Branch held out his phone. Mallon looked around the room. No one else was there. The only thing out of place was a few suitcases.

"I'm sorry, sir?"

"Take this." Branch rolled his eyes. "Help me. I need games and . . . stuff like that. Books? Audiobooks, I think that'd be good. Music. Although I guess I need headphones too, right? Bound to be some around here."

Mallon had trouble reading the situation. Branch seemed happy. Maybe it was medication. The doctors might have prescribed an upper to balance out the sleeping pills. Mallon took Branch's phone from him.

"I'm sorry, sir, but I don't understand."

Branch stretched and brought his hands down on his stomach. He rubbed his round belly and yawned. Happy as a fat little Buddha.

"It's time to make some changes around here. You're coming with us. Lots of work to do, and I trust you. You, Diana, and . . . one other person. That's it. Everyone else is so greedy. Selfish."

Mallon waited. Unsure how to deal with a happy, sober Cody Branch.

"You're lost," Branch said. "As was I. But now I'm found."

Branch raised his palms to the air in mock supplication. He looked at Mallon. "Goddamn boy, you know you're allowed to smile once a week."

Mallon heard Branch's phone vibrate as a message came in.

"It is time to move on." Branch extended his arms like airplane wings. "And move on we will. Have the staff come up and pack for me. I need a few suitcases for winter clothes and a few for summer clothes. You'll have to do the same. We're going to the lodge in Wyoming first. After that, I don't know, I'm leaving those details up to her."

"I should pack?"

"Well, only if you don't want to wear that black suit every day for the rest of your life. Although, maybe you do."

"Sir, I think I need some more information before I can . . . "

"We're getting the hell out of town until the dust settles, and I want you by my side. There will be some delicate maneuvers. And along the way you get to spend some time on a beach. You can find a local girl to hand you coconuts."

Mallon's head swam. "A trip."

"A tactical retreat. I don't want to come back to Santa Fe until construction on the casino has started. Maybe two years. There'll be more lawsuits, but Diana can handle all that."

"Can I ask what happened to spark this change, sir?"

Branch's smile faltered. "I received some information. Distressing information. I'm acting now, before it gets worse. We're leaving tomorrow morning. You can go home and pack."

Two years. Mallon pictured the compound falling apart, being overrun by weeds. He pictured his empty duplex. Claudia would have no one to look out for her. He felt like he was stuck at the bottom of a well with smooth cylindrical walls.

"This is a bad idea." Mallon took a deep breath. "Your wife is having an affair."

Branch folded his arms and let out a sigh. He seemed disappointed, a little sad, but not angry. Mallon had been bracing for fury.

"Does every damn body in town know?"

"It's O'Connell, sir. I'm sorry, I don't know how long but . . . "

Branch waved his hands to silence him. "I know. I even know what they were planning. It's good you figured it out. You're sharp. That's why I need you. But *she* is not coming with us."

Mallon felt nauseous. He had hoped Branch's rage would wipe away these plans, give him the time he needed in Santa Fe, time this man was taking from him.

"What are we going to do about it, sir?"

"Nothing. The hardest thing I've ever done, and I may need you to deck me to keep my hands off his neck, but nothing is exactly what we need to do. I'm paying to make my problems go away. This morning we bombed the Apaches with a settlement offer, and we'll come back after the fallout has disappeared."

"But what about O'Connell?"

Branch smiled. It was cold and terrible. "O'Connell is going to get what he deserves." Branch stood up and pointed at the suitcases. "The staff will probably need to go buy more, I don't know."

Mallon watched Branch walk through the office and into the bedroom. "What about O'Connell, sir?"

Branch shut the bedroom door, leaving Mallon alone with the suitcases.

The phone buzzed again. Branch had forgotten it. There were a dozen new messages about travel, swimming, the Caribbean and Aspen and Switzerland. Mallon's eyes flicked up towards the security camera in the ceiling, worried someone was watching him snoop.

All the messages were from Janice Chávez.

# THIRTY-THREE

THE SIGHT OF THE CUBICLE fish boxing up their stuff made Charles queasy. Salazar did it masterfully. Charles marveled as she swayed the room's emotions. The second she started talking, everyone knew what was coming. She complimented them, made assurances of references, congratulated them on seeing the project through to its next phase. As they checked out with the imperious receptionist, their cardboard boxes of personal belongings were searched for electronics. A few even walked out smiling.

Charles waited until Salazar went back into her office. She was reading a contract, jotting notes in the margins, scratching words out, flipping pages. Charles sat down across from her desk and she flicked her eyes up at him.

"Ah, good" she said. "I had a question for you."

She turned her monitor towards him. An article about Hawley on her screen. "You know him?" she asked.

Charles nodded. "Yeah. Yeah, I did. We weren't close but we'd worked together."

Salazar sat back. "It's a sad story."

"It's hard to believe."

She turned the monitor away from him. "You've done good work."

"I have?"

She smiled. "Yes, you have. We're moving on to the next stage of this process." She indicated the monitor with her hands. "The press doesn't care about the Apaches, so we're putting them behind us. Time to start building again. That's why we didn't need the extra staff."

"Things are quiet out there."

"They were mostly working on the purchase of the land, the bonds, and so on." Salazar held out a thin file folder. "This is the next phase."

Charles grabbed the folder and flipped through the pages. It was a contract of employment. His name was all over it.

"We'd like you to transition to a parallel organization. The Airport Authority is hiring you to finish overseeing the construction."

The pages were a blur. Branch's name was nowhere to be seen, and then he heard Thompson's voice booming through his head. Charles closed the folder.

"I don't get it. What about you, what about Branch?"

"I helped get the bond passed. It was always my plan to exit. I'm not particularly interested in asphalt vendors and driveway cutouts. Cody and I think you're more than qualified to handle this. You'll move to an office down on site. You'll have a few assistants and you can stay in the house and keep the car. There's also a pay raise."

Charles opened his mouth and closed it before finding the words. "It seems a little fast. I've never run a construction operation before."

Salazar leaned back in her chair and tilted her head. "It's not like you're going to be working the forklift. This is managing people, vendors, access to the site. Management skills. This is a good chance for you. If you're not interested, we can move on with someone else and we'll pay you out for the month."

"I know we're not supposed to talk about the bigger idea, the goal for a gaming option on the site, but I'd still like to be involved with that."

Salazar remained stoic, taking a few seconds to reply.

"Details of future site use are still to be determined. There are lots of ideas out there, but none of that can happen until we finish building."

Charles opened the folder again. "And this is my chance to stay involved."

"And your first job is to go back to San Miguel tomorrow."

"I was just there."

"Things have changed. We sent you out there too early. I already apologized to Governor Luján. You'll go out tomorrow and tell them the Apaches aren't a problem anymore."

"How did I miss that news?"

"Everything happened after you left for the site. The Apaches still haven't accepted our initial offer. They'll accept this next one, it's . . . generous. You're not going to have any notes, nothing in writing, but you're going to tell San Miguel that after the Apaches drop their claims, our organization will need an additional fifteen percent to cover cost."

Charles began to wonder if this is how Jim Hawley felt when he heard the boots marching down the hall.

"Fifteen percent of what?"

"This is one of those important meetings. It'll be quick, but it'll also be your best chance to demonstrate commitment to this project."

Something about the Hawley story had been bothering Charles and now he realized what. Jim would never have marched off to his own execution. Charles imagined him crouched behind his cell door with a sharpened spoon or a sliver of brick pried from the walls. Jim would never have waited for Navy Seals to save the day. He would have tried something. If his move had worked, he would have lived, and even if his move had failed, well, he was going to die anyway.

Charles knew a bad chance was still a chance. He picked up a pen from Salazar's desk and signed the documents.

# TUESDAY

# THIRTY-FOUR

DRIVING TO ESPAÑOLA, Olivia pulled over twice to look under the hood, poke around in the trunk and prod anything that looked like a secondary tracker. Nothing. She had taken the first tracker out and left it under a trash can downtown, but she doubted Mallon would be satisfied with just one.

That morning, she tried to follow her usual routine. Coffee and breakfast at a local bakery, running to the gallery to check in with the owner, trying so hard to act normal.

The compound had been different that morning. The household staff spent yesterday and this morning buzzing around and avoiding eye contact. Every time Olivia turned, there was another lawyer or banker slipping into her husband's study. The security staff had been cut way back, and Cody never emerged from his office. Not even Janice had answered her calls. The world was changing, and no one had included her. Olivia needed to go check on Andrea and the kids.

Outside Santa Fe there was hardly any traffic, and her husband's cars were all the same, which should have made them easier to spot. Still, she could not keep her eyes off the rearview mirror.

She blew away a few strands of hair that hung over her eyes. She reached for the coffee she thought was in her center console, but she had thrown it away hours ago. Again, she tried to blow the hair away from her face before running a hand across her head.

"Stop it," she said. "Just stop it."

Then she turned off her car's Bluetooth, and then her phone, just in case.

Andrea's house looked even quieter than it had during her last visit. The grass was longer, and a few pieces of trash had blown into the yard. It took Andrea too long to answer. Finally, she cracked the door and shut it after Olivia slipped in.

"Yesterday, someone was out there," Andrea said. "A guy in a car. He was there for hours, and who knows how long he was out there before I noticed him."

"Why didn't you call the police?"

Andrea shot Olivia a glare that stopped her in her tracks.

"I'm not exactly on solid legal grounds here. I couldn't do anything. I couldn't even keep peeking out at the blinds because I was scared he'd see me."

Olivia sat down at the kitchen table. "What kind of car was it?"

Andrea paced between the kitchen and the living room. "What?"

"The car. What color was it? Two-door, four-door?"

"It was white."

Olivia smiled. "That wasn't one of Cody's. He loves black town cars. Every security guy drives a black town car, I swear."

Andrea chewed her thumbnail and shook her head. "I don't know. He was there a long time."

Olivia looked around. The house was so still. "Where are the girls?"

"They're in the back. I told them to be quiet. They've gotten good at that."

"No, no, they don't have to do that. You're not in hiding. This is supposed to be . . . relaxing."

"We're not supposed to be here. You can't just tell me to relax."

Olivia noticed the empty picture frames on the end tables and the trash can overflowing with paper plates and pizza boxes.

"Have you even unpacked?"

Andrea shook her head and sat down across from Olivia. "Why bother?"

Olivia opened her mouth, wanting to give all the same excuses and encouraging words she had given Andrea time and time again. It was no use.

"They were tracking my car." Olivia felt like she was confessing. "My husband might have sent someone out here, but I don't think so."

"They were tracking you? Has he finally lost his mind?"

"It feels like I blinked and everything's falling apart. Something is about to happen."

"We'll leave," Andrea said. "We have to leave."

"I can put the three of you in a hotel for a couple nights. I'll get out cash."

"I wasn't just talking about me and the girls. You. Leave him now. Assume he knows all about whatever you're doing."

"I'm not ready yet. He'll kick me to the curb, and we won't have anything."

"We'll have safety. We won't be in this holding pattern any more. I can't keep doing this. The girls need to be in school. *You* can't keep doing this. Look at you. Would you really be more miserable living in Albuquerque working as a temp?"

Olivia shook her head. "That wasn't one of Cody's guys."

"Fine, but something is happening, you said so yourself, and . . . I had a dream last night."

Olivia rolled her eyes.

"Stop it," Andrea said. "You know that happens to me. Before I got sick, before mom died, before Ellie broke her arm. In my dream, you were on the road, in a car, and someone shoved the side of it. They ran up to your car on foot and shoved it." Andrea pushed her arms in front of her. "It started to spin out of control, not flip, you didn't flip, I think that's important too somehow, but the car spun and it hit the guardrail and it spun again and again. Someone did that to you."

Olivia took a breath. "Well, now I'm excited to get back on the highway."

Andrea furrowed her brow, then let out a snorting laugh. "Stop it, I'm serious."

Olivia smiled. "We have to hold on a little longer."

Andrea shook her head. "I don't think we can."

⁓ ⁓ ⁓

It took twenty minutes for Olivia to calm Andrea down. Andrea was determined to leave, but at a certain point, she just didn't have the energy to argue. Olivia figured she had a day, maybe two before she needed to jump ship and drag Andrea with her.

On the drive home, she thought about Andrea's dream of her spinning out of control. Whose hands were those that hit her car? Was it Janice? Maybe Charles? Olivia crept closer to Santa Fe. Or maybe they were her own?

When Olivia pulled into the compound, it was nearly empty. There was a moving truck outside and the walkway was full of suitcases and cardboard boxes. No one was home. She went from room to room, calling for someone, anyone.

When she went up to the bedroom, she whispered Cody's name. She was scared to face him but prayed he was there, drunk as usual.

He was gone too.

# THIRTY-FIVE

WITHOUT MALLON LEADING him astray, Charles avoided the winding back roads to San Miguel. Approaching from the highway, the Pueblo looked like any other small town. The houses near the meeting hall were also the newest in the Pueblo, with satellite dishes, new cars, high stone fences.

On the last trip, Charles had seen the back half of the Pueblo and knew the money only went so deep. He pulled into the council parking lot. Part of Charles was screaming to run away, take a flight, let the whole state choke on its own dust.

There were only two other vehicles in the meeting hall parking lot: a new car and a newly repainted truck that was almost an antique. Whoever was in this meeting would be the people who were really in charge: the ones who lived in stone houses.

As Charles stepped out of his car, Addie called. Again. She had called three times on the drive down. He could not avoid her forever.

"Hey babe, just getting out of the car. Sorry I missed you earlier. These mountains wreck the signal."

Charles smelled burning wood on the breeze, felt the gravel crunching underfoot.

"I'm coming out tonight," she said.

"To-tonight? Wow, that's great."

"Is it?" Addie's voice had an unfamiliar hardness. Not angry, not spitting and gnashing, but she sounded ready to punch through any excuses he would throw at her.

"Your flight was next week, I thought."

"I changed it. We need to talk."

222

"Okay. What happened? What's going on?"

"I don't know what you've gotten yourself into out there, but . . . I'm on my way. I land at ten and I'm renting a car."

"You don't have to get a car, I'll come get you."

"No, I don't want you to."

"You're really not going to tell me what this is about."

After a few seconds, Addie said, "I kind of thought you'd tell me. Guess not. I'll call you when I hit Santa Fe."

And then, she was gone. Charles could see someone on the other side of the meeting hall's tinted glass doors. Who knew how long they had been watching him.

The glass door opened and Governor Luján waved Charles in. He flapped his hand, hurrying Charles into the building.

"Sure took your time," Luján said. "Maybe one of the old gossips didn't see you out there."

"I'm sorry?" Charles blinked, his eyes were useless in the dark meeting hall.

"You're not the most popular chap around here."

Charles looked around the meeting hall. There were two vehicles outside.

"Is it just us?" he asked. "I expected more of a . . . "

"War party? Fire dance?"

Charles shut his mouth. He was not going to dig the grave Luján would gladly have filled in for him.

Luján grinned. "Come on out Christine."

Christine Morales, the woman who had started to make a scene during the council meeting came out from behind the curtain on the stage. Yesterday, she seemed like an outsider, a troublemaker, but this was no meeting for outsiders.

"I told you we didn't need to be sneaky," Christine said.

"She was going to stay back there," Luján said. "A witness. Just in case."

Charles rubbed his hand across his face. He knew his role, but he hated everyone else knowing it also.

Charles looked at Christine. "I thought you were opposed to this airport."

Christine held her hands out. "Still saying 'airport'. Not me, I'll say casino, I'm not scared. If this *casino* can help us, then I'll help it. I'm for these people, that's all I care about, and I'm going to make damn sure some of that money goes to the people who need it."

"Why don't you build it yourself? Why get Mr. Branch involved?"

Luján grinned. "That's been my line going on ten years. Save some of our money. Apply for our own loans. It's not going to ever happen that way. The banks won't loan us the cash because they don't want to piss off the tribes that already have casinos. And I can't tell my people that we're not building that school or paving that road so we can save a hundred grand here and there for a casino we hope to build in ten years."

"I'd tear his balls off myself, if he tried that one," Christine said. "Look, I don't want your boss' money. But even if we could fund this ourselves, you know what kind of place that would be? Cheap. And it would bring in cheap people. The kind of guys who'll tear through the village for fun. Drag waitresses into their back seats. *That's* the casino I've been fighting."

"And Branch's casino will help?" Charles asked.

Christine's face fell. "It'll create different problems. But if I've lost the war, then I'm going to dictate the terms of my surrender. If a casino is coming, it's going to be the best goddamn casino in the state, and we're going to get our fair share."

"I almost miss her being my nemesis," Luján said. "She kept me sharp."

Christine pointed her finger at Luján and furrowed her eyebrows in warning. They both smiled. Charles did not understand their relationship, but it was clearly deep and true.

"But you've got bad news for us," Christine said. "You're the delivery boy Diana sends when someone's died."

"He backing out?" Luján asked. "Backing the Apaches?"

"No, no," Charles said. He used a finger to jab each word home. "He's going to make the Apache problem go away."

Charles expected them to look relieved, but Luján and Christine barely blinked.

"But he wants another fifteen percent."

"That's too much," Luján said. "No way."

Christine raised her hands, palms out, to calm Luján. "It's okay, it's okay." She turned to Charles. "No."

"No?"

"Christine," Luján said, "without Branch, we wouldn't have this chance."

"I"m going to call Diana myself with *our* offer," Christine said. "We need an *additional* fifteen percent. I can make the Apaches go away cheap, but we'll need eighteen percent of future profits."

Luján shook his head. "This wasn't the plan," he said. "What can you offer the Apaches?"

Charles stepped back and looked at Christine Morales as if with new eyes. "It's you," he said. "There are no Apaches. You put that group together to make sure Branch treated you fairly."

She almost smiled. "I'll reach out to them. Native to Native."

Luján turned around, a hand to his mouth. "You should have told me."

He paced, trying to find the words, and then opened the door to the parking lot. He stood in the doorway and turned to Charles. "You've done your job. Go back to your master now."

"I can help make sure that your . . . "

"This conversation has nothing to do with you," Christine said. "Sonny and I have a lot to talk about."

"If I tell Branch the truth, he won't move forward with you at all," Charles said.

She laughed. "He already sent his chief goon with a check for ten million. Made quite a show of it, but the Apaches will keep saying no until I tell them to say yes. I'll drag this process out to get what we need. He will still be rich. You'll be rich. And you can't prove any of this."

Charles nodded and kept his mouth shut. He was an easy messenger to kill.

Christine and Sonny walked deeper into the meeting hall. Charles backed out into the bright day, his eyes having trouble adjusting to the light.

# THIRTY-SIX

GABE SOLD THREE OUNCES in an hour. He worked up the nerve by smoking a joint and then downing two quick beers. Steady hands and a calm stomach meant Gabe could finish it all in a quick afternoon. No time for looking over his shoulder when he only had a minute to slap a bag into someone's hand and pocket their cash.

Two of the ounces went to friends. Guys who had swallowed Gabe's story about a friend in Colorado.

The third ounce was a bad idea. A few weeks earlier, all Gabe wanted was a hamburger. The kid who worked the drive-in at the Blake's near the highway had the nerve to ask Gabe, a stranger, if he could score him some weed. Gabe grabbed his burgers and sped off without paying. This time the kid burst into a dumb toothy grin when Gabe showed what he had to offer.

Gabe knew two things at the same time: that this was too easy, and that he should have done it a week ago.

Back at the house, Gabe counted his money. Helen wanted a grand. Gabe had $1,100. Gabe needed a few hundred more for food, new sheets, taking Micah to the movies, but he was almost there.

He tried not to look into his kitchen, where Rose's check hung from an old magnet on the fridge. Gabe promised himself he would not cash her check. He would not even recognize it as a check. That slip of paper was not money to Gabe. It was a note telling him to go back to Rose.

He took the check off the fridge, turned it over to hide the numbers and put it back under the magnet. As he grabbed another beer, he thought about throwing the check away. Gabe sat down on his couch. He could still see the kitchen out of the corner of his eye.

His phone rang. Gabe grabbed for it, hoping for Rose, willing to settle for Helen. *Blocked Number.*

Cold sweat spread across Gabe's chest. Frederick. Gabe stared at the phone, willed it to blink out of existence. Frederick would know he ignored the call. Better to answer and start begging now.

"Yeah?" Gabe's voice was quiet.

"Gabey, Gabe, Gabe. I didn't think you'd answer."

"Fucking Bobby." Gabe let out a deep breath he'd been holding for too long. "Where are you calling from? Why are you calling me at all?"

"Oh my God, this guy, look at him. He begs me to call if we're starting up, and now he's too busy for my call. That's fine, whatever, paying people in cash makes me nervous."

"We starting? When? Monday?"

"Eager beaver. No, we're starting Tuesday, but you're needed on Wednesday. And try not to do anything that gets you on the news, okay?"

"Hey, man, I didn't do anything."

"Story of your life, Gaber. See you in a few days."

The line went dead. Gabe put the phone down and looked around the room.

No more selling weed by the ounce. No more lying to Helen. She would let Micah come up. Gabriel Luna was a respectable member of society again.

His phone rang, and Gabe answered right away. "Do I get a raise too?"

"It's always money with you." This time it was Rey.

"Hey, man, you were right," Gabe said. "I got the call. Going back to work in few days."

"I know, my clients just accepted a metric fuckton of cash. I should be making sure I get paid but I'm talking to you for some reason."

"You didn't take them on for free, did you?"

"We'll talk about that later. Look, I found your mom."

Gabe laughed. "You found my mom? I only asked you yesterday."

"Well, I know how to use the internet. Two Google searches and one call to a buddy on Taos PD. I did it in traffic."

Gabe sat up, his mouth still holding an echo of a grin. "She's out there?"

"Want me to start at the beginning or . . . "

"Just tell me where she is."

"Okay, okay. Celsa Luna, who was born Celsa Ramírez and died Celsa Chávez, is in a cemetery up near Pecos. I'm sorry, man, she died nine years ago."

"Nine? She was alive nine years ago?"

"Yeah, right in downtown Pecos, worked in a hotel. Look, I have an obit. She got written up in the *Santa Fe New Mexican* and the *Journal*. I'll send it your way."

"Who paid for that? Did she have kids? Other than . . . "

"No, no kids. And this wasn't some fifty-word funeral notice. They sent journalists to write a story about her. I got to say, man. I always knew you were down for the cause."

"Tell me what you mean."

"She lived here in town for a few years, doing . . . not much, I guess. But then she fell in with what was left of Reies López Tijerina's group. Remember them in the '60s?"

"Kind of. They took over a post office?"

"National Forest. Armed fucking uprising, man. That land belonged to local families who'd been cheated out of it. Tijerina went to jail, but some of those guys were still fighting the fight. Your mom joined them after she split. She organized Chicanos and Natives north of Santa Fe. Helped bring more services out to Acoma Pueblo, San Miguel, a few spots. The article here quotes all these people: 'She was a great leader,' 'Could have been a national figure,' blah blah blah. The real fucking deal, man. I'm telling you this is in your blood."

"But she worked in a hotel."

"Yeah. I don't know. Something must have happened. She stopped organizing. Dropped all those people. No one seems to know why. Ends up in Pecos. No kids. No husband."

"That's two hours from here. She was two hours away."

"She was." Rey groaned. "I'm sorry, man. Be proud. Seems like she did some good work."

"Why didn't she call me? Why didn't she find us?"

Rey rustled through some papers, as if he could find the answer.

"Hey, I'll bring this stuff by," he said. "Or we can meet at The Pig."

Gabe looked around the house, there was so much to do.

"Maybe later. Hey, can I borrow your truck to go pick up Micah tomorrow? I'll leave you my bike."

"Sure, whatever you need." Gabe hung up.

Two hours away.

One of his strongest memories of her was just an image. He was in the living room, playing next to her rocking chair while she watched TV. When she rocked forward, her leg would graze Gabe's back, soothing, calming, present.

Two hours away.

# THIRTY-SEVEN

CHARLES SAW OLIVIA'S SUV parked outside his cul-de-sac. It stuck out into the road and was oddly far from any of the houses. His stomach bubbled with a stew of excitement and nerves. She made him feel dumb and vulnerable. He slowly walked into the house. She was sitting on a stool in the kitchen, resting her head on the marble island.

"Why'd you park on the road?" he asked. "I almost clipped your front end."

Olivia sat up. She looked exhausted, as if she had spent the day knotted in anger and it had taken hours and more than a few glasses of wine to move past it.

"I don't have the time I was hoping for. Have you found anything? If we're going to make a move, it has to be now."

Charles realized she was scared.

"There's no proof," he said. "Each side is playing the other, and neither side is answering my calls. Also, look, you won't like this, but Addie's coming out here tonight. I'm going to need some help cleaning up."

"Maybe you can testify or swear to a statement or something."

Charles set his wine glass down. "Did you hear what I said about my wife? She'll be here in a few hours. I think she knows something."

"What did you find?"

"Look." Charles glanced around the house, not quite ready to look straight at Olivia. "I'm going to be overseeing the whole project. Salazar is closing up shop and leaving. I got a promotion and I don't think I should be . . . "

"Why did *you* get a promotion?"

He grinned. "Well, I guess you don't think it's because I'm good at my job."

"Did you tell my husband about us? Try to sell me to him for a title bump?"

"No. Hell no. He'd pound me to dust if he found out."

"Maybe." Olivia stood up. "This isn't about you anymore. If they're putting you in charge, it is not because they like you."

Charles held up both hands. "I know, I know, I've heard that's what they do. They're going to burn me if they need to, but they don't need to yet. I can stick around here for months. You and I can keep figuring this thing out. You're right, I need protection, so stick with me and we'll find it."

"I don't know which of us is more delusional."

Charles took a step towards her, arms outstretched, but she stopped him with a look.

"I want to make this work between us."

Olivia laughed. "No, you don't. You're looking for something you can win because you're tired of losing, but you can't even see how screwed you are."

"I'm out here for the long run. I'm not sneaking away with you tonight."

"I don't want you to sneak away with me at all. I want you to be useful."

"Hey, I found out the truth about who's behind the Apaches claim. Branch is being tight with his cash, but he'll pay me for this. It'll help both of us."

"I'm not staying with you. I'm leaving."

While she was running as far away as possible Charles had been digging closer to Branch. At some point, they had passed each other. Years ago, Charles learned how to tell when she was about to run out and slam the door behind her. He figured he had about twenty seconds.

"Are you going to give me anything?" she asked.

"Are you going to give us a chance?"

Olivia crossed the living room in four quick strides. "Cash out, man. Go home. That's my plan. And don't worry about cleaning this place up. I haven't left anything behind."

And then, he was alone. Other than a dirty wine glass and the painting on the wall, Olivia was right.

# THIRTY-EIGHT

MALLON WAS NOT DOING WELL. In the guardhouse, he could hear the buzzing fluorescents, so he went outside. Then, he heard each insect in the trees, and the scent of the blooming flowers was cloying. Every action of the past week loomed as a colossal and compounding error in judgment. Trusting Mrs. Branch and O'Connell had been a huge mistake. After he added a touch of pressure, he expected them to do the right thing. Instead, Janice got to Branch before he could.

Everyone else had left the compound. The other guards had been sent away, most of them for good. The domestic staff had gone home earlier. A moving truck, stuffed with everything Branch might need for a year on the road, sat in front of the house.

Mallon went back into the guardhouse. He assumed Mr. Branch was still at Janice Chávez's, where he had left him that morning. Mallon was alone in the compound, watching the tracking monitor as Mrs. Branch's vehicle left O'Connell's and headed back.

He should go home, tell Claudia goodbye, pack a bag and hope she would be there when he got back. His orders were clear. Stand down. Even worse, look past what was happening all around him. Let O'Connell walk away. Let Mrs. Branch walk away. The boss made it sound so simple.

Mallon hated that he had missed all the signs. Janice Chávez had been clinging to the edges of the Branch empire for years, and Mallon never suspected a thing. He paced around the guardroom, scraping his feet on the floor to drown out the noise of the humming computers and lights.

Maybe he was the one falling apart. Maybe he was the perverted one. He entertained the idea, chewed over the thought that these other people were doing the right thing and he was wrong. He spat it out like a broken tooth.

The orders were simple but they were also a paradox. Do nothing. That's not an order. That's a state of being. So, Mallon asked himself, if he did something, was that disobeying orders? What if he did something to make Olivia Branch go away? And O'Connell. Then, one day, everyone would forget they were ever there and nothing would have to change.

The front gate opened, and Mrs. Branch's car pulled into the compound. Mallon left the guardhouse. He got to the front door just as she was starting up the steps from the parking area.

When she saw him, she tightened her grip on her phone and keys, then shot a glance around her. "Where is everyone?" she asked.

"They're gone. Everyone's gone."

She lifted her chin, defiant. "Move out of my way."

Mallon stayed still.

Anger edged into her voice. "You going to stand there all night? I'm trying to go inside."

Olivia looked at the ground. "What did he ask you to do? Tell me. Am I supposed to drive away? Walk down this mountain? Or are you going to hurt me, like those other people he sics you on?"

She used the back of her hand to push some hair out of her face. Her movements were ragged, nervous. She pointed to the moving truck behind her. "Is your stuff in there? Is he promising to make you rich, too?"

"I don't care about money."

Mallon had never exchanged so many words with Mrs. Branch. Part of him ached that this was how it had happened. None of this was his fault. He was doing his job. She was the one who had ruined everything.

"Mr. Branch wanted me to allow you inside to pack a bag. One bag. His lawyers will be in touch."

"I don't have enough cash to even . . . "

"I don't care." Mallon paused when he saw true fear enter her eyes, the kind of fear he usually stamped out with a fist or a knee. He took a breath and tried again, quieter. "You brought chaos into this house."

"Wait, wait, no, I'm trying to get out of this chaos. You look around and think this is normal? Where is he dragging you? Do you even know?"

"Mr. Branch is leaving town while construction resumes. We'll return soon."

"He's making you go on vacation with him? Oh, you'll love holding his umbrella on the beach and refilling his daiquiris. Cody's about to snap. He won't be able to outrun it. You've seen it better than anyone, better than me."

"It's not my job to judge."

"I was trying to get out and rebuild."

"With his money."

"Of course with his money. I've earned it."

Mallon took a step forward. Olivia tensed but held her ground.

"Who's in Española? You were there today."

Olivia flinched. "We don't need to talk about that."

"How many lovers do you have? Should I go kick in that door?"

"That house doesn't matter. What matters is that Cody thinks he can run our lives. Why should we suffer because he wants to build a casino and go to a beach by himself?"

Mallon broke eye contact. "He won't be by himself. Ms. Chávez . . . "

Olivia squealed as the air was pulled out of her lungs. She smoothed her hair back and grabbed two fistfuls at the back of her skull. She hung her head back, exposing her throat to Mallon.

"Of course."

"You didn't know."

"This is all my fault," she said. "Trusted her."

As she hung her head, Mallon kept quiet. Tears brimmed in her eyes, and she turned red, furious.

"When did all this start?" she asked. "These plans, the travel?"

"Yesterday evening."

"Right after I talked to her. Oh, she's clever. Everyone always thinks they're the clever one. Not this time. Not me."

Mallon wanted to hate her. He wanted to break her in half for bringing O'Connell down here and ruining everything. But he stepped aside. "You should pack your stuff and go. I'll call you a cab. Get you a room for a few nights."

Olivia laughed, dry and tinged with insane humor. "I'm not walking away with just a cab ride and a hotel for two nights."

"What else?"

"What else is . . . you help me. You work for him. You protect his interests and you know what he's doing is a bad idea. Deep down you can feel it. This plan, this casino is getting too big for him. He's cracking up. How many times have you carried him to bed in the past six months?"

"What's your point?"

"If you want to help him, then figure out how we can both get what we want."

"You don't know what I want."

"I'm pretty sure you don't want to see him crack and you don't want to lose what you've built here."

Mallon looked over her shoulder into the woods outside the compound. He had trouble holding her gaze.

"I'm not going to help you run off with O'Connell."

Olivia laughed. "He's the one who wants to stay here and get rich. I want my own life."

"You brought him out here. You used him."

Olivia looked at the ground. "O'Connell's digging in. His wife is flying into town right now. She's probably going to leave him, and he won't have anything to go back to."

"That may be my fault. I sent her some . . . compromising photographs. I hoped it would pull him back to DC."

"Of course you did. How many trackers are on those cars?"

Mallon didn't answer.

"I want money to start a new life," she said. "You want your life to not fall apart. Let's help each other."

Mallon kept his gaze steady. He would let her talk.

"Look." She lowered her voice. "He's swept up in a lot of emotion right now. If we keep him here a few more days, dealing with . . . something, anything, then he'll wake up."

"Last night, this morning, he was happy. He doesn't want to wake up."

"I don't care if he and Janice stay together, but Cody can't disappear and expect it to work out. I'm not trying to break him. I want him to slow down, catch his breath and give me what I need. You deserve the same."

"I will not do anything to help O'Connell."

Olivia sighed and nodded. "He's on his own."

Mallon lifted a hand towards the guard shack. "Let's go talk. It's more secure in there." Olivia turned, indicated he should walk in front of her.

"One thing," Mallon said. "Tell me about Española."

Olivia was quiet, the gravel skittered under her shoes. Finally, she said, "Okay."

# THIRTY-NINE

CHARLES HOPPED OFF the couch after hearing Addie's car pull up. He looked around the house one last time before opening the door. Olivia's fingerprints were all over him, pushed deep into the soft matter of his brain, and Addie would see it the second she looked at him.

He opened the door and walked to the edge of the front courtyard. Addie closed her trunk and took a second to look at the old houses and the thick ropes of stars.

"I told you it was beautiful," he said.

Addie formed a weak, sad smile. "I can see why you like it out here."

She lingered behind her car until a breeze made her shiver. Charles walked to the driveway, grabbed her suitcase in one hand and wrapped the other arm around her shoulders in a forced hug that caused her to stiffen. To hide his embarrassment, Charles turned and led her inside. He wanted to puke. He could not even muster the courage to hug and kiss his wife before she left him.

"Let me show you the rest of the place," he said. "It's amazing."

Addie looked around the house. "Yeah," she said. "Yeah, it's impressive."

She sat down on the couch and pulled her large, boxy purse into her lap. Charles tried not to see in her red eyes that she had already walled herself off. He stood away from the couch and leaned against the top of an armchair across the living room.

"Can I get you some food? Water? They keep the place stocked with groceries and wine. I can open a bottle."

"No, I'm fine. Maybe a water," she said. Her voice caught and Addie brought a hand up to her face. "Sorry, it's just, you're really not happy to see me at all. I knew you wouldn't be, but I thought . . . "

Charles sat down on the couch, but Addie stiffened and pulled away from him.

"No, no," she said. "That's why I came out here. I needed to see it in your eyes. Not over phone or video but actually face to face."

This was it. Everything was happening right now, and Charles was not ready. He assumed they'd wait until morning or maybe a full day would go by before she called him out, demanded some sort of reckoning.

"Things aren't that bad," he said. "We can work on it. I'm making some amazing progress out here."

"Don't even try it." Addie let out a disgusted, angry sigh. "You were never good at spinning people."

She pulled her phone out, opened her email and pulled up a photo. She handed it to Charles and quickly brought her hands back.

The photo showed the outside of this house at night. A time stamp in the corner said 3:15 AM. Olivia, looking very comfortable with her hair pulled up and her clothes rumpled, was leaving the house, and Charles wore the stupid, shit-eating grin of an oversexed teenager.

He looked at Addie. "Who . . . "

"I don't know who sent it. I don't care. Probably her husband. I'd like to thank whoever it was for speeding this up."

Charles closed the photo and looked at the email address: *driverXOXO*. "This is bad," he said.

Addie laughed, angry and disgusted. "You think?"

"No, no, this is . . . " Charles looked around the house, wondering if there were cameras. He went to the window and looked outside.

"Don't try to make this a 'privacy' thing. You got caught."

Charles turned around and leaned back on the front door. It was difficult to put everything in order. Addie was here. Addie deserved an answer, but now he was retracing his steps, wondering what he had been caught on the record saying. Wondering what he had been caught on the record promising.

He had attributed Olivia's dire warnings to her paranoia. Thompson's warnings he had attributed to his jealousy and greed. But a man sitting in front of his house with a camera was solid.

"Who is she?" Addie asked.

His mind spun. "My boss' wife, but no, no it's not what it looks . . . "

"Don't you dare say that."

Charles shook his head. "Wait, give me a second here." He covered his face with his hands and dug his fingertips into his eyes until he saw stars. After he removed his hands, Addie was blurry but incandescent with rage.

"I messed up. But listen to me, listen to me, they're not building an airport out here. It's a casino, and there's going to be lots of money and I was trying to get involved."

"By fucking your way in?" Addie got to her feet and hooked her purse over her shoulder. "I can't be here."

"She wanted help leaving her husband."

"You're involved with something crazy. I don't know what it is. I don't know *who* she is. But you've been trying to worm your way into something crazy and you never even told me."

"Everything has happened very fast."

Addie caught her breath and shook her head. "You're not coming back with me. You're not coming back to the house."

"I was going to get us out of debt."

Addie grabbed her suitcase and moved towards the door with such purpose Charles had to step out of the way. She looked over her shoulder and said, "Why on earth would they want to bring *you* in?"

Then she was gone, and Charles was alone with that question, the same one Olivia had asked, ringing in his ears.

# WEDNESDAY

# FORTY

GABE SPENT TWENTY MINUTES reassembling Micah's room. Helen had relented. She said he could pick Micah up that afternoon. Two nights. Two nights with his son.

He used a rubber mallet to straighten out the bent table leg, threw out the lamp he had broken and did his best with everything else. Most of the pages he wrote were wrinkled but still readable.

He spread his work and the info about his mother out on the card table. He had barely slept, and now the sun was up and the light through the window made everything he knew about her look even thinner. Micah needed to know this.

Rey had brought over two newspaper clippings, each only a few paragraphs long, and a copy of a page from a book. No pictures or anything personal. It was like reading an encyclopedia entry about someone who died two hundred years ago.

Gabe used the eraser end of a pencil to move the documents. *A local, unheralded civil rights leader passed away on Thursday. . . . Celsa Chávez, sixty-seven years old, passed away at her home in Pecos. . . . Many of her neighbors did not know about Chávez's work in the mid-1970s . . . Chávez never married and never had children. Friends recalled that she valued her privacy.*

Gabe had spent the night reading the articles and then falling back into bed until an ache in his chest led him back into Micah's room, where he read the articles again. This was not a mother. At best, it was a collection of shadows and fragments that had broken off of her life to be spat out by a stranger. This woman was a pile of words, and Gabe did not know how to reconstruct her into a mom who had left him, found a cause to believe in and then chose to die alone.

Gabe would be different. He would not die alone. He would not leave Micah with these questions. Maybe Micah would dislike the answers, but he would know exactly who his father was. He went downstairs and counted the money. The $1,300 was boosted by an extra $200 Rey gave him when he brought over his truck and the clippings. Pity cash.

Tight, but with some luck Gabe could swing it. He left the cash in the bowl and wrote Helen a check for a grand. The bank was already closed, so he would deposit the cash the next day. Gabe chewed his lip, an old habit he had outgrown years ago. This was good. He had raised enough money. He had won. Gabe looked around the house. It did not feel like winning.

⌒⊙ ⌒⊙ ⌒⊙

Every time Gabe pulled into Helen's driveway, one of her gray-haired neighbors was out watering the lawn. They always gave him a dirty look.

Helen was waiting, looking ready to be disappointed.

"I swear that truck's the only thing louder than your bike," she said.

Gabe hopped out holding the check. "Yeah, but it's not my bike."

Helen took the check. When she was skeptical, her eyebrows dived towards each other. "Thank you," she said. "I don't have to worry about depositing this, right? I can do that on my phone right now, you know."

Gabe opened his mouth in protest but then snapped it shut. "I'm depositing the cash in the morning."

Helen bit her tongue when Micah came out of the house carrying two big duffle bags. It looked like he had packed for a week.

"Hey, man, that's a lot of bags. Going to leave some stuff with me?"

Micah slid past his mom and tossed the bags into the back of the truck. "No, it's just, I don't know, Mom thought I should bring some things." He disappeared back inside.

"You were supposed to have this taken care of," she said.

"I do. I do."

"'Depositing the cash in the morning is not taking care of it. Why didn't you just bring the cash?"

"I was afraid of losing it."

Helen looked confused. "You don't even know how to be an adult, do you?"

"I'm trying."

Micah came out with a small suitcase. His eyes kept flicking between Gabe and his mom. "Man, you're loading up the wagon train, aren't you?" Gabe said.

"Sheets," Helen said. "Some soap, towels, a few groceries."

Gabe shook his head. "No, no, that's okay. I bought all that stuff. Everything. Dish soap. New sponges. Little air freshener things you plug into the wall. Got it."

"I'm sure you did, I'm sure the house looks just great, but he's already packed. And his video games are in there. That's really all he needs."

Micah tossed the suitcase into the back. "Nice truck," Micah said. "When'd you get it?" He meant, *Thank God, it's not the bike,* but Gabe smiled anyway.

"Thanks for not bringing the Harley," Helen whispered. Gabe felt something give down deep inside.

"Did you see the video I'm in? Online? It's being watched a lot. I'm making T-shirts, figured I'd cash in."

Helen yelled over her shoulder. "Go ahead and get in the truck, sweetie." She waited until Micah climbed inside before turning back to Gabe. "Look, I'm letting him go with you because he wants to, but you need to be real sharp. Don't do anything dumb."

"I'm going to make this work."

"That's easy to say."

"I mean it."

"It's easy to mean."

"Things are changing. I found my mom," Gabe said. "Well, Rey found her for me."

It took Helen a second to react. "Oh. Oh, wow. Where is she?"

"Nowhere now. But she was living in Pecos. No family, nothing, all by herself."

"She sounds like you."

"I'm not like that. She avoided me. I've been trying with Micah."

"I know you think you're trying, but it's not enough. You have to actually be in his life."

"Look," Gabe put his hands on his hips and dropped his eyes to the ground, "you were right. Years ago, I could have changed. Should've done it, absolutely. But I decided not to and spent years feeling like it was too late. Now it almost is."

"I didn't want you to change. I wanted you to focus."

"I'm giving this one more shot with Micah. It'll work this time."

Helen folded her arms and looked worried. "Gabe, I have no idea what you're talking about, but you're putting way too much pressure on this visit. It's a long weekend, that's all. He's already scared this isn't going to go well. He's worried you'll flake on him."

"But I didn't. I'm here."

"That's my point, getting this far isn't enough."

Gabe looked back. Micah was in the truck watching them. Gabe waved. His son lifted his hand and undid his seatbelt. Gabe realized Micah thought the visit was over. He was ready to give up. Gabe turned to Helen.

"I don't know how to do any of this, and I'm an idiot," he said. "But I got to start somewhere."

# FORTY-ONE

THE AQUARIUM WAS EMPTY. Even the iron-jawed receptionist was gone and all the side offices were dark except for Jordan's and Salazar's. Charles turned on the light in his office. A handful of pens and a coffee mug borrowed from Lou sat in the center of the desk. Everything else had been tossed out; even the computer was gone. Charles dropped his bag on the desk, grabbed the mug and headed across the bullpen. Olivia's and Addie's twin warnings had been echoing all night. Why him? Between those alarm bells and wondering if he would see Addie again, sleep became a fantasy he accidentally stumbled into around four in the morning.

Somewhere in the night, a plan developed. Actually, it was less of a plan, maybe a desperate hope. Talk to Salazar, tell her the truth about the Apaches and Christine Morales, negotiate some kind of payout. Three months' salary. Six? Something to keep him floating until something else came along. His constant companion: something better on the horizon.

Charles almost threw the mug against the wall. Salazar's office was empty. It was stripped of everything but the generic office furniture. Even the smiling blonde kids in the picture frames were stock photos. He pictured her disappearing into the mountains with a suitcase brimming over with hundred dollar bills and Charles' guts. He looked back across the bullpen. Only one other person was there.

Jordan slowly, reverentially, placed her stuff into cardboard boxes. She had taken each postcard and campaign sign off the wall and neatly stacked them on the desk. This was a ritual for her, an emotional ceremony.

"Things seem different around here." Charles tried to stay light. "Can't quite put my finger on it."

Jordan jumped, she took her earbuds out and looked up at him like she'd been caught. "Sorry, I didn't think you were coming in today, didn't think anyone was."

"Even Salazar's office is empty, stripped to the bone."

"No real need for us to have all this space. They hired a couple outside accounting firms to balance the books, and then there's, well, you know, your side."

Charles sat down across from her desk. "I don't think I do know. What is my side? I don't know how to run construction."

Jordan stopped packing and looked at Charles, confused. "I thought you negotiated all that. Diana hasn't been looping me in on a lot lately. Didn't even know about the settlement until this morning."

Charles sighed. "They're starting construction again?"

"The Apaches withdrew their claim yesterday."

Charles couldn't hide his shock. Branch must have taken Christine's deal. "Do you know how much it cost? Were there changes to the underlying terms?"

Jordan shrugged her shoulders.

"Do either of us know what's going on around here?" he asked.

Jordan picked the tape off the back of her postcards. "I'm sure everything's fine. I'm meeting with Diana tomorrow to talk about what's next."

"So you're sticking with her."

"There's another election coming up. She says there's always room for me."

Salazar must have seen something of herself in Jordan—the smarts, the strategy, the energy—something she wanted to keep nearby. Jordan was being groomed. One day, she would blink and realize she was in charge.

"You know," he said, "I think you should start looking for something different. Go to Solís' people, maybe. Get out of here. I should have turned around right away."

"What are you talking about? You're getting a new gig. You're going to be right there with Mr. Branch. They love you."

"That's what I was telling myself too," Charles said, somewhat embarrassed. "Look, I'm an asshole, and every bad thing you think about me is true, but listen to me when I tell you to be careful. I'm sure you've heard whispers here and there that make you nervous. You need to watch out."

Jordan picked up the mug Charles had placed on her desk. "Is this Lou's?"

"Yeah. I'm heading back to DC soon, so why don't you hold onto it?"

Charles walked out of the office, wondering if she heard his warning and knowing he was starting to sound a lot like Olivia.

ↅ ↅ ↅ

Making his way towards the Plaza, Charles felt a breeze in the air and allowed the stream of tourists to carry him along. On the walk, he called Thompson. It took too long to convince him to meet, but Thompson relented.

The next call was to Addie. He called twice before she answered.

"I don't think there's much to say," she warned. "I'm heading back to DC tomorrow morning. It was the first flight I could get. We can do the rest over email."

"Meet me, please. I'm going to sit down with Thompson and I want you to hear about how things work out here."

"I don't want to catch up with a friend of yours. I don't want to see you."

Charles cut down an alleyway on the outskirts of the Plaza. Blank, featureless adobe walls loomed on both sides of him, and his voice echoed strangely on the phone. He said, "Look, I know I've messed up and I need to get out before it gets worse. Thompson knows the score out here and he can help explain what happened."

"You're sleeping with another woman. Don't turn this into some grand conspiracy."

"Look, I tried to reach for something I shouldn't have, and they're punishing me. I want to go back with you. I need to go back. Thompson can help me explain."

"What did you do out here?"

"I'm still trying to figure all that out, but I need to get out of New Mexico," he said. "Come meet me in the Plaza, please."

Addie was silent for a full thirty seconds, long enough for Charles to emerge from the alley and onto a sidewalk of vendors selling jewelry from blankets. Tourists cheerfully handed over stacks of twenties.

"I'll give you fifteen minutes," Addie said.

# FORTY-TWO

OLIVIA WISHED MALLON WOULD MOVE. They were sitting in the guardhouse, about to call Cody. She wanted to pace and to chew her thumbnail while waiting, but Mallon sat still.

They had spent the night in the guardroom, pacing, talking through what they knew. It took hours for Olivia to convince him that she was only looking for enough to start over. When Mallon told her he only wanted everything to be normal, she believed him right away. Just before dawn, Mallon dragged his cot across the front door. Olivia moved some keyboards and slept on a table for two hours.

After waking, Mallon had gone to visit Thompson, Charles' only other ticket out of Santa Fe. Cody had already prepared a file on him, so Mallon thought it would be a quick visit. She almost expected Mallon to come back with drops of blood on his collar. When he returned, he was calm, collected. They were shutting down Charles' reasons for staying in New Mexico.

Olivia thought Charles should thank her, but somehow she doubted that would happen.

Now, it was time to call Cody.

Mallon's eyes became dark and he set his chin in an angry, martial pose. Olivia pictured Janice and Cody packing, drinking mimosas and laughing at their unlikely reunion. Guilt crept in, but she brushed it away. Cody and Janice could have their lives together, but she needed her piece first.

"Sir," Mallon stood up so fast he almost knocked his chair over, "We have an emergency."

Olivia could not hear Cody's response, which meant he was not berating his "kid" for the interruption. It meant he was in a good mood.

"I'm sorry it's so early, sir. However, this is a fast-moving situation, and I wouldn't call unless I absolutely needed to. It's O'Connell and Mrs. Branch, they're trying to pull something."

Olivia tried to lock eyes with Mallon, encourage him that they were doing the best thing for everyone, that it would hurt Cody today but position him better tomorrow. "Like yanking a rotten tooth," Mallon had said about her plan. Now, he looked hesitant.

"I know you're aware of their activities, sir, but you don't know about this. O'Connell is threatening to expose everything. Says he'll go to the press, the FBI, anyone who'll listen."

Olivia heard Cody's laughter through the phone. Mallon continued, "Of course, he doesn't have any proof, but he says he's been recording conversations, and Mrs. Branch has been helping him. He played me a tape over the phone, sir. It doesn't sound good. He wants to talk to you directly."

Now the rage. Olivia felt her chest tighten. Cody's rages could level mountains. For a day, he had been happy, and now she was taking that from him. Mallon was quiet. He let Cody exhaust himself.

"I will, sir." Mallon paused. "I agree. I'm afraid so. Yes, I do know where he is." Mallon hung up and looked at Olivia as if she were holding a gun to his head. "It worked."

"Like a rotten tooth."

Mallon nodded. "Grab your bags. We can't be here. He's calling in the rest of the guys. Give it twenty minutes and then make *your* call. Is that everything?"

"Cody's not leaving? Did you get what you wanted?"

Mallon crossed to the door. "Not yet. I have to grab O'Connell."

"Are you going to take him to my husband?"

Mallon did not turn around. "No, I can't do that. Mr. Branch expects O'Connell to have tapes, evidence. He needs to leave before your husband gets to him. Thompson won't give him any money, so the wife will have to."

"After those photos you sent, I doubt she's feeling like investing in him right now."

"If he goes to Thompson, then he should be scared enough to go straight to the airport. I can convince him myself if I need to."

Olivia shook her head. "Poor Charlie. Maybe he'll actually learn a lesson."

"He doesn't seem like that type."

Olivia smiled. "No, no he's not."

# FORTY-THREE

CHARLES FOUND A BENCH near the old stone column in the center of the plaza. Tourists walked circles around him, snapping pictures. He wanted to sneer, make them look at the pictures later and regret not noticing that harried guy trying to stitch his life back together.

He saw Addie enter the plaza before she saw him. There were dark circles under her eyes, and her hair was pulled back in a thin ponytail. Finally, she zeroed in on him, and they found each other in the crowd, the way lovers are supposed to do. For the merest fraction of a second, it was a reflex really, she looked happy to see him, then the wind blew that expression off her face. She did not sit down.

"I don't want to be doing this out here." She looked around. "I shouldn't have come."

"Look, this city, this state isn't normal. Thompson knows it better than anyone. All this will make more sense once he gets here."

"Charlie, you slept with the woman in that photo. I don't need to hear local gossip."

"My boss' wife was trying to get me to help her expose some of the corruption around here." Charles reached for his ringing phone. "This is Thompson. He's going to explain." He pressed the phone to his ear. "I need your help. I need a drink."

"Is that your wife with you?" Thompson asked. "What the hell's she doing out here?"

Charles looked around the plaza. "Where are you? You're going to need to tell her what it's like out here. All the dirt."

Thompson sighed. "Look behind you. See that drugstore there? Kind of old-timey? Let's get a milkshake."

Charles scanned the buildings around the square and spotted the "Apothecary." A chalkboard out front advertised cold soda and hot fudge.

"Are you kidding me? I want a drink not a postcard."

"It's nice and cool in here."

Charles hung up and looked at Addie. "He wants to get a milkshake." She rolled her eyes and turned around.

"Wait, wait," Charles said. "Five minutes. If you're going to leave me, then leave me in five minutes."

Addie readjusted her shoulder bag and walked towards the pharmacy. Charles followed.

Thompson was sitting on top of a small, round stool at the end of a long Formica bar. Charles took a seat next to him but Addie stayed standing. Clusters of families moved through the store pawing magnets and Billy the Kid T-shirts.

"You're out of your mind," Charles said. "What is this place?"

"It's quiet and they make good milkshakes. I'm serious. I got one coming." Thompson put an arm around Addie's shoulders and brought her against him a little too tight. "Surprise seeing you out here."

Addie cracked a small smile. "I've only got a few minutes."

Thompson leaned over the bar to get the soda jerk's attention. The poor guy wore a starched white, short-sleeve shirt and a little paper cap.

"No, we're really okay." Charles waved the server away.

Thompson reached down and adjusted his belt, which only drew attention to his gut. His grin faltered but did not disappear. He turned to Addie. "This place is a hundred years old. Older. You know what happened here? Upstairs. The guy who killed Trotsky stayed here just before going down to Mexico to do the deed. True story."

Charles pounded his palm on the counter. "I need you to tell Addie about how things are done out here. The doom and gloom you gave me last week. Then I'll tell you some very, very important information."

Thompson pulled his mouth back into a frog-like frown and shook his head. "Maybe I don't want to hear what you've got to say."

"You do, you really do. But first tell Addie about Branch and Salazar." The kid brought Thompson a strawberry milkshake in a tall, cold glass.

Thompson smiled at Addie in pity. He faced forward, stirred the milkshake with his spoon and shot a quick glance towards the front of the store. He said, "Your husband is working for two very powerful people. Very rich. Very, very rich and getting richer by the minute. And you don't get that rich, that fast without pushing a few legal boundaries."

Addie set her bag on a stool and looked at Charles. "You know you can't afford to deal with people like this."

"You're right, it got out of hand, but this was my chance to head home with a real stake out here." Charles turned to Thompson. "That's what I want to talk to you about. There's been big movement, and I was hoping you'd pay for some information."

Addie interrupted. "Whoa, what are you doing?"

Thompson scooped some ice cream into his mouth. "My fault. I gave him some cash last week. He's not the only one who gets a bit . . . blinded."

He looked around the drugstore again.

"You expecting someone?" Charles asked.

"Hey, I'm here to say goodbye. I would prefer it if people didn't, you know, see us talking right now."

"That can't matter. Why would that matter? No one knows me."

"I bet you still think that's true."

Addie grabbed her bag. "I'm leaving. Charlie, if this was some trick to get me to stay, then I don't know how it was supposed to work."

"Neither of you are listening," Charles caught himself and lowered his voice. "I know what they're doing, and your clients need to hear this. Isn't that what you wanted from me?"

"What I want," Thompson stabbed his spoon into his milkshake, "is for this project to have never even started. More than that, I wish I had never even heard of airplanes. I'd be safer now running through the desert, throwing a spear at an angry, metal, god-bird."

"I don't understand."

"No," Thompson snapped. "You don't. And maybe I should have warned you louder but I didn't think you'd need that kind of coaching." Thompson pushed the milkshake away so hard it almost toppled over. He pressed his thick fingers against his eyes.

"A few days ago, all I wanted was your inside track. You tell me the whole thing will become yet another half-built ghost town on the edge of the city, then I get my clients out. You tell me all is well, that they're letting the Apaches build a casino next door, letting San Miguel have the parking and Cinnabon revenue, then I would have steered my clients accordingly. That was my dream."

Charles took a deep breath. "I want another check. More consulting fees. Fifty grand."

"You're crazy," Addie said. "You need real help."

Thompson massaged his temples with the thumb and fingers on one hand, forming a clamp around the front of his skull.

"These are our options, aren't they?" Thompson said. "Grind ourselves down like Hawley until we're not even recognizable as humans, or jump ship and get rich and fat like me."

"It's time for me to get my share." Charles whispered, but the anger kept searing his voice. "I've been neck deep in the electoral shit for years. Kids I hired as interns are managing winning senate campaigns. The other day I saw a 'political analyst' on CNN. He was a damn coffee boy on my house race in California. I got steered onto a treadmill and everyone else is . . . "

"Man, after Delaware you should have . . . "

"No, do not tell me what I should have done. I never sold out. I never picked an empty suit and a great smile. The one time, the one time I chose the easy win? I almost go to jail. The one time I chose a corporate assignment, I end up trying to keep my voice down in a drugstore. I deserve to come out of this with something valuable. It's not going to be connections, it's not going to be power, so it's going to be money."

Thompson cast his eyes down, like a scolded child. He smiled and lifted his head, clasping a hand on Charles' shoulder. He looked at Addie and sighed.

"Okay. This morning. Early. I'm alone in the office and I receive a visit from one of Cody Branch's . . . " Thompson stopped to find the right word. "Guys. One of his very large, very scary, guys. The main guy actually. He delivers messages. I mean that literally. He carries folders and hand-delivers them to the governor or whoever, but never me."

Charles' foot was still shaking. The adrenalin was short-circuiting his blood. He knew it had to have been Mallon.

Thompson dropped his eyes again. He tapped the side of his fist on the counter. "This guy told me that you would be reaching out to me. He told me that you would have something for me. And then he told me that if I took what you were offering, well, then he didn't say anything at all. Instead, he showed me a list of every client I have ever worked with. Now, that's not a state secret, but there are privacy issues at stake. You can't just go to my website and get a list of two hundred clients, but he had that list."

"It was a threat?" Charles asked. "To stay away from me?"

"I shouldn't even be here. And I prayed, literally, I mean that, I prayed you wouldn't call. The big guy said you'd be desperate, and here you are, with another scheme."

Addie put her hands over her face. "Charlie, what have you done?"

"I'm trying to help all of us," he said. "It's not an airport, it's . . . "

"Please," Thompson interrupted. "Right now, I go back to not knowing what's happening. If I'm lucky, and I'm obviously not, maybe my clients believe me. Maybe I don't have to see that brick of a man again." Thompson dropped a five-dollar bill on the bar and slid off his stool. He glanced at Charles and Addie but kept breaking eye contact. "If *you're* lucky, and you're obviously not, you go home and get a quiet job. And then you thank the Lord that, despite your best efforts to prove otherwise, you are not Jim Hawley."

Thompson put his hand on Charles' shoulder and gave Addie a weak smile. He left them in the drugstore next to a sticky milkshake glass.

# FORTY-FOUR

GABE WAS IN TROUBLE. He and Micah were not even making small talk. The kid had one ear bud in and was staring straight ahead. Gabe made the quiet even more painful by occasionally reading out the text on highway billboards.

They passed a man walking on the side of the highway with his thumb out. Any other day, especially driving someone else's truck, Gabe would have slowed down and told him to hop in the back. The man wore a big backpack with a metal frame. Hanging from it was cookware, a sleeping bag and a canteen. Gabe had forgotten all about Micah's trip.

"So you're going camping," Gabe said. "I've got some old blankets you can take. Some pots and pans I can dig up."

Micah shook his head: "Well, it's not like how you do camping. There's a dining hall, barracks, you know."

"Oh, that's okay. It's still fun, right?"

"Should be."

Gabe itched for a cigarette. "And it's a church thing, too. Didn't you say that? Like, priests and whatever?"

Micah sunk lower in his seat and looked out the window. "It's a youth group. Service-oriented. You never did that?"

"Stuff like that didn't happen back in my day. If you were out in the woods with a priest, it'd be because he didn't want anyone to hear you scream." Gabe started laughing at his own joke before catching a glimpse of Micah's disgusted expression. He coughed, reached for a cigarette, put the pack back in his shirt and regripped the wheel.

"Things aren't like that anymore," Micah said.

"I know, I know." Gabe shrugged his shoulders. "Bad joke."

"It's a service camp. We learn how to help people. Half the time we spend with kids who have developmental problems. We drive into town to visit retirement homes, feed the homeless."

"That's camping?"

"Sure, yeah, why not?"

Gabe bit his lower lip and looked straight ahead. "Okay," Micah said, "most people think it's cool."

Gabe opened his eyes wide and agreed. "Right, yes, it is. I'm impressed. I'm just confused. When I was your age, I was getting drunk and riding dirt bikes through wheat fields. Where'd all this come from?"

Micah turned red and looked out the window. "It's what I like to do."

Gabe knew the kid was used to being congratulated for stuff like this, but the shock was too much for Gabe. What if he had stuck around? Worked things out with Helen all those years ago? He would have messed the kid up. Micah was better without him.

They drove the rest of the way in silence.

&#x1f650; &#x1f650; &#x1f650;

Micah did not seem impressed by the house. Most people looked curious, at least. The kid only seemed unsettled, like it was a roller coaster he could not admit was scary.

"Been a while since you've been here," Gabe said. "Remember it much?"

Micah nodded. "Yeah, for sure. It's the house. I remember it with a nicer lawn."

"Well, smartass, your mom was the gardener. Let's get your bags inside. I hope you know how to hook up that video game thing."

Gabe hopped out of the cab, but his ankle filled with hot nails. He sat down on the edge of the truck's doorframe, one foot in the dust and the other hanging beside it like an injured paw. He wanted to reach down and rub his ankle, but his back would not cooperate.

Micah was waiting by the front door with his bags. "You okay?"

Gabe blew out a deep breath. "Yeah. Ankle started to hurt fierce. Let me toss you the keys."

"No, the door's open."

Gabe nodded and waved Micah in. He took another breath and, bracing himself on the truck door, stood up. The pain went white, then started to fade. He needed to get inside, wanted to leave the pain outside.

Gabe took a few deep breaths then stood and grabbed the last bag in the bed of the truck.

By the time he got into the front living room, his ankle pain was gone. Frederick was there. He sat on the couch, smiling and nodding along to music coming out of Micah's earbuds. Micah was standing in front of him. Frederick was holding the ear bud just outside of his own ear.

"This is not a good song," Frederick said. "The bass distorts everything. You think that's good?"

"They're called Bass Demons. That's their sound."

"What are you doing here?" Gabe asked.

This was not Frederick's style. It was too early in the day and he never waited for anyone.

Frederick shook his head. "No, sorry, the producer messed this up. They pushed the bass up and forward in the speakers and buried everything else. There could be chainsaws back there for all you know."

"Okay, okay," Micah said. "Here, this one is a lot more mellow."

Gabe came up behind Micah and pulled him away from Frederick. Micah almost stumbled in surprise.

"Whoa, hey, what's up?" Micah asked.

"Now's not a very good time for me," Gabe said to Frederick. "My son is here."

Gabe caught a strong scent of weed in the air. A trash bag sat on the coffee table. He had hidden the marijuana upstairs in his bedroom—near his guns. Frederick had found it and packed it up. Gabe wondered when Micah would catch the smell.

"Oh, but we've got things to talk about." Frederick sounded hurt. "I'd like it if the boy was here for this conversation."

"Micah," Gabe pointed upstairs. "Why don't you go get settled?"

"For real? I just walked in and you're sending me to my room?"

"He's going to make me a playlist," Frederick said. "Aren't you, son?"

Micah shrugged. "If you want, but I'm putting Bass Demons on it."

"I'll give almost anything a second chance."

Gabe knew Frederick would find out eventually, but he hoped it would be after Gabe grew visibly ill. Who would hurt a sick man or a sick man's son? Gabe caught a glimpse of the trio in the round mirror above the TV. He did not look sick. He looked like the kind of loser who would scam his friends.

Frederick motioned towards the seat next to him. Gabe sat down, eyes on Micah. Frederick tracked his gaze, and they both stared at the kid.

"I was going to call you," Gabe said, "explain a few things."

Micah's eyes flicked their way, then back to his phone. He sat cross-legged against the wall. It made him look about ten years old.

"I got a call yesterday," Gabe said. "We're starting construction again. So, I'll have some extra money soon."

"Pay off some bills?"

"Yeah, I know I've got a few."

"A few," Frederick repeated. "I don't have a lot of friends, Gabe. Just a few. I don't think anyone has a lot of friends. Not when it matters. Some people may be more popular, more well known. You, for example, are very well known." Frederick leaned forward and got Micah's attention. "Son, do you know how well known your father is right now?"

"Ugh, that video," Micah said without looking up from his phone. "No one knows that's my dad, thank God."

Frederick laughed. Gabe's throat closed up. "Well, it is a bit embarrassing," Frederick said.

Gabe felt like the man could hear his thoughts and sniff out his fear. His chest constricted and he could barely catch his breath.

"It's not an embarrassing video because of what you say," Frederick said, "but because you can't do *anything* now and not be recognized. Oh, in a week there'll be some other internet idiot and you'll be forgotten. But, right now, I bet you didn't have any idea how famous you are."

Gabe could only exhale and nod.

Frederick turned back to Micah. "Son, your dad ever say this one to you? 'I'm not mad, just disappointed.'"

Micah laughed. "Ha, no, not him. My mom loves that one. Teachers too. It doesn't even mean anything. We laugh when they say it."

"It means something when I say it."

Micah caught the rising tension in the room. He looked to Frederick and then to Gabe before standing. "I'll go unpack."

Frederick waved Micah over. "Before you go, help me up."

Micah came to the couch and took Frederick's hand then, in a spin move, Micah was sitting on the couch and Frederick was standing next to him, with his hand on the back of Micah's neck.

Actions flipped through Gabe's head. A quick shove to Frederick's shoulder. Yank Micah forward and away. Back door.

He knew none of that would happen. Frederick always carried a knife in his sleeve and a gun in his belt. Gabe could only watch Micah's eyes go wide as he realized a stranger was gripping his neck.

"What's on the table is mine," Frederick said. "I'll be taking it back. Also," he pulled a slip of paper and a pen from his shirt pocket, "you'll need to endorse this check over to me. I prefer cash, but I'm making an exception for you. You're welcome."

Frederick tossed Rose's check and the pen towards Gabe. They both landed at his feet. Gabe kept his eyes locked on Micah as he reached down to grab them. Micah's eyes started to tear up as the initial shock of Frederick's grip started to pass.

Gabe signed the back of Rose's check and dropped it onto the trash bag. "That's enough," Gabe said.

"Not quite. There was a bowl in the kitchen that was very conveniently holding some of my money as well. I helped myself. That's almost enough. We'll discuss the rest at a later date."

Frederick looked down at Micah as if seeing him for the first time. "Son, do you know what your dad does for a living?" Micah managed a small head shake. Frederick continued, "Why don't you tell him, Gabe?"

"What do you want me to say?"

"The truth."

"I don't do much. I sit around. I drive a truck on the construction site. I worked in a call center for about a year but I lost that. Lose most of them. Is that what you want?"

"That's part of it."

Gabe's jaw tightened as if he could bite back the words. He looked at Micah, only at Micah. He said, "I wanted to see you. I knew you needed help with this camp, which I'm so proud of you for going to. So, I borrowed money. And I tried to do some work . . . "

"Gabe."

"I sold some drugs. I sold weed. Not very much. Practically legal now, anyways. I wish I didn't have to, you understand?"

Micah's nod was so faint that Gabe worried he had imagined it.

Frederick took a deep breath through his nose and let it out through his mouth. "That feels good, doesn't it? Clearing the air."

Frederick sighed with satisfaction and released Micah's neck.

Gabe saw the color return to Micah's face, but the boy was still too shocked to move.

"Give me your phone," Frederick said.

Gabe reached for his cell, but Frederick waved him off. "Not you. Micah, you were going to send me a playlist and you need my contact info."

Micah reached into his pocket and pulled out his phone. Frederick took it from his hand. "I'll call my number from your phone. That way we can stay in touch. Make sense?"

Micah nodded but still kept his eyes locked on Gabe's.

"That way," Frederick said, "if I need anything from you, or you from me, it'll be a breeze."

Gabe watched Micah's eyes brim right to the top with tears. No way the kid understood what was happening, but the violence hung in the air, a stranger was touching him, and it was his father's fault. Frederick slipped the phone into Micah's pocket. He ran upstairs, the sound brought back Gabe's memories of the kid clambering up the stairs on all fours. Gabe expected a slammed door, but Micah must have caught himself and slipped it shut.

Frederick looked out the back door at the new housing development and then back to Gabe. "You could have really cashed in on this place, you know."

"My dad built it."

Frederick snorted a laugh that sounded like a sneer. Gabe noticed Frederick was holding Micah's earbuds, and the sight of his fingers rubbing the cords made him queasy. Frederick tore each earbud away from the cord and tossed the mutilated wires at Gabe's chest. Then he let himself out of the house, locking the door behind him.

# FORTY-FIVE

MALLON FOLLOWED O'CONNELL from the office to the plaza. From there, he saw Thompson give O'Connell the brush off. He was a block behind O'Connell and his wife. They were fighting, but the not-so-happy couple was about to fly away. They should be thanking him.

Branch wanted O'Connell dragged to the office. From there, Branch would order violence until O'Connell spilled his guts about the conversations Mallon had fabricated. It was nearly two years since Mr. Branch had asked him to inflict pain. Moving away from the heavy approach was part of the reforms, but Mr. Branch was willing to make an exception. Mallon would have loved to oblige him, but there were no recorded conversations, and Charles would have crumbled right away.

Mallon pushed aside all thoughts of morality or duty. O'Connell and his wife were walking down a crowded street that was about to lose half of its pedestrians, exposing Mallon too much. She must be staying in a hotel outside the plaza, he thought. The words they were shouting at each other started to come clear. *Trouble. Too far. Home.*

O'Connell needed to get on a plane. He needed to be any place where Mr. Branch could not talk to him.

Tourists stepped around the bickering couple and turned around to gawk. They stopped in front of a hotel, a cheap joint trying to pass itself off as a ski lodge. O'Connell's hands were up, pleading. She was crying.

Mallon hopped into the hotel parking lot, jogged around to the patio restaurant and took a seat near the sidewalk. He wanted to make sure Charles was smart enough to take his only way out.

"Listen to you," Addie said. "You sound like a criminal. You sound like everything you spent a year denying."

"There's so much money out here. I'm not going to ask for . . . "

"If you want to stay here and go to jail, then feel free. I am tired of bailing you out."

Mallon's fists turned to stone before he even realized it. O'Connell should not be talking about staying.

"You want me to go back with nothing?" Charles asked. "Go back *to* nothing?"

"You were supposed to come to *me*. Now, all I want you to do is beg your mom for a spare bedroom."

"These people will pay to keep me silent. I know too much. Trust me . . . each side is paranoid enough to give me . . . "

Mallon did not hear the rest of O'Connell's words. All he heard was the word *no* echoing. *No no no no no* until the echo was not just in his head, it was bouncing off the passing cars and the plate glass of the hotel lobby. The word *no* bounced off O'Connell's face as Mallon stood up, stepped between the couple and connected his knuckles to O'Connell's chin.

Charles dropped like a stone. Then, Addie was at his side, repeating that same word. *No, no, no.* Charles blinked, not yet seeing but realizing something terrible had happened.

"No," Mallon screamed. "No, I gave you a chance." Mallon brought his fist down into Charles' nose. "Leave. Leave. Leave."

Addie flung herself out of Mallon's way and almost rolled into the street. Cars honked, and Mallon registered an increase in noise and maybe some lights. People were looking at him, watching him do harm, and it was all O'Connell's fault.

"This was your chance." Mallon's fist connected again. "I tried to help you."

Mallon pulled back again, then a clamp was applied to his right bicep and someone's foot went into the back of his knee.

"No," Mallon said. He tried to push himself up. "I am a state trooper, and this man was attempting to extort money from . . . " Then, a knee was on his neck and another was on his arm, and then red and blue lights showed O'Connell being tended to. Mallon went quiet and shut the world out. He would not let the world come back until he was home with Claudia.

# FORTY-SIX

CODY'S SAFE HELD STACKS of bound hundreds, but Olivia was not satisfied. Janice had been right. The son of a bitch still used her birthday as his combination. Well, Olivia thought, the once and future Mr. and Mrs. Branch deserved every second of the torture they would inflict on each other.

The safe was small, holding only the stack of cash and a few documents, including the title to her car. She counted out the money. $160,000. Not what she expected, but enough for her, Andrea and the kids to get a good head start. Taos? Boulder? They could go anywhere. She slammed the safe shut.

She called Cody. This moment—the moment when she called her husband and told him she was leaving, that she was taking what she deserved—had played in her head for months. In the past, she assumed she would be nervous, apologetic, on the verge of tears. Instead, she was grinning ear to ear.

Cody did not answer until the third time she called. "Let me guess," he said, "trouble at the ATM?"

His tone tripped Olivia up. He sounded pleased with himself.

"I was calling with something you'll need to hear."

"Oh, lucky me," he sneered. "Thank you for your concern. You're not calling on behalf of your broke boyfriend? Your broke self?"

"You're the one running off with an ex," she said. "When did all that start?"

"Not running off. Rectifying a mistake. When *did* this start?" Cody went quiet. Janice murmured in the background. A pang went through Olivia's chest. Not jealousy. More like pity.

Cody came back on the line. "It's been about six months, we think. You know, she's the one who convinced me to answer your call."

Janice had first reached out to Olivia six months ago; building up her trust and reeling her in.

"You two are going to drive each other crazy," Olivia said. "You both know it's not going to end well."

"Your concern brings a tear to my eye. She kind of likes you. Says you two have done some chatting."

Olivia lowered the phone and tried to stay calm. This is what he did. She had watched it happen for ten years. Cody drew people in and poked them until they swung at him—handing over all their high ground.

"I'm going to trade you some information for some cash," Olivia said.

Cody laughed, loud and angry. "I'll unlock your bank accounts when your boyfriend comes to meet me. I know all about O'Connell's little scheme and his recordings. You two were clever, but . . . not really."

"What did you do to my bank accounts?"

Olivia's accounts were in her name only, but she supposed having built the bank president's house and half his branches might have earned Cody some favors.

"You're so good at keeping a straight face," Branch said. "I looked you right in the eye when you brought me his resume and didn't see a thing. When'd you meet him?"

"You haven't looked me in the eye for a year."

Olivia turned on her call recorder. "I need something from you," she repeated.

"Get in line, sister. I've got nothing left to give. What the Apaches didn't steal from me is tucked away tight. You're not getting a dime. Everyone gets their tiny little checking accounts back when I get my hands on O'Connell."

"I don't know where he is. Besides, maybe I don't need that bank account. I found more in your safe."

"The safe? Your deviousness is evil incarnate. It'd turn me on if I weren't going to kill you first."

"I'm taking my car. I'm taking the 160k I found in the safe. And then, I want another $150,000 a year, starting next year, for the next five years. I'm cheap. I just want out."

"That's a lot more than the pre-nup you signed. Girl, you're done. You get nothing."

"You know I won't take that for an answer."

"He's really not there with you, is he?"

"He's not." Olivia stepped into the hallway and waved at the camera. "You know he's not. I don't know where he is. Don't particularly care."

"What a lovely wave. I'd love to break your arm. Tell your boyfriend when he meets me at the office, he'll get his life back. The wife too. I can't decide if I'm going to have a go at him or let Mallon have all the fun."

Olivia closed her eyes. Charles had better be running.

"I'm going to email you a document," Olivia said. "You can sign it on your phone and send it back to me. Hell, Janice can sign as a witness."

"You did all the signing necessary when we got married. Whatever you and O'Connell have is worthless. Mallon's grabbing him and . . . "

"I'll tell you what's really going on," she said. "You believed Mallon when he called you. Why not believe me?"

Cody went quiet again. There was an echo on the line, and Olivia realized she was on speakerphone. Janice was probably recording too.

"What are you trying to say?"

"The truth could save you a lot of money," she said.

"Are you trying to keep me from hurting your boyfriend?"

"The fact that you think he and I are in this together proves you're clueless. You know he couldn't keep up with me."

The echo on the line disappeared, but the call was still connected. They must have put the phone on mute. They were discussing, debating. Olivia closed her eyes. It was up to Janice.

Cody came back on the line. "Why are you trying to help me? You'd leave me on the side of the road like a dead dog if you could."

"If you're a dead dog, then I lose my money."

Cody laughed. "You've learned a thing or two from me, Liv. You really really have."

"You're lost, Cody. You didn't even know about me and Charles until she told you."

Cody sighed. "One. Five. Oh. A year. That's it?"

"For five years."

"And you'll stay away from O'Connell."

"You'd have to pay me a lot more to stay with him."

"You're recording this call, aren't you? Mallon told me your boyfriend was into that too. Good idea, I suppose. Tell me what you need to tell me, Liv."

"Mallon lied to you. Charles doesn't have recorded conversations. Charles wasn't trying to blackmail you."

"What the hell are you thinking? You're trying to turn in Mallon? I'm not paying you for this."

"Mallon hated Charles since the moment they met. And also, I swear he thinks he's protecting you. He knew about me and Charles days ago. Even sent Charles' wife photos of me and him. That's why she's in town. Did he send them to *you*?"

"That man is a soldier."

"Then tell me where he is right now."

Cody's silence was so weighted it was almost painful.

"He thinks he's saving you from yourself," she said. "You're going to do something violent to Charles, and you'll end up having to pay him off. After all that, you'll still never hear any tapes because Charles didn't make any."

"If either of them play a single second of a recorded conversation . . . " Branch trailed off.

"He won't. They don't exist. Mallon and I came up with that to keep you in town."

"Am I the only one who's actually open about what he wants?" Branch asked. "I'll sign your damn papers. Send them over."

"Sending now."

Olivia's hands were shaking as she emailed the document. "You have them," she said. "I'll wait."

"I've got something funny to tell you," Branch said.

The document appeared in her email. Olivia opened the file. He had signed.

"You ready for the joke?" he asked. "Janice had convinced me to give you a payout of one million. Now, I got a C in Algebra back in high school, but I'm pretty sure that's more than what you ended up asking for."

Olivia felt a little dizzy. She swallowed her regret and said, "I don't need a million. The rich people I know hate money more than they hate themselves."

"Ah, the wisdom of the poor. I'll unlock your money, but Charlie boy and wife are fucked till I get my hands on him."

They were both quiet. The echo on the line went away. Olivia could hear birds on the other end. He must have walked outside.

"Has it been that bad?" Cody asked. "Have I gotten that bad?"

"Yeah, you have."

She hung up. For a second, guilt for what would happen to Charles pushed its way into her brain. She shook it away, flipped off the security camera one last time and began throwing her clothes into a suitcase.

# FORTY-SEVEN

CHARLES PICKED at the dried blood on the hem of his shirt. The stitches in his eyebrow ached, but not as bad as his nose. All he could smell was old blood. Addie drove them away from the hospital with steady hands, but her eyes revealed the shock.

"I just don't believe you," she said. "They will not let that man go. There were witnesses."

Charles nodded, which caused a sharp pain in the back of his neck. He took another painkiller. "He wasn't even cuffed when they drove away. He's an ex-cop, and Branch will get him out in an hour, if he hasn't already."

Addie hunched forward over the wheel, eyes on the road but with no real sense of where she was going. She muttered, "Dozens of witnesses."

"I'm sure he'll get a stiff fine," he said.

Well, Charles *had* wanted Addie to understand that the normal rules were inoperative out here.

All it cost was a nose.

"These were the people you wanted in with? These were the people you were trying to scam?" Addie's shock was giving way to anger. "What happened to you out here?"

Charles looked out the window at the trucks, the mountains, the grey hairs in their BMWs. Every car belonged to Cody Branch. Every black-haired woman was Olivia. He remained quiet until they got back to Addie's hotel.

They sat in the parking lot, scanning for Mallon and black town cars.

"I can't stay here," Addie said. "Let's get rooms in Albuquerque. Something by the airport. In the morning, we can try the police again."

"I can't go to the police."

Addie rested her forehead on the steering wheel. "The FBI, state police. If something is going on, then someone's got to listen."

"If I go to the cops, Branch and Salazar will flip this back on me. That's why they chose me to begin with. My name's on so many documents. I delivered so many messages. They'll say I was the troublemaker."

"You were."

Charles looked around the parking lot. The sun was setting and Mallon crouched in each shadow.

Addie pushed the tears off her cheeks with the side of her hand. "You invited them. Charlie, you're doing this to yourself. Your mom has bailed you out so many times that you don't even know how to . . . "

"Don't, don't bring her into this. If she'd given me that loan, I wouldn't have even needed to go to Thompson in the first place."

"*You* messed up. You did this. Now it's time for you to go back home."

"Give up. That's what you mean. Punch a clock, write press releases for the FDA." Addie flipped down the sun visor with its mirror in front of Charles.

"Look at yourself. You should be begging for a cubicle right now."

Charles' face was swollen and multi-colored. Seeing it made all the pain come back.

He tried to hold his face still, but the tears came anyway.

ϲᴥᴏ ϲᴥᴏ ϲᴥᴏ

They were almost at the edge of Santa Fe when they needed to stop for gas. Addie's debit card was rejected at the pump. Her credit card too. Charles was broke, but he knew he had enough in the bank for one tank of gas.

Declined.

Sitting in the car at the gas station, Addie called her bank and credit card companies. Her accounts were frozen. The operators were unable to tell her why.

The Albuquerque airport was ninety minutes away. Together, they had about thirty dollars in cash.

Rented sedans full of tourists cruised through the gas station. Farm trucks rusting from the inside out barreled by. A hitchhiker with a big backpack hustled for quarters. They were all moving on, away. But Charles and Addie were stuck, thanks to Mallon and Branch.

Addie refused to believe it. She kept calling different accounts, asking for higher and higher supervisors. Nothing worked.

Charles' phone buzzed. An unknown number was calling. He answered.

"This is Charles."

"You're at the Allsups near Highway 20. Stay there and Lou will bring you to me." Branch's words were stiff and blocky, as if he'd blow his mouth apart by giving expression to his rage.

"I don't think we're going to do that."

"And how far are you going to get? Come speak with me and you get your accounts back."

"Your attack dog already broke my nose."

"I'm sorry he did that. I'm dealing with him separately. Let Lou bring you to the office. We hear your recordings, then delete them, and all is forgiven."

Charles watched Addie pace along the side of the gas station, phone pressed to her ear.

"My wife . . . "

"Oh *now* you're concerned about her? She can drive away, once you're in the car. Her accounts will be turned on before you go a mile. And she gets to keep her job."

Charles hesitated.

"Want to test me?" Branch asked. "You don't think I can call a senator, who calls a third-term congressman from Virginia and tells him to fire someone? I can do that without a call. A text could ruin her. Lou is five minutes away. Stay there."

The line went dead.

Charles got out of the car and walked towards Addie. She looked to him with hope.

"It was Branch," he said. "If I go to him, we get our cards back—everything."

She shook her head. "No, no one can do something like this."

"It'll take days to undo what he did. After that, he'll go after our credit. He knows where you work."

"What does he want from you?"

"He thinks I have recordings of some kind."

Addie cocked her head. "Do you?"

"No, he's nuts. Maybe I can talk to him, convince him I'm . . . "

"These are not people you can talk to. We have to move."

Charles spread his arms and pointed around the gas station, the mountains turning purple on the horizon, the thousands of miles of forest and rocks.

"Where?" Charles shook his head. "When Lou gets here, I have to go."

# FORTY-EIGHT

GABE WALKED FROM THE BOTTOM of the stairs into the kitchen, around the living room and back again. He kept looking up at the ceiling. Micah had locked the door and not come down for hours.

Gabe went upstairs, knocked and tried the doorknob. "Hey, Micah it's me. Can you unlock this? I think we should go get some dinner."

Silence for long enough to make Gabe nervous.

"Can you let me in? Or open the door at least?" Micah could be heard rolling off the air mattress, unlocking the door and then dropping back into bed. "It's unlocked."

Gabe opened the door and looked in the room. Micah had pushed the air mattress into the corner and was sitting up against the wall. He seemed out of place and huge in this room meant for a younger kid.

Gabe pointed to the posters on the wall. "I found some of this stuff in the closet. I know it's not your style anymore but it's still yours."

Micah nodded at one of the posters. "I'd forgotten I was into those wrestlers. That was some kid stuff right there."

Micah sat up and dug through one of his bags. The contents had spilled out in soft explosions. He pulled out a phone charger and plugged it in.

"Hey, let's go somewhere. You brought your video games, right? Let's go over to Rose's. She has a son about your age."

"I don't know who Rose is."

"You'll remember when you see her. I think we should get some air."

Gabe took a step into the room. The small stack of papers he had written and the articles about his mom were still on the table under the window.

Micah lay back on the bed and got lost on his phone. "I called my mom," he said. "Left a message. She wanted me to call her if things got weird, you know?"

Gabe shook his head. "No, no, hey, you didn't need to do that. He's gone. That guy's gone. He's not coming back."

"It's fine. I bet she'll show up in a couple hours. Get me out of your way."

"Look, that was scary, but I've known that guy for years."

"I wasn't scared."

Micah's eyes were so big and watery.

Gabe sat down at the card table. "Well, I was scared. But he's gone and he's not coming back. We had a misunderstanding."

"Dad, you sold drugs. Just weed or whatever, but I can't be around that. I need a scholarship. If I get busted for something dumb, I'm screwed."

"I'm not going to let that happen."

"You blamed it on me. You did something illegal and said it was to help me."

"I needed to see you. It was the only thing I could do."

Micah shook his head. "No, no it wasn't."

Gabe looked out the window, then down at the table. Gabe was losing him. Micah was slipping through his fingers and would crash to the floor any second. But Gabe kept trying. He said, "Fine, let's call your mom. She can pick you up at Rose's, but let's get in the car. I'm buying some hamburgers, and we're going to talk." Gabe gathered the papers off the desk.

"Remember how my mom left when I was real young?"

Micah was lost in his phone again.

Gabe kept going. "Well, I asked my buddy Rey, he's a lawyer, good guy, sharp. I asked him to try to find her." Gabe waved the papers at Micah. "And he did."

Micah looked up at the papers in Gabe's hand. "My grandma? Is she still alive?"

"Grab your stuff and I'll tell you on the way to Rose's."

Micah rolled his eyes and groaned. "Whatever." He started shoving clothes into his bag.

⋘ ⋘ ⋘

If Rose was out, Gabe was screwed. He could not exactly take Micah to The Pig.

Still, he pointed the truck towards her house and crossed his fingers. "You didn't need to call your mom," Gabe said. "That guy . . . "

"Let's just talk about my grandma."

Gabe put all the pages on the dashboard. "Right there. The first few pages are about her. She died a couple years ago but had an interesting life."

"You never saw her after she left?"

"No, she kept to herself. The obituary's in there. She did civil rights work. I'm not really sure about the details. Rey can probably explain better. Something about Natives and land."

Micah's eyebrows furrowed, confused. He grabbed the stack and scanned the first page. "She sounds kind of famous. Wait, what did she do?"

Gabe shrugged. "She helped people. Tried to, for a while at least."

"This is my grandmother?" Micah read the article. "I can tell people at the camp about her. Use her as an example of good service."

"I guess I wouldn't be such a good example, huh?"

Micah didn't look up. "She sounds like you, you know? A little. Like a loner."

"Is that what I am?"

Micah looked at Gabe like he'd asked the dumbest question in the world. Gabe pulled onto Rose's street. Her car was in the driveway, and Gabe wanted to say a prayer.

Micah used his phone to take photos of each of the pages. He even took photos of Gabe's handwritten sheets, unaware of what they were.

"What are you going to do with those?" Gabe asked.

"I don't know. Think I'll post the obit online. People can help find more about her."

Gabe stopped the car in front of Rose's house. The lights were on inside, and Gabe could see a flickering TV. It looked like heaven.

Micah hopped out of the car and grabbed his bag with the video games. He already looked more comfortable. These types of houses, and what went on in them, were his landscape.

"Don't doubt the power of the internet, Dad."

"Hey," Gabe said, "at least tell me you smiled at that video of me."

Micah rolled his eyes. A small smile flashed. "I try not to think about it," he said. "It's real bad." He laughed and then shook his head.

"See," Gabe said, "we can still have fun."

Micah flung his head straight back and groaned. "Oh, no, don't do that. Don't be weird."

"What? I'm just saying we . . . "

Rose opened her front door and leaned on her door jamb. She smiled at Micah and said, "I bet you don't remember me."

She gave him a big hug that caused him to stand up straight and lean away. At the same time, she shot Gabe a glare that spoke volumes.

"So glad y'all dropped by, come in."

Rose kept her arm around Micah's shoulders and led him into the house. As ever, Gabe was a step behind.

# FORTY-NINE

MALLON ONLY KNEW one person at the station: the desk sergeant who used to work at his old precinct in the mountains. He actually smiled when he saw Mallon being escorted in, like it was some kind of joke. Then the sergeant read the situation, dropped his eyes and frowned at the paperwork.

From the start, it was clear the arresting officers had no idea what to do with Mallon. They took him down hard, then uncuffed him once someone saw his retired badge. Still, they took him in. From there, everyone got more confused. They fingerprinted him but did not take a mug shot. There were forms, but he was not processed. Mallon recognized it as the hesitant push and pull of needing to go through the motions of law enforcement. If they let him go right away, these cops would not sleep well. They walked him away from the holding cells and sat him on an office chair next to the break room.

Mallon had time to think. He had time to get angry. Their plan had a narrow path to success and O'Connell had blown it.

A few cops nodded at Mallon on the way to the coffee maker. He watched the desk sergeant try not to look his way. At this two-cell precinct near the plaza, Mallon figured, the worst crime reported was stolen skis.

O'Connell and his wife were probably finished giving statements. Getting stitches too. Mallon's knuckles were raw and one of them had split. A smart man would run. A smart man would have run days ago. Maybe the wife got the message and was dragging O'Connell to the airport right now, but Mallon somehow doubted it.

The desk sergeant was holding a plastic bag. Mallon could see his phone and car keys. His gun was in a separate bag. None of his belongings had been logged into evidence. The sergeant was talking to the younger cop, nodding his head in sympathy, understanding. The younger cop shot a quick, angry glare at Mallon, then threw up his hands and slammed through the station door. The desk sergeant walked over holding the bag. He never made eye contact as he walked past Mallon and into the break room. When the sergeant left the break room, his hands were empty.

Mallon knew he was not released. Technically, he was escaping, but no one would call it that. He slipped into the break room and picked up his phone, keys, wallet and gun. No one needed to feel guilty about letting him go because no one actually had. This was over. Mallon could go home. He could go back to the compound and hope that Mr. Branch was ready to listen.

He hooked his holster back on his belt and poured coffee into a Styrofoam cup.

⁂ ⁂ ⁂

Mallon hit the parking lot the same time as Lou's sedan pulled up. Mallon went to open the passenger door, but it was locked. Lou left the car running, opened his door and got out. Lou kept one foot in the car and talked to Mallon over the roof.

"What is this?" Mallon asked.

"What the fuck did you do?"

"Something I shouldn't have, but it's too late for that. We have to make sure O'Connell got the message."

"This isn't good, man. You're not coming back from this."

Mallon waved off the station behind him. "They didn't even charge me. There's no record this even happened."

"Lucky you, but here's what I know. I got a call from the big man fifteen minutes ago. He says you've been fired and he wants me to deliver the message."

Mallon sipped his coffee and put a hand on his hip. "I'm not fired."

"I don't think it's your call to make."

"He's not thinking clearly. I'll explain it to him."

"He shut down your car himself. Same with your access cards, phone, computer, everything."

"No." Mallon shook his head. "No. It doesn't work that way. I'm not fired."

"Look, I'm sorry, man, but this is happening."

Mallon shook his head again. Lou was wrong. Mr. Branch would let him explain. "No way he cares about what I did to O'Connell."

"It's not about O'Connell. He laughed when he heard about you punching him. It's about something between you and Mrs. Branch. Tell me you're not that dumb."

Mallon felt his whole body turn on a knife's edge. "What did he say?"

"He said that you and Mrs. Branch were lying to him, and that she sold you out."

"Tell me everything."

"It's true? Goddammit, man. That's all I know. I don't want to know any more."

Mallon looked around the parking lot. Streetlights flicked on, and his busted knuckle started to ache.

"Go home," Lou said. "Sleep. I'm picking O'Connell up right now and taking him to Mr. Branch. He'll get what he deserves."

"Give me five minutes with him."

"You had your five minutes with him. I'm supposed to take your keys."

Mallon shook his head. "That's not going to happen."

Lou slammed his palm on the roof of the car. "You attacked O'Connell. You got whatever going on with Mrs. Branch. It's over."

"I was helping."

"Well, it didn't work. Keep the keys, it doesn't matter. The car's shut down anyway." Lou raised a finger in Mallon's direction. "Go home. For your own sake."

Lou hopped into the car and drove away.

Mallon did not turn around. He was worried there would be a crowd on the station steps. He was worried there would be an old,

dirty desk sergeant watching him with folded arms and a condescending head shake.

ᥱᥩ ᥱᥩ ᥱᥩ

The sun was setting as Mallon walked back to his car. His
movements were clipped, mechanical. He waited at every light,
looked in both directions before entering an intersection and
stepped aside for each pedestrian. Each movement was precise
and clean because inside he was shaking with rage.

The car was where he had left it, but his key was useless. Lou
was right. Branch had gathered up years of service, of busted
heads and buried secrets, and tossed it into the fire. Gone.

It would take him thirty minutes to walk home. Long enough
to clear his head, breathe out his anger. Fine, let Olivia disappear.
Let Branch deal with O'Connell however he wanted. Mallon could
do that. He could go home and tell Claudia he did something stupid and trusted the wrong people. She would rub his chest and tell
him it was all right.

She would be lying.

Mallon clasped his hands together and brought them down on
the roof of the car. He did it again and again. He had let bad guys
go before. He had been the young cop pressured to look the other
way. He had let the guy in Pecos go. He had carried water for
Branch and told himself it was the lesser of two evils. He had let
go of his nightmares about war and fleas on dead dogs, and
machine guns and kids that got too close to convoys. But he
would not let this go. Branch would not get rid of him so easily.
The roof of the car started to buckle.

Mallon stood up and gulped air.

Lou said he was taking O'Connell to meet Branch. Only two
places would work for that meeting: the compound or the office.
The compound was up the mountain and secure, but the office
was a fifteen-minute walk. Mallon brushed the dirt off his hands,
touched his gun out of habit and started walking.

# FIFTY

THE CARS ON THE ROAD glowed orange and red in the sunset. Olivia kept looking in her rearview mirror. She expected to see Mallon, Cody, maybe even Janice or Charles, not their cars but actual people barreling down the highway after her, snarling and raging.

She had not felt this free since leaving Charles in Chicago, years earlier. But that whole period was tinged with failure. The failure of a marriage and of limping back to New Mexico with a stack of unfinished canvasses. This time it was not just freedom, it was liberation.

෴ ෴ ෴

Española at night looked even more depressing than during the day. When the sun was up, the eye could be distracted by the mountains, the trees in the valley, the sky. At night, all Olivia could see was the dirt and the broken windows and the people with red splotches on their faces and blue snakes crawling up their arms. Olivia did not want Andrea and the kids to stay one more night there.

She had never visited the house at night. It was a newer subdivision with an aspirational name, Rancho Vista. It was also half-empty. Olivia's stomach went sour when she thought about Andrea in this place. The houses were all dark, like missing teeth, and the few cars on the streets only heightened the emptiness.

Andrea's house was the only one with any kind of movement; a couple cars and a pickup truck loaded with furniture sat outside. A few guys were walking out of the house carrying the dining room table, the same table where Olivia had sat and assured Andrea everything would be fine.

Olivia slammed on the brakes and ran towards the house. She did not see Andrea or the kids anywhere. At some point, her keys slipped out of her hand.

"No, no, no," she yelled at the movers. "You put that back."

The guys froze and put the table down. Olivia did not recognize them. She did not see Mallon. Where was Andrea?

"I am Olivia Branch and I am ordering you to . . . "

"Girl, girl, girl, take a breath." Andrea stepped out of the house with her hands up. "It's okay, it's okay."

Olivia came to a stop in front of the house and looked at the guys, then back at Andrea. "Get away from her."

"They're my cousins," Andrea shouted so loud she started coughing. One of the men reached out a hand to steady her, and Olivia wanted nothing more than to chop the thing off.

"What is this?" she asked.

Andrea turned on her heel and went inside. Olivia followed her and shot a glare that caused the guys to back up several feet. Andrea dropped onto a recliner, still coughing. Olivia hustled into the kitchen and filled a glass with tinny tap water. Andrea's hands shook as she coughed and she spilled almost half of it out, but a few gulps were enough to calm her throat.

"We were going to surprise you," she said, her voice still raw.

Olivia looked around. Everything was boxed up. The house was too quiet.

A little desperately, she asked, "Where are the girls?"

"Look, I know you have some kind of plan, but I just couldn't take it anymore. We're going to stay with my cousin. He's got a place on the edge of town. Big yard. Extra room. It'll be good."

"No, that's not the plan. Cody agreed to pay me out. I got the cash. We can go anywhere."

Olivia handed Andrea her purse. She let out another cough when she saw the cash and then grimaced at the money as if it could slither out of the bag.

"I did it," Olivia said. "I'm gone."

Andrea smiled. "This is good news, girl. Good news."

"I know, I know." Olivia looked around again. "But this will still work. Have these guys follow us. We're definitely taking this furniture. I like that idea. We'll stay in a hotel in Los Alamos or, hell, let's all go to one of the resorts in the mountains, my treat."

Olivia watched Andrea avoid her eyes. It was one of her tells. Back in high school, Andrea would drag out the bad news and spend half the conversation staring at the ceiling.

"This is what we've been talking about," Olivia said.

"Have we? *You've* talked about this. I don't want to move anymore. You're going to end up somewhere amazing, and you'll open a gallery . . . and it's a great plan, but it's *your* plan."

Olivia smiled. It was her own tell for conversations that scared her.

She pointed at the purse in Andrea's lap. "That money is real. It is our chance to leave this place."

"You left twenty years ago, and you should have, but I never did. This is a crappy little town, but it's where mom's buried, and it's where we grew up."

"You complain about this place all the time."

"Everyone complains about where they live. The girls will be fine. The schools are fine. And, look, I don't have a lot of years left. I don't want to spend them on the road."

Tears filled and then spilled out of Olivia's eyes. "You don't want to go with me?"

"I don't want to go anywhere." Andrea's voice caught and cracked. "And you're not going to stay."

"I will go wherever you want to go. If you want to stay, then I'll build a house on the ridge. It'll be perfect."

"Stop it." Andrea smiled and looked straight at her. "Girl, you'll get bored. You always get bored. It may take a year or two in Taos, or in Tucson, but it'll be three months here. Tops. You know it."

Olivia shook her head. She felt gutted. "Why are you doing this to me?"

"You always keep moving. That's your thing. Always has been. Mom was an artist and she loved that spirit in you. I've never been able to keep up. And now all I want is to sit in a chair next to the girls and watch the sun set behind that same dumb mountain range I've spent my life staring at."

Olivia's hands started to shake. "You know what it took for me to get this money? You know how many people I lied to? They're tearing each other apart back there."

"I didn't ask you to do any of that. I didn't ask for this house or for you to leave your husband. I've been trying to tell you. You weren't hearing me. Please stop crying, because I can't. My tear ducts are all messed up."

Olivia smiled, which only made her cry more. "Can I stay with you the first couple weeks? Help you get settled and decorate?"

"No," Andrea said firmly.

Olivia could not stop her mouth from shaking. "Wow, you must really hate how I decorate these houses."

Anger flashed in Andrea's eyes. "Stop. I do not hate this house or any of the houses you've sent us to. I hate hiding."

Even hollowed out by chemo, she was still the bigger sister. Olivia pushed her tears away and tried to open her mouth, but the tears kept flowing. Andrea pushed herself off the recliner and came to her side. She put her arms around Olivia's waist and squeezed.

"You come visit us any time. Come down from where you land and see us every goddamn chance you get, but I am not tying you to us. Have you really never realized you're strongest alone?"

Olivia wrapped an arm around Andrea. "I'll leave half the cash with you."

"I was hoping you'd say something like that."

Olivia laughed, and the floodgates opened. She cried until there wasn't a drop left.

They held on to each other and Olivia drew strength from the woman who had left half her body in a hospital.

Eventually, Olivia started to feel too much finality in Andrea's goodbye, as if she were flying away to Chicago again, or marrying Cody again, or any of her other departures. "I'm not moving to France. I'll end up an hour away," Olivia said.

Andrea looked into her eyes and smiled. "Whatever you say, Liv."

After helping with the final packing and loading of Andrea's boxes, Olivia took off her wedding band and left it in the middle of the living room floor.

Andrea's cousin seemed sweet, and Olivia shook his hand like he was marrying her daughter. He seemed baffled by the whole situation and scared to death of Olivia, but his affection for Andrea was clear.

Olivia followed them to the subdivision's exit. Andrea turned left, deeper into Española.

Olivia turned right, towards the interstate.

# FIFTY-ONE

CHARLES AND ADDIE sat in the car, waiting for Lou to arrive. The engine was running. Charles was grateful for the noise. He thought about putting on music but knew that would be ridiculous. What kind of music do you play on the way to your own funeral?

Addie turned towards him. "There's got to be another way. I mean, if you go, if you *have* to go, you'll be fine, I'm sure, but there has got to be another way."

"If Lou's there, I'm sure he won't let Branch go too far. Lou is solid."

Charles believed it, although he was also aware of what Branch could make people do. His broken nose throbbed.

"The ATF, maybe the FBI, someone has got to regulate casinos," Addie said. "They'll listen to you."

He shook his head and winced at the pain in his neck. "I don't have any evidence. This whole time, I've been looking for it, but these people are too careful. I'd be the jealous, dirty politico looking for a payout."

Addie looked straight ahead. "That *is* what you are."

She was done with him. Still, Charles realized that waiting with him in this car was the nicest thing anyone had ever done for him. If he wasn't about to puke his guts out, he would cry with gratefulness.

"Branch said you'll get your cards back when I get to the office. You can go now. Lou will be here soon. You'll be able to get gas outside of town." Charles laughed, bitter and sad. "There's a pueblo just south of town with a gas station. Tell them I sent you, and they'll charge you double."

Addie shook her head. "No, I'll wait. I want to see the car. I'm going to take a picture of his license plate. They need to know people are paying attention."

Charles smiled and reached for her hand. She pulled it away before he got halfway there.

Addie turned in the driver's seat and looked straight at Charles. Her eyes were cold and serious and she spoke deliberately.

"I'm going straight to the airport. I will sleep in the terminal, I don't care. There's an eight AM flight to Baltimore. I'll buy you a ticket. I will leave it at the counter, okay?"

Charles nodded and opened his mouth, then closed it. Everything he thought to say was hollow.

"I'll be the last person on that flight and I'll ask them to hold the doors if you're not there. But I will get on that plane. After that . . . "

When Lou pulled up, Charles' leg started to shake. He did not want to go. He wanted to hide. He wanted to run into those mountains and burrow deeper and deeper.

Lou stepped out of the town car. Addie took his picture and started the car.

Charles tasted blood in the back of his throat. "This is the right thing to do," he said. Addie nodded and gave his hand a squeeze. It was a small gesture, barely anything at all, but it calmed him. He took a deep breath and got out of the car.

Lou smiled and opened his passenger door. "You look like shit."

"I wish I could argue."

Addie leaned her head out of her open window. "He's not going to get hurt," she said.

"I know ma'am. The boss only has a few questions. Mallon won't be there. Everything's very confusing right now, but we should go."

As Charles looked back at Addie, she said, "I'll see you at the airport."

Charles smiled and nodded, wondering if Jim Hawley's wife had said the same thing.

୧ୠ ୧ୠ ୧ୠ

He watched the back of Lou's bald head the whole drive. He wanted more smiles. He wanted Lou to assure him that everything would be fine, that they would have time to drink some piss beer before he caught his flight. Lou did not say a word.

As they pulled into the office, Charles broke the silence. "Mallon won't be here?"

Lou shook his head. "Mallon doesn't work for us anymore. I sent him home."

"He should be in prison."

Lou shrugged and turned off the car. "He always did what he thought was right."

Charles got out of the car and followed Lou into the office.

"The big man is going to have questions for you," Lou said. "He'll yell and be crazy, you know how he is, but you'll make that flight." Lou stopped and turned around. "Unless you try to get clever."

"I'm done being clever."

Lou laughed. "Yeah, I bet you are."

Branch sat on a desk chair in the middle of the sea of cubicles. Only the emergency lights were on and the room drowned in shadows, broken by occasional patches of red and white.

Branch was leaning back in a chair with his hands folded over his chest. He looked so normal without his mansion and his fawning crowds.

"Quite a day," he said. "You know, I was actually happy this morning. I'm so glad your face looks that painful. Pity there's no fractures. Mallon must be getting soft."

He pointed towards a chair a few feet in front of him.

Charles sat down. "Oh, don't worry, I'm going to get an x-ray back in DC. I'll send you a bill."

Branch smiled. "If you make it to DC."

"I'll make it. Lots of people know where I am. There are cameras in here. You're not going to do anything stupid. I need my accounts unlocked. My wife's too."

Branch nodded at Lou, who pulled out his phone and stepped towards the door. Charles noticed Lou had positioned himself out of earshot but could still see what was happening.

"Even after I let you go, I'm sure you'll find a whole new pile of shit to fall into."

Charles reached into his jacket for another painkiller. Branch's insults would have stung a few days ago, but however nasty Branch got, it was nothing compared to what Charles was thinking about himself.

"I'm not here for you," Charles said. "I'm here so that my wife and I can leave. You don't scare me anymore. Not after this," Charles said, pointing to his face. "And not after everything else I've been through this past week. I should be the one threatening you. If I beat you to death with a paper shredder, at least I'd know where I'd be sleeping the next few years."

Branch raised his eyebrows. He seemed impressed. "Oh I like that. You know, when Olivia brought me your resume, I thought you had balls. I don't know if you had them before but, boy, you've got them now. You're going to do terrible things after you leave New Mexico. Next time you're looking in the mirror, look deep into your eyes. You'll scare the piss out of yourself."

"You paid off San Miguel, didn't you? You got ripped off."

"And I'm sure you will enlighten me . . . for a price."

Charles swallowed and managed a small nod. "Your wife played both of us, but San Miguel has been orchestrating this whole thing."

"My wife has more guts than all of us put together. Mallon included. When did you two cook all this up?"

"I didn't know she was out here when I took the job. She surprised me. I came home to that house you gave me one day, and she was . . . in my bed."

Branch took a deep breath in through his nose and let it out in a rush. "What did she want?"

"You know what she wanted. I'm sure she figured out a way to get it. She wanted to leave you and start over. Did you let her?"

"What I've done with my ex-wife is none of your business." Branch's rage flashed.

Charles felt his heart beat faster. He glanced over his shoulder at Lou, who was still standing in the doorway.

"Lou won't keep me from knocking out those teeth Mallon loosened," Branch said. "Those recordings Mallon told me about. You don't have any, do you?"

"I wish I did. But I know who's bankrolling those Apaches and if you want any of the money back . . ."

"There was always going to be something or someone to pay off. It's already forgotten. There was a problem, it went away. That's a win in my book."

Charles stared at the thin, grey carpet. It was all a game to people like Branch. The people Charles had been working for his entire life.

"So what do I leave here with?"

"You get to leave here," Branch said.

Charles stood up.

Branch stood up also. "You're done, boy, when I say you're done."

"You win. I'm done trying to find an angle. Enjoy your casino and your . . . "

Charles flinched and ducked as the front door shattered. He looked back and saw Lou decked out and Mallon standing over him. Charles backed up, clawing for something to put between him and the train barreling towards him.

Mallon reached for his hip, grabbed his gun, pointed the barrel straight at Charles and pulled the trigger.

# FIFTY-TWO

A RED EYEBALL blinked open on Branch's gut and grew and grew as Branch dropped to the ground and caused an earthquake that broke windows and scared hawks out of trees and cracked a nuclear reactor in Los Alamos. One down. Mallon did not care which one he hit first. They were both in his sights. Once they were gone, then all the chaos would be gathered up and flushed away.

Charles was on his back, dropped by the shockwave and the hand of God that Mallon felt move through him and into his fists, guided by unimaginable power. Mallon could clean up this mess, this one mess. Give everyone a chance to start over. The tribes and Claudia and the people trying to make it through the day and even Mrs. Branch who'd sold him out would have a chance to start over with these two dead.

Mallon advanced, both hands on the gun's grip. He relished O'Connell's blubbering. Suddenly, there was movement over his shoulder. Lou was up. Bad news for Lou. He wanted Lou to stay down, but now Lou was there, pointing a gun at him, coming straight for him.

Mallon kept his gun on O'Connell, and time slowed so much that he could close his eyes and breathe and enjoy the heightening of his senses. He missed that feeling. Branch had made him grow soft. Sorry, Lou, you should have stayed down.

Mallon spun and pulled the trigger faster than Lou. Nothing happened. Click. Click. Click. And then, the ceiling. Mallon was on the ceiling. No, he was looking at the ceiling, and Lou was kicking his gun away. Had he done what he needed? Had he restored balance? Unclear. Then, Mallon remembered the desk sergeant and his gun in an evidence bag. They had emptied the clip and tossed the bullets but forgotten to clear the chamber. Mallon had forgotten to check. The training was never good enough, and he hated that, but not as much as he hated the cold in his chest, the kind of cold Claudia complained about. Where was Claudia? He did this for her. So the world could stay together. Where was she? He missed her. Then, suddenly, she was there. She pressed a palm on his forehead, and he felt his body go soft. Claudia rolled her eyes and smiled at him. Then she curled up on his chest and sunk into his bones, and he followed her. Down. Down there, finally. Where everything was quiet.

# FIFTY-THREE

ROSE HELPED JOHNNY AND MICAH set up their video games in the living room. The two boys had never met, but they quickly established a quiet, spare way of communicating. Nothing about what they were doing looked like fun to Gabe, but he could not deny their smiles.

After they started playing, Rose tilted her head at Gabe and gave him a smile full of teeth.

"Should we make some coffee, Gabe?"

"I don't really think I . . . "

Rose brushed past him and walked into the kitchen. She leaned against the counter and folded her arms. "Fucking nerve," she said. "It's impressive. I slam the door in your face, and you're back with your son and a smile. You knew I had to let you in if he was with you."

"Let me explain."

She shook her head. "I'm sure it was bad and I'm sure it was your own fault."

"Frederick was in the house. He threatened us. He took your check and made me endorse it. I thought he was going to hurt Micah." Gabe lowered his voice. "The kid freaked out. He called his mom. She'll be here soon."

"Then, why'd you come here? Helen never liked me, and now she's going to think . . . " Rose pointed at Gabe, then back to her and back again.

"You said you wanted to see Micah. And I needed to tell you about the check."

"Stop it. The check is fine. I'll cancel the check. Frederick was just trying to scare you. Drug dealers don't cash checks. Why did you come here?"

"I wanted to see you."

Rose sneered. "Uh huh, sure. Why did you come here, Gabe?"

He put his hands on his hips. "I didn't know where else to go. I don't have anywhere else. Rey's stressed out by his case. All my other friends are lowlifes. Your place is so nice and . . . I knew you'd be good to Micah."

Rose kept her arms folded, but her posture thawed. "Why else? There's always something else with you."

Gabe opened and closed his mouth a few times before he could find the words. He felt like a drowning fish.

"Don't freak out again. I wanted you to help me explain to Micah about the cancer."

Rose made her hands into two fists and brought them up to her chest. "Stop it, you stop it, you can't just make up something like that."

"Look, I've had those visions before, and there's always something to them. This one was clear. Even Jefe agreed with me, and everyone knows cancer runs in families. My bones have been hurting. I've been tired, weak."

Rose cut him off with a wave and then grabbed a piece of paper off the top of her fridge. "I looked this up after you left the other day. Symptoms of bone cancer: tiredness, pain in joints, exhaustion."

Gabe nodded. "Yeah, yeah, that's it for real."

"You know what else those are symptoms of? Being an old asshole. You don't have bone cancer. When did you have that vision?"

"Almost a month ago."

"And what was your dad like a month after his diagnosis?"

Gabe looked around the kitchen. "I wasn't there. I didn't show up until the very end, you know that."

"He'd lost twenty-five pounds that first month. He was dead in eight weeks." She pointed to Gabe's belly. "You've been going the other way."

Gabe shook his head and brought a hand to his chest. "No, nooo . . . there's a pain. Right here. Like a lead plate I can't lift. Sometimes I wake up in the night and I can barely breathe. I don't want to die without explaining myself to Micah. I need you to show me how."

"What do you mean *how*? There is no how. You don't have cancer. You feel terrible because you're old and alone, not because you're dying. You don't need to tell him anything. You need to be there for him."

"It's not that simple," Gabe said.

"It really is. They don't actually want big heart-to-hearts. They just want you to be around. They want you to listen."

"I was a crap father when we lived together, and I've been worse since then. My dad would rather smack me in the mouth than talk to me."

Rose turned away from Gabe and stuck her head out of the kitchen. "Hey, Micah," she yelled, "are those papers your dad gave you out there."

Micah, playing the game, spared time for a distracted response. "The what?"

"The papers," Rose yelled.

"Yeah, they're here somewhere, I guess."

"Cool," Rose said. "Bring them in here and grab these sand-wiches I made for y'all."

Gabe heard the sound of the video game disappear and foot-steps come towards the kitchen.

Rose smiled. "Food tends to get a response."

She walked past Micah, who looked around the kitchen, con-fused. "Sandwiches?"

Gabe waved him forward. "Hey, let's look at those papers real fast."

"Yeah, I want to, but I'm real close to finishing this level."

"Real fast," Gabe said. He pointed at the papers in Micah's hand.

Micah looked at them as if he were seeing them for the first time. "Are these all about your mom?"

"No, that's the thing. See, I wanted to do something for you. I wanted to leave you with something."

Micah leafed through the pages. "I don't get it. Did you write these?"

"Yeah, about myself."

"Okay. That's cool." Micah looked up at Gabe. "I haven't read them yet, but I will."

"They're not very good. I wanted to pass on, you know, some wisdom."

Micah looked back over his shoulder towards the living room and the TV. Then Micah's phone rang. He looked at it and grimaced. "Oh, it's Mom, I forgot I called her."

Gabe swallowed hard. "Is she here?"

"I doubt it." Micah answered the phone. "Hey, Mom. No, I'm fine. The what? Oh, no, that's not what I meant. Everything's cool here." Micah looked at Gabe. "Dad took me to his friend's house— nice house—and I'm playing video games with her son." Micah grinned. "I'm sorry the message sounded that way. You know me. I was probably half paying attention, but, no, everything's fine, I swear."

The kid was covering for him. Keeping his mom away so he could stick around longer. Micah was lying to her. He was weaving a story, laughing away her concern. It was how Gabe would have handled the situation and he felt a little queasy because of it.

"Talk to you tomorrow," Micah said. He hung up. "Now what's the deal with these?" He held up the papers.

Gabe shook his head. "Nothing, well, no they're something I worked on, but they're nothing. Here," he said, holding out his hand.

Micah pulled the papers away. "I want to keep the stuff about Grandma."

"That's fine." Micah handed over the pages and went back into the living room. Rose ducked her head back in and smiled. "Well? Easy, right?"

Gabe shrugged and walked out of the kitchen and onto the front patio. Rose followed him. He lit a cigarette. She took one from his pack and lit it herself.

"Look," she said, pointing through the window at Johnny and Micah. "They're having fun. That means you're doing something right."

Gabe let out a cloud of smoke. "I guess so."

Gabe looked at what he had written. None of it made sense. These were not his stories. They were the stories of someone much better. Someone who never sold weed. Someone who never broke his own arm a week into boot camp and spent decades lying about that and everything else. Gabe lit the pages on fire and dropped them into a coffee can near the front door.

"What the heck?" Rose shouted. She ran inside for a glass of water. Gabe smiled as she doused the fire and slapped at his arm.

Rose laughed away her anger and slipped her arm through his. She leaned her head on his shoulder until she complained about it hurting and stood up straight. They smoked their cigarettes and watched their boys play video games. A very small corner of that lead plate in Gabe's chest reluctantly came loose, turned to dust and blew away in the breeze.

# FIFTY-FOUR

CHARLES WALKED OUT of the police station at five AM. The wind had kicked up and it felt sharp and cool against his busted face. Addie was waiting in Albuquerque. Their flight left in three hours.

The cops and paramedics had arrived fifteen minutes after Lou called them. It was another thirty minutes before Branch was stable enough for the ambulance to move him. Charles assumed the mean bastard would be writing a book and cashing in on his recovery within six months.

Mallon lay in the middle of the floor, where he had been felled like a tree. Charles kept staring at the thin smile on Mallon's face. He knew each second he looked at that horrible grin—horrible because it was so happy—would etch it even deeper into his consciousness, but he could not look away.

Charles looked up and down the street in front of the station. There were no taxis this late, and his phone had been smashed back in the office. The cops had let him leave a message for Addie on the airport courtesy phone, but Charles doubted she would get it.

Charles walked back towards the plaza.

It had taken thirty more minutes for his own examination by paramedics and then a ride to a little police station a few minutes away. Then, four hours of delivering statements, being questioned and writing up what he had seen. The ordeal ended with a warning not to leave the state. Charles was going to do exactly that. As he left, he saw Lou in one of the interview rooms. It would be a longer night for him.

Charles found an ATM in the Plaza. His card was still useless. The only other people on the street were some garbage men and a few pre-dawn joggers, happy to speed by the guy with a bloody shirt and black eyes.

Charles found another ATM and then another. Nothing.

Charles wanted to go home. He wanted to get on a plane and fly to his mother's house and let her yell at him and say I told you so. He wanted to sit down with Addie and a divorce lawyer. He wanted to file for bankruptcy. He would walk humiliated down Pennsylvania Avenue, seeing Olivia in each passing stranger. He was ready to leave.

Charles found himself back in the park at the center of the plaza. He took a seat and moaned, his entire body aching. He looked around the maze of streets and the ancient adobe. He wanted to go home. He had no idea how to get there.

# Author's Note

I moved from Washington, DC to Santa Fe in 2007 to be close to my family and take a job on a political campaign. Santa Fe's ghosts and complexities are confusing, yet beautiful. Driving through that old town and those ancient mountains, I knew I wanted to tell a story that combined New Mexico's complexities and my conflicted feelings about politics. If I succeeded at all, it's due to the overwhelming amount of support I've received over the years.

First, thanks to Nicolás Kanellos for plucking this un-agented manuscript from the slush pile. The whole crew at Arte Público Press has been supportive and endlessly patient with my near-constant emailing about every single thing. Thank you, Marina Tristán, Gabriela Baeza Ventura and everyone at that amazing publisher. Joining your roster of writers is the honor of my career.

This book would have shriveled up ages ago without the good folk at Texas State University. Thank you to my thesis advisors for reading an early (and pretty awful) version of this book. Having Nelly Rosario, Doug Dorst, Robert Tally and Elissa Schappell on my thesis committee was a dream. Tom Grimes, Director of the MFA program while I was there, was a constant source of honesty and inspiration. Portions of this novel were also read by the late Robert Stone. My copy of *Dog Soldiers* is never far away. At Texas State, I became friends with Tim O'Brien. We put on magic shows, drank a good bit of scotch and went to Las Vegas for a magician's convention. His notes on a novel draft were the most helpful feedback I've ever received on any piece of writing. I owe you so much, Tim.

Thank you to all my colleagues at Texas State. Ross Feeler gave me amazingly detailed edits, and I couldn't imagine a better community of writers to fall in with.

Writing is a solitary endeavor, which makes me appreciate my writing family even more. Carrie Thornton and Stuart Bernstein are the wisest, and nicest, people in publishing. Becka Oliver, Michael Noll and The Writer's League of Texas have been so helpful. Clay Smith has done more for me than perhaps anyone else I know. I wish I could list everyone in Austin who gave me advice on this project and many more, but the list would be longer than the book itself. I'm so happy to play a small role in Austin's vibrant literary scene.

I've had the privilege of teaching high school English for seven years. My students keep me hopeful about the future, and I hope I keep them hopeful about themselves.

And what's an author's note without a cheesy "I love you" to my mom and sister. Deborah Zamora and Victoria Santos are forces of nature and the rest of us are caught in their wake.

Paige is my love who I marvel at every day. We are so lucky. Turner and Parker are our wild boys, but all of this, everything, is for Zamora.